KNOT HER Fight

an
MVP: MOST VALUABLE PACK
novel
BY *Ari Wright*

Published and formatted by Blue Eyed Books.

Knot Her Fight

MVP: Most Valuable Pack, book 3

ISBN: 9798991446402

Cover Art: Staci Hart

For all the fighters.
We know who we are.
xx

WHAT IS
an omegaverse?

An **Omegaverse** is an alternate universe wherein humans have evolved a biological hierarchy based on three individual designations: **alphas, betas, and omegas**. In an Omegaverse, every person falls into one of those three categories (or "designations") by the time they reach adulthood. Their **designation** then determines certain elements of their physiology, psychology, and physical appearance. The humans in this Omegaverse are not shifters.

Alphas are large, strong, dominant, possessive, and territorial. While civilized, they often struggle with the urge to use force or exert their dominance over others; particularly fellow alphas. Optimized anatomy makes them physically superior in many ways, including reproduction.

Male alphas have a "knot" at the base of their penises. This **knot**, much like the penis itself, becomes engorged when they are aroused and expands to its full size upon completion, "locking" an alpha into his partner. Female alphas have a "lock" inside their vaginas that perform a similar locking maneuver on their partners.

Alphas are biologically compelled to find compatible partners based on individual scents. They also tend to form **packs** with others. Omegas often become the center of packs because they are the only designation capable of creating **bonds** between others. There is rarely more than one omega in a pack. Once a pack bonds with an omega, all of their scents alter subtly. This shift helps protect bonded omegas from unwanted advances.

Betas remain the most similar to everyday humans. They do not have intense scents or the same biological compulsions that alphas and omegas share. Many beta-beta relationships resemble traditional monogamous partnerships. Because they cannot bond among themselves, they often choose to marry instead.

Omegas are smaller and softer in stature, naturally submissive, wary of violence, fearful, emotional, empathetic, and magnetically attractive. Omegas' bodies are built to endure the demands of an entire pack of partners, emotionally and physically.

Omega biology draws alphas in. When omegas are aroused, their bodies send nearby alphas a signal by **perfuming**. Omega perfume is a concentrated hit of their specific scent, intended to lure an alpha to their aid.

Alphas and omegas each have distinctive scents. Their bodies produce these scents at all times, but they are particularly strong when the individual is sexually aroused or emotionally distressed. Alphas and omegas can have very intense, all-consuming physical and emotional reactions to each other's scents. While uncommon, the phenomenon is called **scent-sensitivity**.

Scent-sensitive alphas and omegas are referred to as **mates**. By some twist of fate or biology, they are near-irresistible to one another. Separating from their scent-sensitive mates would cause an omega extreme pain and distress.

Omegas experience **heat cycles**. These "heats" are spurred by the biological imperative to mate/bond with an alpha (or group of alphas) who will provide for and protect them. When an omega goes into heat, he/she will experience intense physical pain unless they are knotted by their alphas regularly. Heats send omegas into a state of limited lucidity that is known as a **heat haze**. This haze makes them extremely vulnerable and unstable.

Omegas can take **suppressants** to lower their hormone levels.

Suppressants help make the pain of heats tolerable for omegas who do not have alphas. Unfortunately, over time, suppressants become less effective.

Unbonded alphas who encounter an unbonded omega can experience **rut**. Rut is a condition wherein an alpha loses his/her mental faculties and gives in to the biological imperative to knot/lock an omega. Rut is often dangerous for omegas.

Omegas **nest** in order to feel secure. An omega's nest should be a soft, round place that feels low to the ground and dark. Omegas take great pride in building their nests to their individual tastes and their alphas' approval. It is their alphas' duty to provide this space and the resources to outfit it.

Courting is the process by which alphas can press their suits with an omega of their choosing. It is generally a task undertaken by the entire pack in pursuit of their one chosen omega.

A **half-bond** can be formed when an alpha attempts to claim an unwilling omega (or vice versa) by biting them without consent. When this occurs, the bond will be incomplete until the one who initially rejected the claim chooses to bite their half-bonded alpha/omega back. Half-bonds are also called "rejected bonds" and can become very uncomfortable for the rejected party over time.

tko

(content warnings)

I'm so glad you're here!

Knot Her Fight is the third installment in the *MVP: Most Valuable Pack* series. If you haven't read Books 1&2, please don't worry, this is intended to be read as a *complete standalone*!

This is a why-choose Omegaverse romance. It includes lots of knots, tons of spice, and absolutely no choosing!

If you don't like rowdy alphas, swoony mates, and group sex scenes (including packmates lending each other a hand), this may not be the HEA for you <3

Content Warnings: sex work/forced sex work, abandonment, past/childhood neglect, PTSD, slut-shaming, rejection sensitivity dysphoria, parental abuse, violence (cage fighting/boxing), neurodivergence/touch aversion, adoption, previous thoughts of/attempted su*cide (off-page), Dom/sub relationship, bondage, breath play, double penetration/DVP, age gap, dubious consent, pierced/tattooed genitals.

knot her fight playlist

"Slut!" (Taylor's Version) — Taylor Swift
Big Dawgs —Hanumankind, Kalmi
Headlines — Drake
I Hate Everything About You — longlost
Make You Mine — Madison Beer
Jungle — X Ambassadors, Jamie N Commons
Hide Away — Daya
Smells Like Teen Spirit — Coopex, Nito-Onna, CPX
Je te laisserai des mots — Patrick Watson
False God — Taylor Swift
Prelude 12/21 — AFI
I Feel Like A God — DeathbyRomy
Whatever She Wants — Bryson Tiller
Shower — Becky G
Unsatisfied — Nine Black Alps
Don't Blame Me — Taylor Swift
Falling Like The Stars — James Arthur
Freak (feat. REI AMI) — Sub Urban
you should see me in a crown — Billie Eilish
Gravity — Sara Bareilles
Start a Riot — Duckwrth, Shaboozey

wet dreams — Artemas
Till Forever Falls Apart — Ashe, FINNEAS
Sweet Ophelia — Zella Day
Roses — The Chainsmokers, ROZES

prologue

YOU WOULD THINK, if a guy knows his junk is going to be in someone's face, he would wash it.

You would be wrong.

Here at *Wally's Boom Boom Room*, the smell of man funk hangs thick in the air—a musk as inescapable as the neon pink fluorescent lighting and carpets stained with God-knows-what.

Come to think of it, I bet the smell is *coming from that carpet*.

Well, it's either that or the—*one, two, three, four, five, six*—seven dudes who have their dicks out right now.

I wrinkle my nose at the threadbare material under my shiny

silver heels. Six inches of platform still isn't enough for me to feel safe from all the cooties swimming around down there.

Blech.

It's actually amazing I can still get the ick from something as innocuous as a dirty floor. Especially when there's a guy literally beating off three feet away from me.

He's small and wiry for an alpha, but the overwhelming scent of pizza rolls makes his designation clear. Along with the fact that my perfume has apparently driven him into a frenzy.

What, does he think he's *special*?

Guess again, bucko.

My perfume drives them all into a frenzy. That's what I'm here for.

I'm still not entirely sure what all these guys think *they're* here for. I see the wedding rings and bond marks while I traipse through the crowded tables. I know that, most of the time, the ones who step the farthest out of line are the ones who have someone waiting for them at home. Trusting them.

In fact, Cheap Pizza Rolls has a wedding band *and* a bite mark.

A familiar, sick feeling swirls through my middle. Disgust and fear—but also guilt. Because, as Wally *loves* to remind me, *I* do this to them. I'm the one they all come for.

Still, I'd really rather not witness my perfume's effects any more than I have to.

So I lock my eyes on the wall across the room, keeping my steps slow and sensual. Wally has always made it clear what would happen if any of his patrons catch even the faintest whiff of distress from me.

Little do they all know—this scent? The one they all go feral for?

It *is* me distressed.

Lyrics and music play in my mind while I sashay around the dingy, ill-lit room. I smile. I flip my hair over my shoulder. I turn and pretend to shoot saucy looks at patrons.

Really, I'm looking at the door.

Specifically, the *guard* at the door.

Because tonight is the night.

It's taken me way longer than I'd care to admit to find a way out of here...

But *tonight is the night*.

The bouncer—whoever he is; no one has ever bothered to tell me their name—sips the same coffee he always makes. About ten minutes later, I notice him squirming in his seat. Five minutes after that, his eyes start darting to the bathroom.

I've taken a very careful path, one that puts me right in the thick of all the nasty alphas, but gets me as close to the doors as I can without seeming suspicious.

Because the second the dude who just downed five liquid doses of Makes You Go medication finally abandons his post?

I bolt for the exit.

SOME PEOPLE really don't know when to tap out.

Rolling my eyes, I step over the guy passed out in the middle of the gym's octagonal cage. He could have walked out of here, if he'd just had the sense to quit while he was behind.

Eh. Maybe.

Depends on my mood, I guess.

After winning four straight sparring matches, I *should* be feeling pretty fucking good right now.

That's when I hear them. Two of the little bitches from the featherweight division. They've been watching me for the last three rounds, whispering in the corner like middle-schoolers at a dance.

"They call him *Ghost*," I hear one of them hiss.

Jesus. Again with the nicknames.

Ignoring them, I shove my shit into my duffle bag. Gym rules dictate that we clean up our own bodily fluids, so I swipe my sweat off the bench and then my chest.

I'm not thorough because *fuck this place*. I've always said it's too nice in here, but leave it to the Thorne Pack to make my punk ass fight in a bougie gym like this one.

There aren't even any beat-up lockers or smelly punching bags. No, this place is all shiny black vinyl fencing and steel pillars. With the gym's logo printed on the custom canvas stretched on the bottom of the cage.

Huh.

Guess I *did* get a lot of blood on that.

Not my fault this fucker is a bleeder, though. He can clean it when he wakes up.

If he wakes up.

Whatever. With what my pack pays for my membership here, they can afford a new canvas. Besides, no one would miss the printed one. Their dumb logo is all over the place. Some pretentious bullshit displaying the name I've never bothered remembering because I don't belong to this place.

I don't *belong* to anyone, and that's the way I fucking like it.

The bitch boys in the corner keep talking their shit. "I heard he doesn't even have a coach. How the fuck did he get called up without a coach?"

I almost smile. On the inside.

News must be getting around. I figured it was only a matter of time before they all heard about me moving up. I wonder when the crows will start circling. Looking for tender places to pick meat off my bones.

Idiots. Don't they know why people call me Ghost?

The second I look at them, they both clam up. The metallic

tang of fear fills the room as I sling my bag over my shoulder, shove past them, and leave the guy I defeated lying in the ring behind me.

As a warning.

WHY THE FUCK *am I here?*

I ask myself all the time.

Every morning I shower under a rain faucet head in a marble fucking bathroom. Every time I start the 1965 Mustang Tristan bought for my twenty-fifth birthday. Every time I have to put on a goddamn tie.

Why. Am. I. Here?

There's something wrong with me. Many things. I know that. Alphas are supposed to want a pack, other strong alphas to have their backs.

I never wanted it. People are annoying. Other alphas *enrage* mine.

Those dominant instincts lying dormant in my chest? They hate breathing air with these guys. They want me to *fight*.

Which is really all I ever want, too.

Plus, I hate fish.

I'd bet my left nut that the sea bass filet Jonah has in the pan costs more cash than I have in my wallet.

Okay, so I don't *have* a *wallet*. But whatever. My pocket.

At the moment, I don't have those, either. Exercise shorts and tank tops ripped halfway down the sides are about as close as I get to dressing around here.

I'm not sure what my aversion to "real clothes" is. I'm sure Spencer has his theories.

Audacious for the guy to spout psycho-babble at us while he's the most fucked-up person in this house.

Maybe.

It could be a three-way tie.

Jonah is the only normal-ass alpha around here. Came from a good family, finished school. No arrests. No scandals.

And now he's "successful" and bored out of his fucking mind. So what does that tell you?

Seems like his only form of amusement these days is getting on my ass. "You have blood on your cheek. Use a napkin," he grunts, tossing one at me.

My scowl pulls into a full-on glower. But the bastard just smirks.

He thinks the fact that I'm a roiling volcano of rage is *hilarious.*

If I had to point to one specific reason why I ended up here, it would be his unconquerable amusement. When we met, I was twenty-one, fighting in underground matches because I had too many arrests to get into the real ones.

I got the absolute shit kicked out of me one night. And while I was lying on the concrete outside the ring, waiting for my soul to leave my body, some big-ass Jason-Momoa-looking motherfucker stepped right over me. He stopped and glanced down at my bloody hamburger-esque face.

And then he *smiled.*

It was deranged.

I liked that.

I wouldn't exactly say we were friends at first. He started coming to my matches. Told me he liked watching my "punk ass" get "beat to hell."

Then, it was a flask ringside after a couple victories. A couple rounds of pancakes at shitty diners. He didn't even tell me he was a famous NFL player until the day he came into the shop where I worked my day job, demanding I sketch up a sleeve of tribal tattoos for him.

I would have told the guy to get fucked, but it was a slow day.

Now, he has ink all over his arms, shoulders, and chest. Nothing like my blackened body. But most of his work is mine.

Since that first appointment, he refuses to go to anyone else. Says my designs are "visionary." And "shocking, for someone who gets hit in the head so often."

Dick.

It's his fault I'm about to choke down some precious fish dish. His fault that I'm *here*, in this fancy-ass townhouse. The ugly, jagged scar on the face of this otherwise good-looking pack.

He simply doesn't take no for an answer. Never gives up on any of us.

Like a fucking weirdo.

Or maybe just someone... *nice*.

Oblivious to my seething—or, probably, ignoring it—Jonah moves on to prepping asparagus and asks, "You have a fight next month, right?"

I flash two fingers, making a point not to look at him. After five years as an amateur champion, my first UFC contract is about to come into effect. Meaning next month's fights are the real fucking deal.

About time, if you ask me.

Jonah leaves his amber eyes on my face, frowning under his dark brown beard. "You hire a coach yet, Ave?"

Jesus Christ. Not him, too.

The pack has been begging me to hire a coach for fucking ever. Well, Tristan and Jonah have; Spencer doesn't care. According to him, it's my business if I want to be "an obvious idiot" and/or "a suicidal lunatic." As long as I don't get blood on any of the furniture, he usually acts like my career never occurs to him. He's never deigned to attend a match.

Tristan, on the other hand, never misses one. Our pack leader has always treated the fighting as a profession. I guess that's technically true now, but I still want to smirk at that phrase.

My career.

Ha. More like finding a way to get paid for liking pain.

Because, fuck me, *I really do.*

The giving, the receiving. I'm not picky.

Seeing my answer all over my face, Jonah grumbles his disapproval for a second and then smirks again. "Excellent. I'll get some cash out to bet on the other guys."

He says that every time. Even back when I wasn't good enough for the amateur league, he perpetually placed ridiculous bets on me and gave me all the money when I won.

It's ironic as hell that I'm a paid fighter now. After years of scrapping and starving and whatever other bullshit—I'm making money when I don't really *need* it anymore.

Being a part of the Thorne pack comes with limitless credit cards, cabinets that are always full of food, and a butler who does all our chores and runs every errand. I quit my old day job at Suburban Ink two years ago and haven't touched any of my prize money in years.

I snort, trying not to be too amused by this asshole.

After all, my greatest strength as a fighter?

I don't care.

About me. Or anyone.

And that's why I win.

JONAH

"EAT IT."

Avery glares at me across the kitchen island. The dark anger in his light eyes matches the black ink covering his pale chest, shoulders, and neck. "Didn't I tell you to get fucked?"

I shove the plate closer. It's a flat disk that blends right into the onyx counter. If not for the bright green vegetables and steamed white fish on top of it, you'd never see the damn thing.

"It's good for you," I grunt, flexing a bit of dominance. "*Eat it.*"

Avery has two moods—Outright Murderous, or I'm Plotting

Your Demise. When he realizes I'm not going to give in, he shifts from attitude A to option B.

With a hard yank, one tattooed hand tugs the plate over while the other snaps out to grab the fork I left for him. Staring me down with all sorts of homicide in his eyes, he stabs an asparagus stalk and shoves the whole thing into his mouth, his square jaw working around it.

He tries to hide his wince at the taste, knowing a fear of green things makes him seem less "Metal". But I laugh anyway. "Atta boy. Get that protein in, too."

"I hate you," he tells me, poking at his fish. "So much."

"Yeah, yeah."

I hate you, is Avery for, *I must like you because I'm using words instead of pounding your face in.*

We've all tried to teach him manners, but since we basically pulled him out of a gutter, it's been a slow, painful process.

I've been trying to remove his head from his ass for the better part of three years, and sometimes it seems like I've accomplished nothing. Until he drops his ghostly blue eyes to the plate and mutters, "Thanks, I guess."

Carrying my dinner to my usual place at the long island, I pause to swat the back of his close-cropped head. "Any time."

He spears another piece of asparagus like he's a gladiator and the fork is a javelin. "You got practice tomorrow?"

Now, it's my turn to try not to cringe. "Yeah. First one back for the season. Looking forward to it."

Avery doesn't buy my shit any more than I buy his. The corner of his mouth twitches up. "Sucks to be a living legend."

I'm starting to hate that term. *Living legend.* Implying, what, exactly? That I should be *dead*?

Because I'm thirty-five and I still play football? Or does it mean that most people who play longer than I have *dropped dead*? Either way, I can't figure out how to not be insulted. And Avery knows it.

I talk around a mouthful of sea bass. "Sucks to be a fighter without a belt."

He glares. Back to Outright Murderous.

Eh, just as well. Keeps me on my toes.

As I chuckle, two sets of footsteps approach from either side of our townhome. I could probably pick them out of a lineup at this point. After fifteen years as a pack, there isn't much I don't know about the Thorne brothers.

The slow, distracted shuffle from the left will be Spencer. Holding a book, I'd bet. Or a stack of papers. He probably has a red pen behind his ear, too. And muttering—he'll be muttering about something.

That shit always makes me laugh. It reminds me of the day we met, two freshmen assigned to be college roommates. I walked into the room and found the guy muttering about his socks, pissed as all hell that the tiny dorm didn't have "a proper armoire."

The horrified look on his face when I suggested he stash his socks in a shoebox next to his bed still makes me snicker.

Most people who met us didn't understand how the hell we lived together. Sometimes, I still wonder. There probably haven't been many sets of best friends who are more opposite than us.

But it just... happened. Spencer helped me with classes. I helped him not get his shit kicked in over his know-it-all tendencies. I made food, and he cleaned the room.

It worked.

When our first year of courses came to an end and we decided to get a place off campus, I knew he and I would be a pack. Meeting his older brother, Tristan—who seamlessly stepped in and rearranged our lives until they were exactly what we wanted them to be—only sealed the deal.

Tristan has always been powerful. I was second-string on the university football squad until he took a few meetings, made some calls. Three years later, I got drafted to the exact team I hoped for.

When I asked how he pulled that off, he pretended not to understand the question.

I assume it's the same way Spencer got into every doctoral program he applied to. And how he landed a prestigious position as a researcher and professor, despite not having a single people skill to speak of.

If the permanent scowl on his face isn't enough of a clue, his students usually figure that out within two or three clipped sentences.

His intensity scares the shit out of people. It's for the best that he's usually too engrossed in his work to notice or care. Although, I do hope his TAs get some sort of therapy disbursement.

Opposite Spencer's shuffles, I hear quick, focused paces. That would be Tris, our pack alpha. Likely coming from his study, where he holes up and does whatever a senator does.

Years later, it's still not clear to me. But it must be important because he never seems to relax.

The second he appears on the threshold, his ever-present phone in one hand, I can tell he's looking at it but isn't even seeing it. With his free fingers, he clutches what appears to be a dead fern.

Who knew we had a plant in this house?

I would have watered it.

To break him out of whatever trance he's wandered into, I force a cough. His head snaps up, revealing a serious face and dark blue eyes. "Yes?"

"Got a victim there?"

He nods absently, staring at the plastic pot like he can't remember how it got in his hand. "It was in my office."

He drops the carcass on the counter and blinks the sheen of exhaustion out of his eyes.

Shit.

The guy needs to sleep, but I know he won't. Just like Avery won't eat any more greens, and Spence won't do any breathing exercises to lower his blood pressure.

These idiots will be the death of me long before any football bullshit.

"Here," I say, pointing to the stove top built into the island and the plates on it. "Dinner."

Spence finally wanders in, his sharper features an odd mix of light and dark. Without glancing up from his papers, he makes his way to the counter, grabs his plate, and sits between Avery and me. The second his butt hits the stool, the papers go down, and his attention shifts wholly to his food.

"Thank you, Jonah," he offers, crisp. "Looks excellent."

He eats three bites, then notices our pack alpha is still lingering and shoots him a patented Spencer Scowl. All disapproval, no empathy.

"Tristan, it's rude to hover."

When he doesn't get a response, I laugh, "Tris. Food. Eat."

Our pack alpha shakes himself out of his own thoughts and cuts us an annoyed look. "Beg your pardon," he mumbles sarcastically, "But I have to run out."

It's nothing new. Neither is the way he can't tell us exactly what he's up to. He has feelers in place all over the city, scouting for all sorts of bullshit. Sometimes, he'll catch wind of a situation and swoop in to intervene.

"I'll be back as soon as I can." Tristan's long-lost focus snaps into place as he reaches for the suit jacket hanging over our fifth barstool.

It's basically a coat-rack at this point. My Orlando Ospreys jacket, Avery's ever-present black hoodie, Spencer's embarrassing elbow-patch blazer. I stare at the empty seat for a long beat before shaking my head and shoving another forkful into my mouth.

Tris sighs at his dinner and casts me a look. "Put it in the fridge for me?"

I feel for him. He's always running off to put out fires. And I know he hates missing time with the pack. "You got it, Tris. Movie night this weekend? It's your turn to pick."

He offers a hearty nod, his WASP-y version of gratitude. "This shouldn't take long."

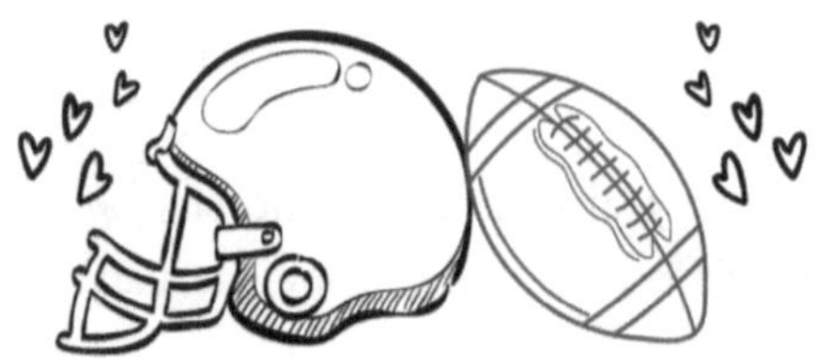

"LET ME GET THIS STRAIGHT."

The woman sitting across from me clearly has *opinions* about my clothes.

I really can't say I blame her. I'm in a thong leotard and fishnet stockings, for Christ's sake.

Silly little slut.

Silencing the hiss looping through my memory, I blink at the police officer glowering back at me. She's annoyed. And probably disgusted.

Why am I surprised?

I ran thirteen blocks in platforms and almost took out a family holding ice cream cones who gaped at me like I was an escaped zoo animal. Something poisonous.

I guess I sort of am. Because the second I walked into the police station, every head turned.

A sane person—or maybe just someone with a speck of real-world experience—might have realized, *Oh, right, I'm the unbonded omega with the super-perfume. Maybe I shouldn't walk into a government building that will likely be full of alphas.*

Well.

Whoops.

There were growls. Snarls. A few of them even lurched up from their posts.

I spent so long trying to get away from Wally and that filthy dump, I forgot to make a decent plan for what would happen if I ever *succeeded*. Mostly because I didn't actually believe I would.

Thankfully, the woman at the front desk of the police station was a beta. She got two of the bonded alpha officers to escort me into a room before anyone decided to make me into a chew toy.

Maybe I already am one. I'm squeaky. And covered in rubber. And apparently, I smell to alphas the way a liver treat smells to a dog. So.

"Miss?"

My lashes flutter as I attempt to focus. Again.

It's hard—my chest feels like it's caving in, and I can't seem to get enough air through the narrow passage of my throat. My mind keeps racing, coming up with stupid jokes and song lyrics and all sorts of other crap I've used to cope for years.

But every time I try to speak, I can't eke out any *words*.

This lady doesn't even know my name. Gray eyes that match her tight police-issue bun scroll down my body with some mixture of distasteful suspicion and muted concern.

Damn this dark-red rubber thong.

And the bodysuit attached to it.

And the inconvenient fact that *I can't talk.*

Actually, I can't remember the last time I *wanted* to talk to someone. Two months? Three?

I open my mouth, sputtering silently. She sighs, dropping her pen to her clipboard. "Sweetie, if you have a drug problem, we can get you some help. There are—"

I shake my head frantically, black hair flying around my chest and shoulders.

Her gaze takes on a hard, frustrated edge. "Listen, I can't help you if you won't speak. Now, I need to know, are you in danger?"

I have to stop to consider that.

Am I?

Wally is surely out there looking for me right now. Not because he *cares*, but because I make him *a lot* of money. I ignore the pang that pounds through my stomach and nod my head.

She ticks a box on her form. "Are you seeking refuge from an abusive situation?"

Those words are... *hard*. Does anyone want to think of themselves as someone who let themselves get mixed up in "an abusive situation"? And, worse, took *years* to figure out a way to get out?

It hurts, but I force down a swallow, nodding again.

When I confirm, she hands me her clipboard and the pen. "I'm going to need some of your personal information. Especially your name. If you can't say it, you'll have to write it out for me."

That, I can do.

With careful letters, I fill in the appropriate line, scrawling the name I've always hated for too many reasons to count.

Serena Swanson.

BEFORE I WALK into any room, I have to remind myself who I am and why I'm there.

Here, I'm Tristan Thorne, a senator and the man who plans to bring omega workplace rights into the twenty-first century.

At this moment, I'm also a man who's about to be $50,000 poorer after bailing out this week's group of omega-rights advocates.

It's always amazed me how cruel and oppressive alphas can be toward omegas without a single hint of rebuke. But the second omegas start rallying to defend themselves or forge a new path forward? They're radicals in need of quashing.

Incidents like this aren't rare, unfortunately, but for the public defender to call me down here on a Sunday night? It must have been bad.

I've been in the back of the office for some time, my stomach grumbling while I fill out two dozen bail receipts. The sheriff explains that, since I've chosen to remain confidential, their office is legally obligated to take cash only.

I nod along and pull an envelope of money out of my jacket pocket, anxious to leave. I'm missing Sunday evening with my pack; and my instincts recoil from the energy in here tonight. Especially the way several of the unbonded officers have abruptly vanished. While the other half keep looking toward an interrogation room on the other side of the wide, cubical-filled floor.

I swear two of them even lick their lips.

My eyes narrow as I peer through the small window in the door of the office we're in. Some indistinct urgency rears inside of me.

"What's going on here?"

The sheriff winces—and adjusts the front of his pants. "Got an omega in off the streets," he twangs in a Southern drawl. "Made half my officers go feral. Some sort of super-perfume, I reckon. You know I'm happily bonded myself, but... it is *potent*. So far, none of us have been able to go into the room. Our beta receptionist tried to talk to her, but she couldn't say one single word. Needs someone to bark her into speaking, I suppose, but none of us can even go near her."

The poor girl. She's so traumatized that she can't speak? And they're just letting her sit in there?

I work to keep from growling. "Did she tell you where she came from? Maybe someone is looking for her."

The sheriff rubs at the back of his head, wincing. "I suppose someone is. Hell, if I had an omega that smelled like *that*, I'd never let her out of my sight."

Jackass.

Irritated, I sweep my papers into a tidy pile and fold them into my jacket pocket as I ask, "Well, did you contact her guardian?"

He grimaces. "That's the thing. She can't say much, but she managed to tell us she was being mistreated somehow. She looks *just fine* to me, but..."

If they call her last known guardian, they might be handing her back to an abuser on a silver platter. If there even *is* a guardian to call...

Christ. Do I have to do *everything*?

While these assholes are thinking with their dicks, I once again remind myself who I am. Why I'm here. What my purpose is.

Sighing, I fish a card out of my pocket and hand it to him. "This is my pack's personal physician. Please contact him and let him know we have an abuse victim in need of medical attention. Use my name."

His silver brows snap down. "How do you know she needs medical attention?"

I scowl. "Her perfume is abnormal, and she currently cannot *speak*. Sounds like a situation for a doctor if ever there was one. Contact Dr. Monroe, and I'll go speak to her about who we can call to come get her."

With a begrudging sniff, he takes the card. "I should warn you: the other alphas have been in a frenzy since she walked in here. Had to send half the force home before any of them snapped into a rut."

We step onto the main floor and I freeze, trying to sense if there's anything to be wary of. From across the room, given the amount of neutralizers they have filtering in here, I can't scent her at all.

That's standard for government buildings. The fact that the others even got a whiff long enough to be affected is odd. Luckily, my doctor friend is bonded. He should have no issues.

"Get Dr. Monroe," I insist. "I can handle myself until he arrives."

That's the thing about being a senator. People listen to you. Do what you tell them. Assume you have your shit together.

Maybe that's why it's so easy to convince myself.

Even though I've certainly never been in a small room, alone, with a young, unbonded omega in a crimson thong.

I see her through the window of the random interrogation room they've placed her in. A flash of ruby rubber; a silk curtain of black hair; naked, ashen golden-brown limbs.

But I'm Tristan Thorne.

It's fine, I think, straightening my tie and dropping a hand to the doorknob. *How good could she be?*

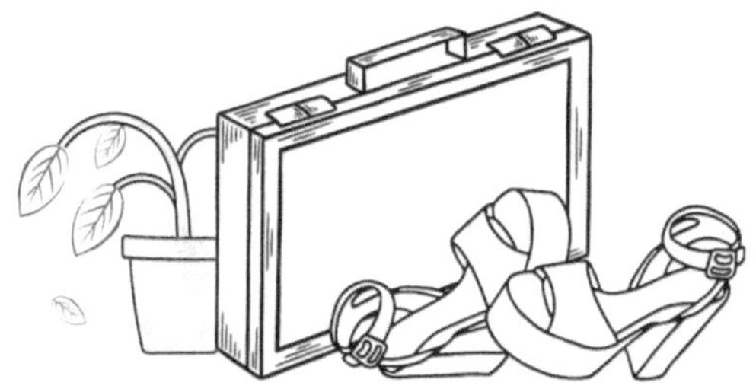

I **SENSE** an alpha looming outside the door.

He's wearing a suit. Which, in this place, means he's probably a lawyer. Or, at best, a nice doctor to inject the crazy omega who won't speak with tranquilizers. Or truth serum.

My heart flies in my chest, beating so hard I swear I can see it tick when I glance down at the pale-brown boobs smushed under my teddy. Fear tastes familiar, a bitter tang welling behind my teeth while I try not to shake out of my seat.

What if this guy's a detective? What will happen to me? Will they figure out where I came from and call Wally?

You're my property. I have paperwork that says so. Anyone who found you or tried to help you would just hand you right back to me.

It's the main reason I didn't try to leave sooner. That and the super-perfume. And the whole no-money, no-phone thing.

Now? No words, either.

This alpha looks word-y. He's as fancy as Wally always pretends to be, only his wealth seems genuine—bespoke suit with shiny thread, polished shoes. A full head of slicked-back espresso-dark hair. Under thick, matching brows, his eyes burn—intense, even from the other side of the door's glass inlay.

The prickles in my gut bloom into full-on ripples. They roll out to my fingertips and toes until I'm pretty sure even my *hair* is quivering.

I don't get it. I spend every miserable night walking around rooms full of the most despicable alphas on the planet. Why would some pretty lawyer make me feel like I'm coming out of my skin?

He doesn't even have his dick out!

The crease between his brows quirks tighter. His gaze drops to the old-fashioned telephone bolted into the interrogation room table, then shifts to something hanging beside the door.

When he moves, I flinch. Chagrin burns through my gut as I realize he isn't *attacking me.* He's just reaching up to take a matching telephone handset off the wall. He holds it up where I can see it and then nods at the one beside my hip.

He wants to talk to me.

Fear rears up, an instinctive flash of *fuck no.* But then I realize —he could have just waltzed right in.

Everyone else has. *This* alpha is trying to give me *a choice.*

Which is... a first.

My hand vibrates while I paw at the phone, my numb fingers barely capable of grasping the smooth plastic. I bring it up to my ear and hold my breath, afraid to even let him hear me *breathe.*

The alpha doesn't seem to have the same concern, though. He

exhales into the receiver, still staring hard through the slice of glass in the heavy metal door.

"Hello."

It's such a normal thing to say; I find myself answering automatically. "H-hi?"

His mouth is chiseled and sort of... *stern*. But it curls up at the corners slightly. "They said you were having trouble speaking."

If he weren't looking at me with a deep kind of concern in his eyes, I'd almost think he was teasing me. My fingers twitch around the phone handle, clammy sweat misting my palms. "I-I am."

This time, I get a small smile. "Could have fooled me, Miss Swanson."

Miss Swanson.

No one has ever called me that before. It sounds so strange that I blurt a correction, although it's barely loud enough to qualify as a whisper.

"Serena."

The lines around his eyes soften. "Serena," he repeats.

It's the first time my own name has ever made me short of breath. I press a sweaty palm to my chest to make sure my lungs still work and end up clutching the necklace dangling there. Fisting it has always been my nervous habit—one Wally didn't mind because it drew attention "where it belonged"—my mashed-down tits.

But this alpha doesn't even glance at them. He just stares at my face... and then stares some more.

His frown is fierce, and it occurs to me that I really ought to be afraid of him. But I'm just...

Not.

There's something else happening inside of me. It sends a shiver through my whole body while the alpha watches on. His brows tweak tightly, and he starts to move for the door.

But then he... stops himself? Again. He looks through the glass, that dark gaze more intense and his voice an octave deeper. "May I come in?"

Some desperate part of me wants to scream *yes*.

I don't understand that impulse at all. I usually hate having alphas around me. I went through this whole miserable night just to get the hell away from them. So why is my body suddenly clambering for *this one* to come closer?

I try to shrink down, making myself smaller and hiding my quivers. "Why?"

When he sees the wariness in my expression, his goes soft again. "You look cold. I can lend you my suit jacket."

I really am. It's freezing in here, and I'm sitting on a metal table in a rubber thong. Which suddenly makes borrowing a jacket all the more appealing.

"I—I guess that's fine."

He nods and hangs up. I do the same. A sudden burst of nerves shakes me off the cold surface and onto my feet. Scuffed silver platforms scrape the laminate while I back away from the door, moving instinctively.

But I've gotten good at reading alphas, knowing how aggressive they're feeling at any given moment. I've had to learn the hard way a few times. And this one doesn't look like a brute.

Powerful and dominant; but not *angry*.

If anything, he seems more agitated on my behalf than his own.

The door snicks open. He steps inside. Harsh fluorescents bounce off all the polished parts of him. A gold Rolex. Shined leather shoes. The gleaming belt buckle that matches his tie-clip. His thick mahogany hair.

I can't open my mouth. To talk *or* breathe.

It goes against every impulse urging me to lower myself in submission, but I have to know—what color are those dark eyes? So I raise my gaze to his.

The navy irises are unique. Almost fascinating. They seem *alive*. Swirling, shifting. Shades of silver moonlight slicing through a restless sea.

He holds himself with authority and strength, even as

compassion shifts in his depths. Somewhere, down in the deep, dark hole burrowed under my stomach, I feel a stir. It's indistinct and as wordless as the rest of me, but for the first time in years, *I feel it.*

My Omega has been hiding for a long time. I don't know much about her, but I know she's silent and scared. She's been that way for a long time.

So it's weird for her to poke her head out now. When I'm in a strange place, alone, with an alpha, who doesn't seem to have any bond marks on him...

The TV shows I used to sneak mentioned this sort of thing all the time. Some cross between fairy tale and biology that supposedly makes certain alphas and omegas destined for each other.

A scent-match, they call it.

Or, in really serious cases, scent-sensitive *mates.*

That word sinks through my middle, clicking into the place where my Omega likes to huddle down.

Mate.

There was a time, years ago, when a group of strong, sexy mates swooping in to rescue me was my literal dream. A secret hope I never even had the courage to admit in my own head.

Could this be... *that*?

My brain loops as fast as my heart pounds. And I don't know *much*, but I know there's only one way to test the insane theory that's taken root in my mind.

So I breathe.

And he's *perfect.*

Summertime, without the heat. Fresh-cut grass, young mint leaves, the faint brush of orange blossoms.

It's lush and cool. A shaded hammock, maybe.

Or a dew-damp garden just before sunrise.

It's more than how good he smells, though. It's a *feeling.* A memory I don't really have, but loved to pretend I did. A fantasy that kept me sane in the darkest moments.

And the fact that *this* alpha's scent immediately brings me back to the only peace I've known in years feels like it *means* something.

My body reacts first. A deep, sucking sensation yanks his scent from the bottom of my lungs, pulling it so far into me that I don't know where it goes. I gasp, dizzy from it, needing more. A high-pitched whine scales up my throat.

The more I breathe, the less control I have. My quivers turn into outright spasms. Everything below my navel contracts on a painful pulse of emptiness, then gels in a way I've never experienced.

It feels *wet* and *hot*. Like melting wax, only more slippery. Sliding out of me, into the thin red strap where most people would probably have panties.

The space around me tilts and blurs. My gaze loses focus, going dark at the edges. My perfume—the true, sharply sweet, richly creamy version—floods our small room.

Through my soupy tunnel of vision, I can only focus long enough to make out the alpha I thought might be an exception to all my rules.

Lunging right at me, with his teeth bared to bite.

DEAR GOD.

This incessant buzzing.

Make it *stop*.

I know I should answer. There are only three people who can call me when I have my phone in work mode.

Avery, who has never called any of us, ever.

Jonah, who would simply barge in here if he needed me.

And Tris.

My older brother, who also happens to be the biggest pain in my ass. If we hadn't formed this pack together, I swear I would have submitted him as a research subject by now.

Would it be fair? Likely not. God knows he's the sane one between the two of us. He carries this pack on his shoulders most days.

But he still has the most infuriating timing.

Damn it, Tris.

I'm busy. I have forty-two hours of data to review before my grad students can plot it. Not to mention the four stacks of papers sitting on my desk at the university. Eventually, those will need grading.

The painful pinch in my chest is familiar. Jonah would tell me to breathe. Avery would roll his eyes. And Tristan would be the only one in the whole world to understand what I'm feeling with just one look.

Damn it... it's Tris.

So I answer.

"Every time one of you interrupts me," I start, pressing the cell between my ear and my shoulder so I can re-roll the sleeves on my white button-down. "I have to start whatever I was doing from the very beginning. You know that."

"Spencer—"

"And, unlike your work, mine isn't as simple as reading emails and shaking hands with old bastards. Each time I have to go back to the beginning, it costs me *hours*, Tristan—"

"*Spencer.*"

Anxiety swells while I think about my commitments. "This research is due Monday," I snap, shoving a hand through my silvery-blond hair—the one major difference in appearance between my brother and me. All the other dissimilarities are below the surface.

"That's another thing you don't have—deadlines."

"*SPENCER.*"

His tone finally sinks through the tension stretched taut in my middle. All of my indignation leaves on a deflating exhale. "*What?*"

Low and urgent, he replies, "I need you to get the others and come to the police station on the corner of Mills and Robinson. It's ten minutes from the townhouse. Bring one of Avery's hoodies. Once you're in the car, I need you to call Myles and have him come back to the pack house. Tell him to await instructions."

I blink at the wall my desk faces, absorbing the list of tasks. Why does he want our butler to come back? Myles always leaves at five. He barely has enough work around here to keep him occupied for the eight hours a day we employ him.

"It's an emergency," Tristan adds.

Unnecessarily. Of course it's an emergency. It has to be, or he wouldn't be issuing cryptic, rapid-fire instructions.

It takes monumental effort for my mind to shift gears, but I force it. Abandoning the data laid out in front of me, I think back to dinner. Tris was running off for one of his silly vigilante adventures.

"Did something go wrong?" I ask, already on my feet.

Our pack townhome is dark. We designed it that way. All matte black—the walls, the floors. It's stark and clean, with square edges and modern tinted glass.

During the day, light comes in through the skylight strips cleverly concealed along the edges of each room's ceiling. But at night, solar-powered LEDs come on. It was overcast today, so the lights along the walls glow a low orange.

Tristan is too quiet for too long. By the time he speaks, I'm stepping out of the eastern wing into the huge living room at the center of the house. Avery and Jonah are sprawled on our charcoal leather sofas. They both look up at me as I snap out our pack alpha's name, barking.

"*Tristan. Speak.*"

Under ordinary circumstances, Tris's dominance would put any of us on our backs. He usually doesn't even flinch when someone else barks. But, this time, I hear his breath catch.

"I bit her, Spence," he groans, shoving out the impossible words. "I accidentally bonded our pack to an omega."

seven

YOU KNOW WHAT?

I'm not surprised.

Finally finding a way to leave Wally's, only to get jumped by some random alpha-hole in a super fancy suit? Because I was dumb enough to think, for one minute, that he might be my knight in shining armor?

That sounds like something that would happen to me.

I still have no grasp on the specifics of what just occurred or who any of the voices around me belong to, but one seems pretty darn insistent. "Tristan, you're going to have to calm down. Your distress will only make her condition worse. Please, try to sit."

Whoever Tristan is, he doesn't listen. I hear footsteps pacing close by.

The voice drops into a mutter, hovering right at my side. "Or we could continue to ignore the doctor," it says. "Outstanding."

A doctor?

I've never been to a doctor. Maybe I'm dreaming I'm on General Hospital again. That used to be one of my favorite shows to sneak at three a.m.

A dream would explain why everything feels foggy and surreal. It could also account for all the strange sensations racing around inside of me. The pain carved into my neck is particularly annoying, but it's nothing compared to the *feelings* ricocheting around my abdomen like pinballs.

Fear. Dread. Pain. Regret.

Fear again. Agony. More dread.

Holy shit. *What* is happening to me? And why can't I seem to get control of my body long enough to open my eyes?

When I try my hardest, all I get is a twitch.

"She's *moving*."

An answering sigh speaks of great patience. "Yes, Senator. I told you, she's very much alive. The twitching likely means she's about to come back to full consciousness. You should prepare yourself. She'll likely be panicked and in pain."

Well, he's got the pain part right; I'll give him that.

It's hard to decide what's worse; the open wound pulsing on my throat or all of the horrible emotions seething in my stomach.

Actually, scratch that.

I know what the worst thing is. And it's absolutely *mortifying*.

Because *whyyyyyyyy* in the world would I be *horny* right now? Like—*what?! Where* is this wrenching *ache* in my pussy coming from?

Silly little slut—I bet you're nice and slick, too.

I cringe away from the lash of my memories, trying not to let them touch me.

It's hard when that cruel voice has a *point*, though.

Because unless I'm some desperate, insane nympho, there is literally no reason for my pussy to be desperately sucking at nothing right now.

Did she not get the memo here? We're in a strange place, surrounded by strange alpha men, basically naked. Unconscious? Half-conscious? And, now, in mysterious pain.

Like, come on, ma'am.

Read the room.

But, nope. I guess I really am an insane, desperate nympho because she's melting like a popsicle on a summer sidewalk—all sticky and wet and, if the air in here is any indication, sweet, too.

Unless that's the mystery doctor?

Doubt it; he seems to have a spicy scent layered with a thick slab of *absolutely not*, which means he's bonded.

Thank the *Lord*.

He also seems fairly calm, given the vibes in here. "Hmm. You said you scented her and blacked out?"

Guilt swells in my middle. For a second, I think it's my usual reaction whenever someone scents my ultra-strong perfume. It takes a second to realize this feels different. And I have no idea where it's coming from or what's causing it.

"I walked in and we looked at each other. She perfumed, and it just—" His voice cuts off with a hiss. The shame roiling through me doubles, then triples, along with a burst of pleasure that connects with the pulsing pang in my core.

A second later, I hear a mortified croak. "My apologies."

The doctor clears his throat. "Perfectly natural. Most alphas and omegas bond in heat, during intercourse. Spontaneous climaxes are typical. Your body is just confused by the half-bond."

Okay, now I know I'm dreaming. Most of what he said made no sense at all.

The husky voice asks the question I can't. "Half-bond?"

Another quiet sigh. "You bit her, but she didn't bite you back. The bond is incomplete. To complete it, she would have to claim you in return. Preferably before her next heat ends. If she goes through the heat without bonding with you fully, the half-bond you've formed tonight will cause you numerous... symptoms."

My mind spins as I listen, trying to absorb medical mumbo-jumbo that cannot be correct.

Right?

The doctor's concerned voice drops lower. "In the meantime, you'll be able to feel each other's emotions, but they will be indistinct and lack any sort of context. You won't be able to speak internally or show one another images, such as your surroundings or memories."

"What about my pack?" the first man whispers.

"Fundamentally, pack bonds run through omegas and pack leaders," the calm one replies as something presses into my wrist, hunting for my thready pulse.

"*You* have a half-bond with her because *you* claimed her, and she has not claimed you back. Your packmates will likely experience an increased attraction to her—beyond that of normal mates—because she's been claimed by their alpha. But as she hasn't bitten any of them and none of them have bitten her, they don't have any bonds. *Yet.*"

Claimed. Bonds.

Mates.

An embarrassing spike of hope impales my heart, but my stomach drops and clenches. Or is that the alpha's?

The doctor continues, "If, for whatever reason, she eventually chooses to bond with them and not with you, she'll have internal bonds with each of them individually. But, because you are the pack leader, none of you will have a pack bond—where you will all sense one another through her—until she chooses to claim *you* in return. *If* she chooses to claim you."

I can sense alpha distress the way bomb-sniffing dogs sense gunpowder. I feel it now, even before the delectable scent of summer—which is already sour and sunburnt—starts to smell like a flaming pile of lawn clippings.

The doctor must sense it, too. "I wouldn't fret about it too much," he reassures. "If you're truly mates, your omega will likely want to complete the bond soon."

Silence beats in the air, thick as mud. "And if she doesn't?"

Doctor Alpha clicks his tongue. His voice drops into a solemn mumble. "It's your job to make sure she does."

JONAH

TRISTAN IS WAITING for us when we get to the police station.

I've been part of the Thorne Pack for close to fifteen years, but it still boggles my mind to see the way he gets things done. This place should be buzzing. Especially in light of what has apparently just happened here.

Instead, it's deader than a doornail. Almost every cubicle sits empty, the front desk manned by an apathetic beta woman who answers the phone in a monotone.

No press, no detectives swarming, no flashing lights or drama.

Damn.

The devil works fast, but Tristan Thorne works faster.

"Over here," Tris mumbles, leading us to an abandoned corner.

He looks like shit. Twitchy and pale, with his shoulders hiked up. I note the way his hands keep clenching into fists at his sides, and a bolt of dread strikes my throat.

He really bit her.

I sort of didn't believe it. Even as Spencer ranted the whole way over.

He told us the short version of the story at least three times. Some omega with "Super-Perfume"—whatever the hell *that* is— came in and needed help. Tris walked into the room, took two breaths, and wound up biting her on the spot.

That's *insanely* out of character. If you'd asked me which one of us was most likely to do something like this, I could have made a case for *anyone* else.

If I believe in anything, it's scent-sensitivity, which is why I've never pushed the guys to look into omegas. I figured there was no point. If our true mate was out there somewhere, we would find them whenever it was meant to be.

If *I'd* been the one to stumble across him or her... I wouldn't have meant to, but I may have been tempted to bite first and ask questions later.

And Avery? His Alpha is a *beast*. Fucking *feral*. If he slipped his leash for half a second around the wrong omega?

Yeah, I can see it.

Spencer, too. He may seem the most controlled, but how long can a guy rein himself in before he snaps? I've known him for the better part of twenty years, and I've never seen him with *anyone*. He has to be lonely as fuck. If someone told me he'd lost his shit, I would easily believe it.

But *Tristan*?

Tris is *careful*, not controlled. He listens to his instincts but also tempers them. Gives his Alpha just enough, never too much.

And under all the senator shit, he's kind and empathetic in a way most people never see.

Not to mention... *all of that senator shit.*

He's in the press. He has a reputation. People counting on him. Important laws he's trying to pass.

Tris rarely gets angry at any of us, but when he does, it's usually regarding optics. Because if our pack gets a bad rep? All of his work goes to shit.

I don't know if I can think of something that would be worse for his position than this. Assaulting and biting an omega? A strange, younger woman who came down here to get help?

We are so fucked.

A door opens and closes. Dr. Archer Monroe appears, frowning, with concern behind his square-framed glasses.

I clap his shoulder. "Arch, hey. How are you?"

After playing for the Ospreys for years, I know our team doctor well. In the off-season, he also conducts research at the same university where Spence teaches—but, of course, our pack-mate would never try to socialize with anyone.

Instead, they offer each other professional nods. Spencer holds his gaze. "What's the situation?"

Archer gives him a look and politely addresses our pack as one. "In terms of where she came from, I'm afraid I don't have good news. She's physically fine right now, but she has a lot of healed bones and several scars. She's dehydrated and needs vitamins, particularly vitamin D; so I wouldn't be surprised if she's been kept out of the sunlight. For the next few months, she'll need a rich diet, lots of fluids, and adequate time outdoors. "

My head spins.

Scars? From *what*?

And *kept out of the sunlight*? As in, she hasn't been allowed *outside*?!

Holy fucking shit.

She hasn't been allowed *outside*. She hasn't been *eating*. And now Tristan has traumatized her to hell.

Archer sighs, wiping his glasses on his shirt. "As for the current situation—she's awake and very frightened. She's also severely touch-starved, which causes a lot of underlying distress for omegas. She can feel Tristan's emotions, as well, which isn't helping. He needs to get a feel for the half-bond and figure out how to shut his interior doors to keep his feelings from affecting her. At least, for now."

Tristan's fists turn white. "I'm *trying*," he mutters. "I swear."

Archer places a steadying hand on our pack leader's shoulder. "Incomplete bonds are tricky to disconnect from. Overriding that will likely take several hours, if not days."

Avery is a ghost behind me. He has been this entire time. Silent and deadly. Absorbing the scene with his ice-blue, unreadable eyes.

Now, he finally speaks. And it isn't great.

"How do we undo this?"

Archer grimaces. "Well…"

Ave scowls. "What?"

Spencer shoots our youngest packmate a venomous look. "There *isn't* a way to undo it. The omega will either bond with Tris during her next heat, or the half-bond will begin to jeopardize his health."

Archer crosses his arms with a shrug. "I suggest you work on how to stop that happening. As a pack. In the meantime, Tristan's body won't tolerate being away from her for very long without extreme pain."

So… not ideal.

"That's not happening," I huff. "If she's our mate, we need to be taking care of her. And if Tris can't be away from her, then we'll just invite—"

Oh God. What is her name? We're standing out here discussing her entire future and I don't even know the poor girl's *name*?

Archer reads my panic. His lips quirk into a sad smile. "Serena."

Serena.

Goddamn, that's pretty. I can tell Avery agrees because he hates that he does. It's written all over his face.

I nudge his elbow with mine, and he turns his murderous eyes on me. "Oh, come on," I grumble. "It's a good name."

"Fine," he snaps. "Doesn't change the fact that our dick-head pack leader just basically bonded with a *total stranger*."

Tris groans, his head falling back. "It was an *accident*."

"An *accident* is parking in a tow-away zone," Spencer snarls, low and even—and somehow all the more vicious for it. "This is a life-changing catastrophe, Tristan. None of us are ready for an *omega*. None of us have prepared or discussed what we're looking for! And you just—"

He's spinning out. Of all of us, Spencer is the one who would have needed the most time to prepare. He's complicated.

"Tris didn't do it on purpose, Spence," I murmur, trying not to touch him even though I want to pat his back. "You know he isn't impulsive."

Understatement of the century.

Tristan never makes mistakes. The vultures in the media will have a field day with this.

Spencer turns his cool, dark eyes back to Tris, the veins along his forearms standing out as he crosses them. "We have no option, now, anyway. She has to stay near you or you won't be able to function. Not to mention all the heat-spikes she's going to have and all the easing she'll need. And a half-bonded heat without alphas to tend to her would be *agonizing*."

Fuck, that's right. A half-bond will send her Omega into a tailspin once her haze kicks in.

I don't even know this woman, but my instincts balk at the notion of leaving her to suffer. Especially since none of this is her fault in the slightest.

It's more than that, though. Hearing what Serena has been through, I can't imagine walking out of here without a backward glance. She obviously needs help getting out of whatever terrible situation she's been in.

It'll be fine.

Probably.

Archer shrugs at us. "You may want to meet the omega before you all decide how you feel. Given Tristan's reaction, I wouldn't be surprised if your whole pack is scent-sensitive to her."

Damn.

Could that really be true?

A mate is the dream I gave up on. So long ago, I barely remember wanting it. But if it's here and it's happening...

It's easy to smile. "See? We can find a silver lining here, guys. Bad circumstances, but, you know, everything happens for a reason."

"Nauseating drivel," Spencer bites out.

"Fuck *off*," Avery spits.

Tristan manages to turn paler. He swallows hard, his features hardening. "How will I ever make this up to her? If you all could *feel* how—she's so *scared*," he rasps, dropping his chin to his chest and breathing hard. "I don't think I should go back in there."

Archer agrees. "Best not. And I'll administer emergency doses of rut-blockers to each of you beforehand. Jonah, I'll sign off on yours for the team, so you don't have to worry about that. We have more than a month before the season starts anyway."

Avery rolls his shoulders, the tats under his tank top moving with his muscles. "What, are we all just going to walk in there? Isn't she, like, *traumatized*?"

"Quite. I would recommend meeting her one at a time."

Ah, shit.

I know what that means. Even before all three of my pack-mates turn and look right at me.

But Archer interrupts, chuckling quietly. "It's not as simple as choosing the friendliest of you all," he tells us. "You aren't the ones making the choices anymore. *She'll* decide who she needs to meet first."

Surprise echoes through all four of us.

Holy shit.

We have an omega.

And she's *in charge.*

Spencer is about to strangle himself with his own outrage. "How do we allow her to choose without going in there?"

Archer has the grace not to outright smile. Or maybe he just doesn't want Ave to kick his ass. But I see a spark of humor in his eye. "Well, Professor, you could start by taking off your shirt."

OKAY, seriously.

Why *the fuck* am I here?

I know I ask myself that question way too often, but *come on*.

This is like some sort of bad lineup. The four of us, bare-chested, sporting band-aids on our biceps, leaning against the wall of the local police station.

Except for Spencer, who refuses to touch the wall. Or, you know, anything.

I put joggers on before we left, so at least I have pockets now. My fingers clutch at their seams while we wait, listening to

Spencer's foot tapping and Tristan's heavy breathing and Jonah's bullshit positivity.

I could bail.

The thought is way too familiar. I estimate it pops into my head at least once a day. Whenever I look around and wonder how the hell I wound up in a pack when I swore I never would.

I *could* leave. We aren't bonded. And I'm the last-minute addition no one asked for. I lift right out. No one would miss me much, aside from Jonah, and he's famous for his Zen resilience.

My gaze only makes it halfway to the exit before the door across from us swings open. Dr. Monroe stands there, holding up a tattered scrap of black.

My tank top.

Oh *fuck* no.

A panicked laugh leaps out of Jonah. "Uh, Arch, I don't know if that's a great idea. Our little thundercloud here tends to—"

Holy.

Fucking.

GOD.

What *is that*?

All of us snap to attention, four sets of focus locking on the open door behind the doctor.

We can all sense the scent swirling around in there. With the neutralizers in the air, it's just a bit. Just a tease. But more than any of us should be able to catch.

It doesn't even matter *how* I'm scenting it, only that *I am*. I drag more into my lungs and feel everything in me *lurch*.

Lush and bright and smooth and sweet.

It has the others in an absolute chokehold.

But me?

I'm *dead*.

Or maybe I *was* dead, and now I'm *alive*.

Because I feel *everything*.

My chest cramps, caving in and staying that way. The fists in my pockets tear through the seams. My cock springs up, hardening along with all of my muscles. They bulge out as my feet carry me closer.

"*Move.*"

The word cracks out of me without connecting to any of my thoughts. I'm not sure who's in charge here—my Alpha and I both feel equally determined to find the omega who smells like *that*.

Jonah's doctor must value his life because he steps out of my path—only pausing long enough to remind me, "Careful. She's very upset."

Noted.

I think.

Can't really stop long enough to be sure.

The door falls closed behind me, hanging just a little ajar. I'm lucky I notice it at all.

Because the girl in front of me is *unholy gorgeous.*

Fuck me hard.

Her black hair looks like a waterfall of ink. Shining, perfect darkness that flows over her back and shoulders like liquid night. Her skin is ashy but golden. Whatever true shade lurks underneath has been leached out by fear or something else. When she hears me, her head snaps up, revealing an oval face and big, scared eyes.

Both of my hands float up automatically.

In *surrender.*

I've never surrendered to anyone. They have to knock me unconscious or die trying. But in this moment? It comes as naturally as breathing.

And then I'm on my knees.

You bow to her, my Alpha says. *Only, always her.*

I don't understand it.

Until I breathe, inhaling for the first time since I stepped over the threshold.

Creamy, fragrant coconut. Sticky-sweet fruit, tropical and

fresh. Pineapples and mangos. Juicy, with an acid edge to balance the succulence. A top note of sunshine—warmth and depth and *gold*.

My lungs spasm. Pain and pleasure rip through my body, exploding, imploding. So *good* and so *sharp*.

It *cuts*. And I bleed. And I *love it*.

I can feel the oxygen carrying her scent, track its path through my blood. Every cell it touches sparks and smolders. Flames. *Burns*.

Am I ash? Or am I a phoenix?

Panting, my head falls forward. Waiting for her to let me come closer. Wanting to crawl on my hands and knees. Praying to a god I don't even believe in.

Then I remember—she can't talk.

As slowly as I can, I lift my chin and find her gaze. It's green, woven with threads of gold. Like an emerald.

Striking eyes, rimmed by kohl lines, upturned slightly. She looks sort of like a black cat—all sleek and mysterious with those wide, gorgeous eyes.

I've spent my entire life asking myself why I'm here. Because wherever I was felt *wrong*.

But the second our gazes lock, my soul snaps forward.

Oh.

That's why.

IT'S possible my Omega has a death wish.

Girl, I scream internally, *What. The. Fuck??????*

First, she decides to come out of hiding just to make me *actually* perfume for the first time *ever* and sends a strange alpha into a raging rut that gets us *mauled*.

Then, she selects *this* alpha out of the lineup of shirts?

Ma'am. MA'AM.

I'd like to speak to your manager.

Why did we pick *him*?

He has more tattoos than skin. They absolutely *cover* his chest. His neck; his arms, hands, shoulders.

Between that and the midnight disarray on top of his head, his face looks like it's in a frame of black. Which is fitting, since it's a *picture* of rage.

Light skin and lighter eyes, flared nostrils, slanting cheekbones, and a tight, solid jaw with a bruise splotched along its edge.

He looks *dangerous*.

Mean.

Terrifying.

Until he goes to his knees.

Just—*thunk*.

His whole big body crumbles down, prostrate on the linoleum. His head falls forward, far enough for me to see that his ink extends over both cut shoulders and all the way down his back. Dizzying patterns expand and contract while he breathes deeply, his body armored by plates of muscle.

Muscle and ink.

And the scent of *jasmine*.

My Omega chose it for reasons she currently cannot or will not explain. I allowed it because, well, I didn't imagine an alpha who smelled so floral could ever be so *scary*.

The scent is infinitely better in person. Warm jasmine—spicy but, somehow, petal-soft. Layered over the richest, deepest amber. Then there's a smoky quality woven through it, one that feels almost *holy*. Woody and sweet, like sacred spaces and quiet reverence.

Frankincense.

The tickle of it strokes the back of my throat and pricks my nipples. Fresh slick douses my non-existent panties. An empty punch of pain clenches my pussy.

Inky Alpha raises his eyes to mine. They're so pale. The lightest blue. And the look in them only tightens the cramps in my core. A pitiful whine gets lost somewhere in my clogged throat.

He lumbers to his feet slowly, his gaze never wavering. The blue *burns*—white fire snapping in his irises while he takes four long-legged strides to reach the table I'm perched on.

Is he going to bite me now?

Will I have to feel all of *his* shame and regret, too?

A bruised, tattooed hand flies up. After years of taking blows, my whole body ducks reflexively. I shake so hard that the tears clinging to my lashes quiver down my cheeks and soak into my shoulder while I cower.

But his tattooed fingers don't close over my wrist or tear at my hair. They brush the tear tracks off my face before molding around my jaw, his touch so light and gentle, it doesn't feel real.

"Hey," he says.

My lips roll together as I blink, dizzy with the scent rising off his hot, inked-up chest. The alpha lifts my face, straightening my spine. He stares, unshakable.

"No one's going to hurt you ever again." His ghostly blue gaze spears right into my soul while he grits, "*Never. Again.* Do you understand?"

More than that, I *believe*. The weight in his light eyes sinks right into me. A steadying pulse of solid *trust*.

Oh, I realize. *That's why.*

❤

THE TATTOOED ALPHA only drops my gaze long enough to peer down at the small pile of clothing Dr. Monroe left next to me. He reaches in and plucks out a worn black hoodie that, judging from the scent, belongs to him.

"Put this shit on," he says. "You're cold."

That's rich, coming from him and all his nude nakedness. When he catches my eyes flickering to his chest, something almost like amusement touches his sculpted mouth. "Cold doesn't bother me. Do I look like a pussy to you?"

It's such a stupid *boy* thing to say. I glower before my brain can communicate that maybe it isn't such a good idea to antagonize the beat-up, muscle-bound alpha.

But he *likes* it.

The tiny hint of amusement lurking in his features suddenly flashes into a wild grin. "You have claws hidden, huh, kitten?" His eyes lock onto mine again, pale blue flames sinking and singeing. "I like claws."

For half a second, I'm almost... *happy*? Well, not miserable, anyway. In reply, the dread dragging through my guts dissipates a bit. Curious relief prickles in its place.

The tattooed alpha is still holding out his hoodie. A pissy part of me—the part with *claws*—wants to shove it back at him on principle.

But none of this is his fault, really, and actual *clothing* would be good. When he sees that my hands are too shaky to even take the zip-up sweatshirt, he steps closer, reaching behind my body to wrap it around me.

Every movement is gentle in a clumsy sort of way. He clearly isn't used to this at all, but that doesn't douse the cool determination blazing behind his features.

Once his sweatshirt is draped over my shoulders, he carefully frees my hair from the collar, almost snagging the necklace around my neck.

I forgot it was hiding under all my hair. Does the gold chain have blood on it now? Will I be able to clean it later?

Considering it's currently my one possession apart from a red rubber bodysuit, I really hope so.

His eyes track the way I fist the charm at the end. He looks closely, his full lips ghosting up a bit.

"What do you have there, kitten?"

Even if my words worked, I wouldn't have any. No one has

ever spoken to me like this. With a cute nickname. And, moreover, like it's a... conversation? Like I'm... *interesting*?

And, for all his intimidating traits, this man is *beautiful*. Some amalgam of angel and demon—the dark and light all twisted and smoldering and smoky.

I have no idea what I would say if I could speak, but I realize I don't even know his name. My entire arm trembles as I try to float my empty hand up and stretch it halfway to his chest.

In a decisive move that makes me a little dizzy, he flattens his bruised, inked-up fingers over mine, spreading them against one of his hard pecs. Those light eyes stare into me, his brow creasing while he somehow reads my unspoken question.

"Avery," he says.

Avery.

My Omega peers out of her hole again, nudging me. Telling me, even without words, that this one belongs to us, too.

Because that went so well *last time, babe.*

But then he flashes that lopsided smile again. "So, do you want to meet these other assholes or what?"

THE FIRST TIME I ever played a game in the NFL, I was as ready as I could have been.

Practices, workouts, drills. I geared up with a smug sort of pride in my chest, ready to jog out and take the field by storm.

I still remember the minute I realized how out of my league I was. Mid-stride, coming out of the tunnels, when I looked up and saw the enormous stadium, the thousands of screaming fans, the dozens of lights.

This moment feels the same.

Humbling. A little intimidating. But also completely life-changing.

Instead of stadium lights, I'm caught in the green beams of the two biggest eyes I've ever seen.

The rest of her is so small. Avery's hoodie practically swallows her. I can only imagine what my clothes would look like hanging off her little body.

That thought sparks a purr in my chest. The sound is deep and rusty. It's been ages since I purred for someone. I'd forgotten how effective it is at settling my Alpha down.

Serena seems to like it, too. Her wide, curious eyes blink at me several times as Avery crowds into her side, making space for me to step a bit closer but hovering protectively.

My mind barely has time to process that shit—Avery *protecting* someone—before her heavenly scent washes over us again.

Fuck. Me.

But she's *perfect*.

Warm and tropical, cool and sweet. Her essence seems to sink into my lungs and expand, forcing out deeper purrs.

She sways toward the sound, a tiny whine trapped in her throat. I fucking hate how scared she is. Which is when it occurs to me—if she's terrified and she smells like *this*; what the hell does her *arousal* smell like?

Holy shit. I might not *survive*.

The thought puts a rueful twist in my lips while I close the final step between us. She has both hands on Avery's body, but she doesn't cringe as my denim-covered thighs brush her knees. There are goosebumps prickled under her net stockings. I frown at them, worried she's too cold on the sterile metal table.

Avery's light eyes glow while they snag on hers. "What do you think?" he mutters, conspiring with her. "Do we kick his ass out or let him stay?"

Leave it to Ave to already be plotting with our omega. He's

only been in here for two minutes. But as she looks up at him, there's a shaky sort of trust in her gold-green eyes.

Avery's eyebrows pinch while he gazes back. Poor kid. He probably has no idea how to deal with his feelings—because it's clear he already has *plenty* for this little omega.

"He's a good alpha," he tells her, voice dropping lower. "Better than me, for sure."

Her instincts must be drawn to his in a special way because she scowls, leaning closer to him. The half-smirk hanging on his lips flashes into a real smile—one he usually reserves for taunting his opponents in the ring. There isn't any malice in it now, though. Just amused surprise.

He's already whipped. Not that I have a leg to stand on—at this point, my purr is practically a dull *roar*.

Her big emerald eyes slowly trace my face, taking in my thick beard and wide features. I almost wince, suddenly all too aware that I'm likely the least attractive guy in our pack.

Maybe we should have sent Spencer in here first. He's a dick, but he has a much prettier face.

"My name is Jonah," I tell her, blurting, "and I know I look scary, but I promise I'm not. Really. I mean, I play football, so I plow people down for a living, but I would never do that to you, obviously. Or anyone. Except, you know, the other players."

Avery's smile ticks into a shit-eating grin. "You made Tubs nervous, kitten," he drawls. "I don't think I've ever seen him nervous."

I shoot him a fuck-you glare before I realize how aggressive I probably look. When I glance back down at Serena, though, she isn't cowering. She's glaring, too.

At Avery.

"What?" he asks, backtracking. "You don't like Tubs? Neither did I, at first, but he grows on you."

She shakes her head at him, frustrated, before turning back to me.

One of the hands clasped around Avery's joggers starts to drift up toward me, and I go utterly still, wanting her to feel safe as she brushes her fingertips over my arm.

"*Jo,*" she says, mouthing the nickname so quietly it almost isn't even a word.

No one has ever called me that, but hell if I'm going to correct her. "Tubs" has never exactly been my favorite, anyway.

It takes me a moment to realize that she guessed that the second she heard Avery say it. She's *correcting* him.

For me.

It's the first word she's said since Tris bit her.

And it's just for me.

That has to mean *something*, right?

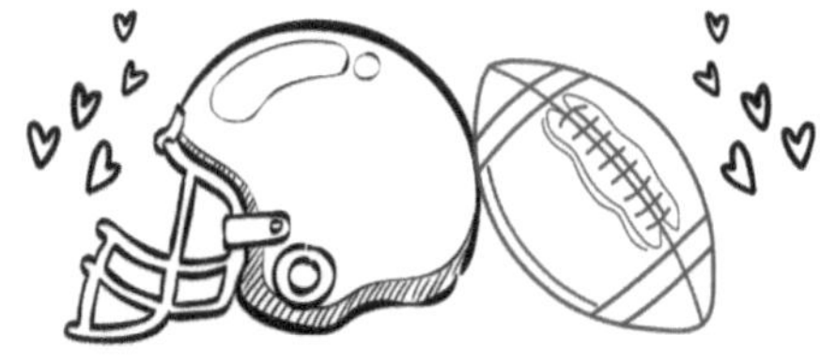

chapter
twelve

THERE'S an omega in the next room who now belongs to me.

And I don't know if I can go in there.

Not just because I don't *want* to, in general, but because I've never felt less prepared for anything in my entire life.

If I had known this was going to happen, I would have—

Well, I would have locked Tristan up.

But, if I had had time to *prepare*, I would have done some research. Set up special doctors and therapists. Made sure we at least had an empty guest room.

At that thought, I whip my phone out and send Myles a

disordered list of tasks. Hating that there isn't time to categorize them by importance or send more detailed notes.

My brother buzzes in place beside me. When his restless gaze shifts over my phone, he mumbles, "Tell him to order blankets. Pillows. And *underwear*."

While my brain stumbles over how absurd and unacceptable this situation is, Archer Monroe ducks back into the interrogation room. I hit send on the message and scowl at his back, rankled.

Isn't this whole thing bad enough without being *humiliated* in front of one of the few colleagues I respect?

But no. He's here to witness me shirtless and squirming.

It's almost worse that he's been so kind about this. No mocking or scorn or even judgment. I suspect it's less for my benefit and more for Jonah's—since Dr. Monroe actually *likes* Jonah.

As a rule, people do not like me.

Especially the ones who have to work with me.

I suppose it may also have something to do with Tristan, though. Despite the absolute mess he's caused, my brother is typically a very respected member of the community. Happily bonded alphas like Archer tend to support his politics because he's the foremost advocate for omega rights in all of Congress.

Which would make this extremely ironic, if I currently had a sense of humor.

"She's agreed to go home with you and stay through her next heat," Dr. Monroe reports, nodding as he strides out of the room. "Which I'd estimate will be here in four to six weeks. I'll prepare some notes on her care and email them over to you all."

Tristan's face doesn't flinch, but his eyes shift. I'm probably the only one who can sense the relief buried there. That's a logical reaction—any distance from Serena will cause him pain until the half-bond is completed. And being *away* from her during her heat would be miserable for both of them.

"It will be best to keep her out of the public eye," I mutter.

"Less risk of a scandal if she decides she wants to leave after her heat."

Tristan's voice drops into a warning snarl. "*Spencer.*"

I gesture around the abandoned police station, narrowing my eyes at him. "Don't start with the self-righteous bullshit. You cleared this place out for a reason. You—the senator leading a *national* charge for omega workplace rights—*biting and half-bonding* an unwilling omega? It's the scandal of the century, Tristan."

"No one will find out anything we don't want them to know," my brother replies, some of his innate dominance returning. "It's my job to protect her now. *And I will.*"

I lean to the side, peering through the window strip into the small, sterile room. Archer is there again, holding his tablet, explaining Serena's birth control options as Jonah frowns in concentration and the small, underfed omega hides the lower half of her face in Avery's sweatshirt.

Something unfamiliar pangs in my breast.

Serena.

It *is* a pretty name.

There's no denying she's beautiful. Well, what little of her I can see, that is. So far, it's just the full, dark fall of her hair and the shape of her down-turned face.

I follow the line of her gaze to the platforms dangling from her ankles. They're thicker than anyone should ever wear—*a safety hazard*—and thoroughly scuffed, with duct tape holding one of the buckles together.

Something about them clenches everything inside of me until I can barely breathe.

My brother stares, grim and determined. "From now on," he says, "she gets whatever she wants."

LISTEN, I might be clueless, but I'm not *stupid*.

And when the nice doctor tells me that I can either wait at the police station while they "sort me out" or "go home with the Thorne Pack"...

Well.

Is it even really a choice?

If all of Wally's jeers over the years are every bit as true as I feared, the only reason he isn't already here is...

Him.

Tristan.

I'm not sure how he's managed to run this place so smoothly, but it seems like every time he says "jump," people pull out their pogo sticks.

The doctor—Dr. Monroe—sees me blinking at the outline of the suited alpha through the door's window and offers me a small smile. "Senator Thorne is a very nice alpha. I think, if you were to decide to give him a chance, you might be pleasantly surprised."

Senator Thorne.

The name sounds familiar, but I'd have to borrow someone's phone to look up why. Dr. Monroe also told me that the one with the white-blond hair who won't stop glaring at me is Tristan's brother, Spencer. He's a professor, I guess.

A professor is one thing, but a *senator*? And *two* pro-athletes?

Their pack is famous.

Highly inconvenient, given I'm an urchin.

I'm still inclined to believe the doctor, though. He's been really nice so far, and since I can currently feel *everything* Tristan feels, I know he's *horrified* by what just happened.

His scent has burned to *ash*. Every time a twinge of panic shudders through me, he flinches. And the emotions rolling through his side of this flimsy, pinched bond are... *desolate.*

He hates himself for doing this.

Is it because of what he's done? Or who he did it to?

I've spent my whole life around alphas, so I know exactly how all of them think. And this? This should be my fault. For not covering my body, properly de-scenting, and keeping my guard up. For ever perfuming at all.

So, it's hard for me to believe he'd feel like this because *he bit* me.

But maybe because he bit *me.*

After all, I can't think of a less-suitable match for someone in the public eye than... whatever I am.

Oblivious to the terrible tangle inside of me, Avery and Jonah stand by my side, getting more agitated by the second. It takes me a moment to realize it's my fault—I'm filling this place with my distressed scent, the one that makes the alphas at the club so wild.

These guys only seem angry, though. They each direct a pointed look at the blond man sneering at me.

Jonah's big hand hesitates before it cups my shoulder, squeezing gently. "Don't mind Spencer," he murmurs. "We'll talk to him."

Tristan seems a bit beyond talking. He interrupts whatever his brother is muttering. The pack alpha's bark is quiet but hard as diamond. "*Enough.*"

I wish I could say that that burst of alpha dominance scared me as much as the thought of four grown men fighting because of me... but instead, a humiliating burst of wetness seeps out of my core, along with a wave of fresh, true perfume.

Behind me, Jonah grunts like a cannonball has just collided with his stomach. Avery bites out a vicious curse, sinking his teeth into his fist as he spins away.

I hang my head and manage to force one word around the lump in my throat. "S-sorry"

Such a sorry little slut, perfuming all the damn time. You must love these alphas all over you. Bet you're slick for them, too.

Wally's voice prickles down my spine as Dr. Monroe offers me a kind look, conspicuously devoid of any judgment or second-hand embarrassment.

"That will happen," he informs, calm and collected. "Now that Tristan is your alpha, his barks may have that effect. In fact, you will generally experience more potent physical cravings and heat-spikes because of the half-bond. It's natural. Nothing to be ashamed of. But it's also no reason for you ever to feel pressured into anything. Ultimately, you'll have to decide what feels best for you."

He really is nice. Whoever bonded him knew what was up. Unlike my looney Omega, who clearly wants us to get ripped to shreds like beef jerky.

I can tell the second my fresh perfume slips under the door, because the Thorne brothers are suddenly very quiet. Avery turns back to me, jaw flexing, eyes wild.

And I should be afraid. That would *make sense.*

But the second we look at one another, I just feel my nipples pebble harder.

He cuts a clean path to the table, going back to his knees and cupping his rough palms over my fishnet-covered knees. "You don't have to come with us," he growls, low and fervent. "Fuck those assholes. I'll wrestle them out of here right now."

I try to picture that—Avery, rolling Tristan and Spencer out of here. The image is almost enough to make me huff a laugh, but then I remember: If they go without me, I'll have to wait here for Wally. Or take my chances on the streets.

A frantic whine whips up my throat before I can stop it. Avery's beatific face creases. His fingers twitch against the sensitive skin on the insides of my knees.

"Okay, kitten, we won't leave without you," he husks. "You sure you want to hitch your wagon to all this crazy?"

My Omega is numbly terrified, half-gripping my reins in a frozen fist. She can't speak or think or really even breathe. Nothing scares her like Wally does. She wants me to get the hell out of here and hide where he'll never think to look for us.

I wish I could reason with her.

Then again, how would I do that? I know, logically, that I should be safe at a police station, but...

Well, I wasn't, was I?

Being here didn't stop an alpha—*Tristan*; and, no, we are *not* thinking about how hot that name is—from taking what he wanted from me.

Who's to say it couldn't happen again? These guys are still *oozing* pheromones, but at least they've been shot up with God-knows-how-many rut-blockers. Any other alpha who walks in here won't be as safe as these four.

And, Lord, what would Wally do with me now that he wouldn't have to worry about making sure no one bites me?

I look into Avery's eyes and try to breathe. It's hard, and I don't quite manage it—but the baby blue streaks carved into the ice of his irises help my lungs expand a tiny bit.

I nod. My hand falls on his, squeezing.

Please don't throw me to the wolves, dude.

His gaze glints, understanding. "I'll be there," he vows, answering the question I couldn't scrape out. "No one will touch you." He looks down at his own hands and gives me that one-quarter-smirk. "Much."

SERENA RIDES home in Avery's car, and I don't let anyone argue.

When I said she gets whatever she wants, I meant it.

Even though, the second there's more than half a block between us, a sharp pinch of pain embeds itself in my center.

By the time we reach the Bentley, it's so bad I can't think around it. Jonah must have been listening to all of Archer's warnings, because he doesn't seem surprised. He shakes his head in a you-poor-bastard gesture and slides into the backseat with me.

The ride home is silent and seething. Spencer drives, his fists tightening and relaxing reflexively on the wheel. I focus on the way his knuckles blanch to keep from groaning in agony.

Fuck.

It feels *unnatural.* Like there's something being ripped from the spot where my soul should be.

The fact that this isn't hurting Serena the same way is the only reason I manage to stay calm. According to Archer, she'll feel the loose bond, but it won't harm her because she isn't the one being rejected.

Her emotions swirl somewhere below all of the pain, dull but readable. She's still scared and overwhelmed, but she seems to be able to think now.

Avery must be keeping her comfortable because her anxiety is much more manageable—but every time she experiences my small bursts of relief, she seems distinctly surprised. As if she doesn't quite believe I could be comforted by her comfort.

Clearly, no one has ever been *kind* to her. And I'm no better than any of them.

I'm *worse.*

Beside me, Jonah distracts himself by looking up omega courting techniques. Dates, dinners, nesting, and gifts. All of the things Serena should have gotten before someone tried to claim her.

He still wants to do those things for her now, and I'm not even surprised—under all the menacing muscle, Jonah is easily the softest of us all.

And tonight? I made sure he'll never get to properly court anyone.

"I'm sorry," I rasp, pressing my hand to the pain in my abdomen and forcing words out.

Jonah looks over at me, his wide features reflecting the blue light from his phone. "Tris, you didn't do it on purpose. And you know we ruled out an omega years ago. I wasn't sitting around wishing and hoping I'd get to pick one or anything..."

I hear a "but" in his tone. Which is news to me.

We *did* decide against an omega. Ages ago. With my work representing the interests of omegas in the workplace, it seemed almost like a conflict of interest for us to court one. Not to mention all of Spencer's intimacy issues. And Avery's *rage*.

... Dear God. What have I done?

My gut clenches, full of guilt-ridden misery. A second later, there's an answering pulse of dismay. I've scared her again, shoving pain at her without any context.

I hate myself for it.

I'm sorry, sweet one.

I don't know if I'm relieved or devastated that she can't hear me.

❦

BY SOME TWIST OF FATE, cruel or fortuitous, our Bentley SUV rolls into the garage two seconds before the throaty rumble of Avery's Mustang echoes down our driveway.

He takes the ramp to our underground garage without slowing much, whipping into his usual spot between Jonah's fully-loaded Bronco and Spencer's spotless Volvo.

Typical Avery. I'll have to have a talk with him about keeping the omega safe.

Or maybe not.

Because instead of slamming his car door and loping off, Avery rounds the vintage Mustang and opens Serena's door for her. Then, he stoops low to fuss over her seatbelt, unclicking it carefully. He silently offers a hand to help her out of the low-riding vehicle.

And she *takes* it.

The rest of us exchange confounded glances while Avery tucks her hand against his bare chest and drops his face to kiss her small fingers.

His pale blue gaze snaps up to us, immediately filling with cool rage. "She's cold."

He says it like I'm personally responsible for the chill in the concrete garage. I suppose that's fair—I may not control the temperature, but Serena wouldn't be suffering for it if I had controlled *myself*.

It makes sense that she's uncomfortable. It's been raining for most of the evening, cooling the summer heat and leaving Orlando wet and gusty.

Not to mention her clothes. Or lack thereof.

My eyes skim down her bedraggled body, noting the tears in her stockings, the tangles in her hair.

I've dated some of the most beautiful women in the world. Supermodels, actresses, pageant queens. That's always been my type—the high-achieving, glossy sort of good looks that land magazine covers.

Couture lingerie. The highest quality grooming products. Bespoke gowns. Elegance, grace, and carefully cultivated loveliness.

Were any of them ever as beautiful as this scared, dirty young woman?

I truly don't think so.

I can barely focus on her beautiful face, though. Each time I try, my gaze flickers to the angry, red half-moons clamped around the left side of her neck. An unfamiliar bolt of urgency strikes my center, along with something equally as dire that swells lower.

I didn't think I could hate myself much more, but that isn't true. Because the second my eyes rove over that claiming mark, a spark of desire catches fire in the pit of my stomach—

No.

I stop the train of thought in its tracks, deeming it wholly unacceptable. She's endured enough of my unwanted attention without adding that aspect to it, surely.

It's too late, though. She feels my "interest" and huddles

closer to Avery. He cuts me a glare, letting her hide behind his body.

"We'll go right upstairs," Jonah chips, tossing in a wide smile. "Can't let our guest get chilly."

Serena's expression doesn't flicker one bit, but her sick swoop of dismay echoes in my gut.

Hmm.

The emotion is so strong, I'm surprised it isn't all over her face. Wherever she's been, whatever she's been through, she's learned to keep her feelings buried.

It reminds me of myself—and, even more, *Spencer.*

At the moment, *I'm* the one doing everything in my power to repress my desires. But every time my brain catches up to my body, my eyes are already lingering *there*, where her throat is torn and those dried pricks of blood—

No.

The elevator is a special kind of hell. Spencer takes the back corner, crossing his arms over his rumpled white shirt, refusing to touch anything. Avery stabs the button for the main floor of the townhome and then stiffens. Beside me, Jonah's grin freezes into a brittle grimace.

Because her *scent.*

Holy fucking *God.*

In the small confines of the lift, Serena's lush sweetness is otherworldly. Creamy coconut thickens the air while bright fresh-ness swirls off her. The sweet edges instantly darken into some-thing tantalizing.

Ave mutters a curse, dropping his chin to his heaving chest and squeezing his eyes shut. Spencer's stay wide open, his inten-sity stabbing at the side of Serena's face while his nostrils flare repeatedly. Bright interest lights Jonah's gold gaze while it sweeps over her.

And me?

I'm *dying.*

That's the only explanation for the pain. A searing tear at my center. The caving cramp in my chest. The aching pulse of arousal that stiffens my cock.

I do everything I can to swallow my groan, but it comes out as a strangled growl. The sound seems to snap everyone out of their own heads.

"Fucking *try it*," Avery snarls at me, stepping in front of Serena again. "I'll rip *your* throat out. See how *you* like it."

His threat barely registers. I'm too busy trying to sort the avalanche of emotion barreling through my abdomen. Mine and Serena's. It takes a moment for me to realize—

Spencer beats me to it. His eyes narrow at her, somewhere between accusing and confounded. "You aren't even aroused right now."

No. She isn't.

She hasn't been *at all* since we left the station.

This is just what she smells like. All the time.

Serena hangs her head. Her shame scrapes at my throat before slithering down to curl in my gut, joining my own. "M-my scent has always been s-strong. I'm s-sorry."

Poor baby.

It isn't as if she's done anything wrong. I step between her and my brother, leveling him with a look. "She isn't doing it on purpose."

Avery's jaw ticks. Just before the elevator slides to a stop, he turns and catches Serena's eye. Something unspoken passes between them, and she grabs at the waistband of his sweats with her free hand.

For some reason, the sight of her touching him suddenly *enrages* me. I smother another growl, my gaze snapping back to those teeth marks. Saliva wells in my mouth. My cock jerks harder.

Fuck. No!

The first-floor elevator empties into the kitchen, right beside the hallway to the Omega Suite and the stairs leading up to the second floor. The wide space is all black, much like the rest of our home. Aside from the "wall" behind the stove and refrigerator, where a long partition of thin wood slats serves to divide the kitchen space from the huge, sunken living room beyond.

My study is off that main living area, along with the proper foyer and sitting area, the formal dining room, Spencer's library, Jonah and Avery's gym, and Myles's work room.

Our valet hovers just behind the slatted wall, calmly awaiting instruction. If he's surprised we have a mostly naked omega with us, he doesn't let on. Then again, calling ahead to tell him to ready the suite was likely an obvious giveaway.

The second Serena sees him, she balks, backing into Avery's chest. A fearful whimper trembles out of her. Ave wraps an arm around her body and growls low.

But I'm the one who *roars*, "Myles, *get the fuck out*."

My packmates all gape at me, but I don't see them. I don't see anything but my unhealed bite, branded into my omega's throat.

RUN, *hide*.

My body moves before my brain can catch up. I scurry blindly into the first hallway I see, my mind racing.

Will these alphas come in after me? Will they take it as an assumption that they can all bite me? Knot me?

And—OH MY GOD—why does that make my thighs even slicker?

What is *wrong with me*?

"Serena!"

Tristan's bark impales me right between my shoulder blades. I stop instantly.

He's so dominant—one of the strongest alphas I've ever met, in terms of the sheer *force* of his will. But I get the feeling that this?

This is him going easy on me.

Barely daring to breathe, I turn back around, bracing for the pain that usually follows an alpha barking at me. When they see the way I quiver, all four of them fall silent.

Jonah scratches his beard, wincing. "Sorry about that, omega. I promise Tristan doesn't usually bark at our housekeeper. And we don't usually fight with each other like this."

Avery snorts.

"Much," Jonah amends, shooting him a look. "But we won't fight at all, now. We just want to talk to you a little. Figure out what you need since you're going to be living here."

The rest of his words fade into a buzz while the situation rolls over me.

Living here? Oh my God, but he's *right*. I don't have anywhere else to go, and even if I did...

I can feel echoes of Tristan's need radiating through my middle. It's bad enough to have me wishing he knew how to turn off the tap—which means it must *really* be bad for him.

And I'm *here*. What would happen to him if I walked out the door?

The concern I feel is almost manic. Hysterical. The room spins and blurs as a harsh sound scrapes out of me, almost a shriek, but not quite.

The others all frown, not understanding. But Tristan's face smooths into an unreadable mask, dark blue eyes glinting while they fall to my neck.

He keeps staring at the mark he left. And every time he does, a strange, jittery panic runs through me. Or maybe that's... *a thrill*?

Whatever the sensation is, it must echo through him because

he curses viciously under his breath, his stomach dropping along with mine.

Jonah whips his head back and forth between us. "What? What's happening?"

The mean, ice-blond one—Spencer—stares at me in his odd, calculating way, then does the same to his brother. His mouth twists in distaste. "Oh dear *God*."

Beside me, Avery bristles with tension. The professor turns to him and Jonah, explaining, "Her claim mark. Tristan hasn't tended to it. Which means she'll be in a half-haze and he'll be useless until it's healed. His Alpha is likely in a rage, and her Omega won't let her settle until the bite is properly tended."

Jonah's amber gaze widens. "And what does that mean, exactly?"

The professor makes sure we can all see his glare before gritting out his answer. "It means things are about to get very familiar, very quickly."

All four of them tense for a long moment. Tristan's unreadable eyes flick back to the throbbing bite. His voice drops low. "There has to be another way."

He doesn't want to do it.

If I were in total control of my body, I might find some way to feel angry. *Outraged.* I was good enough for him when I perfumed and he lunged at me, but now I'm not? Now that he's had time to think about it, he doesn't want to touch me anymore?

But I'm not in the driver's seat. And my Omega is *devastated*.

A soul-deep stab of hurt forces a whine from my throat. Tristan instantly comes toward me, his features creasing.

"She *wants* Tris to touch her?" Jonah asks Spencer, appalled.

It's a great question, but right now, I can't *think*. That same sensation from the interrogation room washes over me as our eyes meet—dark blue to green.

Safe. This alpha is safe.

Even though he's proven that he *isn't*.

When I whine again, shriller and louder, they all jump into

action. With everyone in motion and all the black walls, the room starts to blur around me.

"Shh," Tristan hums. "Shh, Serena. I'll take care of it."

Strong hands grip my hips, and then I'm weightless, being lifted into a leather barstool with a curved back. I realize it was Jonah when his voice rumbles right behind me.

"Her pupils have blown. Can she still hear us, Spencer?"

There are more murmurs, then Avery's beautiful face appears, my vision tunneling around him. "Is it okay for Tristan to tend to that bite, kitten? After he's done, it won't hurt anymore and you might be able to chill a little bit."

Seconds after the words leave his lips, I can't remember the question he asked, but every time I blink, his white-blue irises are the only thing I see. The only tether I have to reality.

I see the hesitation there, remnants of whatever his question was. And I don't know what he said, but I know the way this alpha makes me feel, deep down in the place no one else has ever touched me.

So I nod.

He almost looks soft for a moment. "That's my girl. My little fighter, huh? You take whatever you need from this knot-head. I'll be right over here."

A full-body shiver wracks my frame as the pack alpha steps behind me. His hands—large and warm—find my shoulders. "I'm sorry," he murmurs, so quiet I might even be imagining it. "I'm *so sorry*. I'm going to try to make it feel better, okay?"

That deep, vibrating regret surges through our half-bond again. I swallow hard against the answering shame and fear that squirm in my middle, focusing on the weight of his palms as they smooth down my upper arms.

Prickles of pleasure break over my buzzing skin. The empty pulse in my pussy pulls tauter and *throbs*. My hips writhe, trying to find friction in front of me or under me to relieve that damn, insistent *ache*.

"Shhh," he murmurs again, bending his head over my shoulder. "Shhh, sweet baby."

I know I must be delirious when I hear him say something that sounds like a pet name. Before I can think about it more, his lips graze the side of my throat.

And whatever thin string was doing a shitty job of tethering me to this earth?

Snaps.

sixteen

THE ALPHA behind me feels familiar—and that's all wrong.

It has to be, right? How could he be *familiar*? I don't *know* any alphas like this.

Not one who would rub his fingers along the insides of my arms while he bends to brush his mouth over my pulse. Not one who would groan softly against my skin or shudder when he tastes me.

Then, I feel his lips graze the burning ache in my throat.

His bite, some quiet, foggy part of me prompts. *He has to*—

Oh, but he *knows* what to do. The soft warmth of his upper

lip skims the very outside of the tingling teeth marks, sweeping over them in a soothing brush. When I whimper, he hums another deep moan.

The sound straightens my spine, pressing my head back against something solid and broad that smells like...

Him.

His shoulder. It cradles my skull while my chest thrusts forward on a pant. One of his hands slides up from my arm to thread into my loose hair, tilting my head so he can *lick* me.

Oh. My. God.

Hot wetness slides over my thin skin, slowly dipping into each of the burning grooves his teeth left behind. My breath snags in my lungs as cold shivers race down my back and heat slips from my core.

I feel dizzy and depraved as my heartbeat pounds between my thighs, pouring more slick out of my pussy while I squirm. Needing, *needing*—

"Alpha!"

The sharp cry has a jagged edge. There are more noises around me. Growls, shuffling.

"He isn't hurting her," someone clips. "But bonding bites are touch-sensitive. Every time Tris touches it, she'll feel..."

"Horny?" someone else guesses.

The serious voice replies, succinct and entirely correct, "Desperate."

As if it's agreeing with him, my body gushes more slick and perfume. Muffled curses blend with the serrated groan vibrating against my neck.

The fullness of the alpha's lower lip begins rubbing at the other edge of his mark, gently grazing the indentations with slippery warmth and summer-scented breath.

My nipples peak into hard, stinging points, poking at whatever terrible material is covering them. I try to reach up and touch, but I have no coordination. My palms slap at the rubbery fabric until another whine rips from my throat.

"Shhh," the low growl behind me rumbles. "Shhh, sweet one."

Large hands slip into whatever material's wrapped around me and engulf my breasts easily, their long fingers rolling my nipples into tingling points. Stars dance behind my eyelids, flashing in flares of light every time he pinches the sensitive tips and strokes them with his thumbs.

The haze feels thicker with every jolt of pleasure that streaks from my tits to the steady thump between my thighs. Another sound—high-pitched as the chilling screech of nails on glass—fills the room. It's so jarring, a spike of panic impales my chest... which somehow makes the terrible noise even worse.

Oh God. Is my body *melting*?

All of my muscles are jelly. Slick puddles under my bare butt. And there are alphas nearby, fighting.

I can suddenly sense them all—three, arguing urgently. "She needs you, Ave."

The reply is heavily gritted. "If I move one single muscle, we'll be dealing with a whole new bite. Spence should do it. He's the most in control."

Someone else disagrees. The serious alpha drops his voice into a low murmur. "It has to be you, Jonah. Avery shouldn't risk it, and I... can't—"

The teeth at my throat scrape lightly over their pulsing indentations. Another whine blares through the room. There are movements and more mutters.

Until suddenly, a big, burly alpha looms right in front of me. He's toasty and sweet, something unfamiliar and delicious that pairs perfectly with the summery smell enveloping me from behind. When I suck his scent into my lungs, they vibrate, my haze doubling.

His features swirl and blur, but I make out a wiry black beard and amber eyes. They flare wide, bewildered, and for a second, I want to *cry*.

He doesn't want me. There's something wrong with me. He probably thinks I'm just a silly little slut, too. And now—

The alpha dives to the floor.

Even kneeling in front of whatever I'm perched on, he's tall enough to put his face level with my knees. Brawny, rough hands completely cover the sides of my thighs, flexing restlessly.

"Tell me what you want, *manamea*," he grunts, chest rattling.

Lord, I must really be losing it. Pretty sure that last word he said wasn't in English, but maybe I'm just insane.

Insane and having a complete omega meltdown in some strange pack's kitchen while their alpha tends to his bite mark by *swirling his tongue* around my pulse. Oh my *God*.

When I whine higher, the burly alpha's eyes darken. His scent gets thicker, reacting to my need. "Do you want me to help you stay still? Or touch you?"

A sharp stab of relief slips into my gullet. *Touch me*, I want to scream. But another unintelligible screech is all I can scrape out.

As if testing my reply, his palms skim higher. I buck against the open air, trying to get closer to him.

The alpha behind me grumbles approvingly. His body presses into the seatback so tightly, I feel his suit jacket brush my sides. The hands on my tits tighten, kneading as the guy between my legs hesitates.

A snarl of frustration snags in my chest... and the next thing I know, my hands are gripping a full head of hair. Tugging at the dark roots. Guiding the big man's face right to my pussy.

There's a long moment of stillness. My breath stutters to a stop, and the alpha rubbing at his claiming mark pauses. But then the man I'm yanking on moans, deep and every bit as desperate as I feel.

The groan sinks between my hips. Perfume and slick pour out of me, drawing a snarl from the alpha lunging at the apex of my thighs.

"Fuck," the one behind me says into my skin, sucking at his bite. "*Fuck*."

Brawny hands snap my legs open. One broad finger hooks into the red strap covering my bare pussy, tugging it aside. I thrust up toward him, gripping the long coarse hair between my fingers even harder, pushing him exactly where I need him.

Even though there's nothing I can do about it—no way to reason with my Omega when we're this far gone—the fear is still there. Coiled tightly in my chest, telling me I have no right to demand anything from this alpha.

Or anyone, *ever*.

But the pack leader skates one of his hands off my tits to smooth a soothing caress down my sternum, almost like he's trying to blot my anxiety out.

And the one between my legs? The humungous guy I'm manhandling?

He *praises* me.

"Good fucking girl," he grinds out, yanking me to the edge of my seat. "Telling your alphas what you need, even when you can't talk."

He sounds like he's panting. When I look down, I see that he is—his enormous shoulders rise and fall sharply while he stares between my legs like I'm a gateway to heaven.

And—God—how is that possibly making me even *needier*?

I tug at his hair again. His teeth gnash, somewhere between a smile and a snarl. But his eyes leap over my shoulder and hold.

I don't realize he's waiting for his alpha's permission until the muffled voice at my neck mumbles, "Kiss her, Jonah."

Right, Jonah.

Jo.

Half a breath later, his wide, full mouth seals over my glistening pussy lips—and he freezes. A choked, pained sound reverberates over my mound, teasing my clit until a fresh burst of slick quivers out of my opening.

A deep, rougher roar echoes in his heaving chest. His body tweaks tight, twitching hard while his eyes flutter shut. Behind me, the other alpha makes a similar sound, sucking my neck and rolling my nipples harder.

As quickly as he froze, the burly alpha snaps his eyes open and looks down at everything he has in his mouth. With another broken groan, he flicks his tongue out, skating it between my lips and grinding the tip against the ring of muscle clenching at my core.

"So goddamn *good*," he husks. "Fucking perfect, *manamea*. I want this sweet little pussy to *drown me*."

My fingers flex against his scalp, a whine breaking the tension in my lungs while the fingers kneading my breasts soften.

The lips at my throat alternate between sucking and rubbing, wet heat dipping into every mark. Soothing and setting me on fire at the same time, especially when he murmurs, "That's a good omega. You going to ride my packmate's face? Make him come in his pants again?"

Is *that* what just happened?

I don't have time to process it because the strong, wide tongue between my thighs smooths a slow path up to my buzzing clit. And wraps around the whole thing.

The taut coil in my center pops, exploding in a white-hot flash of pleasure.

"Mm," the alpha hums, lapping at me harder. "Give me another one. I'll put my fingers in this perfect little pussy so it has something to clamp down on."

An embarrassing squeal sloughs out of me as he doubles down, working my clit in soft nudges and hard licks, hooking two of those thick fingers into my soaked slit.

The roughened pads glide through trembling heat, my muscles clutching desperately at him. He loves that—delving his touch deeper while he moans against my swollen bud, plucking it gently between his lips and smoothing the top with his tongue.

Slick slides down his fingers and past his wrist. The hands cupping my breasts squeeze while the standing alpha fits his teeth back over his bite and clamps just hard enough to make me dizzy.

Their tongues work in tandem, the sinuous circles lapping faster and harder, sending my body into a violent spin cycle that I swear will break me apart.

Instead, all of my tension erupts again. Harder and deeper than before. Wrenching pulses contract in my core, tugging those big fingers as deep as they'll go and earning another round of growls from both men.

My haze doesn't burn off, though. I sway as the teeth at my throat and the lips brushing my core disappear. Four strong hands glide over my sides, my legs.

A rough voice floats into my brain, its words lost to the fog that pulls me under.

WIPING CUM out of my joggers was not on my bingo card for today.

Neither was becoming a complete simp in, like, twenty minutes—but here we are.

Having tucked Serena in, Jonah and Tristan shuffle back into the kitchen. By then, I've cleaned up the worst of the mess, but Spencer is still glaring at me from the bottom of the stairs. As if he didn't want to take his dick out and come all over the floor just now.

If he's fooling anyone, it's himself. I can see the boner pressed into his pants. And the way he's gripping the stair rail with two hands, like he doesn't trust what he'd do if he let go.

I get the feeling.

When Serena started whining for relief, I wanted to be the one to give it to her so goddamn bad. But even the *thought* of licking her made my teeth ache. If I had lost focus for half a millisecond, Tris wouldn't have been the only one tending his bite mark.

And then she might hate me.

Which would be inconvenient, considering I'm *obsessed* with her.

When the others catch me grinning, they look at me like I'm a lunatic. Well, Jonah does. Tristan is too busy looking sick, and Spencer is glowering down his nose.

"This will never work," he bites out. "We need to bring the omega back out here and give her an overview of our expectations. She needs to know—"

"—that she's free to do anything she wants," Tris interrupts, equally fierce despite the way his hand clutches at his center. "She's under no obligation to any of us."

Spencer blinks at him, his mouth actually falling open for half a second. "*No obligation?* Are you delusional or suicidal? If she were to leave or get hurt, what, exactly, do you think will happen to *you?*"

Sometimes, when you're in the middle of a Thorne Brother Smackdown, you might get the distinct sense that you're missing some crucial shit. Their family is all sorts of fucked-up, but they never talk about it beyond vague allusions and this sort of prep-school debate club bullshit.

Wouldn't it just be easier if they punched each other?

Tristan gazes at Spencer for a long beat before gathering himself. With a roll of his shoulders, he's back to his full pack alpha power, smothering the room with a thick layer of cool dominance.

"I know what will happen," he answers simply, staring his

brother down. "And it will be my own damn fault. None of this is her burden, least of all *me*. If she wants to leave, we'll let her go. Her safety is my only priority."

Tingles squeeze my lungs, burning deep. Fervor, I think, which is an emotion I'm wholly un-fucking-familiar with.

But keeping Serena *safe*? Shit. That might be my new religion.

She isn't even in the room anymore and her perfume has soaked into the place—bright, creamy sweetness. But I don't think that matters anymore.

Clearly, my Alpha knows perfection when he sees it. And that means there must be a hell of a lot more to her than her scent.

"We need to figure out how to court her."

My packmates all cut me suspicious looks. Like the fact that I'm trying to be a part of their conversation is some sort of conspiracy. I roll my eyes.

"You know," I prompt, "ask her what she likes. Doesn't like. Who she is and why she was at the station tonight. We should, like, ask what happened."

Spencer openly seethes. "We *know* what happened. She escaped an abusive situation."

The words fall between us, landing in the middle of our stupid black kitchen with a *splat*.

Fuck. He's right.

I've seen some grotesque shit in my life. Broken bones, gore, guys who didn't make it out of the ring. But nothing—*nothing*—has ever made my stomach sink and twist and *squirm* like this.

Someone hurt *our mate*.

It doesn't even matter when or why or how. The simple fact that it happened makes me murderous.

Jonah catches my eye. He looks every bit as sick as I feel, but dazed, too. Can't say I blame him there. The second I get my chance to taste our omega and make her feel good, I might just check-out permanently.

Well, world, it's been real, but I live between this omega's thighs now.

Tristan's broken rasp breaks into the conversation. "I'll try to find out. But we should be prepared for what might happen when she wakes up. If she wants to leave, we can't force her to stay."

"Like hell we can't," Spencer snipes. "You bit her. You're *half-bonded* to her. That means she *stays*, Tristan."

Again, I feel like I need some subtitles for whatever they're actually arguing about. But Jonah interrupts before I can ask.

"Come on, guys," he mutters, rubbing at his slick-shiny beard. "Let's not fight about this. She hasn't said she *wants* to leave. I think that means we should be planning how we're going to win her over right about now. This is our *mate*. Are we seriously not going to *try* here?"

Tristan stares at him, gears spinning, but Spencer scoffs. "I think *courting* ended when Tris's teeth broke her skin."

"Jonah's right."

All three of them freeze again, whirling to look at me with those same stunned expressions.

Assholes.

I shrug, playing off their surprise. "We have to grow some balls. I know this situation is fucked-up, but we should still *try*. That's what people do when they care about someone, right?"

Jonah's brows crunch. His mouth quirks so he's speaking out the side of it to the others. "Am I losing it, or was that actually inspiring?"

chapter **eighteen**

OKAY.

Okay.

Where am I?

My eyelids squeeze while I think through the options. *Well, I'm either going to wake up at Wally's and realize the whole gorgeous-pack-of-mates, accidental-bonding, riding-an-NFL-player's-face thing was a dream...*

Or I'll be in some strange room. Which would mean that all of that insanity actually happened, and I'm—I just—

Oh God.

Can you die of embarrassment? Asking for a friend.

If all of that really happened, it explains why the emptiness in my middle feels so strange. At first, I think it's just because my Omega has retreated, back to whatever corner she's been holed up in for years. I wonder when she slipped away and if she'll come back.

Then, I realize that there's also a noticeable lack of earth-shattering regret. Which means Tristan Thorne has left the building.

Fragments from his conversation with the doctor alpha swirl through my hazy memories of the moments after he bit me. The doctor wanted him to shut down the bond from his side, to seal his emotions off and keep me calm. If all of that was real, then he's definitely figured it out.

I'm sure my thoroughly mortifying behavior earlier helped motivate him, but I don't care. I'm just relieved. At least, for now, everything I feel is my own.

The first sensation isn't a feeling, though.

It's *hunger*.

The painful, queasy kind that tells me it's been a while since Wally deigned to provide me with a meal.

There may not be a Wally anymore, I think, dazed and, somehow, sicker.

I try to take a deep breath and force my eyes open, but a swirl of heavenly scent curls down my throat. Four different alphas, all blended into an aroma so rich that my pussy instantly slicks all over again. My head spins, a stab of fear impaling the whine that wants to scale the back of my throat.

I've spent years around every type of alpha there is. Rotten ones, metallic ones. The sort that smell musky or sickly-sweet. Popcorn, cardboard, wet socks. Egg salad, cheap beer. Asphalt. Sawdust.

None of them—not a one—had any sort of positive effect on me.

It made sense. I was broken. Fractured or fucked-up or freakish. Whatever you want to call it—my ass was never *normal*. I'd accepted it.

I *liked* it, because, no matter how those alphas at the club treated me—no matter how they leered or catcalled or groped or smacked—I didn't care. None of them could touch me *inside*—where it counted.

Which is why the smell of this pack *terrifies* me.

Why do they smell *so good*?

What if I'm making them up?

Is that even possible? They seem so *real,* and I honestly doubt my imagination is *this* good.

All blurred together, I can't even tell where one scent ends and another begins. There's the summer-sweet grass and orange blossoms that I thought belonged to Tristan, but it's layered with a cool freshness. Rain and wet stone. Dew-soaked gravel or a wet brick road. The electric *snap* of a thunderstorm on my tongue.

That ominous, otherworldly scent was the smell clinging to Spencer's dress shirt. It overlaps perfectly with Tristan's—almost like they're one scent instead of two.

Avery's masculine perfume winds through it in a teasing, mysterious sort of way. A lazy curl of jasmine smoke. Musky amber. Spicy and sweet.

Or... or is that sweetness from something else? Jonah, the big, burly one, made my mouth water just as much as he made my body gush. Sticky and toasted, but rich and golden, too. With... chocolate?

What *is* that?

In the end, I decide I have to figure out what the hell is happening. I can always blame it on my stomach later.

Keeping my eyes shut, I scrabble upright, my trembling hands sifting through something soft and sumptuous piled around me. Once I'm sitting, I blow out a long breath and crack one lid open.

Holy. Fucking. Shit.

Where am I?

This couldn't possibly be... a guest bedroom? *My* guest bedroom?

Who *lives* like this?

Politicians, my brain sneers. *And NFL players*. Not to mention the professional MMA fighter and a professor at some prestigious university.

So maybe the room makes sense.

If my hazy memory serves, I didn't see much of their townhouse, but everything I saw was black. This room has the same luxurious, impenetrable feel, and the palette is every bit as dark. But the similarities end there.

Because this room is... *cosmic*.

I've never seen anything like it. Big and open and *beautiful*.

Midnight walls stretch high on three sides. The paint is a rich, purply black infused with some sort of sheen—glittery and subtle. It reminds me of the photos of constellations I've seen in books, the way stardust seems woven into the darkness but also stands apart from it.

Not that I need a picture of the stars in here.

Not when the entire back wall *and* ceiling are *made of windows*.

My neck cranes back while I follow the matte metal frames and clear, shining glass—all the way from the floor of the back wall to the ceiling seam over the entrance.

"Wow," I murmur, awed.

"You're awake."

I jump, screeching. "Holy fuck!"

A dark rumble answers across the room. From the broad shape of a man sitting on the chair in front of the room's antique vanity.

He stands slowly. Shadows shift until the tailored lines of Tristan Thorne's body come into view. My stomach plunges to my feet.

"You're real."

It is, quite possibly, the stupidest thing I've ever said. Tristan's face creases into a frown, the expression more intimidating than before, with shadows surrounding his square jaw and settling over the thick ledge of his brow.

"I am real. You're in our pack house. And you've been asleep for about two hours."

Okay. That makes sense. Or, at least, it all fits with the fantastical story I thought I'd made up. I nod, but the motion is shaky.

"You're speaking again," the alpha staring at me points out. "I was wondering if you would when you woke."

And because I'm stupid and awkward, I do this weird, seated half-curtsy thing that does not achieve the casual air I was striving for because my voice shakes. "Ta-da."

Good Lord.

Kill me now.

Tristan doesn't even crack a derisive smirk. In fact, his frown *deepens.* "Are you—" He pauses to clear his throat and tug at the sleeve of his dress shirt. "How do you feel?"

I assume "wet" isn't a great answer, even if it's true. Honestly, I need a shower and food and some clothes to borrow, but I'm too chicken to say anything other than, "F-fine."

His scowl just gets more severe when he sighs. "You shouldn't lie to me, Serena. I can still—"

My stomach starts to roil, and he cuts himself off, narrowing his flashing eyes and scanning over my body. "Did we harm you earlier? I know it must be difficult for you to believe, but none of us would ever hurt you on purpose. If what Jonah did wasn't welcome..."

I notice he omits any mention of his own role in the whole thing. Which makes sense, right? Why would a powerful, beautiful man like Tristan Thorne want to admit to an attraction to *me?*

I'm still in this STUPID RUBBER THONG.

My cheeks burn. "He didn't do anything wrong. I should probably apologize to him, though. I was..."—*unhinged*—"Is he okay?"

For the first time since the whole biting fiasco, the side of Tristan's mouth twitches. "He's fine, omega. Jonah is used to taking hits from three-hundred-pound linebackers. I'm afraid having a tiny omega grind into his face doesn't rank high on his list of concerns."

Oh. Of course. *Stupid.*

These are, like, grown men. They probably have sex all the time.

I mean, I'm no virgin, but I know I have significantly less experience than most people my age. Especially other omegas. I've never even had a knot, real or fake, and—

A low sound echoes in Tristan's chest. I think it's a growl, but he douses it too quickly for me to feel sure.

The air in my lungs freezes over. Is he... angry? With me?

Shit. I can't piss this alpha off. I have literally nowhere else to go, not to mention he's already marked me, and his pack smells like heaven and—and—

"*Breathe, omega,*" he barks, low and firm. "There are a few things you should know."

I DON'T OFTEN FEEL stupid.

Guilty? Yes. All the time.

Guilt has been my constant companion since Spencer was old enough to talk to me about what he went through in the same household that raised me like a prince.

It only got worse when I got older and realized how privileged our family was. And then even worse, again, when I got into politics and saw just how much I wasn't doing. *Couldn't* do.

I'm also all too familiar with doubt. I've always wondered if I was doing the right thing. For my brother, my pack, the people who elect me. Hell, the people who didn't elect me, too.

But stupid? Embarrassed by my own cluelessness?

No. This seething burn of humiliation in my stomach is brand-new.

Well-deserved, though, for many reasons. Chief among them, at the moment, being the fact that I honestly thought this omega might not hate me.

Back at the police station, before everything went wrong, it felt like we connected. I felt it again when I was tending her bond mark. And the instinctive reaction my body had to hers is undeniable.

I knew what to do. It felt perfectly right to care for her like that. I wanted it to mean something.

And the longer I sat in her suite, looking around at all the furnishings I chose ages ago, wondering how she would feel about them... I don't know. Maybe I just *wanted* to believe in the best-case scenario. Or needed to.

Either way, I'm doomed to disappointment.

From the second she realized I was in the room, she's been terrified. Filled with shame, regret, doubt, and anxiety.

The best thing I can do for her right now is leave. But I promised the guys I would have this conversation. Avery was right; we need to know what led her to the police station tonight.

Spencer also had a point—there are practical matters at play here. If she doesn't choose to stay, I'll begin a slow, painful unravel. If she *does* stay, then I'll have to deal with those consequences too.

The press won't like it. Neither will a lot of my constituents.

But, of all of us, Jonah made the best point of all.

We have to try.

Even if it means humbling myself to her every single day, I want to try.

Her sweet, sad face pinches as a wave of apprehension swamps us both. Thankfully, it doesn't seem like she can feel my emotions anymore.

Figuring out how to stop assaulting her with my feelings took much more effort than I ever expected. Even now, it feels unnatural. Instead of a closed curtain, the way Dr. Monroe described, it's more like a door I have to lean against at all times.

She isn't blocking *me*, though.

Which means I feel everything she does.

It's a one-way street, but at least it won't cause her any distress. I almost told her about it a moment ago, but she's already so overwhelmed. I don't want to burden her with one more thing. Ever.

That's what the noble part of me argues, at least. The less-gallant piece hisses that there's a chance this omega will never let me get close to her any other way. Experiencing the frayed fragments of her feelings might be as close as I ever get to a real bond with her.

And I would deserve that rejection.

"W-what do you want to talk about?" she stammers.

Everything.

The word sticks in my throat. Pitifully, painfully true.

I want to *know* her, so badly it literally feels like it's killing me. But why would she ever want to share anything with me? I've already proven, beyond a shadow of a doubt, that she can't trust me.

It's better if she doesn't, anyway. I no longer trust *myself.* And her safety is now this household's top priority.

"A variety of things, but we'll stick with the essentials," I hedge. "Obviously, you'll need decent clothes, shoes, and other personal effects. I have an iPad here that I'll give you to use until we're able to source a proper phone—on it, you'll find links to our pack's personal shoppers. They upload options, and all you need to do is choose whatever you like. I'll make sure it all gets here as quickly as possible."

Serena blinks, her face carefully blank. Hiding the nausea shifting in her stomach. "What will I do? While I stay here?"

Of all the questions I expected—*how could you do this? What the fuck is the matter with you? How far away from me can you move within the next twelve hours?*—I never expected that one.

What will she *do*?

I look right into her eyes, flexing all the alpha power I possess. "Whatever you want."

I've never meant anything quite so much. She can literally have anything she asks for. If she wants a private plane to Tahiti, I'll book one. If she asks for a limitless credit card, I have four in my wallet. If she wants to work or study or book daily appointments at every spa from here to L.A., she can have it all.

Any of it.

But she just stares at me as her insides fill with *dread*.

I don't understand why. What does she think I mean? Or maybe she just doesn't believe me. I can't say I blame her.

So I try one more thing. "I can get you your own apartment, even," I offer, repressing the way my entire body wants to cringe at the thought. "Anything you'd like."

Serena's emotions are a thorny tangle, but she bites her lower lip slowly, her face still carefully blank. "I—might like to stay. For now."

Relief swamps me, and then doubles when I remember she can't feel how enormously thankful I am. "Very well. I'll leave the iPad for you to make your wardrobe and food selections. Jonah didn't know what you'd like to eat, but he was worried you may be hungry, so he made you a sandwich. It's here on the nightstand for you."

When she bites her lip harder, I see that her teeth are relatively straight and white. Which strikes me as odd, given how poorly she was cared for in other ways.

Then again, her hair is perfect, too. Long and smooth. I've known enough women to know that there's some sort of chemical straighter and shining lacquer on it. Her brows are neatly threaded; her nails are long, almond-shaped, glittering with nude polish.

And when Jonah shoved that bodysuit aside earlier, I couldn't help but notice that she's waxed perfectly smooth—

Jesus, Alpha. Not now.

I force myself to focus, squinting at her in the dark.

What sort of situation would leave an omega underweight, nutrient-deficient, and riddled with healed injuries... with perfect hair and nails—and the prettiest pussy I've ever seen?

Fucking hell—not now!

"Would you tell me..." I prompt, speaking through gritted teeth while I ignore my throbbing knot, "what happened to you?"

She huddles lower on the bed, looking so small and tired suddenly. The feelings that swirl through her are devastating, but her voice is so soft. "I'm sure you can guess."

I don't want to guess. I want to know.

Mostly so I can assure her that no matter what she did before or wants now, there's no reason for the self-loathing swarming her stomach.

As I stare at her, trying to summon patience, the sick swell in her gut doubles, and a matching pulse of guilt fills me. There's so much *shame*. Mine makes sense, but hers? I don't understand it.

This omega looks like she's wasting away. She needs to *eat*. And sleep more. If I keep pushing her, she may not be able to do either tonight.

"We can discuss it some other time," I decide, stepping away. "I'll leave you to rest."

That nagging feeling of unnaturalness assails me. I don't really want to leave her—but relief rolls through her half of our incomplete bond, so I turn to go.

"Tristan?"

Her quiet little voice says my name for the first time, and my heart clenches.

I look over my shoulder in time to catch her swallowing hard.

One of her manicured hands floats up, tracing the mark I left in her neck. "Th-thank you. For letting me stay here."

The words are daggers. They sink into my middle and twist. I've done nothing—*nothing*—to deserve this woman's gratitude.

"Don't thank me," I order, unable to bear it. "*Never* thank me."

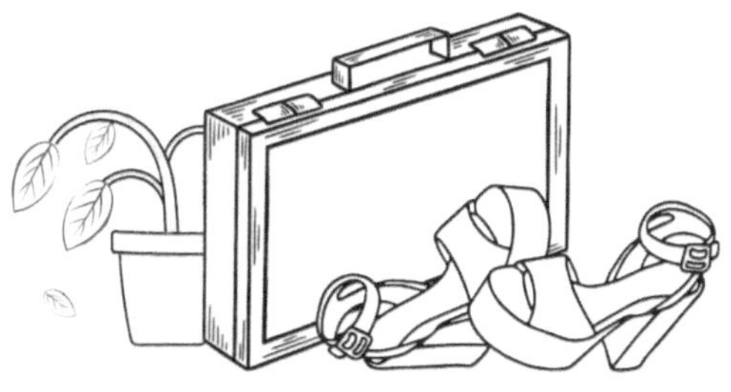

chapter
twenty

NEVER THANK ME.

My Omega gives a quiet whine as Tristan's words sink in. He's long gone by then, the door to the beautiful guest room firmly shut.

He seemed pretty dang eager to get out of here.

I'd be more insulted if I weren't still in this ridiculous bodysuit.

The reality of the situation gradually sinks through me. I left my old life. I got away. And then—I sort of got my dream.

A pack, mates.

But they're basically gods, and I'm homeless.

Just imagining what they all must think of me—weak, damaged, dressed like a sex doll, oozing perfume I can't control—brings tears to my eyes. I draw my knees to my chest and set my forehead against them, hoping the silk sheets can handle my self-pitying sprinkle.

Really, I know this isn't so bad. I could have been bitten by alphas way worse than these. They could have passed me around earlier when I was so out of my mind, but they didn't. None of them even took anything for themselves, did they?

No. No, they couldn't because I *grabbed one by the hair and shoved him between my legs.*

...

Oh, *God*.

Remembering the stunned look on the burly man's face as I desperately dragged him by his beard makes me feel like I've been stabbed. A hopeless wail flies out of my mouth while I curl tighter around my legs.

The door bursts open. I scrabble back, panicked until I see it's just Avery, standing on the threshold with murder in his eyes. He flashes them around the room as if looking for a threat and then skewers me with his gaze.

But only for a second, because Jonah *tackles* him.

Um...

Is this normal?

"I told you *no*," Jonah roars, pinning him to the ground. "You can't just walk into her *room*! You have to *knock*."

They're wrestling... over manners?

My mouth hangs open, tears forgotten. Everything forgotten, really, except for Jonah's huge, flexing body on top of Avery's inked muscles.

With uncanny flexibility, Avery somehow flips his packmate off him and pins his legs with his knees.

"I was *checking on her*. She's *crying*."

Avery snaps the words out like I'm bleeding from the head,

not leaking tears. Jonah stops struggling and turns to look at me. When he sees how puffy and gross I must look, he goes limp.

With one final shove, Avery gets up and offers a begrudging hand to help Jonah lumber to his feet, too.

Lord, they're *huge*.

Earlier, when my silent Omega was in charge, she noticed a lot of things about them, but not their sheer *size*.

Which might be impressive—if I wasn't alone and unprotected.

And covered in my dried slick.

My scent shifts into the version that I pumped out for years—darker than my usual aroma, but also sweeter. The one that drove all those alphas wild.

Both guys freeze, staring. Seconds pass before Avery starts to lurch forward. He catches himself, raising those otherworldly eyes to mine. "Can we come in, kitten?"

My head feels floaty as I nod. It's their house, after all. Besides, having seen what they do to one another when they disagree, the last thing I want is to piss them off.

Jonah shuffles in behind Avery. While the latter comes right over to my bed, the big football player looms in the shadows where Tristan stood earlier, looking around.

It seems like he hasn't been in this room before. He absorbs everything in it with a blend of approval and... longing?

Maybe this isn't a guest room after all. What if it's actually the *Omega Suite*?

Would Tristan really put me in the special room reserved only for his pack's omega?

Avery answers my unspoken question as he pouts, grunting at the glass wall behind the huge bed. "Damn windows. Stupid thing to put in your suite. Sunlight's gonna wake us up every fucking morning."

Us?

As in they'll be staying in here?

My heart trips over a beat of excitement before my mind

catches up. Do I want two alphas I don't really know sleeping in here?

Maybe?

My scent gets darker as I fret internally, doing my best to keep my face smooth. But Jonah's shining topaz eyes catch my gaze from across the room. His solid features crumble into a frown.

"In the elevator earlier, I wondered what that darker edge to your scent meant, and now—You're *scared*," he mutters, moving closer. Pain tightens the laugh-lines at the corners of his eyes. "Oh, *manamea*, don't be scared. Avery and I won't hurt you, I promise."

There's that word again—*manamea*. The one I thought I heard but didn't understand. I don't have time to worry about it, though.

Avery cups his hand around my jaw, the now-familiar gesture just as soft as the first time he did it. "Are you really afraid of us, kitten? We can leave you alone. I just heard you crying from the hallway and couldn't stay away."

I blink at his beautiful face. "You were in the hallway?"

Jonah nods. "The whole time. We wouldn't leave you alone with Tris like that after what happened. We didn't know how you might feel about him being in your space, but his Alpha couldn't calm down with you out of his sight. So we had to compromise."

That's actually... really sweet. Especially considering I basically assaulted this guy in his own kitchen earlier.

Shame burns the edges of my scent. I tuck my legs in tighter, attempting to hide how much skin I have on display. I try to meet his eyes, so he knows I'm talking to him, but I only manage one brief glance.

"I—I'm so sorry about earlier."

The toasted sweetness in the air plummets into a burned, gooey mess the same second Avery's expression blinks into total blankness.

Have I made them angry? Already?

A whine I can't bury ekes out. I shrink down instinctively, shaking. Jonah's chest rumbles in a growl.

A long growl.

A... *really* long growl.

Holy shit, *how* is he still growling? It just goes on and on and —*oh.*

Could that be a *purr*?

JONAH

I CAN STILL TASTE SERENA.

Warm and tropical, but cool and sweet. A rainforest as green as those wide, gorgeous eyes. A paradise every bit as lush as the glory I found between her thighs.

Mate, mate, mate.

My mind chants, my teeth throbbing along with my knot.

It helps that she's still soaked onto my lips. The luscious sweetness honeys every breath I take, sinking into my lungs while they vibrate on rough purrs.

It should be perfect.

But the look on her face is *killing me.* And the fact that she's apologizing for the *single greatest moment* of my entire life feels like a gut-punch.

My Alpha's urgent need to care for her ramps up. The only thing I can think of is food. She must be starving, and the sandwich I made her is untouched.

In the pale moonlight, those emerald eyes are Serena's only spot of color. So big. So bright. The rest of her looks puny and downright colorless by comparison—dark features and ashen brown skin.

Getting something in her belly suddenly feels more important than breathing. I hustle, lurching toward the bed, and she—

Cowers.

Crouching down into the mattress, with her baggy sleeves piled over her face and head. A whine shatters the air.

Avery and I both go still, staring at each other. It's honest to God the first moment I've ever seen fear in his eyes. And also the first time he's ever voluntarily looked to me for help.

I'm not sure how *I* know what she needs, but I do.

Moving slowly, I lower myself into the mountain of pillows stacked behind her. Reaching over, I gently stroke my palm along her trembling back.

"Come here, omega."

She shakes harder, peeking at me with one eye. "I—I'm sorry. I—I—"

She thinks I want to *punish* her somehow. For needing relief while my pack leader tended her bite mark. The claim he made *without her permission.*

The need to protect her—from any other harm, from her own misplaced *shame*—vibrates in my blood. My purr revs louder as the hand on her spine slips lower. In one motion, I scoop her straight into my arms.

Avery goes stiff, watching me warily, but my Alpha isn't concerned. His intuition blurs with mine, smoothing the edges of my purr while I hold her against my chest.

She's so light; it's a miracle she hasn't blown away. She needs to eat *now*. But I want her to feel relaxed first.

Soothing sounds blend with my purr while I cuddle her tenderly, waiting for her body to realize she isn't in danger. Not with me.

The second my chest touches the side of her face, her whine dies. A shudder of pleasure rolls through her, but it still feels like she's bracing.

My purr rolls on anyhow. Serena's shakes turn into shivers. When she sniffles, I realize she isn't just quivering; she's *crying*. And trying to hide it.

"Aww, baby," I whisper, folding her closer. "You don't have to hide how upset you are. Get it out."

The poor sweet thing deserves to cry as much as she wants. She's been through hell. And then the guy who was supposed to help her hurt her. If she feels like wailing for a week, I'll stay here in her bed the whole time.

I run both of my hands over her skin, skimming her thigh and her back. Feeling how unbelievably small and fragile she seems against all my brawn.

My purr deepens, and she sways, letting her weight press into me. Her wet face finds its way between my pecs, nuzzling closer while her breathing hitches. I cup the back of her head, petting the thick black hair.

"I can take it," I promise, nestling my face into her crown. "Just leave it all with me."

I might not be as refined as Tris or Spence; and maybe she didn't click with me the same way she clicked with Avery. But Serena hides her sobs against the middle of my chest, soaking her tears into my sternum.

And it's enough for me to know that I'm *never* letting go.

I'M GOING to owe Avery for this later.

When Serena finally cried herself out, he whispered something into her ear and shot me a meaningful look while he vaulted out of bed.

Meaningful—as in, "Don't fuck this up or I'll kill you and have fun doing it."

I nodded as he loped out, noting the way his muscles twitched with every step. If I had to guess, I'd say he needed to blow off steam in our gym. Which, all in all, seems like a pretty healthy reaction to everything that's happened tonight.

Part of me expects Serena to panic when he leaves, but she actually huddles closer to me. I can feel how embarrassed she is about it, though. I don't know if it's because of what happened in the kitchen or the fact that we were strangers just hours ago. Either way, she clearly doesn't feel like she should be accepting comfort from me, even when her body craves it.

"You know," I rumble quietly, doing my best not to startle her. "The doctor said you're touch-starved."

Her voice is small and ragged. "I don't really know what that means."

What sort of omega doesn't know what touch starvation is? Worried, I hold her a bit closer and explain, "I'm not an expert like Spencer, but touch-starved omegas can get sick. Your hormones and nervous systems are out of whack. Basically, you need affection. Hugs, cuddles, back rubs. Anything that feels good."

She curls down, the edges of her scent burning into the sweet darkness that makes my insides ache. "I guess that makes sense. I've always had issues with my perfume. And I don't know if anyone else has ever hugged me before."

My stomach caves in on itself. No one has ever *hugged* her? *No one?*

No wonder she trembles and perfumes when I run my fingers through her hair.

I can tell she's still uncertain, though. It probably feels scary to let a strange alpha tend to her like this, but I can't *stop.*

My mind reels, trying to come up with some way for her to get comfortable accepting this from me. "You know," I start slowly. "This doesn't have to mean anything. I'm an alpha; you're an omega. You're touch-starved. If you want me to help, it can be as simple as that."

Big green eyes blink up at me, warm with gratitude and shot with slivers of fear. "Are you sure?"

For an omega who had me by the hair a few hours ago, steering my face between her thighs, she's a shy little thing. I smile, even though my heart feels like it's cracking. "Very sure."

When I brush my lips along her forehead, she perfumes *hard*, her spine snapping straight. I run my hand along it, hoping my warmth will chase the chills away.

Before she can feel embarrassed, I hum, "Mm, *manamea*. Reminds me how perfect your slick tastes."

She's still mortified, ducking her face against my pec. "What does that word mean?" she whispers. "Y-you said it earlier, too."

The way her voice wavers makes it seem like she might think it's an insult of some sort. Or a taunt. I hitch her higher up my body and scent-mark her crown.

Fuck it—if I'm the one treating her touch starvation, I'm going to be thorough.

"It means sweetheart," I admit. "It's a Samoan word. My mother used it when I was little."

"She's Samoan?" she asks.

I nod, unable to contain my wistful sigh. "Yeah, she was."

She hears what I don't say, squeezing me with her thin arms. "I'm sorry."

I bury my face into her hair and inhale her. It's insane how much it helps the ache in my chest—how absolutely *right* it feels to hold her this way.

"It was a while ago. Right around the time we formed our pack. She had been sick for a long time. I'm glad she isn't suffering anymore."

I'm also glad Serena can't see the way I grimace before I go on, asking, "What about you, *manamea*? Where are your parents?"

Her miraculous perfume somehow gets sweeter, even when she's upset. That might make it hard for other alphas to parse her feelings, but I'm finding I can already tell the difference between arousal and distress based on how it makes me feel.

This is *definitely* distress. My nose itches while my insides flip.

Which makes sense as she tucks her face lower and murmurs, "My parents... I think I should probably wait and tell you all at the same time. It's not—it's not a nice story."

Something in my brain snags and tears. My purr follows suit, catching when I drag in a gasp. "Did they—"

She cuts me off, whispering, "*Please*, Jo."

The deep ripeness of shame touches her coconut creaminess again. Like it's her fault that her parents harmed her?

But I hate how much sense that makes. She's clearly touch-starved as hell. Underfed. And whoever she tried to get away from was keeping her locked inside.

I purr louder to cover a growl, leveraging both of us upright. Those big green eyes blink at me, her pretty face bemused as I pull her back into my lap and reach for the plate on her nightstand.

"You need to eat," I grumble, balancing it on her legs. One of my arms bends so I can keep petting her head. My other hand snatches the grilled cheese I made and brings it to her mouth.

She nibbles at it tentatively. Her eyes go wide. "Oh my God."

A smile breaks the tension tugging at my features. "Yeah?"

She nods and takes a much bigger bite. "It's so *good*. What is it?"

My grin stays in place, even while my brows pinch. "It's a grilled cheese, baby. You've never had one before?"

She shakes her head, looking back at the plate. "Three firsts in one night," she mumbles, "I knew professional athletes were over-achievers, but this is crazy."

I tuck a strand of her silky dark hair behind her ear, studying her profile. My cock jerks, undeterred by the fact that going down on her earlier made me come in my pants. *Twice.*

"Three?" I ask to distract myself. "The sandwich, the hugging, and what else?"

When her complexion warms and her gaze drops, my stomach freefalls. "Wait. What I did in the kitchen, was that your first—?"

She chokes on a laugh. "Oh. No. I mean, not really. I'm not a virgin or anything. I only—well, no one had ever, um, *gone down* there—"

She cuts herself off, cheeks visibly darker. "Have I mentioned how sorry I am about that?"

I decide I'm going to scent-mark her every single time she seems embarrassed. While I nuzzle my forehead into hers, I reply, "I'm not. Best thing I've ever tasted. I can't wait until you need me again."

She frowns a little, looking adorable. "You don't have to do that for me again. I'm sure it's... weird? And I basically made you..." Something suddenly makes her eyes leap wide. "Oh God, I didn't even offer to do anything for you, did I? Do you— Should I—"

Sweetheart. I press a soft kiss to her lips, holding just long enough to calm her down. When I pull back, all I see is the honest panic all over her face.

She's really *scared*. Because she thinks she didn't *please* me?

I cup my hands around her face. "Kissing your sweet pussy is my new favorite thing to do," I husk. "So anytime you want me to do it again, *please* fucking tell me. And I don't want you to worry about repaying me. At all. Okay?"

We have plenty of time. Forever, if we can convince her to stay. We'll get to me when the time is right.

Her pupils expand, telling me that her Omega is watching. Which explains why her voice shakes again. "Y-you don't want me?"

I hug her hard. "*Of course* I want you. But I get the feeling that no one's ever made it all about *you*. And I want to be the man who does that, okay?"

I'm also a lot bigger than most guys. If the way she strangled my fingers earlier is any indication, she'll need to work up to taking me.

Which just means more of her sweetness on my tongue. And more time to learn all about her.

I might be the luckiest alpha in the world.

She still doesn't seem like she quite believes me, but that's no problem. I'll prove it to her. Thinking so, I pick up the other half of her sandwich and lull her back into my arms.

While she eats, I tell her about our big backyard and pool. She must like that idea because her scent gets lighter and brighter by the second. When I mention the overgrown garden and she actually *smiles*, I decide that will be my first project for her.

After she's done eating, she can barely keep her eyes open. I tuck her into her bed, arranging everything so she'll be comfortable and leaving her the clothes we gathered so she'll have our pack's scents on her sheets.

She's already dozing when I pull the comforter up to her chin and bend to kiss her forehead. "I'm sorry that it happened like this," I whisper against her skin, hoping she'll hear me. "But finding you was my dream."

chapter
twenty-two

Tris?

Too soon?

AVERY

too soon

SPENCER

Is the omega secure in her room?

AVERY

she has a name, asshole.

JONAH

I tucked her in an hour ago and just spent forty-five minutes in the shower trying to convince my dick to let me sleep.

AVERY

samesies

think that's where Tris is now?

JONAH

Probably. This mate stuff is no joke. I would have stayed to cuddle her more but I was afraid my knot would explode.

Which reminds me: you're on cuddle duty while I'm at practice, Ave. She's touch-starved as fuck.

AVERY

not for long

THE WORST PART of all of this isn't having an omega to consider, or even watching my brother burn.

It isn't the mind-bending list of things I'm not prepared for or all the ways this half-assed plan to woo a complete stranger could go horribly wrong.

No.

Twelve hours in?

The worst part is how I thought I knew myself.

And, as it happens, I didn't have one single fucking clue.

All the instincts that I spent years subverting... I thought resurrecting them would be a gradual process. Or, at the very least, one that would take longer than two hours.

But by the time I finish pacing my room, fuming, and force myself to get into bed, all of my assumptions are disproven.

All night, raging *need* vibrates under my skin. I feel hot. Aggravated. *Aggressive*, even.

Everything I've done my best to suppress for so long.

All of that work. Years of control. With Serena's scent clinging to the dress shirt hanging over the back of my desk chair, it all amounts to nothing.

Which brings me to the second worst part of all of this—how much I understand what happened to Tris.

I hate that I *get* it. Hate that just *breathing* the faint traces of the poor girl's perfume on the sleeve of my button-down is enough for *my* teeth to ache.

Fucking hell. I'm practically salivating. And she isn't even in the *room*.

And then there's the last, final piece of completely inconvenient fact:

This is my field of expertise. I've spent years of my life studying exactly this. Which is how I know, down in the nauseous, seething depths of my stomach—this omega isn't just our scent-match.

She must be our mate.

I always hoped we didn't have one. So much so that I all but *convinced* myself we didn't.

How did I manage to deny the possibility so thoroughly? Why wasn't I prepared?

The question haunts me while I roll from one side of my bed to the other, pounding my fists into my pillows, throwing the covers off, and then pulling them right back up.

Anything to ignore the way my stiff cock presses into my pajama bottoms.

By morning, I've gotten two hours of *terrible* sleep. When I wake up and roll over—onto yet another throbbing erection—I'm *angry*.

For fuck's sake.

It's been over a year since I even felt the need to relieve myself. A steady regimen of rut-blockers and two hours in our pack's gym every morning typically banish any stray impulses.

They've done studies on that, too—how gradually reducing sexual releases over time eventually alleviates the need altogether.

Of course, those studies weren't conducted using mates.

Or even individuals in complete packs.

And they *may* have focused on single, elderly alphas.

I was still optimistic, until now.

Jonah used to ask about it. Why didn't I ever bring anyone back to our dorm? Why didn't I ever date? Why didn't I seem to notice when girls reached over and flirtatiously stroked my arm?

Because I was doing my best not to snarl at them. Trying hard *not* to feel their fingertips on my skin or the sick swoop that echoed through my stomach when I did.

He once asked if I liked men better; I didn't know how to explain that I only preferred them insofar as their touch made me want to *fight*. Sometimes, rage is easier to take than a roiling gut.

I shower and shave, ignoring the aching pulse in my knot while I dress in my usual slacks and a fresh shirt. Every few moments, I have to pause to take deep breaths, reminding myself that the lingering sweetness buzzing in my sinuses isn't real.

It's a phantom sensation, one that's common for unbonded alphas who find their scent-sensitive mate. It won't go away until I bite her and she bites me back.

I honestly can't decide which step in that process sounds worse.

I debate how much I'll regret skipping my workout while I pack my leather messenger bag and shrug on a blazer. The truth is, our gym is on the first floor, and I can't risk running into Serena until I've made some sort of plan for how I'm going to handle this.

Her.

If I take the elevator, I can go straight down to the garage without chancing a run-in. Skipping my daily exercise, coffee, and breakfast will likely have disastrous results for the students in my ten a.m. lecture, but these are desperate times. More desperate than I'd ever admit to anyone.

With a few final breaths, I slip into the hallway.

The dark slate floor and matte black walls are cool and dark. Our solar-powered LEDs barely glow, which means last night's thunderstorm has bled into morning. That puts an edge on my foul mood—I spent the better part of the night listening to the rain. If I have to hear it all day long, I'll be constantly reminded of why I spent hours tossing and turning.

My mind plays tricks on me while I stride down the hall. Serena's scent swells, a richer, sharper version than the traces she left with me last night.

I grit my teeth, irritated with myself for being so surprised. Omega pheromones have been my life's work. I'm well aware of the many phenomena associated with scent-sensitivity. Yet, *knowing* all of this would happen hasn't made the reality any less jarring.

Muttering chastisements to myself, I turn the corner and run right into a small, scurrying body.

"Ah!"

A squeal-like whine rips out of Serena while she reels back, jumping away from me as though I'm a human branding iron. I recoil, too, trying to process the sensations that swarm me. The outline of her figure lingers along mine while her scent pours into the air between us, rising in a cloud of cream-soaked sweetness.

I wish I hated it, but it's fucking *paradise*. Everything warm and exotic and so *delicious* that my mouth waters.

Goddamn it.

I grapple for control, barely managing to find my reins and yank myself back from the instinct to pounce on her.

For her part, Serena shrinks down, her knees wobbling until she's forced to steady herself with a hand on the nearest wall. She opens her mouth, but nothing comes out.

Jonah texted to report that she spoke to him last night, though I'm sure he didn't glare at her the way I am right now. I know I should stop, but I can't quite keep the sting out of my voice as I scowl down at her.

"*What* are you doing here?"

"WHAT ARE YOU DOING HERE?"

Great question, Professor.

I don't know what I'm doing or why—I'm too busy trying not to throw up on your Oxfords.

This is not the first impression I wanted to make with the alpha Jonah described as "the most particular."

For one, I'm still in this stupid bodysuit and Avery's hoodie because there are no clothes in my room that fit me. I suspect the joggers and athletic shorts folded on the suite's dresser are intended to get me through the day, but they're all so large, they immediately fall off my body when I try to wear them.

I ditched my fishnets last night, but at the moment, that feels like a mistake. Sure, they didn't exactly cover me. But having bare legs while I stand here, invading these alpha's private spaces, somehow feels worse.

Silly little slut.

What was I thinking?

Spencer awaits an answer to that very question, raising one of his silvery-blond brows in a stern arch. It pairs nicely with the hard set of his chiseled lips and the sharp cut of his ticking jaw.

I try to tell him that Jonah left me a note, but my voice suddenly cuts off as my Omega snatches the controls from me.

His rain-soaked scent simmers, turning darker and more electric. It's difficult to process what, exactly, he smells like. Lightning. O-zone. The way the air cracks when static splits it. Either way, it tingles in my nose, and my body reacts, releasing an embarrassing tidal wave of perfume while my entire core contracts.

Spencer's features look just like Tristan's—straight and aristocratic, if more severe. And more beautiful, too. His nostrils flare, inhaling me. A low, rumbling growl starts in his chest.

I flinch, my head turning to hide against my shoulder and the black hoodie bunched there. My body folds in on itself, cowering against the wall I'm using to keep myself upright.

But he doesn't come at me.

Instead, he takes a measured step backward and locks every muscle into utter stillness. Until only the hard bulge at the back of his jaw twinges.

"I will not touch you."

The way he snaps the words makes me peek at him. It sounds less like he's trying to convince me and more like he's reminding *himself.* Those dark eyes—a bottomless brown instead of Tristan's deep blue—snap down my body and back up again. They zero in on the piece of paper crumpled in my left hand.

Since I can't find my words, I force my arm to jerk out

straight, offering him the note I found next to my bedroom door when I woke up.

There's no doubt it was Jonah who slid the paper under the crack. His haphazard handwriting and crude drawings made me smile when I first saw them.

It's a map. Their whole townhouse, laid out and labeled, with a dotted line for me to follow up to Avery's room and a note reminding me that Jonah would be home at three.

Spencer studies the page, his shoulders unwinding a fraction. "I see." He pins me in place with his dark eyes, brows crouching low. "You came up to find Avery?"

I try to force a swallow, but I feel like I might gag. Instead, I settle for a lightheaded nod. Spencer's frown deepens.

"He typically sleeps well past noon." The alpha's tone is brusque, but matter-of-fact. His eyes skate over me again, a hint of uncertainty flaring in their depths. "Did you... need something?"

Can I admit the shameful fact that my body is *wired* and the only thing I can think of to quiet my mind is Avery's cool eyes and inked fingers?

I really don't think I can.

But, again, my Omega seems to have other ideas. She peers out of her hiding place, eyes wide on Spencer's handsome face.

And a new gulf of perfume *pours* out of me. Along with enough slick for all four of these alphas.

Plus maybe like three of their friends, too.

Such a silly little slut.

Spencer looks like he would agree with Wally. His scowl pulls into a snarl. "*Miss Swanson.*"

It isn't a sexy snarl. Not a Serena-what-are-you-doing-to-me-you-gorgeous-creature sort of snarl. It's *pained.*

Pissed.

Appalled.

I don't blame him. *I'm* appalled.

Stupid, weird, silent Omega. It's like she *wants* him to bite us, too.

Panic joins the tingly flood of heat in my middle. That gelling, jittery warmth settles between my hips once again. A sharp stab—more painful than any arousal I've ever experienced—impales my pussy.

I whine, the loud sound shattering the tension pulled taut between us. Spencer starts to lurch toward me, but he catches himself, backing off immediately.

"Your perfume," he husks, teeth grinding. "It's different. Stronger. Do you feel dizzy? Or warm?"

Warm and dizzy would be a blessing. At the moment, I feel *hot*. And *delirious*.

When I try to open my mouth to explain why my entire body is suddenly shaking violently, another pitiful whine escapes. Spencer growls out loud this time, fisting his hands at his sides.

A bark snaps out of him. "*Omega. Focus.*"

An answering fission of fear cracks through my chest, but my eyes fly to his automatically.

"Focus on me," he orders, quieter. "Nod your head—are you hot?"

Will he be angry at me? What's *happening*? Whimpering and shrinking down, I squeeze my eyes shut and nod.

But he only hums, clipping over another question. "Dizzy?"

I try to nod again, but it feels more like a loll. My eyes blink open, finding Spencer closer than before. His voice softens into a rasp. "You're having a heat-spike," he murmurs. "You need—"

An alpha.

He doesn't say the words, but I already know. The second he said heat, I knew. That's what this is—this familiar feeling that I've done everything in my power to block out.

Only, it's somehow worse than usual? Dr. Monroe tried to warn me; he said my heat symptoms would be "exaggerated" now that I've been claimed. I didn't believe him, only because it didn't seem possible for heats to be worse than the ones I'm used to.

Spencer frantically flicks his gaze over me like I'm a bomb that's about to go off. One that he *knows* how to diffuse—he keeps looking at the place where Avery's hoodie skims the tops of my thighs—but, for some reason, he doesn't want to. Doesn't want *me*.

Instead of coming closer, he backs off again. His throat works on a swallow as my vision blurs, giving him two extremely pissed-off faces.

For a moment, everything wobbles and wavers. Then, a sharp slice of pain stabs my empty insides. I whimper, doubling over.

The strange, stern alpha mutters, *"Goddamn fucking hell."*

And then he lunges for me.

SOMEBODY BETTER BE DEAD.

That is the only acceptable reason for anyone to be pounding on my door at eight a.m..

If no one is dead, someone is about to be.

I open my mouth, fully intending to tell whoever is there to *fuck off*, but a sweep of sensation prickles over my body, leaving my hair standing on end.

Sticky-sweet, creamy lusciousness.

Serena.

Not bothering to put anything over my black boxer briefs, I

force myself upright and grunt. My hands are sore as fuck from my last spar. Ribs, too. Not to mention that kidney shot I took. And the gnarly blotch on my hip bone.

Day two is always the worst day for bruises.

"Not cool, kitten," I grouse, shuffling to the doorway, kicking a pile of clothes and a stack of sketch pads out of my way. "Next time you wake me, it better be with your gorgeous—"

Oh.

Shit.

"*The fuck*?" I bark at Spencer. He's standing in the hall, holding our limp omega around the waist like she's a corpse and he's trying not to get his ugly-ass blazer dirty. When he doesn't answer me, I realize he's holding his breath.

Which I suddenly understand—because good fucking *God*.

Serena's perfume is so mind-meltingly perfect, the cock I spent last night repeatedly draining instantly hardens into steel *again*. My knot pulses while my dick kicks up, almost busting through my boxers.

Some foreign sense of urgency snaps through my body. I reach for her right away. The totally un-fucking-familiar feeling of relief vibrates inside my bones the second I touch her. My injured, inked fingers curl around her jaw and lift her bleary eyes to mine.

"Serena?" I murmur, pulling her into my body and bundling her against my chest with my free arm. "What's wrong, baby?"

She whines softly, nuzzling her hot little cheek against my palm, then my naked chest. Scent-marking.

Fuck. Me.

I'm down *bad*. And this girl has barely even *spoken* to me yet.

In fact, I need to ask her what the hell is up with that shit. Talking to Jonah before she talks to me? Not cool.

Nothing we can do about that right now, though. Because my little kitten seems to be having trouble *standing*, let alone speaking.

I swear to God, if Spence hurt her or scared her, I will use that stupid elbow-patch blazer to mop his blood off my walls.

When I glare at him, he snarls right back, outraged. "I didn't *do* anything. She's in a heat-spike! She needs—"

She just fucking *needs*. I can smell it. *Feel* it.

Adrenaline spikes in my blood, the way I only feel right before I step into the ring. It's pumping through my body now, though, sharpening every sense.

Spencer's throat catches. "You," he chokes out. "She needs you."

Because he can't do it, I see, noticing the way his eyes don't quite make it up to mine. He isn't ready to touch her yet. Especially not the way my girl needs to be touched right now.

We're a pack. This is what we do, right? Help each other and shit? Make up for each other's issues?

"I got it," I tell him, nodding.

Serena whines again, nuzzling closer. Spencer's gaze flickers over her while he hesitates, opening his mouth and then closing it again.

I raise a brow. "You wanna watch or something, teach?"

He snaps straight, puffing up defensively. "*No*. No. I need to go. Call me when she's... stable."

Call him after I make her come until she passes out.

Got it.

As I start to close the door, he claws it back open. This time, his dark eyes flash at me. "Remember: no knotting. We don't know what she's been through, and she can't consent like this."

Jesus. Do I really come off like this much of an asshole?

I roll my eyes. "Knotting on the first date is just bad manners, Spence."

He doesn't look convinced.

That's fair. Bad manners are sort of my thing.

MY OMEGA and I are so not friends anymore.

If we ever were. It's difficult to say; and I can barely remember where I am or how I got here, at the moment.

The cold-fish alpha dragged me to one of the flat black doors in the flat black hallway. He practically kicked the thing down, pounding at it with the toe of his shiny, fancy shoe since he couldn't use his hands. Those were busy keeping me from slumping into a puddle of my own slick.

Eventually, the tattooed one threw his door open, glaring

until he saw me there. They sniped at each other for a minute. Most of that went over my head, except for the mention of a knot.

Which had my silent Omega shoving desperately at me. If I weren't so dizzy and overheated, I might try screaming at her.

Because *seriously*?! A heat-spike? In front of the one alpha in the whole house who's literally *vowed* not to touch me?!

The inked alpha whisks me away from him easily, slamming his door behind us. Some foggy, stilted part of my brain recognizes that his room is different from all the others.

The walls are covered in drawings, here. I wish I had the ability to parse exactly why, but I can barely keep my feet under me.

There's a hollow, aching pain carved up into my core. It pulses and pounds, dribbling warm, slippery tingles down my thighs. I press my palm into my lower belly, clenching my fingers against the rubber fabric of the cursed red bodysuit.

Now is the time to talk. I know that. I need to *say words* to tell the alpha that I need him to help me. That it's okay for him to do whatever he wants as long as he gives me his knot.

Maybe I'm just delirious, but at this point, it would be a relief. I haven't been a virgin in years, but the handful of beta busboys and bartenders at the club didn't have the ability to knot me. I remember being relieved by that. I can't quite remember why, now.

I can't tell if *any* of my thoughts make sense. They float through the haze in my head, not quite sticking long enough for me to really consider them. Every time I try, needy squeezes pull my pussy tight.

Deep breathing only fills my lungs with the smoky mix of amber and frankincense. A teasing note of jasmine tickles my nose and pricks my nipples. I whine again, close to tears.

Why isn't he touching me? Does he not want me, just like the blond one? Do they all know that there's something wrong with me—

"Hey, kitten." The inked alpha stands in front of me, stripping off my hoodie and running his bruised, tattooed hands along my arms. "You're shaking. Shh. It's okay."

No, it's *not*.

I'm not okay. This *hurts*—outside, inside. On the surface and somewhere down deeper.

I can't believe how much I care what these alphas think of me, how much they want me. After just one day?! If they don't want me now, what's going to happen once they find out where I came from?

And this alpha thinks I'm *okay*?!

None. Of. This. Is. Okay.

My hands don't feel attached to my body as they fly up, clawing at his broad chest muscles, shoving him hard.

The edges of the room blur, colorful papers swirling with dark walls. A strange sob clogs my throat. But my body doesn't stop. I do it again. And again.

Just as quickly as the insanity set in, it drains out of me. My fingers slip against his bare skin, losing any strength they had. My heaving lungs stutter on his scent, sending another burst of slick down my legs.

I'm afraid to look up at him. Afraid to see how angry he is, how much I've fucked up any chance I had at him... liking me. *Wanting me.* If he still does, it will be all twisted with rage, probably. He'll want to make it hurt, now.

The hand settled on my hip flexes while the other floats up, cupping my jaw in that demanding, no-bullshit way he has. Lifting my face so I'm forced to see the aftermath of my outburst.

But he doesn't *look* mad at all.

He looks *proud*.

A bright, burning light flares in those ghostly opal eyes as they trace my face. When our gazes lock, the instant connection I felt with him yesterday comes flooding back. My gasps turn to whimpers.

His fingers soften against my face. "You are so fucking beautiful," he murmurs. A drop of humor soaks into the set of his mouth. "Terrible fighting form. But I can fix that."

Whatever face I make has his eyes smoldering. He leans down, brushing the top of my ear with his lips. Dazed, all I can think is that they're so much softer than I expected any part of him to be.

"I can teach you how to really leave a mark," he rumbles, "Because I want your marks all over me."

A shiver tingles down my spine. The alpha follows it, fingertips skating over the bare skin covering my vertebrae, down to where the red rubber onesie sticks to the small of my back.

He plucks at it. "Can I burn this fucking thing?"

The far-away, sane piece of my brain registers that he isn't joking. In fact, when I manage to loll my eyes up to his face, I find him staring back intently, his black brows arched eagerly.

He really wants to burn it.

My Omega and I finally agree on something—because just as I'm wondering why arson suddenly sounds *so hot*, a rush of my real perfume rises off me.

The inked alpha's pupils blow wide, yawning to consume his pale irises. Amber warmth and petal-soft spice swell between us, mixing with my cream-soaked sweetness. The combination sinks into my body, obliterating all sense of reality.

There's a shrill, manic noise. A whine.

Is that me?

It must be because the alpha immediately snaps me off my feet, bending my legs around his bare waist. His hot, patterned skin rubs between my slick thighs. My pussy cinches, a deep, steady throb beating under the wetness.

My back hits something soft. I don't care if it's a bed, a couch, or a chair. I can't care about anything except the sudden flash of a blade catching the weak light. Three snapping sounds—and the pressure against my pulsing pussy and my tight, aching nipples suddenly ceases to exist.

Like magic, the pinch of the red rubber thong disappears.

Crimson goes flying off to the side. The blade clatters to a nearby table.

"*What. The. Fuck.*"

Now the alpha sounds angry. I frantically search for his face, my Omega desperate to see if I should be afraid.

For a long beat, he balances on his hands; his head bent over my chest while he looks down the length of my naked body. When his chin finally snaps up, his eyes are blue fire—the very hottest part of a flame.

"*Who* did this to you?"

Everything is too fuzzy. I don't know what he means until his fingers graze under my breasts. A dizzy memory floats through my brain—bitter and sickening. Pain and failure and fear from a long time ago.

I always forget about the damn scars. There are a fair few, most of them placed there strategically. Any alpha who eventually took me off Wally's hands would have to undress me to know I was damaged.

"Who," the tattooed alpha demands again. "Did. This?"

Some of them were my own doing, actually. The result of being locked up alone during my heats. I usually came to with some scratches on me. And broken bones, a time or two.

My Omega panics at the memory... and the thought that maybe, if these alphas find out that no one wanted to be with us for our heats before, they won't want to be with us either...

The alpha on top of me watches my face fall and reaches over to thumb at my lower lip.

"Stop that," he grits. "You're the most gorgeous goddamn thing I've ever seen. A fucking *warrior*. These scars won't stop me from sinking my knot so deep inside you that you'll never get it out. But when I get my hands on whoever did this to you, death will be *the least* of his worries."

Dear Lord. Am I turned on by murderous destruction?

Guess so.

A sharp sound vibrates up my throat while more perfume

soaks the air. He groans, dropping his forehead to mine. "Jesus, kitten," he gasps. "I think maybe *you're* trying to kill *me*."

Maybe I should be. But all I can think about is getting something hard and thick into me. I hook my ankles around the backs of his thighs and try to drag him down, drawing the hard length between his legs to the apex of mine.

Settling our hips together, he growls low, skimming his lips down my cheek and finding the pulse beating on the un-bitten side of my neck. He sucks it right between those overly-soft lips, tugging on the thin skin until my vision blurs and swirls.

"Alpha!" I cry.

His cock kicks against my core, hot slick seeping into his tight, black underwear. I can feel his knot, full of scorching blood, beating like a separate heartbeat.

The rhythm in his chest is even faster when he grazes his pecs over my nipples. My own heart leaps into overdrive, thrashing like it's trying to fight its way out of my chest and to him.

He brings his face back to mine. Our eyes lock, his filling with that smoldering softness he only seems to possess when I look right into him.

The entire universe stops as those plush lips finally find mine, brushing in teasing tastes before dropping into a slow, delving kiss. His tongue strokes deep, smooth, and hot against mine. I taste his smoky flavor and swallow it down, moaning in desperation when he pulls back slightly.

"I'm going to take care of you," he promises, voice dropping low. "And then I'm going to fuck you as hard as you'll let me."

Yeeeeeeeees.

I whine and buck, grinding myself against his cock. He roughs out another snarl, slipping his hand over my hip, the blunt nail of his thumb scratching a line along the crease of my thigh.

I'm aching. *Melting.* Whimpering and moaning and squirming so hard under him, I'm surprised it doesn't hurt.

Or maybe it does. Maybe that's why his eyes have glazed over with pleasure and pride.

"Such a perfect little kitten," he grits. "You gonna give me those claws?"

When I sink my nails into his shoulders and drag them down his chest, he rewards me by settling his huge hand over my pussy and grinding the thick ridge of his cock into my thigh.

The wet boxer briefs clinging to him give me quite the preview. Surprising texture rubs through the damp fly, but I can't focus on it for long because two strong fingers push between my lower lips.

The second his thumb skims over my clit and his other fingertips breach my opening, I scream. The orgasm is quick and brutal, a flash of white that's too quick for me to do anything more than bite down on the hard flesh of his shoulder.

He grunts, hips stuttering. Instead of stopping, though, he keeps skirting my pussy, teasing me with one fingertip at a time. "You needed that one," he rasps. "Let me give you more."

Some of my heat-spike haze has burned off. Enough for me to look up at him and feel the tears that gather in my eyes at the fervent, focused look in his.

A name rings through my mind like a bell and comes out of my mouth without permission.

"Avery."

Feeling explodes through my chest—so confusing but completely all-consuming. The strength of it terrifies me, but it flows into all the cracks streaked through my soul, soothing and electrifying at the same time.

It's *scary*. I've never felt anything like this. To have come on so fast, so completely... How can it possibly be real?

One of my tears escapes, and he catches it, licking at my cheek gently. I didn't think it was possible for him to be any sweeter to me, but then he nuzzles my nose.

"I know," he husks. "I know, baby. Me, too."

Could he possibly mean that he feels *all of this*?

It seems that way. Especially when he rolls us onto our sides a moment later. Hitching my bent leg over his hip, he starts to push his boxers off, giving enough of a glimpse for me to wonder just how far down these tattoos go.

A thick swallow sticks in my throat. I've seen a lot of alpha cock. Way too much. And none of it from anyone I knew or liked.

For a second, I'm afraid of myself. What if this amazing guy takes his underwear off and I freak out? Will I hate it? Feel as ambivalent about it as I did all the assholes at the club?

Avery definitely isn't shy.

Two seconds later, he lifts his other hip to whip the black boxers off. Settling onto his back without hesitation, staying close but giving me a bit of space to process everything I'm seeing.

And I do mean *everything*.

Because *holy. Shit.*

That is *a lot*.

First, there's the sheer *size* of him. Long and brutally thick, he stands perfectly straight and high, sprouting from an impressive knot and balls large enough to match.

Like I said, I've seen a lot of dick. But this one is... *beautiful*.

Or it would be. If it wasn't also *savage*.

Because, of course, Avery doesn't just have a normal, pretty penis.

No.

It's *covered* in black ink patterns, all the way from the edge of his knot to the underside of his cockhead. And there, at that ridge? There's a piercing.

One of *eight* piercings, actually.

Two silver balls, right under the domed head, followed by a ladder of smooth silver bars. Seven of them studded along the underside of his tattooed erection.

It really is a sculpture. *Modern art.*

And all I want to do is touch him.

Avery beats me to it, wrapping his hand around himself and giving his beautiful cock a long, hard tug. I watch in fascination as he twists his palm around the head, squeezing a bead of pearly pre-cum out of the tip.

My tongue skims my lower lip. He works his fist over those piercings, pausing to roll the silver balls on his frenulum until he hisses. My hand twitches, half-raising before I catch myself.

Avery smiles, a crooked flash of amusement. "Did you want to do this part?"

I have to fight the wedge in my throat, but he deserves an answer. "I don't—" I start to admit, hiding my eyes. "I—I've never—"

The arm under my torso flexes, leveraging his big body back on top of mine. With the hand he was using to stroke himself, he tilts my face back in his direction.

Intense emotion swirls in his eyes, asking the one question that keeps streaking through my thoughts. "How the fuck did I find you?"

If that were some sort of line, it would still be enough to make me blink back more tears. But it isn't. He means it.

He's looking at me with a suspicious sort of awe. Like I can't possibly be real. Or here. *Or his.*

Maybe I'm not. Maybe this is all dust and it's going to blow away the second the wind shifts.

Right now, that just seems like the best reason to give in to it.

Before more tears escape, I wrap myself around him. He doesn't miss a beat, catching me against his chest, sinking his mouth against mine instantly. His tongue slides in, thick and hot against my tingling lips. When I moan, he groans back, eating at me as he tangles his fingers in the hair at my nape.

"Fucking perfect," he grunts into my mouth. "You smell like sex-soaked heaven. I want it all over me."

When I gasp at his filthy encouragements, my teeth nip his lower lip accidentally. I start to recoil, but he just bites me right back, the sudden sting sending a throb to my clit.

The wild light in his eyes tells me he's figured out exactly how much I like his dirty mouth. His smoky, floral scent rises off his inked chest while he skims his lips along my jaw, murmuring, "You gonna grind that sweet little cunt all over my cock?"

I cry out and he pulls back slightly, piercing me with his intense eyes. "I want to pump you so full of me, you'll feel it all day," he roughs out. "But only if that's what you want."

It is.

It's the only thing I've wanted since this haze broke over me—his thick hardness, filling all the places that ache.

If I'm honest, I've been desperate for that feeling for *years*. With every heat I went through alone, the gnawing emptiness got worse and worse. Physically... and deeper. Higher. In the pit that dug itself into my middle with every lonely whine.

"I—I—" My hand reaches between us, skimming the swell that's already expanding at the base of his studded cock.

His eyes glow, snapping with blue fire. "My knot?" he grits out.

When I nod, he doesn't balk or laugh. He groans, leaning his forehead into mine. "Baby, you have *no idea* how much I want that. But then I'd have to fight Spencer and you'd be down one nerdy alpha."

He's funny, even though I can tell he isn't entirely kidding. At the moment, though, I can't even smirk.

I'm too embarrassed to ask for his knot again or explain why I need him so badly. A pitiful whimper is all I manage, nodding in defeat.

But Avery scent-marks my forehead with a sweet nuzzle. "Let me fill you up another way," he murmurs. "Yeah?"

He doesn't say please, but his ghostly gaze does, filling with a burning sort of entreaty. A dizzy rush of feeling floods me as I nod, the motion shaky.

"That's my girl," he praises, lowering his hips between my thighs. "You want my dick?"

I whine, hooking my ankles around his thighs to drag him down to my center.

Wild need flashes in his light eyes. The hand cradling my nape slips down to my hip, adjusting the angle of my body while the other palms his pierced cock, positioning it.

The first touch of his warm, flared head has me squirming for more. He flashes a wicked grin and drops his hips, flattening himself over my slit.

Ah!

Every one of those smooth silver bars glides through my slick, teasing the spread lips of my pussy. I moan and buck, desperate for more friction.

Avery bites the corner of his plush, pink mouth and looks between our bodies, watching me gush against every rung of his ladder.

"Fuck me, that's pretty," he mutters. "That's it. Get your slick all over me, and I'll get my cum all over you. You and me are going to be a *mess*, baby. I fucking love it."

Before I can think of a reply, he tucks his hips back, grinding the head of his dick right against my pulsing clit. The two silver balls pierced underneath fit around me, rolling over both sides of the throbbing bud while the rest of his metal glides more firmly between my swollen folds.

It's insane. Burning hot and metallic cool. Smooth and slick and textured and hard.

My body works, pumping myself along everything he has, pressing my pulsing entrance into the lower edge of his knot. When he feels me clenching against him, he growls and impales me in one deft move.

Like a cobra striking. One second, he's just there, and the next, he's *there*. So deep his knot presses right against my slit. His shaft buried inside my desperately cinching muscles, stroking those thick silver bars against my inner walls.

And I'm *full*—for the first time I can remember, I don't feel alone or empty or cold. The aching chasm that's been pounding for so long clamps around him, trying to hold his thickness where I need it.

But he doesn't stay still. His broad, inked body works against mine in rolling thrusts, building speed until I can't tell if he's in me or about to be—I just feel *him*, hitting that ache head-on with every pound.

All the air sloughs out of my lungs as he reaches between us and thumbs at my clit. His hips keep thumping, but his lips find mine in the sweetest kiss. A combination of wild need and tenderness that has my pussy pulling taut, along with the bundle of burning pleasure in my core.

"Right there, yeah?" he pants, smoothing his touch over the top of my clit while he sinks himself deep and rubs his ladder along the place inside of me that begs for more. "Fuck, you feel perfect when you're about to come. So goddamn beautiful, baby. Give it to me."

On the next plunge of this body into mine, I fly over the edge. Relief bursts through my middle as I come, my body finally able to clamp down on the exact thick hardness it craves. Sparks of euphoria fizzle out from my core, rolling all the way to the top of my head, the tips of my fingers, the pads of my toes.

Before I've caught my breath, Avery roars, rearing back. While his wide, inked chest heaves on snarled breaths, he grips the base of his cock and starts coming. Thick, slippery release jets into my pussy before he pulls out, shooting ropes of hot cum all over my bare belly.

The feel of him marking me, his scent melding with my own, pinches the new tender place in my chest. I scrabble for him, and he comes right to me, falling into my arms without any care for the mess spreading between our bodies.

Avery turns us onto our sides and pulls me into an embrace. His rough, rasping purr vibrates against my breasts, a perfect match for the ragged voice murmuring into my hair. "If you wake me up again," he says, "You better have bacon."

IT'S NEVER APPEALED to me, this game.

I find it tedious and immature. People are suffering. And these "public servants" stand around boardrooms, eating exquisitely catered meals and measuring their dicks.

Figuratively.

There are actually more women in here this year, and a couple of gender-fluid representatives, which pleases me. What good is the concept of representation if elected officials don't reflect the people they serve?

Unfortunately, there isn't a whole lot of public service

happening in here at the moment. Plenty of bagels being eaten, though.

The cogs of government move slowly. It can be painful to watch. But I have a plan, and it's working. If I can just convince—

Fuck.

The hole drilled into my middle has been plaguing me since I opened my burning eyes at four-thirty this morning. Dr. Monroe told me to expect the pain. He said it would only grow the further I get from the omega.

My bedroom is right on top of hers, so it didn't really start to pull from a dull throb into a sharp, piercing *tug* until I left the townhouse. Ever since, I've walked around the capitol building with a crease between my eyebrows, playing off the discomfort as a bad mood.

It's bizarre to be so fundamentally changed and not have anyone notice. They can't see the steel cord sewn into my center. There are no bite marks for them to smirk at, no changes in my scent.

Although, if the half-bond has changed Serena's scent, I can't sense it. When I walked into the kitchen this morning, mouthwatering paradise perfume still spun through the air. And when I loitered outside her bedroom for twenty minutes before tearing myself away, she certainly smelled just as irresistible as ever. Even through the fucking *walls*.

Jesus.

According to the brief research I managed to conduct last night, there's a chance other alphas won't be quite as attracted to her... but she'll only continue to smell more appealing to *us*. Her pack.

Oh—shit.

Out of nowhere, dazed panic spears me. Serena's.

She must be remembering where she is. And why.

The next burst is a tangled jumble. I only get a few seconds into untying it before our breakfast meeting is called to order.

I'm the host, technically, meaning I have to sit at the head of the table and look formidable. Which isn't fucking easy with all of Serena's fear and shame seething in my stomach.

It reminds me of last night in her room. The way she kept her features smooth while her insides *heaved*.

Because of me.

There's no context for it now, but I can guess why she's scared. It would be terrifying for an omega to wake up in a strange house and remember all of the things that happened to her yesterday.

Still, the *shame* doesn't make much sense to me.

At first.

"Senator?"

An alpha woman who represents the Sixth District stares at me expectantly, her heel tapping against the floor. The rest of the table has turned in my direction, too. I ignore the sensations squirming low in my abdomen and flip open my tablet.

Some aide uploaded our agenda, thankfully. I only have to speak for a few moments and flex a bit of my force before I can turn the floor over to the beta man who runs District 17.

Which is fortunate. Because the reason for Serena's embarrassment and self-loathing is suddenly—*viciously*—clear.

Heat impales my groin and *pulses*. Waves of warmth and a shivery, vibrating need that instantly floods my cock with boiling blood. It hardens along my inseam, jerking so hard I'm surprised the stiff material doesn't rip.

I nearly double over in my chair. A grunt sloughs out of me. The entire room of state representatives turns to stare.

Fucking hell.

My scent blasts up several notches, along with the air of dominance I've done my best to cultivate. There's nothing subtle about it now. Instead, it's a blanket of steel, suffocating the entire room.

My Alpha is off his leash. *Feral.*

And *confused*. The poor, stupid bastard. Pumping out pheromones for his omega, not understanding why we can sense her need if we aren't *with* her.

I barely manage to throw my entire weight at that flimsy internal door, holding all of my feelings in my own body instead of funneling them down the frayed, throbbing connection between us.

District 17 starts backtracking, nervously mopping at his sweaty forehead while he stammers. The rest of the room holds its breath, assuming anger is the reason for the noticeable shift in my mood.

I let them believe it. If I'm going to pass this Workplace Protection Act, I have to be extremely careful about the way I introduce Serena to the world.

The second she's seen in public with my claim on her? People will assume she's ours. *Mine.* Which will officially make me "biased" about omegas and their rights.

I'm not sure it would have been better if we'd courted publicly prior to this clusterfuck. It would have made news of our "bonding" less shocking, but courting would have given the media and political pundits plenty of time to poke holes at the concept.

She would have been subject to severe scrutiny. She still will be; possibly more than usual, if anyone catches wind of where we met. Or *how* we met.

Goddamn it.

I spent most of the night wondering if I should tell her what's at stake here. She seems bright and sweet—she might understand if I tell her. Jonah seems to think so. Avery thinks I'm an asshole for caring about anything other than the woman I took a bite of.

And Spencer is probably halfway to insanity at this point.

"Senator?"

Motherfucking *hell.*

I'm flooding this room with pheromones. Aggression and need, all tangled and twisted around the roots of regret. Remorse. And this pulling, piercing *pain.*

Whatever Serena is doing, the arousal only rises. Higher and hotter and harder. Blood pounds in my ears, echoing the angry thump in my dick. I have to cover it up, keep anyone from getting suspicious.

Playing my pain off as disapproval, I make my face as severe as the stab in my center. "Yes?"

Whoever dared to summon me falls silent. Tension stretches over the table, but I can't really feel it—because the pressure pulling at my groin *doubles*.

Goddamn it.

I could close her out. I've learned how to do it, but I chose to keep the passage from her to me unobstructed, needing to know she was okay. Trying to give her space without abandoning her.

But if I shut that final door, there's no guarantee she won't notice when I go to reopen it later.

And I won't risk losing this connection to her.

Even if it means I'm about to lose control of my baser urges in a boardroom full of important people.

One of my aides wades into the fray, coming to murmur into my ear. I can't hear what she says, too focused on the way her hand lands on my arm and the sudden, insane urge to *rip it off*.

She's a beta, but the synthetic omega perfume she has on makes me see red. How dare she taint the scent of Serena that's clinging to my jacket? Why does she think she can touch me?

My Alpha bucks and strains against his binds, desperate to roar in this woman's face. Tell her all about the omega setting our blood on fire. Make sure no one else ever touches what's *hers*.

But I'm Tristan Thorne.

It takes longer than usual to remind myself *why* that matters, to keep from losing my shit. Instead, I roll back from the table and smoothly stand.

I can't stay long enough to come up with an explanation. Let the perfumed beta deal with that. *I need to—*

My polished shoes eat up the hallway. I clip into my office and growl something about not being disturbed, unsure who's even there to listen or follow my orders.

Not caring.

Beyond the ability to care.

I flick the lock and stride to my desk, ripping at my belt as I go. My pants bunch around my quads while I shove them down, freeing my throbbing erection.

It bobs upright, curving to reach my navel, forcing me to pull my shirttails up before they get smeared with pre-cum.

A bolt of relief sails up into my stomach. For a moment, I don't know if it's mine or Serena's.

When I go still, my hand hovering beside my cock instead of grasping it the way I want to, I know for sure. It's her, not me.

And if the accompanying notes of confusion and desperation are any indication, she isn't alone.

One of the guys has her.

Fucking hell, but why does that make the pain *worse*?

Or better, really. The vicious pulse pounding in my cock kicks up, inflating my knot. Until I'm sure that, even if I just stand here and watch my package twitch and swell, I'll end up coming all over my desk.

I consider it. Consider waiting, watching what the little omega can do to me without even realizing.

But then she sends a lick of languid heat through the bond.

My control shatters.

I press one palm along my hot, pulsing length and use the other to squeeze my screaming knot. The wetness seeping from my cockhead lets me glide in and out of my fist without resistance.

I imagine Serena's slick, her swelling scent. A growl snags in my heaving chest. My knot expands, pushing through my kneading fingertips, growing heavier in my hand.

Fuck, she would take me all the way down to the root. Squeeze me and slip against me again and again and ag—

My entire core flexes as a rough roar bursts from my lungs. Scalding pleasure washes over the pain pulling at my middle, whiting it all out for one blissful moment. I squeeze myself tightly, imagining her body strangling everything I have...

...and come all over the polished mahogany in front of me, shooting thick ropes of white across the dark wood desk.

Dragging in a shuddering breath, I close my eyes and drop my head, trying to come down from my climax.

But the painfully incomplete tether in my center rips at my insides. And Serena isn't done. Her arousal assails me all over again, sending trembling jerks through my spent dick, drawing my aching balls up even *harder*.

So we can start all over again.

"DID you want to keep your toes?"

The cool blue flames in Avery's eyes flare as he levels a look at Jonah. The big man stretched out underneath me rolls his eyes and grumbles, angling his legs to drop his feet to the floor, well away from Avery's left thigh.

A few days ago, I might not have had the balls to say anything, but after four days in their house, I've learned that the easiest way to make Avery happy is to blurt whatever sassy nonsense pops into my head.

Because he *likes* it.

I narrow my gaze at the tattooed alpha. "He was here first, you know."

Pale, fiery eyes roll over my black cut-offs and Jonah's borrowed jersey, up to my pouting face. His mouth twitches, the plush pink lips betraying a hint of his crooked grin. "You telling me to get lost, kitten?"

Jonah's brawny hand continues massaging the back of my neck. He's been true to his word ever since my first night here—steadily doing everything he can to treat my touch starvation without even a trace of expectation.

Today, he got home from practice and decided we needed to veg out on the couch. Of course, his version of "vegging out" includes a stuffed-crust pizza, buffalo wings, cheese fries, and absolutely no veggies to speak of.

He offered to let me pick anything I wanted to watch, but he's done that every day. When I insisted he choose, he asked if I'd mind watching an old game so he can review the tape.

Which is how I wound up sitting upright in his lap while he reclined in the cushions, massaging my neck and shoulders as he explained the finer points of his plays.

Until Avery busted in, tearing through our food like a tornado and claiming a spot close enough to feed me fries from his inked-up fingers.

"I never said that," I scoff, reaching for his plate and snatching his pizza crust. I tear a bite off and watch the way his eyes sparkle, full of danger and something a bit more intense than admiration.

"I'm just saying," I mumble, chewing and skirting my focus back to the game tape. "You can't take a seat next to Jo's feet and then complain about them."

Jonah's smile is wide and warm. "Yeah," he agrees, lifting his feet and dropping them right into Avery's lap, next to his food. "Listen to our omega."

Our omega...

Oblivious to the tingles frothing though my insides, Avery glares down at Jonah's toes, then glances over at me. "Fuck it," he grunts, scooting closer, until Jonah's calves are over his groin and he's close enough to loop an arm around my waist.

Nerves simmer in my stomach as I turn to Jonah, worried he'll be annoyed. But he only gives me another kind smile, slipping his hand from my nape to lace his fingers through mine.

He nods at the screen. "Next we should watch one of Ave's old fights. I have a few recordings."

Avery sets his empty plate aside and scowls. "That shit is so boring."

They bicker like this all the time. It's actually sort of cute, given how they both clearly enjoy the back-and-forth.

While they keep debating, I look over at the two empty chairs positioned on either side of the sofa, wondering where the Thorne brothers are.

I've barely seen Spencer. After the incident in the hallway, he's started keeping odd hours—leaving very early in the morning and coming home in the middle of the afternoon. I suspect he's figured out that I'm usually with Jonah and Avery at that time, leaving him free to slip past without feeling obliged to check on me.

That's what I am to him, I've gathered—an obligation. I'm fairly sure he only tolerates me living in their house in order to keep his brother in one piece.

I have no idea if it's working. Tristan Thorne is every bit as evasive and mysterious as the professor. Sometimes, I catch him hovering in nearby rooms, observing the way Jonah and Avery interact with me. Probably trying to decide how he feels about the monumental mistake he made by biting me.

His regret is still palpable. It hurts my feelings, sending me into a pit of dread and shame every time I catch sight of him.

Honestly, my reaction doesn't even make any sense.

Why do I let the way he feels about me affect my self-worth? It's not like he *knows* me. He hasn't even tried to.

Then again, he didn't bite me for my *personality*. Maybe my scent is the only value I'll ever have, for the senator. Which makes the fact that he hates himself for being lured in by it even more complicated.

As if sensing I need a distraction, Avery snatches my wrist and pulls my forearm over, propping it on Jonah's slightly bent knees. He extracts a Sharpie from his joggers and starts sketching, tracing fine lines over my skin.

I look over at Jo. "Is this normal? Should I be concerned?"

Jonah grins and shows me some of his own ink. Implying, I think, that Avery did the piece etched into his own wrist. "I think it means he likes you."

Avery's opal eyes flick up to mine, warm and teasing. "Was that really in question, kitten? After last night?" His pretty lips quirk as they remind me of *all* the heat-spikes he's eased me through. "And yesterday? And the day before?"

He's just *kidding*. I *know* that. This is our thing—being sassy, clawing at one another.

But my scent still darkens as my belly squirms, filling with the familiar sensation of shame. I duck my head, hoping no one will notice if I can compose my face before they—

Jonah kicks Avery's thigh. The pen tip marking my skin pauses.

For a second, I think I'm about to be in the middle of one of their smackdowns—*over me?*—but then Ave reaches for my chin, lifting my face the way he always does. Wanting to see my eyes.

"Hey," he murmurs, leaning over to rub his forehead into mine. "I'm sorry."

"You're just joking," I dismiss, forcing a smile. "And I've probably been way too needy—"

He sighs, kissing me softly. "Fucking *never*," he roughs out. "I don't ever want you to think that."

He pulls back, a wince marring his black brows, creasing the pale skin between them. My eyes mist when I see the genuine concern in his.

When he sees the tears, Avery's face cracks into a pained expression. "Come here, baby."

Jonah helps, lifting me right into Ave's lap and sitting up behind me. While he rubs soothing circles on my lower back, Avery presses his lips into mine again, whispering, "That was a stupid fucking thing to say. I'm sorry."

He shouldn't even be the one apologizing. It's me—my problem, my fault. My perfume. My heat-spikes. My hang-ups. That little voice inside of me that tells me sex appeal is all I'll ever be to anyone.

It isn't true, though. I can already see that.

Jonah's been a perfect gentleman, giving me more affection than I ever dreamed and never so much as letting his hands wander. And twice, during my spikes, Avery's put me in his tattoo chair and spent nearly an hour between my thighs, getting me off without any reciprocity.

He holds me after and purrs for me, tells me jokes and funny stories. Or he gets one of his sketches out and works on it while I melt against his rumbling chest.

They both act like they're truly happy I'm here. It isn't fair for me to be so sensitive about this.

"I—I'm sorry, too. I shouldn't feel so—"

Jonah moves in closer, his own purr vibrating against my spine. "But you do, *manamea*. It's okay. We all have our stuff."

Avery pulls back just far enough to give me a solemn look as he shudders. "Yeah, *never* tease Spencer about the freckles on his shoulders. Trust me."

My giggle sounds watery, but it makes him smile. "And Tristan is weird about his ears after that one haircut," he adds.

Jonah sighs. "I told him not to cut his hair that short."

I laugh again, but my heart feels heavy. Will Tristan ever tell me any of his own stories? Am I going to have to hear them all from his packmates?

Jonah's phone buzzes. He checks it quickly and then chucks it aside, his expression softening as he moves closer to me.

I don't know how he senses my feelings, but he snuggles into my back while Avery drops more kisses onto my mouth. Before long, we're making out while Jonah keeps up his steady, soothing touches.

Their purrs press into me, melting the tension I can't seem to shake. Making me believe, for just a few minutes, that I'm the center of their world.

When my perfume winds into the air, I expect them both to press their advantages. Instead, Avery's mouth curves against mine. He hums, his voice rough with desire. "You know what I think?"

Jonah answers before I can. "What?"

"I think our girl needs a foot rub."

The big man behind me grins at Ave. "You'll have to fight me for it."

twenty-eight

JONAH

"TUBS LOOKS like his ass is on fire."

Chortles echo through the locker room while Theo Matthews, our tight end, busts my balls. I narrow my eyes at him.

"How are those chin pubes coming along?" I clap my hand on his shoulder. "Don't worry, little guy, they'll grow in eventually."

His packmate and our quarterback, Declan Howard, snorts while Theo sputters. We have a long-running joke about how much thicker my hair and beard are.

Matthews may have the Viking thing going on, but my Samoan blood makes his facial hair pitiful by comparison. I'm also the only guy on the team who's both taller and wider than him.

He always gets back at me by pointing out how ancient I am. So, I'm not surprised when he laughs, "Your beard is only better because you're, like, a thousand, Father Time. How much slower were you in the sprints this morning?"

I snap my towel at him, covering for the fact that his question actually makes me frown. I *was* slower than ever this morning. Usually, I'd make a point of getting him back by pointing out the very obvious rug burn on his ass, but I'm too busy trying to yank my clothes out of my locker to do much else.

It's 2:40 and I promised my omega I'd be home by three.

"You're not even going to ball-tap him?" Declan whines, then notices how I almost shove both my feet into the same pant leg. "Damn, you really are in a hurry."

Theo looks suspicious behind all of his blond facial hair. "Got a hot date or something?"

I can't tell if he's still kidding. The guys on the team normally give me plenty of shit for dating. I am old, after all. And enormous.

Actually, one of their quips about me crushing the last chick *was* sort of hilarious. And unfortunately accurate.

But now, a squirmy panic settles over my stomach. *Fuck.* I'm going to have to be so careful with Serena. She's as small and delicate as that little hummingbird charm she wears around her neck.

"Not a date," I admit, shrugging my T-shirt on. I glance around us to make sure no one else is listening and lean forward. "We met a girl. An omega."

Declan and Theo freeze. Look at each other. And then they both *whoop*.

Dec slaps my arm while Theo bounces up and down like a teenage girl at a Harry Styles concert. "Holy shit! GET IT TUBS!"

The whole locker room is staring now. Of course.

I give them all my best impersonation of Avery's death glare until they go back to their own shit. Then I hiss, "It's not public information yet, you knotheads. Tristan has to tell the press and all that stupid shit."

If anyone will understand, it's them. Their pack leader is a high-profile tycoon who also happens to own our football team. They're all used to dealing with the media.

Declan nods, unbothered. "That's cool. Meg will still want to meet her, though. You know she loves you, Tubs."

Their omega does social media stuff for the team and I'm one of her favorite players to film. Apparently, I'm, as she puts it, "one juicy beefcake."

Will Serena be okay with me working around another omega? Will she want to meet Meg? Or is that weird?

Jesus. We really were unprepared for this shit.

Theo's face loses all traces of teasing. He gives me a little shake and a reassuring smile. "She'll like it. They can all talk shit about us."

I cringe. "All?"

"Meg will want to bring her best friend," Declan says. "But she's cool. Her pack runs the Timberwolves hockey team."

Well, as long as they're all packed up, it shouldn't be a big deal?

I don't know, but my five minutes are up.

"I'm late." I shove my shit into my duffle and make sure Coach isn't looking. "Make up some excuse for me."

♥

I FIND Serena in the backyard.

That isn't a surprise at this point. When she isn't cuddled with Avery in his room or watching me cook dinner, she loves being out here in the sunshine. She also loves movies—even the really bad ones—nature documentaries, and taking little walks around our neighborhood.

And me? I love to watch her.

On her knees in a sunny patch of grass on the other side of our pool, she closes her eyes and runs her palms through the springy green. Feeling the blades, letting them tickle her hands.

When she brings her hands to her face and inhales, I wonder if she's thinking about Tristan and his summery, grassy scent.

From what Avery and I can tell, the Thorne brothers have all but ignored her since she got here.

For Spencer, it's fear. He's never told me why, but I know he has issues with people touching him. I'm sure, with how much he must want this woman, he's terrified of what will happen once he gives in.

The inevitability of it can't be easy for him, either. He's always so in control. Knowing that it's only a matter of time before he loses it is probably fucking with his head.

Tristan is a whole other beast. I feel him sometimes, watching from the next room, observing her with gut-wrenching sadness in his eyes.

I'm not sure if Serena realizes how scared she is of him. Whenever he walks into the room, her scent descends into the delicious darkness that makes me queasy. I know Tris has noticed it because he's steadily started avoiding her.

Not wanting her to suffer. Taking whatever pain it causes him to walk away. Believing he doesn't deserve to try to woo her.

I can't decide if that makes him noble or stupid.

While I watch, Serena shifts on her knees, sunlight slanting over her dark head. Recapturing my complete attention instantly.

God, she's fucking beautiful.

Glossy brows match her thick black lashes. They twitch against the apples of her cheeks, which are underlined by high, delicate cheekbones. Her nose slopes adorably, ending in a little button. And her lips are a dark, dusky rose that goes with her complexion.

I like that we sort of match, both of us with richer coloring than the rest of the pack. Mine is more russet, though, and hers has gold undertones. Our hair is similar, too. Coarse and black—but mine kinks and waves while hers falls in straight swoops.

I wonder what her heritage is. I wonder if she knows. I should order one of those DNA kits. We could all do them, like a little pack project.

My mind spins, conjuring all sorts of things I could do with her. All the stuff she's probably never had a chance to experience.

We could go to the beach. I could teach her to drive the boat our pack only uses twice a year. There's a chance she doesn't even know how to drive a car...

I'll show her that, too, I decide.

We can travel. She should see *everything*.

While I think, she looks around, a small smile pulling at her lips. Which makes the extra creaks in my knees and the healing cuts on my hands so fucking worth it.

Planning a surprise for our cunning little omega wasn't easy. I had to distract her with stuffed crust pizza while the landscaping company delivered everything; and Avery kept her occupied most of the weekend so I could clear out the old, overgrown garden beds to plant fresh stuff for her.

I may have gone a little overboard—rose bushes, tomatoes, tons of herbs. Toward the back, she even has her own little grove —orange, lemon, lime, and mango trees.

I finally finished up last night and took the tarps off everything. This might be the first time she's seen all of it—and now I'm very glad I cut out of practice early.

While I lean into the back door's jamb, she rises to balance on her knees and gingerly reaches out to touch the basil plant closest to her. The little curve on her lips splits into a real smile.

So worth it.

I can't stay away anymore, lumbering down the lanai's steps to the pool deck. She hears my heavy tread and turns, her hand flying up to grasp something on her chest.

Her necklace, I realize.

Along with *manamea*, I've started calling her hummingbird in my mind. Partly because of small gold charm she wears all the time. But, also, she sort of looks like a flighty little hummingbird when she floats around our house, hovering at the edges of every room like there's a flower she wants to land on but isn't sure if it's safe.

We had lots of hummingbirds back home. My mom used to take me out early in the morning to watch them zip through her garden. They really do hum when they do that, their wings a blur of color and sound.

Our eyes meet across the pool. A deep slice of longing cuts through my chest.

She's let me hold her every day. Treating her touch starvation —at least, that's what I said, and she's never corrected me. Since Avery has mostly taken responsibility for her heat-spikes, I make sure she gets all the non-sexual affection she wants, even if it means my dick and I live in a constant state of desperation.

At least being around her perfume has gotten easier to take. Which just makes it better, somehow. Now that I'm used to it, I can appreciate all its subtle nuances.

And sometimes, when we're cuddled together on the couch or in her bed, and I've breathed her in enough, I find myself forgetting about it.

And then it's just... *her*.

Which I love even more.

As soon as our eyes lock, hers sparkle. She gestures at the new plants. "I think we might have gardening fairies. Or gnomes."

She makes little jokes, but only when she's extremely relaxed. The fact that I did that for her, today, fills me with more pride than fifteen seasons in the NFL ever has.

"I hope not," I grunt, playing along. "Gnomes are a bitch."

She giggles, but the humor quickly falls off her face. Intensity brightens those big green eyes. "Jonah, did you do all of this yourself?"

I nod, coming a few steps closer. "It was no big deal. I planted some tomatoes and a bunch of herbs over there. If they like this spot, you and I will go to the garden center and get more. Maybe a few more fruit trees, too. They look nice, right?"

She just stares at me, gaze swirling as her scent sweetens. I'm too far away to tell if she's happy or upset, so I do my best to give a casual shrug. "If you don't like it, I can—"

With my eyes cast down, I miss the way she darts toward me.

Which is how the Orlando Ospreys center winds up getting thrown to the ground by an omega.

twenty-nine

JONAH IS every bit as comfy as he looks.

I lie in the crook of his bare shoulder, resting my head where it meets the broad expanse of his chest. Tracing a finger along the thick black lines inked over his heart, I turn and look up at the copse of oak trees swaying overhead.

He catches me peeking again, chuckling quietly over his purr and pulling me in closer. "I'm glad you like your garden, *manamea*."

Sweetheart. He calls me that all the time. And, sometimes, when I'm feeling extra shy, *hummingbird*. Either way, everything he says is layered with undeniable fondness.

Which I still don't understand.

He won't let me do *anything* for him. Every time I offer, he just tells me we have time. Like there really isn't any rush—like he actually wants... to get to know me?

I feel like we've made some pretty good progress on that. He quizzed me about all my favorite foods, the types of music I like the most, how I feel about all the clothes Tristan's personal shoppers sent for me.

I've learned about him, too. The big man loves any sort of sporting event—even things most people don't usually watch, like surfing and bowling. He's passionate about cooking and spending time outdoors, which means he loves to grill on the enormous gas range the pack has in the backyard.

I've only been here for a week, but it's already clear he's the peacemaker of the pack, with a deep understanding of all the other guys and tons of insights he has no problem sharing with me. That's how I learned that Spencer has a touch aversion and Avery used to be a tattoo artist.

He's also been the source of all my Tristan intel. I haven't had the nerve to ask many questions, but so far Jonah's told me that their pack leader may seem fussy, but he's really the least-picky eater of them all. He's also not at all particular about what they do to spend time together as a pack and prefers making most decisions as a group.

Other than that, the other info I've gleaned is pretty useless. He likes to change into comfortable clothes the moment he gets home; he's a bit of an insomniac; and, according to Jo, he has "a black thumb" that can kill any houseplant, no matter how hardy.

Something this big man clearly doesn't struggle with, if this beautiful garden is any indication.

Every time I look around, I can't control my smile. So I hide my face against his pec instead, scent-marking him before I realize what I'm doing. His purr deepens, his hand spreading wide over the small of my back.

Bearded lips graze my forehead before he nestles his chin against the crown of my head. We stay there, content, for a long moment before he rumbles, "I've been thinking about things we could do together. Places to take you. Things you might want to learn."

No one's ever been as kind to me as this alpha. In fact, I doubt anyone's been this kind to another human, ever. And without expecting a single thing in return. Not even an explanation as to how I ended up here.

Why do I suddenly feel like I might cry?

"Jo?"

He turns his face into my hair. "Mmhmm?"

"I'm sorry it's taken me so long to talk to you all. I know I promised I would. I'm sure you're all getting frustrated..."

It isn't really a question, but he hears what I'm asking anyway. Hitching me closer, his voice lowers into a soft murmur. "Serena, where you've been doesn't matter to me. I only need to know where you want to go. So I can take you there."

His words sink in slowly—their meaning and his absolute, mind-boggling sincerity.

"Jonah..."

Nerves flutter in my stomach, my scent smoldering while I fret over the phrase I've been thinking about all week. Every time he holds me or kisses me. Every scent-mark. Every kind word. I keep hearing what he said the first night and wondering what he meant.

This doesn't have to mean anything.

Was he trying to give himself an escape hatch? I sort of assumed so, at the time. An out for both of us, I figured. Because I was clearly scared, and he was clearly too good for me.

But, then, why has he said such beautiful things; and gone to the trouble of making me gifts?

Is it possible he really just wants me to be comfortable?

There's only one way to know.

"I know you said this doesn't have to mean anything. But what if—" I start and pause to swallow hard. "What if... I want it to?"

For a long beat, the alpha under me goes still. My mind races, trying to come up with some way to take back what I said. Play it off as a joke, maybe? Or—

He rolls me faster than a man his size has any right to, putting us face-to-face. Lord, he really is handsome. All his strong, broad features perfectly balanced with his thick, dark brows and beard.

His rich amber irises shine in the afternoon sunshine. Dropping his forehead to mine, he flashes a grin that's pure joy.

"I'd say *thank God*." He nuzzles me sweetly. "Isn't it obvious that I'm crazy about you, *manamea*? Finding you is everything I've ever wanted."

As soon as he says the words, it seems insane that I ever doubted him. He's made it abundantly clear—just as obvious as Avery, in his own unique way. Cooking for me at every opportunity, holding me every time I seem even the least bit unsure. All of his scent-marks and forehead kisses. And now, this garden...

Am I really so broken that I didn't think he could care about me? Even after *all of that*?

This poor alpha.

I brush my lips along his and settle in, really kissing him for the first time.

It's nothing like Avery in the best way. My tattooed alpha kisses with carnal intent, always making it abundantly clear just how much he wants more.

Jonah, though... He's slow and soft, his lips teasing mine until I moan and arch up, desperate for more pressure. He smiles, then, his beard prickling my chin while his mouth pulls into a wide, pleased grin.

I feel his cock through the jeans molded to his lower half. I've spent the week mentally sizing it up every time it makes itself known, and I'm more than a little intimidated.

His dick can't possibly be proportional to his enormous body... right?

Oh my God.

Right?!?

His scent thickens, sweetness bursting on my tongue while his smokey, toasted goodness gets deeper. *S'mores*, Avery told me. That's the name for Jonah's rich blend of chocolate and golden brown and gooey deliciousness. I've never had s'mores before, but they promised we could make them one night when the weather gets cooler.

I truly can't wait. *Maybe I won't have to*, some depraved piece of me thinks. *Maybe his cum will taste like he smells.*

I haven't tried Avery's yet to confirm. In fact, for someone so inherently sensual and spontaneous, my fighter has been alarmingly polite. He never demands anything from me, happy to get me off with his hands and his mouth and his pierced cock as many times as I want him to.

Sure, it usually ends with his cum glazing my belly... or my thighs... But still. He's a *giver*.

Just like Jonah, he's made a point to make me the main priority. Because, I'm beginning to suspect, they might actually... *like* me.

Me.

Not my scent or parts of my body that they can use. But... like me *as a person*.

I almost can't believe it. Maybe that's why my small voice asks, "What are the things you wanted to teach me?"

Will he say something sexual? Maybe he wants to teach me how to take knots. Or swallow them. I should probably figure out both if I really am staying here for my heat...

Jo's large hand comes up to pet my head, stroking my hair back while he looms over me. "Well, I want to take you to the beach. That's a *must*. Do you know how to swim? If you don't, I can teach you. It's not so hard."

He wants...

To teach me to swim?

I blink at him. My Omega peers out at his face, nudging at me the same way she did with Avery, only this time I feel like she's almost rolling her eyes at me.

If she could speak, she'd be saying, *See? Told ya so.*

When he sees whatever my face is doing, his creases in a frown. "I know it might not sound like much fun, but it really is a safety thing, hummingbird. We live in a place with a lot of water, and we have a pool. I should maybe get you professional lessons or—"

I arch up, kissing him harder than before. He grunts, catching me against him and holding me there effortlessly.

When he pulls back with a bewildered blink, I start to shimmy out from under him. "Come on."

He sits up and watches me stand. "Where are we going?"

I reach for the hem of my T-shirt and strip it off, flashing the nude sports bra underneath. For half a second, my usual shame starts to creep up.

Stupid little—

But Jonah purrs, the sound sinking into my center and unraveling any anxiety there. "*Manamea,*" he murmurs, his eyes skimming my bare torso with unrestrained adoration. "You are so damn gorgeous."

It only makes me more sure of my decision. I hook my thumbs into my shorts and shove them down, leaving my lower half in a lacy pair of black briefs.

Jonah's mouth actually drops open. I smile wider. "You want to teach me to swim, right? Well, we have a pool, but I don't have a bathing suit. Is that a problem?"

His throat works as he reaches his brawny hand to his fly and grips the long, thick ridge there. Something that manages to be both dark and light flashes through his eyes as he quirks a brow. "You flirting with me, omega?"

I guess I *am.* And I don't even feel ashamed of it.

A happy laugh bubbles up my throat. "Yeah, I think so."

Honest softness fills his gaze. "Then I'm the luckiest man alive."

That look gives me enough confidence to reach for my bra. Just before I pull it off, I pause, looking around at the high brick walls protecting their property. Jonah follows my train of thought and stands, coming to block me from anyone's view.

"We have cameras, and we own all the land around the fence," he murmurs, reaching to pull his own shirt off. "No one will see us...except maybe the guys. If they're home."

Thick brows lower in consternation. "Is that okay with you?"

Again, I can just tell he *means* it. If I'm uncomfortable, we won't do it.

As simple as that.

His sincerity touches me all over again, bringing back my bravery. I whip the sports bra off and toss it aside.

Even Jonah's growl somehow sounds *warm*. Possessive and approving. "You sure, baby?" he roughs out, the inked russet skin of his chest shifting while his muscles bunch, hands reaching over to skim along my bare sides.

He drops his voice into a teasing rasp. "They could be watching right now... seeing your perfect perky tits bouncing. The way you're pressing those pretty thighs together. All the naughty glances you keep sending down here."

He cups himself, the motion just careless enough to make my breath catch. When I lick my lips and accidentally look down at the outline of his erection again, he laughs quietly.

But he isn't laughing *at* me. Or mocking me for wanting him.

He doesn't think I'm silly or stupid. Instead, he *praises* me.

"Such a good omega," he murmurs, stepping closer. "You want to see what's yours? Show whoever's watching in the house that you like big alpha cocks?"

Desperate desire floods my core, pooling between my hips as I perfume. The thought of Avery—or one of the Thorne brothers, *oh my God*—seeing what Jonah does to me is enough to have me on the edge without even touching him.

When I nod, Jonah's eyes flash. His scent gets sweeter than ever before, the burned, toasted outline of it adding to how mouth-watering he is. Not missing a beat, he unbuttons his jeans and shoves them off. Without any boxers underneath, his cock immediately springs free.

And it's—

A monster.

Holyyyyy—wow.

The wide wall of flesh juts from between his hips—so big, it manages to make the rest of him look narrow. Which would be incredible, if it didn't also terrify me.

Tap out. Tap out, my thoughts squeak.

But my Omega? She's *proud.* Sizing up this magnificent specimen with a cocky air I've never gotten from her before. Almost like, *Yep. Nailed it.*

Ma'am.

We really need to talk about your life choices.

This man will *split us in half.*

I have the thought, but then I see the look on his face. Warm amusement touches his mouth while his eyes take on an intent sort of heat.

"It'll fit," he murmurs, somehow soft and rough.

He steps closer until the thick, dark head smears pre-cum against the curve of my belly. "You were built for this cock," he tells me. "My knot. Everything. You're my mate, *manamea.* We'll fit together."

Jonah smooths his hands over my hair, leaning down to scent-mark my forehead. I smile into his bare chest, nodding at the crystal water behind us. "You'll have to catch me first."

I FUNDAMENTALLY DISAGREE with just about everything I've ever heard people say to justify poor behavior.

Most of it is nonsense, or outright untrue. *I didn't mean to. It just happened.*

And then, my least favorite:

You never know how you'll react in a situation until you're the one in it.

Well. I thought I knew how I'd react to this, but here I am.

Jonah knows I'm here. He looked at me when he stood up

and took his shirt off. I heard him ask the omega, too, pressing her about one of us watching until she admitted she liked the idea.

Serena.

I never expected to like that name so much. Never thought it would randomly slide through my mind while I was supposed to be busy with other things.

Like now.

I'm supposed to be reviewing applications for my student research team. Instead, I'm looming at the back door of the pack house, watching Jonah show his dick to the omega.

Serena, my brain unhelpfully supplies.

Miss Swanson, I correct internally.

Though, I admit, it does feel a little bit ridiculous to stand on ceremony when she has her tits out.

Beautiful tits. Jesus.

My cock pulses along my inseam, straining as those ripe, rounded breasts bounce. They're perfectly formed, tipped with dark nipples that stand out so clearly on her golden-brown skin.

Fucking hell.

I really should go back to work...

Jonah holds his cock out for her. I'm sure I saw it a few times when we roomed together in college, but it never occurred to me how large he is.

It seems like it should be physically impossible for someone so small to take anything that large inside of her. I know she'll be able to, though. Omegas are built to take their alphas all the way to the root.

Gushing and clenching around our cocks and knots, and—

I force my body into stillness, snapping my eyes closed and breathing through my mouth until I feel like I have control. It's pointless, though. This close to them, Serena's real perfume carries along the breeze.

I can *taste* it.

Coconut cream and pineapple paradise. My knot swells, the beast inside of me snarling.

Watching her cup his length and gently skim her fingers down it doesn't help.

He groans, pushing his hips forward for more. She adds her other hand, touching him all the way down to the mass of hard flesh inflating at his base.

Jonah touches her, too. Running his large hands over her back, dipping his touch into the lacy panties spread over her rounded ass.

I should leave.

But I can't.

Especially when Serena suddenly flashes him a smile so beautiful that I lose my breath. It gusts out of my lungs, leaving me with an aching twinge in my chest as she backs toward the pool. She turns away from Jonah, flashing him her backside before she slides out of her lacy scrap of underwear.

His eyes drop right to her ass, which I think may be her intention. Because when I keep my gaze on her face, I see the fear there.

For a moment, I don't understand. My Alpha lurches forward, trying to snap his binds and run to her. Comprehending before I do that—

She's never been swimming before.

I'm about to launch into motion when she visibly inhales and steps over the edge. She's smart—going for the shallow end, feet first, close enough to the wall that she can grab it if she needs to.

Still, my mind is blown by the notion of just… jumping into something. I'm sure I've never done that. Usually, people who do seem stupid to me.

Right now, though, all I see is bravery.

And *beauty*. God.

Naked, with the water lapping at her luminous skin and her hair spreading over the water like ink, Serena looks like a goddess.

Jonah must agree. He stares at her with his mouth ajar, his big body heaving on deep breaths just like mine is.

Her green eyes sparkle knowingly. Sharp in a way that makes my blood burn. "You coming in, big man?"

My packmate growls softly, sliding into the water without pausing to take a breath. The second he starts plodding a path to her, she shrieks a giggle and darts the other way, making him chase her.

Or, maybe, *letting* him.

It's part of alpha biology, wanting to hunt down our mates. A current cracks through my limbs while I watch her dodge his hands, weaving through the water much more quickly than he can, even though she can't go under.

Jonah clearly loves it. The grin on his face just gets wider and wider, until they're both laughing, sloshing water onto our deck while they play with each other.

That's what this is.

They're *playing*. Having fun together.

Why does that make my stomach drop?

Finally, Jonah has enough. He opens his arms and sweeps Serena right up, carrying her to the pool steps and settling her over his lap. Totally naked and unbothered, he pulls her face to his and sinks his tongue into her mouth.

Damn it. Why doesn't this seem messy and senseless to me, the way sex usually does? Why am I *watching* and *throbbing* and *what the hell* is this *burn* in my gut?

Envy, my mind supplies, factual as ever.

And it's correct. That's what this feeling is.

I'm *jealous*. Seething desire flares hotter and higher while Serena keens, rolling her hips against Jonah under the cool, blue water.

He lets her use him, groaning and grunting gentle, encouraging sounds even when he manhandles her ass, her breasts, her hips. Murmuring to her about how they need to go slow, let her practice before she tries to take him inside her.

It makes sense. I know he promised Tristan he wouldn't try to fuck her until she's better prepared for everything he has to give. Serena must agree to behave herself, because she nods and presses her mouth back over his, her hands grasping at his shoulders as he gentles her.

A sick sort of sadness joins the burn below my diaphragm.

Because—dear God—*I want* to kiss her.

By the time Serena starts to rub herself against Jonah's length, I've accepted that I can't walk away. So, instead, I watch even more carefully. Wanting to know what will please her. Trying to see how she might feel.

The way she falls into him, trusting him, letting him guide how fast she goes with his iron grip on her hips...

Fucking hell.

We really have a mate.

chapter
thirty-one

IF SHOPPING WERE Jonah's idea—or even Avery's—I would not be shocked.

But when *Spencer* issues three no-nonsense knocks to my bedroom door and announces that we're going out to furnish the nest...

Well.

He does not seem like the sort of alpha I should argue with.

So I put on one of the simpler ensembles in my new Tristan-approved wardrobe and hope it isn't too fancy or too slutty.

I didn't pick the clothes, so I know I shouldn't feel guilty about whatever they do or do not reveal... but some deep-seated part of me whispers that my scent is already alluring enough. I don't need these black jeans to be so tight or the deep-V cut of this black blouse.

The fact that I actually like the sleek, sexy clothes only makes it worse, somehow. Because... *of course* I like them. These are exactly the sort of fancy clothes a *silly little slut* like me *would* like, aren't they?

Not wanting the guys to tower over me any more than necessary, I strap on a pair of platform heels and pray I don't look ridiculous. One glance in the mirror hanging beside the Omega Suite's door tells me that my prayers have once again been forwarded to voicemail.

I cringe at my makeup-less face and limp hair. Tristan's personal shopper may have been able to source all the clothes I could ever need, but I really do need to grab my usual beauty supplies if I don't want to look like a hot mess.

For all his scowling, Spencer does seem like the only sane, rational person around here, sometimes. He informs all of us that we're heading to a store that will have all the practical things I need. Namely, toiletries and "proper" nesting supplies.

It definitely doesn't feel romantic or even emotional, but as we ride over, I begin to suspect this might be his unique brand of care-taking.

He certainly seems concerned with my well-being, checking his Volvo's rearview mirror every thirteen seconds. Jonah fills the gaps in conversation, giving us a play-by-play of his practice while he sprawls next to me in the back, taking up more than half of the seat between us with his massive body. Avery sits in the passenger seat, glaring at the radio every time a new pop song comes on.

On the other side of the sedan's tinted window, I watch the world slip by. It was one of my favorite things to do, as a kid, but I haven't driven around during the day in *years*. Wally always fetched me for the club after dark and usually brought me home before the sun came up.

The pack townhouse is in Orlando's historic downtown area. I watch it give way to the suburbs—larger, grander homes and pristine lawns. There are lakes and fountains and parks and gardens. When we drive past one particularly pretty patch of flora, I press my fingertips into the cool glass.

For the first time since we left the house, Spencer speaks, interrupting my musings. "Serena, where would you prefer to go for nesting supplies? As I understand it, there are two popular stores. Do you have a preference?"

I feel like a deer in headlights, unsure how to answer or admit I've never been to a nesting store. But Jonah goes to work, typing away at his phone until he looks up with a warm smile. "The one on Colonial has the best reviews."

Right. I could have looked that up. Avery gave me my very own phone days ago. It's wedged in my fist, but I keep forgetting I have it.

While we all get out of the car, I try not to let myself wonder where Tristan is and why he hasn't been around at all.

Maybe he's just going to ignore me forever.

Spencer's phone chimes, and he frowns at the screen before glancing at me. I start to ask him what he's staring at, but my words get choked up again. It seems to happen when I get over-whelmed—and this place is the definition of overwhelming.

I've never been anywhere so *big*. It's *endless*. Just yards and yards of shiny white linoleum and hundreds of rows of shelves stacked two stories high.

My body tries to freeze on the threshold, but Jonah settles his big hand over my lower back and gently propels me forward. While Spencer leads us toward a customer service desk, Avery closes in at my other side. He doesn't reach for me, but his eyes lock onto mine.

"You good, kitten?"

I nod, but he doesn't buy it. I get a raised eyebrow instead. He leans closer and grumbles, "I fucking hate this place, too."

Jonah rolls his amber eyes. The sticky-sweet scent of his skin toasts a bit, but that just makes him even more mouth-watering. Especially when his fingers knead my spine through my thin silk shirt. "Give her a chance to form an opinion, Ave. Omegas *like* this place."

Avery stares at him, level as can be. "Not my omega."

Damn it, but he's *right*. I hate it here. The fluorescents overhead are *blinding*, and whatever scent-neutralizer they pump into this place gives me a headache.

Spencer returns to our group within a few moments. He has a tablet in his hand and starts ticking things off the screen. "Pillows, cushions, stain and moisture resistant covers, bath supplies, hair products, blankets—"

My temples throb dully as my chest tweaks tight. All three of them stare, waiting for me to say something, until Jonah's phone goes off. He barely checks the screen before he sighs, stashing it away and reaching for my hand.

"I know it's a lot," he whispers, stepping close enough to block out the chaos of the store and the lights and smells. For a moment, I can only see his wide chest and inhale his toasty scent. He cuts Spencer a dirty look. "We'll go through one thing at a time. *No lists.* And whenever you feel done, we'll leave."

Spencer watches, his pinched expression collapsing into something darkly contemplative. He keeps the troubled look on his face while we go through the first few aisles.

By the fourth, he seems more confident. He still doesn't touch me, but he looks me in the eye and explains little tidbits of omega knowledge he's acquired through his research.

"You'll want at least four of those. Omegas typically require three to five blankets for their beds. I'd feel better if we selected six."

"Choosing a variety of cushions may help you build your nest faster. Most omegas like more density toward the center and less around the edges."

And when Jonah picks up a pillow with tassels (that, admittedly, I hate the feel of), he simply snatches it away and mutters, "Preposterous."

Attitude aside, it's actually sort of fascinating. If he didn't intimidate me into silence, I'd like to ask him what he teaches at his university. Or if he'd be willing to lend me some of his books.

I can probably sneak some when they all go to work one of these days.

Avery's the only one without a normal job, but he seems more like an accomplice than a narc. Every time I have a thought I wouldn't want the others to hear, he's already staring at me, smirking. Especially when we make it to the "toiletry" section of the store.

It has all the usual stuff—and I'm thrilled by the idea of a shower with the scent-masking body wash Wally always forbid. But it also has a lot of *other* items. Like industrial-sized vats of lube with hand pumps.

Spencer looks stiff as he adds one to the cart without comment, but Avery sends me a scorching smile, and Jonah *blushes*.

Which is actually *adorable*.

I can't resist reaching up and touching his cheek. When he sees I'm biting back a smile, a warm grin stretches across his broad features.

He really is the definition of a team player—content to be the butt of any joke as long as his pack is happy. He doesn't make me speak, either; he just bends down to rub a fresh scent-mark along my cheek, nuzzling me with his soft, thick beard.

The sensation sends prickles to my nipples. They stiffen and graze the fabric of my shirt. Without warning, piña colada perfume swirls around us.

We all freeze for a moment.

Spencer's dark eyes flash, angry and almost... *wild*.

Avery grunts, ducking to sink his teeth into his closed fist.

I start to scramble for an apology, fighting the squeeze in my windpipe. But Jonah's gaze softens. He pulls me into his body, hugging me close.

"Mmm, hummingbird," he husks, purring. "Like a slice of heaven every single time."

I only manage a couple of words. "B-but people can smell me. M-my perfume—"

"—is nobody's business but ours," he finishes, as if that's that. Smoothing one enormous palm down the back of my head, he folds me closer to that deep, rusty purr.

Avery's voice is about as smooth as 20-grit sandpaper, but he grinds out, "What's next, Spence?"

I lose the thread of their conversation, falling into Jonah's rumbles, letting him break the ache between my eyebrows. When I nestle my face into his shirt, I feel the front of his jeans strain over an erection. But he doesn't get pissed about it or press an advantage. He only clasps me closer and drops his face to my hair while he continues talking and purring.

We leave a thin trail of my perfume behind us while I fill the cart with the makeup and hair stuff I desperately need. I'm starting to feel like we might actually get everything done when I hear it.

"I *knew* it."

The voice is just familiar enough to raise the fine hairs on the back of my neck. My body locks into stillness, accidentally stopping short and forcing Avery to run into me. He snaps an arm around my waist, scowling, until he sees my face.

"What—"

But it's too late. The approaching footsteps turn onto our aisle, revealing two alphas I wish I didn't recognize.

"I told you it was her," Cheap Pizza Rolls crows. He elbows the taller, balding one I've always thought of as Spray Cheese. "*No one* else smells like this little snack."

I flounder, my mouth opening and closing. Thinking over and over, *No. Not here. Not now. Please no.*

It's too late, though. Jonah's brow crouches low as Spencer

snaps straight. Avery's arm flexes across my middle, holding me against his body. When he speaks, there's a growl layered into his voice. "These friends of yours, *kitten*?"

I try to speak, but my silent Omega has me paralyzed. A thick wedge blocks my throat and nothing comes out.

Unfortunately, that does not stop the alpha across from us. "We know her from the club," Pizza Rolls scoffs.

He flicks his muddy eyes to mine. "Didn't know Wally had started lending you out, babe. Does he charge by the hour, or do you do overnights like the other girls?"

Oh God.

OH. GOD.

My mind reels, imagining what the alphas surrounding me must be picturing. *No*, I want to scream, but a quiet whine is all that escapes.

Usually, I'd expect Jonah to reach for me when my scent darkens this way. But he's frowning at our interlopers, the gears in his mind visibly grinding.

And Avery? He keeps his arm around me, but he's staring at the side of my face like he's never seen me before.

Their scents are a burned, gooey, sopping *mess. What if they don't want me anymore? What if they shove me at these other alphas and walk out of here? What if—*

But, then, *Spencer* grabs my hand.

And I forget how to breathe.

THE GUY across from me should probably be on a stretcher.

I slam my fist into his jaw anyway, imagining someone else's face as his shredded, bruised mug swells bigger every minute.

I don't care. I land a kick to his ribs and sweep his legs. It will be easier to pummel the absolute shit out of him if he's on his back.

Is it fair to use some other fighter at my gym as a stand-in for the dickheads who scared my omega so much that she nearly passed out in that godforsaken store?

Better question:

Who gives a fuck about fair?

Nothing else is. It sure as shit hasn't been for my girl.

So this won't be, either.

"Avery."

I hear him. But fuck him.

My opponent—if you even want to call him that—has his hands up over his face, shouting some bullshit about yielding. I don't fucking care. I rattle his shit harder, both of my aching fists flying.

"*Avery.*"

My name echoes through the cage, louder this time. Pissed.

But I've always *liked* pissing people off. Anger is an emotion I understand. When someone wants to kick my ass, I actually feel like I understand them for a few minutes.

The only exception is Serena.

All she has to do is *look* at me, and I know she sees everything.

When I peer down at this guy's hamburger face, it occurs to me that maybe that isn't such a good thing.

What would she think if she saw me savaging this random dude? Would she be afraid, the way she was today?

Or that first night with—

Tristan's bark slices through the gym like a cleaver. "*Avery. That is enough.*"

With a growl, I shove off my latest victim. There are three more limping around on the sidelines somewhere.

Damn. I've been at this for a while. I'll probably get a fine.

Again.

Ripping at the tape around my hands with my teeth, I snarl at the only asshole wearing a three-piece suit in this shithole. "The fuck are you doing here?"

Tristan has mastered glaring without frowning. His mouth stays straight, but his eyes *rage.* "Jonah told me you stormed off after Serena got upset."

I scoff as I climb out of the ring. "Oh, now you fucking care? She didn't 'get upset.' She had a fucking *panic attack* because some random assholes walked up and tried to start shit. But you weren't there, so."

I slam my bare shoulder into his while I pass him, hoping it hurts. Dropping onto a bench, I bore my eyes into his face, demanding, "Do you even realize what she's—"

Survived.

I don't need to know the details to know she's a mother-fucking survivor.

As much of a fighter as I'll ever be.

Tristan's voice drops, low and urgent. "I'm trying to do the right thing, Avery. I know I have to do more, but she's afraid of me. I don't want to force my presence on her. Or make her feel obligated to accept me."

I fix him with my harshest glare. "And ignoring her is your big solution? You think that's going to help?"

He blows air out of his nose and looks back at me, ignoring the blood soaking into my towel as I wipe at my cheeks.

"I don't know her very well. Clearly." He clenches his jaw, the muscles ticking in a way that always reminds me of Spencer. "Can you tell me anything about her?"

A harsh laugh scrapes out of me. "You came to *me* for *help*? Jesus Christ, this really is a new low."

But Tristan stares back at me, steady. Waiting. Truly asking for help, which is mind-blowing on so many levels, I can't process it properly with adrenaline still pounding through my ears.

Maybe that's why I answer the prick.

"When we ride in the car, she looks out the window like she's soaking up every blade of grass we pass," I blurt.

It's a pretty stupid observation, but Tristan nods solemnly, like I've just started rattling off nuclear codes or something. When he keeps looking at me, I scrape out more.

"She isn't sleeping at night. I don't know if it's what happened or being in our house or being alone, but she spends most of her days napping in my bed and she seems to like that.

"She doesn't mind when I draw on her, and she smiles at

Jonah's jokes. Spencer scares her a little, but he's a scary mother-fucker. Plus, he looks like you."

Tristan winces slightly. "Fair. What else?"

I scrub my bloody towel through my hair and over the back of my neck, mopping up sweat. "She loves junk food, especially anything smothered in cheese. She wears little outfits, even when we're just hanging out at home. I think she likes to look put-together. We got her makeup and shit, but I bet she'd actually like shopping somewhere nice instead of that big-box bullshit we did today."

Tristan hums in agreement. "Noted. Anything else?"

I ignore the lump in my throat, grunting, "Yeah. Her touch starvation is *bad*. Jonah spends half of every day with his arms around her because she told him no one else had *ever* hugged her. Like, in her life."

The color leeches out of our pack leader's face, which perversely satisfies me. He deserves to feel like a dick.

I go on, "In bed, she's always shocked as hell whenever I do anything for her. I still don't know what she did during her heats, but I'm pretty sure *no one* took care of her. Spencer thinks because her perfume is so fucking good, there probably weren't any alphas who could handle it without biting her."

I look him dead in the eye when I say that last part. To his credit, he takes it like a man, gritting his teeth but not dropping my eyes. "Did she say when her last heat was?"

Shaking my head, I squirt some water into my mouth. "Didn't ask. Isn't that, like, rude?"

There are some moments when Tristan really does feel like a big brother. As his mouth quirks up in fond amusement, I feel young. He tilts his head slightly. "Not for the men having sex with her, no."

"Well, so far, that's just me," I snap back. "And it's going to stay that way until she decides she wants to climb someone else's knot. Or I'll be kicking all your asses."

Tristan takes the hit again. I have to give him credit for that, at least—he doesn't have a big ego. When he fucks something up, he'll take all the shit I can pile on him. And he never tries to defend himself.

It's still blowing my mind that *he* did this.

His face hardens back into an unreadable mask. "Jonah also told me that you waited until they got Serena into the car, and then you bolted." He glances at the guy laid out in the ring behind me. "I assume you were trying to control your temper so you didn't scare her?"

He's right, and I hate that. "We were only two miles from the gym, so I ran here," I mutter, hanging my head and pressing my forearms to my thighs. "She's been through enough shit. She was already upset. I didn't want to make a scene by unleashing my Alpha in that place."

Tristan's hand lands on my shoulder. He doesn't say anything, but I hear it anyway. *Good job, kid.*

"Jonah called me. He said she's been hiding in her room, but when he brought her dinner, she asked if we could all talk. She wants to explain what happened today."

I ignore the pang of relief that strikes my gullet, shoving to my feet. "You gonna give me a ride home, then?"

He almost smirks. "Maybe I should make you walk."

"Fuck you," I chirp, tossing my shit into my duffle and strapping it across my back. My gaze catches on the Octagon, and I roll my eyes.

"Hold on."

Tristan watches while I jog over and kick the guy lightly until he groans, lolling his head to try to look at me. "Sorry, man," I shrug. "Better luck next time, eh?"

By the time I'm back by his side, Tris looks like he just witnessed the parting of the Red Sea. I trudge past him, shrugging. "Serena would have wanted me to."

chapter
thirty-three

I'M TRISTAN THORNE.

But that doesn't mean shit right now.

Right now, I'm just a man who wants to tear the world in two but can't fit my hands around it.

Serena asked if she could talk to all of us. I never expected *this*, though.

I've been keeping an eye on her all week, making sure she seems as settled and happy as she feels through the bond. Until I walk into a room, that is. Then her panic and shame lash at my insides.

It's been easier for me to watch from a distance. Absorbing her quick smiles and intelligent eyes. Seeing how she relaxes into Jonah's nurturing and rises to meet Avery's attitude.

I've even seen glimpses that I know Spencer would love—her thirst for knowledge, the careful way she reasons through situations, hovering at their edges before acting. Which is why I suspect she's been thinking about this carefully since she arrived.

What to tell us, *how* to tell us.

She chooses the living room. That feels obvious, since the only other place we'd all fit and have a place to sit is the nest she hasn't even opened yet. I was hoping Spencer's shopping trip may encourage her. Not because I want to go in there—*although*—but more because *she* needs that safe space.

I'm starting to think she's never had one.

As we all shuffle into the living room, I can't help but run my eyes over her outfit. It's one of the new ones—tight pants that hug her hips and a silky low-cut blouse. I might appreciate the ensemble more if it wasn't soaked in the scent of her stress.

Sweet baby.

It really isn't fair to her, the way she smells aroused when she's scared. If I didn't have her distress churning a pit in my stomach, I might never have figured out the difference between her perfume and this darker sweetness.

The rest of my pack has figured it out, too. I can tell they're all on edge.

Avery sits on the edge of the sofa with his elbows on his knees, shifting restlessly. Jonah drags his palms over his jean-clad thighs. And Spencer stands in the far corner of the room with his arms crossed, motionless.

It's telling that Serena chooses one of the individual reading chairs instead of wedging herself between Jonah and Ave. Until tonight, she's seemed content to take every opportunity they've given her for affection.

Now, the small omega-sized space between them remains vacant.

I'm the last one in the room, coming to the only chair left open, across the coffee table from Serena. She bites her lip while I sink into it, chagrin and apprehension clanging through our frayed tether.

Her right hand curls protectively around her hummingbird necklace and she starts to talk, her words slow and halting.

"Those alphas today. They know me from the club I used to... work at." She swallows, her stomach flipping as she winces. "Wally's Boom Boom Room.

"It's a—" Her voice cracks. "It's a strip club. Downtown. They have dancers and private rooms and... *other things.*"

She lets those words land in the middle of the room and suck half the air out of it.

"Like me," she adds. "I was one of the *things* alphas could only get at Wally's—an omega with super-perfume, walking around, delivering drinks, free for fondling or pictures..."

God, I can't *breathe.* The slicing shame carving her insides to shreds has severed my airway. When I try to look her in the eye, she ducks her head and bites her lip harder.

"How did you end up there?" I force out. "Did you *want* to be a dancer?"

Dear God, please say *yes.* Please say this sweet omega wasn't there against her will for God knows how—

"No. No, I *never* wanted to be there." She shakes her head, casting desperate looks at Jonah and Avery. Begging them to believe her.

As if this is somehow *more* acceptable because she didn't want to do it.

Which makes me *furious.*

"*Look at me.*"

My bark flies out and her head snaps to the side instantly. Fear spikes hard in her belly, forcing out a whine.

As soon as her eyes land on mine, I lower my voice. "Do you think," I rasp, "that we'd be angrier if you'd had a choice? That knowing you *had* to work somewhere—*anywhere*—against your will isn't the most horrible thing any of us can imagine?"

Aside from death and assault. Although, what she's describing would legally qualify as the latter. Especially since—

"I never wanted to be there," she repeats, shriller. "My—Wally made me start when my designation came through. He—he'd been planning it all along."

A low buzz begins to hum through my ears. "All along?"

She nods, her wild desperation tearing at my gut. "He chose me because he thought I'd be an omega."

Chose her.

The words spiral through my brain until Spencer puts it all together, his frozen voice clipping out, "He *adopted* you."

It isn't a question, but Serena nods anyway, darting a quick look to my brother before turning back to the floor. "He knew my mom, I guess. And she had the same strong perfume. He thought —he thought I would be like her. So when she decided to surrender me, he swooped in."

Jonah looks sick. His russet skin has a faint grayish cast as he scrapes, "And you were—*raised* by him?"

Serena grimaces. "Nannies, really. Then, tutors and babysitters. For a long time, I had no idea anything was weird. I lived in a house, I went to school. I didn't know that other kids' parents always spoke to them or spent time at home. I thought we were normal.

"But then, right around junior high—when I started to figure out that most kids didn't sleep in their parents' basements or go months on end without seeing them—Wally pulled me out of school and got me virtual tutors. For a long time, that was the worst part; I really wanted to go to school, but I wasn't allowed."

Spencer speaks again; no doubt because his linear mind is the only one capable of thinking straight at the moment. "Did he say why?"

Serena sighs. "He told me that my designation bloodwork

indicated I would be an omega and claimed keeping me in the house was the best way to *protect* me. Said a lot of people did it."

Sadly, that really isn't far from the truth. Many families pull their omega sons and daughters out of school when they designate. It's one of the things I'm trying to change with my work—making it illegal to cut an omega's education off before they've finished high school.

"Wally always told me how lucky I was that he adopted me in the first place," Serena remembers, tracing her toe in circles on the floor. "Everyone else—teachers and neighbors and whatever—all said the same time thing, so I believed him. I felt *grateful.*

"At first, when he asked me to work at the club for him, I wanted to make him happy. When he made rules about how much I could eat or who I was allowed to talk to, I did my best to follow them. For years, I didn't even notice all the locks on the doors and the windows because it never occurred to me to try to get out... Once I figured it out, I did *everything* I could to try to get away from him. Even when he would... punish me."

Avery has been still and silent this whole time, but he finally moves. Standing without a sound, he takes five heavy steps around the table.

And drops to his knees.

His tattooed hands mold around her face. "I knew there was a fighter in here," he says, rough and earnest. "There she is."

Serena's eyes fill as she stares back at him. "You're not mad? You don't want me to leave?"

"*Manamea,*" Jonah gasps, lurching to join Avery on the floor in front of her. "*Never.* None of us would ever want that."

She doesn't believe him. I feel doubt expand inside her chest. Golden green eyes blink at Jonah before slowly turning to Spencer.

Waiting, I realize, for him to disagree.

My brother doesn't, though. He gazes back at her, steady and intense. Saying, without words, *None of us. Not even me.*

Which only leaves—

Serena chooses to look right at me for the first time in days. Tears sparkle on her lashes, but she seems grimly determined, otherwise. That flawless poker face of hers locks into place, hiding how sick she feels.

I can't think of a better reason to let the door blocking my feelings collapse.

WHEREVER I AM, it's dark.

I can tell before I even open my eyes that the sun has set and I'm inside. Probably somewhere in the pack house because, through the crack in my eyelids, I feel like the walls are all kinds of black.

I'm also... *wet?*

But not in a sexy way.

"—but the sample was not considered statistically significant."

The low voice speaks in the crisp cadence of someone reading aloud. While it goes on, reciting variables from a research study, something smooths over my head in rhythmic strokes.

A page turns. The dim light seeping through my eyelids flickers. I inhale, filling my lungs with sudsy lavender and the fresh scent of rain.

Spencer.

And he's *touching me.*

After the way he's dodged all physical contact, that's surprising enough to turn my head and open my eyes. I find him sitting on a short wooden stool with a thick book spread open in his lap. He looks as coiffed as ever, but somehow more intimate.

Maybe because the sleeves of his white dress shirt are rolled up his impressively vascular forearms. When I look closely, I see that his silvery-blond hair is hanging a bit looser than usual, with one lock curled over his forehead. He also has a pair of frameless glasses balanced on his nose.

I must be in his bathtub because I don't recognize the grand, onyx bathroom. It's almost as big as the one attached to the Omega Suite, but this one has an egg-shaped soaking tub. No jets, but enough depth to give me the illusion of privacy.

Of course, someone must have *put* me in here...

When he catches me staring, he pauses his reading and slowly retracts the hand resting on my head. His gaze narrows, assessing my expression before he finally says, "You're awake."

For some reason, hearing someone as articulate as Spencer say something so painfully obvious makes me smile. Well, almost. My lips curl up a little as I sink into the warm water and the thin layer of bubbles floating on top.

He notices the shyness in my posture and clears his throat, straightening up a bit and removing his reading glasses. "Tristan opened your half-bond to try to show you something and you lost consciousness." He clears his throat and adds, almost defensively, "That's very normal for omegas who find their—"

"Mates."

It's the first time I've said the word. And the only one I've ever said *to him*.

He blinks, throat working. "Yes," he rasps. "Mates."

Who knows if it's the passing-out thing or the fact that I feel so emotionally drained. It could be that, after finally telling them all my horrible truths, nothing else can touch me.

Hell, maybe this lavender aromatherapy really works.

Whatever the reason, I feel calm. More words float out easily.

"Did you not want a mate?"

It seems like a sensible question to me. After all, he clearly doesn't like having me in their house. And he didn't choose this.

Or me.

But he's so obviously thrown by my question that it's almost funny. He opens his mouth and shuts it twice before finally admitting, "No. I didn't."

With a nod, I sink lower. "I get that."

Odd, disbelieving silence stretches over us. Blond brows crunch over those dark, endless eyes. "You... do?"

I snort, accidentally blowing bubbles into my own face. "Yeah," I mumble, wiping at my nose. "Don't get me wrong—a pack of big, strong alphas to save me was my dream for a long time, but once I actually *met* some alphas... No offense, but they were overwhelmingly horrible. The idea of being saddled to a bunch for all eternity because they liked the way I *smelled* was my worst nightmare."

My lips twist in a rueful smirk as I turn back to him. "Joke's on me, huh?"

Here I am, thinking I'm being blasé and maybe a tiny bit charming—but Spencer stares at me so intensely, I swear the flesh on my face melts a little. He has a way of looking right *through* people that's so unnerving.

I shrink back a little, and his jaw clenches. But his voice is even. "It must have been difficult. Having someone you trusted turn on you like that."

It's a strained attempt at empathy. Unnatural for him, I think. But he's trying. So I feel like I sort of have to answer.

I lean my head back along the edge of the tub and stare up at the patterns glowing overhead, echoes of the candles flickering on the counter. "The hardest part has been trying to forgive myself for how stupid I was. Accepting that I was so clueless for so long."

Spencer makes a low humming sound and dips a washcloth into the water. He hovers over my arm for a long moment before blowing out a breath and running it over my skin, his eyes snapping back to mine. "How did you finally figure out you were trapped?"

I cringe lower, feeling a pang of embarrassment for the first time since waking up here. I want to lie, but it's impossible with him staring into me like that.

"There was a storm one day," I whisper, dropping my gaze to the bubbles. "When I was a girl, I—playing outside in the rain was one of my favorite things. And, one day, I tried to remember the last time I'd *felt* the rain on my skin, but I couldn't. So, I tried to leave the club, to go outside. For the rain. And I wasn't allowed to."

Spencer's mind doesn't work like the others. Instead of crumpling in pity, his face stays smooth while he processes. And then he says, "I smell like rain."

Why does this uptight, intimidating alpha saying all the wrong things make me want to *smile*? I bite my lower lip and hum, "Mmhmm. You sure do."

His brows drop again, furrowing while he ponders that and glides the washcloth up to my shoulder. "Was he planning something else for you, if you hadn't gotten away?"

I'm grateful the bath covers the way shame swirls into my scent.

"I think he originally planned to—" I turn my face away. "Lend me out. Or have me dance. But then my designation came in, and once the hormones hit... I don't know what happened, but my perfume made them all *rabid*."

Spencer shifts, clearly uncomfortable but listening closely.

"Wally decided he could make more off me if he used me for enticement instead of letting other alphas sully my scent. So, every night, I had to walk around in the skimpiest outfits he could find, serving drinks and letting alphas paw at me while I passed."

The man next to me stifles a growl, letting me finish. "I did that for a long time. Then, I found out that he had *big* plans for my twenty-fifth birthday."

For some reason, I feel the need to turn back and look at him as I finish, "An auction."

Spencer is quick. It takes him less than a second to understand. "For you," he realizes. "He was going to let packs *bid* on you?"

My head falls back while my eyes slide shut. I nod, feeling oddly hollow. "During my next heat, so I wouldn't put up a fight. I guess he thought I was getting too old."

Like I said—I can sniff out an angry alpha from a mile away. Traditionally, those were the ones who wanted to hurt me. Of course, none of them were allowed to—other than Wally.

But he isn't here now. And a shiver skirts down my spine as Spencer's scent darkens.

His voice sounds jagged. "These scars... Did they all come from him?"

I laugh, but it's a bleak sound. "No. He wanted me to be *pretty*, so he mostly kept his hands off me. Except for the times I tried to get away and he had to teach me a lesson. A few of the scars are from that. But most of them are my own fault."

Beside me, Spencer has gone unnaturally still, his chest barely even rising on shallow breaths. When I meet his eyes, they're dark oceans. I suddenly feel like I'm in a confessional... but I know I need to finish the story. To have it all out there, once and for all.

"When my heats came," I whisper, "he would put me in a room with food and water and leave me there for the week. Alone. I still don't know what my Omega did or why, but every time I woke up, I had new injuries."

His brows pinch, and his hand rises from my shoulder. He holds it near my face for a beat before setting it on the crown of my head, sifting my hair back.

"I'm sorry," he roughs out, snapping those never-ending eyes to mine. "For many things. But especially that you ever felt pain like that."

I don't know how I can tell what he *isn't* saying. It's a murky instinct, indistinct and halting, but I feel so *sure*.

He knows what it's like to have someone he trusted hurt him, too. And he knows what it's like when you hurt *yourself*.

"My father wanted alpha sons," Spencer tells me, turning for the washcloth again. He carefully picks up my other arm, sending a rush of tingles to my fingertips.

"*Only* alpha sons. He came from a long line of them, in a family with a lot of money and no regard for omegas whatsoever. They were breeding vessels to the Thornes and nothing more.

"When I was young, though, my personality concerned him. I was quiet, and I preferred hiding in my room to being around others. When he began to suspect I might be an omega, he was horrified. Once Tris left for college, he spent the next four years bringing in omegas to try to entice my Alpha out of hiding... and, when that didn't work, attempting to beat the weakness out of me."

A terribly wry smile curves his mouth. "I still hate that it worked."

When I make a face, his expression smooths back into its usual mask. "Not really, of course. Environment has no bearing on our designations—a fact my research has all but proven—but he still got what he wanted when I designated as an alpha after all. And that's always rankled me."

Of course Spencer felt drawn to studying designations after enduring all of that. And he set out to prove that what his father attempted to do to him couldn't be done. Probably in the hope that his research might prevent others from repeating those sins.

For a moment, I try to come up with something to say back.

But my Omega makes one of her rare appearances, peeking out at him. She nudges me, showing me what we should do, projecting calm certainty that seeps into my center.

So, I don't speak. Instead, I lift a wet hand out of the bathwater and carefully skim my fingers over his forearm, looking into his eyes.

I'm sorry, I tell him silently. *There was never anything wrong with you.*

The intensity shifting in his depths sparkles while the rest of his face falls slack. Awe and a dark flame ignite in his irises. His other hand flies up, long fingers wrapping around my elbow.

My Omega may be sure, but I'm not. I'm thinking he'll toss me back into the water and storm out.

But, instead, he growls, "*Serena.*"

Then hauls me up, bubbles and all, into a kiss.

chapter
thirty-five

KISSING SERENA FEELS like drowning and hyperventilating at the same time.

I think I can't breathe, then I think I'll never need to again. Because I can taste her on my tongue, feel her softness pressed into my sternness. And this—*this*—

This is the one type of chemistry I haven't studied.

Her skin is wet and soft as I *feel* parts of her that I haven't even let myself *look* at. My cock kicks, my thoughts spiral.

Lavender soap is no match for the lush perfection of her scent.

And even though I managed not to look while I got her in the tub earlier... I have a feeling I won't get away that easily this time.

My body is in *chaos*.

Arousal courses through my veins, racing through my extremities. But the fear welling in my middle has teeth. It snaps, vicious. Demanding tribute.

That doesn't surprise me. I expected to hate this. What I didn't anticipate was the *want* underneath. It's rooted deep—maybe even deeper than the fear. And while the two sensations battle it out, Serena whimpers against my mouth.

Fucking hell.

What have I done?

How do I take it back?

How do I make sure she *never stops*?

A pained, pleasured groan vibrates through my chest, and Serena pulls away, panting. For a second, without her lips on mine, fear wins out. I want to snarl at her, but it seems like she's expecting that.

Her eyes go wide. She blinks up at me, so scared and vulnerable. My Alpha roars, infuriated that she feels afraid because of me.

I look down at the way I'm holding her—with a hand clamped around her wrist and the other buried into her hair. It's hardly romantic or even *nice*. Is that why she's uneasy?

But no. When my fingers flex against her scalp, a burst of her true perfume snakes into the humid air.

She *wants* this. *Likes* this.

And she's *dripping* on the *floor*, goddamn it.

I grind my teeth, my mouth watering, and say the only thing I can think of. "You need a towel."

Serena blinks. A small laugh tumbles out of her. "Um, yeah. Sure. Thank you."

I want to punish her for laughing at me, but I also want to reward her for laughing at all. It's hard to decide which notion is more insane.

I don't *want* a mate.

I shouldn't be kissing her.

Or manhandling her.

And I most definitely shouldn't be watching the way soapy water sluices over her curves.

But I do. I have. And I will.

My gaze trails over her perfect nipples, memorizing the way the dark buds point slightly upward. The feminine sweep of her waist and soft stomach. Her flared hips. And lower—

Fuck, I can't *breathe* in here.

Hiding a gasp, I pivot and practically rip a towel off the nearest rack, keeping my head turned while I hold it open for her. Her fingertips graze mine as she takes it from me. A moment later, she peeps, "Coast is clear."

I turn back to her with a sharp nod. Her hair catches my eye first—specifically, the way I mussed it. Since I suddenly exist one thought at a time, I turn toward my bathroom counter and snap, "Come."

She drifts to my side, lingering nervously. I watch her toes curl into the bathmat under her feet while she waits for me to reveal my plans for her. When I show her the comb in my hand, her lips wobble. Then they spread into a bright, wide smile.

I feel my brows pinch. Do I have something on my face? Why is she looking at me like that?

"What?" I demand.

Humor twitches through her expression. "Nothing." She shrugs a shoulder. "I like you."

She—

I glower, waiting for the punchline. "You *like* me?"

Serena nods, brow pinched in confusion but eyes clear and earnest. "Um... yeah."

Why? And, more importantly, *how*?

No one *likes* me. And why would they? I'm smart enough to know how insufferable I am.

But Serena's smile softens into a distinctly fond face. "You're surprised," she says quietly, then grins again. "That just makes me like you even more, actually."

Before I can attempt to process that impossibility, her little hand grazes my cheek. I stiffen, some blend of shock and apprehension skittering down my back.

I can't remember the last time a person touched my face. And once my mind tells my body there's no reason to fear, it feels…

It feels…

I grasp her wrist carefully this time.

"I can't do that," I tell her. "*Not yet*. But there are other things we can try."

A way to learn her body and give her what she needs. Test her limits and my control.

Because I may not have wanted a mate, but based on the way my body burns for hers? I have one. And every instinct urges me to *show her*.

Her teeth sink into her lower lip. Those clever green eyes dip to the floor, shy, but more perfume gives her away. The luscious scent swells and brightens. I inhale roughly, a growl rumbling behind my sternum.

It's ironic. Jonah and Avery have both fucked more women than I ever cared to count. Tristan is well-known in certain circles for his sexual proficiency.

But I'm an *omega expert*.

And, in the way of any true "expert," my knowledge is vast and largely theoretical. Sure, I took the time in my twenties to put some of it to good use—always at heat clinics, with strangers, where I knew no one would try to touch me back. None of it was ever done in a real-world setting, though.

Most of it seems to be working so far. The dim lighting, the warm water. The way I stroked her hair. Those are all tried-and-true omega-taming tactics.

I have many more I can show her.

But only if she can keep her hands off me.

Small and wet, with her eyes cast down, she looks like the perfect little supplicant. My Alpha claws at my insides. Wanting to taste her. Sink her onto our knot. Fill her until our scents meld together.

"Come," I order, waving her into my room. "I'm going to teach you."

chapter
thirty-six

THERE'S a desperate surge my middle.

Panic?

No, it's too... solid.

Urgency, maybe.

I can't decide if it's mine or if Tristan has accidentally let himself through, but I decide to take it as my own.

When I step out of Spencer's bathroom and into his dark, pristine bedroom, a slow, heated wave of need rushes up my abdomen. Frothing against my insides until familiar tingles race down the backs of my thighs.

Spencer holds himself with a controlled, condescending air. But his nostrils flare wide, his chest heaving on every breath.

And his eyes *burn*, bottomless.

"You want a lesson?" he husks, looking down his nose at me. "Can you control yourself?"

He wants to know if I can keep from touching him. Considering my sexual experience is pretty much limited to what Jonah and Avery have done with me—neither of which like for me to keep my hands to myself—I don't really know how difficult that will be.

But I do know one thing: after working at the club, I will never be the kind of person who touches someone if they don't want me to.

I nod at him. It's harder for me to speak now, with him glaring. He seems less angry with me and more pissed off in general, but he's just as intimidating as ever. Especially in his dark bedroom, with shadows filling his sharp features.

Jonah is a thick slice of manly perfection, and Avery is *art*. But Spencer is... lovely. As beautiful as a sculpture by a master, shaded with stern shadows.

That isn't the only difference. Avery has no discipline, but he always treats me like I'm made of glass. Spencer is the opposite—his air is controlled but not *careful*. There's a roughness to the way he regards me.

And I *like* it.

He jerks his chin at his desk, the motion almost callous. But utterly in command. "Get my chair."

My body moves without even consulting my brain. I grab the chair pushed under his wide, cluttered desk. It's heavy—a solid wooden piece with a velvet cushion. I struggle a little, but force myself to carry it over, scared to drag the legs along the floor and displease him.

Which is wild.

Why do I *care* if I piss this alpha off? It's not like I couldn't walk out of the room. Or call for one of the others. Or—in an emergency—try to signal Tristan internally.

I don't do any of that, though.

I just... *obey*.

And it feels *good*.

Calming. Like I don't need to have a hundred thoughts and fears swirling in my head all at once. I just need Spencer's dark gaze and his deep, even orders.

"Set it here."

His foot taps a spot on the rug under his iron bed frame. I drop the chair there, and he nudges it back until it's only six inches from the footboard.

"Wait."

I grasp the towel knotted over my breasts, watching while he clips to his armoire and returns with two neckties. Without pausing, he secures each to a different iron slat along the end of his mattress.

When he's finished, he turns and glares at me again. "I will sit here. You will be in my lap, facing the room, with your hands on the back of the chair. If you move them or try to touch me without permission, I will use the ties to bind you to the bed." His silvery brow arches. "Understood?"

"Yes, Professor."

Oh. My. God.

Whyyyy did I just say that?

I don't know, but the air between us pulls taut. And for a moment, I'm sure he'll laugh at me. Or—more likely, in Spencer's case—kick me out.

Silly little—

Instead, he curses under his breath. A ragged exhale rolls out of him. He lowers himself into the chair and spreads his long legs.

"Come here, darling."

I move without a thought. Again. Until I'm between his bent knees, looking at him for more instructions.

When he sees my searching expression, something in his softens. His voice gets quieter but no less stern. "Drop the towel."

My fingers pluck at the knot holding it up, shucking the whole thing. Spencer's throat works, but he keeps his chin tilted up, watching my face closely instead of looking at my naked body.

"You like this, don't you? Obedience."

I swallow, not wanting to admit it out loud. Or even to myself.

It seems wrong. After everything I've been through, all the alphas who wanted to control me—it's almost shameful to enjoy it.

When I start to hang my head, Spencer's fingers hook under my chin, angling my face back up. Black eyes smolder into mine.

"We like what we like, Miss Swanson," he murmurs. "You can't control the way you enjoy obeying any more than I can control the desire to direct you. It's part of our biology."

I've heard about an omega's urge to please their alphas, but I've never experienced it like *this*.

It helps that Spencer is a true educator, through and through. Hearing him explain omega biology in his crisp, matter-of-fact way helps settle some of my guilt.

The truth is, I can't imagine anyone not hanging on his every word. He has... *power*.

Just like the other Thorne, when Spencer speaks, I feel compelled to *listen*. But I also feel like I'm truly *learning* something. He's so clearly brilliant—how could I not?

"I'll show you," he says, his tone brokering no argument. "Sit astride me, facing outward."

The tweed fabric of his pants chafes against my thighs as I whirl around and lower myself onto his lap. I move carefully, but he still hisses when my ass settles over his groin. The hard twitch against my left butt cheek makes me gasp a little, too.

For a long moment, he stays still, breathing hard enough for me to feel his chest expanding and contracting behind me. I hear a hard swallow just before his hands find my wrists, guiding them back to the chair frame.

He wraps his fingers around mine and squeezes, showing me how to hold on. His voice takes on a harsher bite. "These will not move. Is that clear, Miss Swanson?"

I start to nod again, but one of his hands flies up, wrapping around my throat to halt the movement. He squeezes carefully, growling into my naked shoulder. "*Say it.*"

"Yes, Professor."

"*Fuck.*" The erection pressed into my backside swells. His other hand comes up to grip my hip. "Spread your legs. Hook your knees over mine."

It's a little tricky, rearranging my lower body without moving my hands for balance. They stay wrapped around the chair back, my fingers throbbing from my white-knuckle grip. My pussy echoes the pulse, pounding dully as I spread myself over Spencer's lap.

The fingers at my throat give another squeeze—this one softer. Approving. "Very good."

His touch ghosts over my hip, up to my waist. It tickles, and I start to rear up a bit, but he closes his palm over my windpipe. "*Down.*"

Oh my GOD.

Why do his one-word commands make me so *wet*?

My body pours slick into his lap, soaking the fabric between us. He rumbles his satisfaction, breathing deep while I will myself to relax, settling back against him. His chokehold loosens, his thumb skating over the wild pulse in my throat.

"You will stay still," he tells me.

And—Lord help me—I believe him.

His free hand resumes its leisurely glide up my abdomen. He watches over my shoulder, gaze riveted to the way his fingertips dip into my navel and stroke up to the bottoms of my breasts.

Spencer reaches the scars branded along my ribs and stops. His eyes sharpen while he stares at the thick, raised lines and works on a swallow. "You said you got those when you tried to leave?"

A beat passes before he slowly raises his arm, holding the translucent skin close to my face. It's faint, but I see what he means for me to see—a thin, silver-white line. Long and deep. A scar.

His voice drops to a murmur. "I tried to leave once, too."

For a moment, my lungs forget how to expand. My heart *shatters*. His father really *hurt* him—so much deeper than any outer wounds.

He made Spencer feel hopeless. Had him believing there was no way *out*.

I should probably feel pity. Instead, relief bleeds across my mind while desperation claws through my body.

He gets it. He understands.

And, suddenly, I *need* him.

A frantic whine scrapes out of me. I buck forward, just barely managing to remember to keep my hands on the chair. Spencer likes that. His scent erupts, more glorious than ever before.

He drops his arm to band around my waist, pulling me tight to his body. His lips skim along my shoulder.

"Hush. You'll get what you need."

More slick seeps out of me. His teeth graze the soft part of my neck. "Do you even know what that is, Miss Swanson? Or shall I make that part of my lesson, too?"

My slick? Or what I need? I don't really care either way. The thought of hearing him discuss my body in his detached, haughty way makes me crazy.

"Please," I beg.

"Mm. Please, who?"

He's toying with me. I sort of love it. Not just because it makes me wetter but because it's a new side to him.

"Please, Professor."

He straightens, focusing. "Very well. We'll begin *here*."

The fingers wrapped around my throat slide to the side, their pads pressing into the healed bite from Tristan. The second he touches it, a new whine bursts out of me. My hips writhe, looking for weight and pressure.

"Claiming marks," he explains, every bit the professor lecturing a student. "They're linked to our pleasure centers, but the connection is especially strong for omegas. So, when I do this —" He lightly scratches over the scar tissue, and my entire core clamps on air— "your body responds."

My perfume is so thick, I can almost taste the way it swirls with his clean freshness. I think he can, too. Every time he exhales, a slight purr rumbles on his breath.

His control remains absolute, though. Which is impressive, with his cock pulsing against the back of my thigh and his pants drenched in slick. Something about his steadiness makes this feel even safer than it already did.

One second later, he brings his mouth to the tingling mark, scraping his teeth against it until I whimper.

"When you have *all* of our claims on you," he half-growls, "stimulating them at the same time will be an interesting experiment."

I gasp at the thought, relishing the way his scent pours into my lungs. So clean and thick. It's like a balm for all the hyperventilating I did earlier, cooling any lingering sting.

But it's also *too good*. My nipples harden to the point of pain, and I struggle, shifting as much as I can without moving my hands. Need edges my perfume. His chest rumbles louder.

"You need more."

It isn't a question, but I bob my head. He keeps his grip on my throat and moves his other hand to the curve of my belly. When he grazes his touch over my mound, I bite back a frustrated scream.

"This pussy seems very needy, Miss Swanson," he comments, dry and disapproving. "Perhaps if I teach you what it requires to be properly satisfied, we can avoid dousing another pair of my pants."

I can't tell if he's still teasing or if he's actually annoyed—and right now? I can't care. Molten arousal dribbles from my center, and I moan, grinding my ass along his hard cock.

Spencer's fingers finally drift over my spread lips, tracing the swollen, soaked edges. He snarls under his breath, stiffening beneath me. When he speaks, his even tone just makes me more desperate for him.

"This is *perfect* omega slick," he hums. "Silky and slippery. Exemplary, really. Very good, Miss Swanson."

I moan quietly, squirming to get more friction from his hand. He ignores me, dipping two fingers into my folds and skimming them over my entrance. It cinches tight, my pussy clenching in desperate squeezes.

His put-on disapproval returns. "You're too tight. We'll have to work on that."

Spencer's fingertips press inside. Just a bit. Just enough to make me crazy. I start to let go of the chair but force myself to hold on, crying out from the way my fingers ache and the feel of him pushing into me.

"And here, about three inches in—" His words break off as he finds his mark, touching a place inside of me that whites out my vision and forces a shrill whine. Another tumbles out half a breath later when he hooks those fingers against the front wall of my pussy and starts to rub in a wide oval.

Everything burns and buzzes. My nipples feel like sharp darts of pain, my thighs quiver from straining, and my knuckles start to scream. But Spencer's mouth lands on that godforsaken claiming mark again, his lips dragging in time with the fingers inside of me.

"This is where you'll take my knot," he says into my skin. "It will expand to fill you. Here." He finds a new spot to torment and I whimper. "And here." Everything starts to gel and tighten. "But most especially here."

The last place turns my breath to golden dust. My vision sparkles while pleasure snaps in my core. *So close* to everything, but not enough.

I pant and squirm, making an even bigger mess of his lap, but he rears back, sitting up again. "Have you ever *watched* a knot inflate, Miss Swanson?"

I start to shake my head, but he squeezes my throat in reprimand, demanding words.

"No, Professor."

He *tsks*. "That won't do." His touch slides away from my center and presses under my ass. "Lift up."

He's not—

He won't—

But he is. He *does*.

And ten seconds later, his trousers are unfastened, his underwear is shoved down, and his cock bobs between my spread legs.

Oh holy fuck. It is *thick*. Not quite as big as Jonah, but more proportional. With veins pulsing up the shaft and a head that flares as wide as its root. I'd expect nothing less than perfection from this alpha.

Perfume rises off my chest, my pussy tightening with *want*. Slick gushes out of me, sliding down to where his girth parts his fly. He grunts softly, his solid length twitching as pre-cum dribbles from the purple head.

His free hand clasps around the base, strangling it. I watch in awe while he strokes up to the tip and collects the pearly liquid there. "Open your mouth."

My lips are already slack. He slips his wet finger in easily, feeding me a mixture of him and me. The taste should be repulsive, but it's *perfect*. For the first time in as long as I can remember, my Omega actually purrs, satisfied.

"Is that good, Miss Swanson?" Spencer hums, his voice as dark and delicious as his cum.

When I whine, he slowly drags the pad of his finger against my tongue, lecturing, "For scent-sensitive mates, slick and cum often taste like concentrated versions of each other's scents. You'll want more later."

I want more *now*.

I turn my head before I can think. My lips find Spencer's, pressing them open and slipping my tongue against his. He goes rigid, fist flexing around my throat until I gasp into his mouth.

For a moment, I think I've ruined everything, but then he groans and adjusts to kiss me back. Our tongues collide, stroking one another while our lips cling.

I can barely keep my grip on the chair; there's no *way* I can stop myself from sliding lower in his lap, until the wide base of his hot hardness presses against my aching clit. He snarls, kissing me savagely while I start to glide against him.

We both pant, growls vibrating through his chest while whines build in mine. His free hand cups his cock, pressing it against my slit, letting me use it.

I grind and moan. Slick gushes against his girth. The bundle of need in my core pulls so tight that I practically sob into him when tingly relief finally bursts through me, snapping the cord.

While I come all over him, Spencer stiffens. The hand at my throat grips my chin. With a sharp motion, he guides my face away, forcing me to look down. His voice is gravel.

"*Watch.*"

I look down at his cock, riveted by the way he squeezes it. Trying to stop himself from spilling.

But it doesn't work. He comes in an impressive eruption, shooting blast after blast onto my body.

While he's still coming, the rounded mass at the base of his cock expands, growing wider and thicker. It must feel good because he makes a serrated sound, sliding his fist down to knead at it, milking himself until I'm glazed in his scent.

"*Omega,*" he grits. His head falls forward, his jaw clamping over the place below his brother's bite, teeth pressing into my throat.

chapter
thirty-seven

A MONTH AGO, I wouldn't have believed this.

Serena burrows closer to the body next to her, sleepily rubbing her face against Spencer's thigh. When she moves her head, the dark purple love bite he left on her neck catches the low lamplight. His hand on her head doesn't even flinch, continuing its rhythmic strokes as he squints at the newspaper in front of him.

When she slowly blinks her eyes open and rolls them up to his face, I have to hold my iPad in front of my mouth to hide my grin.

Absolute shock colors her pretty eyes as her lashes flutter in disbelief. For his part, my best friend simply glances down at her with something almost like... *warmth*? Then, he fixes his features into a dry look and nods over her shoulder.

"Your dog snores."

Serena cranes her neck, finding Avery snuggled into her back, snorting in his sleep. A bright grin fills her face.

And Spencer actually *smiles*.

He covers it by snapping his paper up. But I still see that shit.

With a sweet little curve still gracing her dusky lips, Serena finally turns her emerald eyes to mine. "Big man," she mumbles, groggy. "Am I having a *crazy* dream, or are we all in *Spencer's* bed?"

Avery mutters something about killing us all and huddles closer to her bare back, tucking his face against her nape. She reaches back and pats his head, lulling him back to his snores within seconds.

Our omega is officially a snake-charmer. Winning over Avery is one thing—but Avery *and* Spencer? In one bed?

She's my miracle.

I set the iPad loaded with all the plays I've been reviewing aside and reach over Avery to cup her warm cheek in my palm. "How did you sleep, hummingbird?"

She softens for me in a way she doesn't for the others. Vulnerability swells in her gaze. "Better than I ever would have expected, after everything."

My thumb brushes over her lips. "I'm glad. Spencer thought having all of us in here would be good for you. If you like it, we'll do it again tonight in your bed."

She glances up at Spence, looking nervous until he meets her gaze and gives a steady nod, sending a noticeable burst of alpha dominance to her as he says, "You'll behave for me, Miss Swanson. No touching unless I say so."

He's done incredibly well, actually. Avery and I slept on the other side of Serena, but Spencer managed the whole night beside her without an issue. He slept in a long-sleeved shirt and pajama pants, but he snuggled her close and held her all the same.

The fact that he's giving her orders, now, only seems to make Serena more comfortable. I swear our girl gets little hearts in her eyes as she gazes up at his stern expression. "Yes, Professor."

He pets her head in approval, snapping out a crisp "very good" before returning to his paper.

Between us, Avery's arm flexes around Serena's waist, hauling her closer as he kisses her nape. "Mm. Smells so fuckably good when she's happy."

Serena grins again, rolling her eyes this time. I stretch over the pillow Ave's abandoned and replace Spencer's hand, stroking my fingers into her hair. After tossing me a shy smile of my own, our omega looks over at the newspaper, scanning the front page's headlines.

Oh. Fuck.

She jerks upright with a gasp, whipping around to lean closer to the words splashed right under the middle fold of the front page.

Senator Tristan Thorne Announces His Pack's New Omega.

"He did *what*?!" she gasps. "Oh my God!"

I read the article on my tablet earlier. With a wince, I recall a few key phrases that probably won't reassure her.

Senator Thorne has long claimed his pack would not consider bonding with an omega, as such an arrangement may present a conflict of interest.

Critics have already begun calling for Thorne to recuse himself from the upcoming vote on his Omega Workplace Protection Act.

When asked if he is worried that his pack's personal life could discredit his work, Senator Thorne had no comment.

"Why would he *do* this?" she cries. "Now everyone will know you're all courting a—a—"

"Goddess," Avery mumbles, nipping her hip with his teeth.

She gapes at Spencer, expecting him to disagree or launch into a panic, but he only blinks at her. "An omega? Yes, I believe that was his intention."

"B-but—" she sputters, turning to me. "He can't just—*why* would he *tell* them?"

He had two reasons, actually, and they were damn good ones. So good that none of us could argue with him.

After Serena passed out last night, our pack leader sprang into action. He called the county's lead investigator for omega abuse and had Walter Swanson brought in immediately. While the police raided his club, Tris pivoted and went on the offensive, announcing a big press conference to divert the media's attention, trying to ensure that no one would link Serena to that dumpster fire she used to work in.

And it *worked*.

When Spencer finishes explaining how Avery and I spent the night helping Tris get all of this taken care of, Serena leaps out of bed and snatches the first shirt she finds—*mine*—off the floor.

Avery groans his disapproval while Spencer frowns after her, and I call, "Where are you going, *manamea*?"

She waves her hands in an angry gesture and stomps out the door. "To see the *senator*!"

"I DON'T GIVE A FUCK," I roar. "Get it done. On *my* authority."

Hanging up, I drop my phone to my desk and shove my hands into my hair.

Fucking incompetence. I need Serena's adoption paperwork dissolved immediately. She shouldn't have to live one more goddamn minute with that scum's name attached to hers.

I'm not waiting for our lawyers to get their heads out of their asses. As far as I'm concerned, if they can't figure it out today, I can find new lawyers tomorrow.

The iPhone clatters down beside the spot where my fern used to sit. The latest in a long line of victims. With a wistful pang, I wonder what Serena would think of my inability to keep a houseplant alive.

She probably wouldn't even be surprised, given how bad an alpha you've been.

The bitter truth swirls around my mind, darkening my mood even further.

I'm already pissed as hell about what she went through. And my entire back is aching from sleeping on the floor of Spencer's bedroom.

I didn't want to wake anyone when I got in from the press conference, but when I found them *all* sleeping in the same room for the very first time, I knew I'd never forgive myself if I walked away. Not to mention—after six hours out of the house, the pain from missing Serena was *gutting* me.

I would sleep on a bed of nails if it meant being closer to her.

After I tried to open our shuttered bond and accidentally flooded her last night, I begrudgingly put the partition back up. So I know my rage isn't flowing through to her right now.

Which means this sudden urgency snapping through her blood is *all* hers.

I brace myself for her fury, knowing I deserve it but not regretting my latest decisions one bit.

I need to know that man will never see the light of day again. And the press needs to know she's our pack's omega.

Most importantly, she needs to know that I'm *proud* to have her. That I have never—not for one second in this entire sordid mess—been ashamed of her.

I claimed her. And I will do it over and over, in every way I'm allowed.

Footsteps patter down the hall, moving too quickly to be casual and too lightly to be one of the guys. When my office doors fly open, I'm already waiting for her, standing beside my desk, ready to take whatever she wants to dish at me.

She pauses in the doorway, her breasts heaving under Jonah's rumpled T-shirt. My mouth opens, ready to explain calmly.

But she moves faster, scurrying over and looping her arms around my waist, ducking her head against my chest.

"Thank you," she breathes, shaking. "Just—thank you."

I embrace her automatically, even while shock echoes through my body. She's here to *thank me*?

And this swell of urgency I feel isn't anger or hatred it's... *gratitude*?

Dear God—What else have I gotten wrong? How accurate are these feelings coming through? Or is it just me, thinking I know what's happening without ever really *asking* her how she feels?

One of my palms cups the back of her head while the other winds around to her opposite hip, securing her against me.

"I don't want you to thank me," I reply.

I truly can't stomach it. Every time she offers even a speck of appreciation, I want to flay myself alive.

Something about hearing me say so must upset her, though, because her scent darkens and her stomach flips.

I sigh, trying to explain, "I'll never deserve it, after what I've done to you. I'll spend the rest of my life trying to make all of this up to you, but I don't want your gratitude. It only throws everything even more out of balance. *I owe you*. Let me try to make good on that."

But our little omega just presses herself closer and whispers the words again.

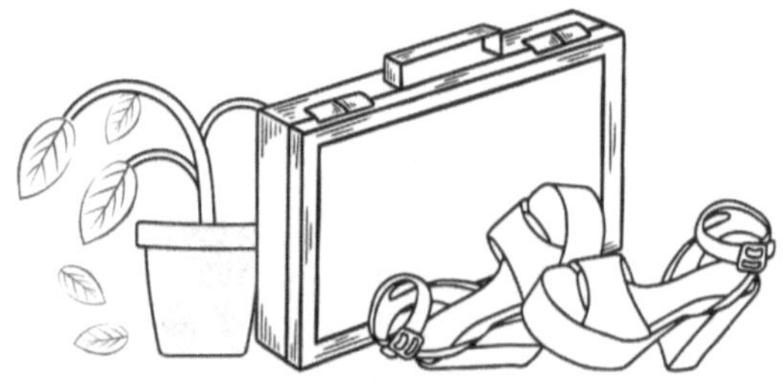

chapter
thirty-nine

AVERY NAMED THIS CHAT SNITCHES GET
STITCHES (NO THORNE-Y BITCHES)

SERENA

Avery...

AVERY

yeah, baby?

SERENA

why did you make us a side chat?

do you have some sort of secret scheme or
something?

AVERY

me?

never.

JONAH

Ave, I stg if you get Serena hurt, I'll kick
your ass.

AVERY

simmer down, old man.

eat some jello or something

SERENA

anyone care to fill me in on what's happening?

JONAH

it's a surprise, hummingbird 🖤

AVERY

just meet me in the garage in ten, baby

don't wear anything nice

you and me are gonna get messy

I'M NOT sure why I'm surprised.

Crossing my arms, I make a face at Avery. "You expect me to believe that Tristan won't care."

"No," he quips, lowering his black aviators over his eyes with a smirk. "Because you're not stupid."

My glower intensifies. "But you want me to come with you anyway?"

Sitting in his vintage Mustang, grinning with his sunglasses on, it's truly unfair how hot he is. A fact that only gets truer when he flashes a crooked grin.

"C'mon," he taunts. "You know you want to, kitten. Be my bad girl and get in the car."

I bite my lip, considering. "I'm in workout gear. Do I need to change?"

He eyes my spandex shorts and the artfully torn crop top I have on over a blood-red sports bra. Feral interest gilds the ghostly blue. "If you do, I might cry."

Well, then.

I glance around, as if the other alphas and their cars might somehow materialize on the spot. When they don't, I sigh in defeat.

How bad could this be?

"Okay, fine." He keeps that wild smile on his face the whole time I spend buckling myself in. I shake my head, muttering, "Menace."

I SHOULD KNOW BY NOW—WHEN it comes to Avery, I need to expect the unexpected.

When he told me he wanted to bring me to his gym, I didn't picture anything quite this grand. His outfit wasn't exactly a hint —the man wears his tattered, basically-naked workout gear every minute of the day.

Unless he's *actually* naked.

No, I scold myself. *No perfuming in the gym full of aggressive alphas beating each other up.*

Luckily, the underwear Tristan provided comes with a handy scent-absorbing feature. Avery still senses my thoughts shift, cutting me side-eye while we stride into the building. "Whose ass am I kicking first? You're not supposed to smell like that for anyone but me."

He has a jealous streak that I probably shouldn't find so damn sexy. Actually, most of Avery's appeal probably shouldn't be so damn sexy. Including the fact that I fully believe he would challenge any alpha I pointed to.

And then kill them.

Yeah, this whole not-perfuming thing isn't going so well.

I start to feel self-conscious, darkening my scent as it winds into the air around the entrance. Avery turns to face me, shifting his gym bag from one shoulder to another before wrapping his arm around my waist and dropping his forehead to mine.

"Hey. Kidding, kitten. Mostly."

It hits me then—this is the first time I've been out with any of them alone. *I could embarrass him. Or send another alpha into a rut. Or—*

"Serena." Avery's voice is more serious than I've ever heard it. When my gaze skitters up to his, I find that his face matches—the starkly gorgeous features set into solemnity that looks all wrong on him.

Those blue, blue eyes scan my expression. Heat and outrage spark there. And even though I know—*I know*—he would never hurt me, I still brace, waiting for him to lash out or lunge or—

"*Listen up, assholes!*"

He's clearly *the* alpha in this gym because all the others immediately freeze when his bark rends the air. He steps in front of me and nods at a side exit. "Everyone get the fuck out."

No one moves, but I do hear some derisive snorts.

From my place partially behind him, I barely catch Avery's rabid smile. "Let me rephrase that: The last one out of here is going to fight me. Right now. No tapouts."

There's an odd moment of silence.

And then people *move*.

I gawk around the inked-up curve of his biceps as a dozen grown men gather their things and haul ass out of the sprawling, impressive gymnasium.

After the side door swings shut for the final time, deafening silence sweeps through the cavernous room. Or, warehouse, really.

The place is a giant rectangle with concrete floors and metal walls three stories high. I spot a traditional-type gym off on one side, a few boxing rings, a corner filled with rows of punching bags, and then, in the center...

The Octagon.

At first, it looks like an enormous cage. Rubber-coated chain-link stretches up from the solid black base, with some sort of padded canvas stretched across the floor.

Avery steps up beside me, bumping my shoulder playfully. "You're not ready for the Octagon, kitten. As a spectator *or* a participant."

I turn to scowl at him. "What do you mean? You didn't bring me here to watch you fight?"

He laughs. "*Fuck* no."

My tattooed alpha turns to me, his hand coming up to hold my jaw in his soft, demanding way. His eyes scan mine, reading me so easily. "Look, my Alpha may be a total simp for you, but in general, he tends to be a complete psycho. I promise I'll show you what I mean some day, but I have another idea for us right now."

Avery and his *ideas* have gotten me into trouble all over the pack house. But when recalling all of those instances makes my scent a little thicker and sweeter, he only quirks a knowing smirk at me.

Narrowing my eyes, I toss out a cocky hip. "Okay, Menace. Do your worst."

"Oh, baby," he whispers, brushing his soft, full mouth over mine. A shiver runs down my back as he steps away, his light eyes darkening. "No one wants to see that."

With one last teasing glance, he lopes off, waving a hand over his shoulder. "This way."

My stomach sinks as he hoists himself into one of the smaller, square boxing rings that dot the corners of the cavernous gym. I stand beside the platform, my throat drying while he reaches a hand down to pull me up.

"Avery..."

He flashes that crooked grin that gets him out of everything. "Trust me?"

It's a complicated question and he knows it.

Do I trust him with my actual life? Yes.

Do I trust that he won't have some sort of insanity up his sleeve?

Not in the slightest.

But I set my fingers in his and let him help me climb into the ring.

He pulls me straight into his arms, twirling me right into his chest and giving me a squeeze. "My girl is brave," he whispers, kissing my brow.

We've had more and more moments like this, where I feel like he's saying one thing, but he's trying to tell me another.

It reminds me of the night we met. How we connected so fiercely without saying much at all. Just like that, when he leans back far enough to look into my eyes, I see so much more than I ever expected to.

On the surface, he's still cool blue fire. *Pride, passion.* Those are two things I always see when our gazes lock.

But there's more, today. A solid sort of determination I've never seen him turn *on* me—only *for* me.

It's there now, though. Cold and steely behind the cornflower flames.

And somehow, I know exactly what he wants me to do. "Avery," I start, voice shaking. "I—I don't think I can..."

Fight.

I don't think I can fight. Because every time I've ever tried, I learned it was better not to.

But certainty flexes over his face. "Try."

The word, his tone, his eyes—it's a *command.*

Only, is it? Because there's something—deep down in the invisible cord between us—that makes me think this is the closest I'll ever see him come to begging.

I feel light-headed as I nod. He wastes no time, bending to

pluck two shiny black boxing gloves from the ground. He tucks one under his arm while he reaches for my hand, sliding the second glove onto it and strapping me in tightly.

The nylon strap chafes my wrist, the padded material weighing my hand down. It instantly sinks to my side while he straps on the second one, pausing to lovingly brush his thumb over my pulse. The second he lets me go, my left hand drops to join my right, dangling uselessly.

Avery drops back, peeling his shirt off and tossing it away. The spotlights angled onto the ring illuminate every dip and hollow on his muscled form, casting shadows under his cut collarbones, the ladder of his abdomen, and his bulging pecs.

Black ink swirls and curves. Skulls, roses, crosses, crowns. My favorite is the monarch butterfly branded right at the top of his sternum; its wings spread under each clavicle.

He must have gotten some new ones because there are two white band-aids plastered on either side of his chest. And Jonah once joked that the only injuries Avery bandages are the ones that come with ink.

Normally, I might ask him, but my throat feels as tight and dry as it did the night they found me. When I open my mouth, I feel like I'll choke on my tongue.

Avery slinks into a fighting stance that looks every bit as natural on him as standing normally. He holds up his own fists, which now have red gloves on them, demonstrating how to pose.

He tosses me a tilt of his head and another cocky grin. "Put 'em up."

I try to swallow, but it hurts. Wincing, I shake my head, stepping back.

Avery's eyes glint dangerously. "Serena."

He never calls me that. Not unless something is wrong. Fear squeezes my throat as I shake my head harder. The two french braids holding my hair back fly around my shoulders.

He takes a step, closing in. "I'm not just fucking around

here," he mutters, scowling at me. "I want you to learn this. Put your fists up."

I flinch, forcing a raspy word out of my sticky gullet. "Why?"

Fervor shines his gaze, filling all of his features. "Because nothing scares me, Serena. *Nothing*. But every time I take your clothes off and I see those scars, *I can't fucking breathe*."

My whole body trembles as he steps into me, putting us chest-to-middle as he holds my eyes. "Because if anyone ever tries to hurt you again and I'm not there," he growls, "I need to know you're going to *fight*."

He falls away again, glaring at me as he lifts his hands. "If there's even a *chance* I won't be there to defend you, then I'm going to make sure you know how to defend yourself. Now, *put your fists up*."

It's the only time he's ever barked at me. Another order—but his gaze doesn't match it at all.

He really is *begging* me. He *needs* this. My safety. His peace of mind.

And I'm starting to suspect that I need *him*.

So I put up my fists.

FOR THE FIRST TWENTY MINUTES, she just... pummels me. Punch after punch. When they start getting harder and faster instead of slowing, I know she's working something off.

I've never related to anything more than the harsh lines of her face as she loses track of where she is and just lets me have it. Grunting and snarling while she hits me again. And again.

That sexy-as-fuck body is quick and graceful. Half an hour after I teach her the proper stances, she's already moving on to footwork. Once I show her how to balance and where to step, she's turning circles around the ring within the hour.

That shit took me *weeks* when I first started.

I've never been prouder.

She must know it because I can't keep my fat, stupid mouth shut.

"There she is."

"Such a fucking *badass*."

"That's *my girl*."

When she finally starts to wind down, I see the sadness creep into her stance. *Defeat*. Because even though she just crushed that workout, it didn't get rid of her pain.

Fuck, I get that. It's my big secret—the fact that I never feel weaker or less sure of myself than I do after I win. Because winning meant I threw everything I had at my demons.

But they're always waiting for me when I climb out of the cage.

Once she loses steam, I talk to keep her from getting in her own head. It seems to work—the more I go on about how I started fighting, my weight class, and my most hated opponents, the easier she flows through the drills.

My kitten lands a hit to my shoulder, and I try not to smile like an idiot. Narrowing her eyes, she goes in for another one, harder. I block it, turning us in a pivot that has her grunting in frustration.

"How did you start doing this anyway?" she grumbles, dodging a super-slow-mo version of my right hook. "You just decided one day to kick the crap out of people?"

I grin. This is my favorite side of her—the no-bullshit, sassy, smart woman she keeps buried under all her fear and low self-esteem. Whenever I manage to tease my kitten's claws out, she never fails to make me fall harder for her.

"No," I reply, leaning out of a jab to the left. "They made us fight in school."

Fuck.

Too late, I realize I've said too much. Serena drops back, her gloved hands falling to her sides like stones. "You had to *fight* in school? What the hell kind of school did you go to?"

I hate talking about this shit. But after everything she told us last night... I owe her this much, right?

"Reform school," I grit. "Put your fists back up."

She follows my order, but her eyes stay wary as I circle her. "Why did you have to go to reform school?"

My shoulder rises in a shrug. "My parents are betas. When my Alpha started to come through, they were pissed. Hated that I couldn't control myself. The aggression, the possessiveness, the sex. All of it disgusted them, so they found a military school that was supposed to wrestle kids' Alphas into submission."

Even now, I almost snort at the irony. They sent me away to get me under control... and wound up turning me from a beast into a monster.

They never expected that my Alpha would like the pain. Crave it. And they didn't know me well enough to know that spite was basically my entire personality at that point.

They didn't want an aggressive alpha for a son, so I decided I would become the most aggressive alpha there was. A pain professional. *A fighter.*

They decided I wouldn't be their son anymore.

Fair enough, right?

Serena is quiet while I tell her my story, letting me lead her through drills and bullshit punches. If she's trying to keep me talking, it works. Which is when I realize—that's exactly what she's been doing this whole damn time.

Humoring me, to get me to keep running my mouth.

Brilliant, bad little girl.

It makes me want to knot her right here on the floor of this ring.

And, *fuck me,* watching her throw punches is making me harder.

"That's enough for today," I decide, pulling off my gloves. "Your arms are going to hurt like a bitch tomorrow."

She rolls her eyes at me like that's somehow my fault but follows suit, tossing the gloves near mine and taking the water bottle I offer her.

After a swig, she nods at my chest. "Did you get new tattoos?"

Without an ounce of shame, I pull one bandage down, showing her what's underneath.

The pieces took some doing. I had to work fast, after the day she had her first heat-spike—tracing the scratches she left along my pecs with a permanent marker until I could make a proper transfer.

Now, there are four jagged scars branded into each side of my chest.

I used white ink, making sure the lines sliced right through whatever shit I had underneath. A skull on one side. Some crown on the other.

Fuck it all. I only need her marks on me.

"I told you I wanted your claws. You didn't break the skin, though," I explain. "So I did."

She sets the water bottle down, stepping closer. With care, she fits her fingertips into the tattoo's gouge-like lines, tracing them. When her head falls back to lock our gazes, her eyes are dark.

She *likes* this. And I—

Fuck.

I *love* her.

It snaps through me like an electric current. So intense, I know she must be able to feel it; especially when her lips part and she gasps.

But I let her see. She needs to know.

Especially since I'm about to fuck her like I hate her. Right here in this boxing ring.

Her perfume winds into the air, pumping adrenaline through my blood. If any other alpha in this gym scents her, they're sure as hell going to smell me, too. By the time I'm done with her, they won't know where I end and she starts.

Tilting my chin at the ropes, I ask, "What about *my* claws, kitten? Think you can handle those?"

Who even knows if I'm teasing her anymore? Truth is, I don't think I am. I want her to see me fight. To know she'll still see the guy she likes and trusts after she watches what my Alpha and I can do in that Octagon.

Serena absorbs the look on my face, her own softening. "I want to," she whispers. "Can you show me?"

My heart clenches, fear and frustration and fucking *want* jolting through me. "Take off your shorts. Panties, too."

Biting her lip, she casts one last nervous glance around the empty gym but starts to shimmy out of her clothes. I close in, backing her into the ring ropes while I growl, "I'd never let anyone live after seeing you like this. So we better hope no one walks in. Or they won't be walking out."

I hear her swallow as she nods, stepping out of her shorts and her shoes, leaving her in just that ripped-up black top and the blood-red bra under it.

The bra I like—but this shirt is pointless. With one tug, I rip it right in half, letting it fall off her.

"You could have just told me to take it off," she teases, raising a brow. "Menace."

I like her nickname. It feels right. Like me.

I flash a *menacing* smile, proving her point as I clamp my hands around her waist and lift her.

Her squeak is short and quiet, swallowed by the silence of the gym pressing around us. I balance her round, perfect ass on the second rope of the ring, making sure it lines up just right.

Then I start working on her hands and feet, winding her wrists and ankles around the top rope and the lowest one. Pinning her open with her knees bent and her gorgeous pussy on full display.

Goddamn it.

I'll never be able to box without getting a boner again.

Kicking off my pants and shoes, I pad toward her with my

cock at attention. The spotlights catch on the bars bolted through the underside while it kicks up to my navel.

Mouth-watering piña colada fills my mouth with saliva. And I just… go to my knees, like I have so many times for her.

Only her. Always her.

She whimpers while I stroke her thighs, holding them spread for my mouth. Roughing out uneven purrs while I lick her smooth, slippery pussy lips.

Ungh. FUCK.

Her taste rolling over my tongue feels like being hit with a defibrillator. A hundred volts, right to the heart. Need crackles through my limbs, lighting every nerve it streaks across.

Yes. More. Burn me up. Melt me down.

Make me into something new.

Something hers.

The sounds she makes while I work my tongue over her clit have me pumping my cock into my fist, slicking my palm with pre-cum.

Her back arches, lifting her hips higher. Pressing herself into my ravenous snarls. Letting me *devour* her.

When I hook two fingers into her opening and press where her body throbs for a knot, she lets out a high-pitched moan and comes, dousing my face with her slick. It dribbles down onto my chest—another mark of sorts.

My Alpha lunges, trying to break off his leash. He wants that scent all over us, soaked into my knot, dripping down my balls.

Fuck. Fuck. Fuck.

I'm used to fighting other people, but fighting myself for someone else is new to me. Squeezing my eyes shut, I lean my forehead into her belly, doing my best to just *breathe*.

But my girl really is perfect for me. Because instead of sagging into the ropes, she squirms, bucking her soaked center into the middle of my chest.

Rubbing more of her scent onto me.

Jeeeeesus.

My hands snap up to her hips, holding her still as I growl, "You're pushing it, kitten. How am I supposed to resist knotting this sweet little cunt if you keep waving it in my face?"

"Don't," she pants. "I—I want you. *Please?*"

Something between a laugh and bark scrapes up my throat. "*Here?!*"

So fucking perfect for me, my kitten. Because she nods hard, her braids whipping forward. "*Please, Avery.*"

I haven't taken her yet today. After all the shit she had to wade through last night, I had all these stupid notions of romance. A bed, a candle.

But this is better.

This is *us*.

I'm already panting, knowing exactly how she'll feel when I slide in. So wet and warm, gliding around my piercings. Heat and softness, gripping and pulling at every inch of me. Rolling all the metal bars. Clamping with the sweetest squeezes.

She whines, working her hips into mine while I watch the space between our bodies. I'm fucking addicted to the way she swallows me. Watching my tattoos sink into her pussy, her dark lips spread around my growing knot.

Her head is thrown back over the top rope while she keens and writhes in my grip. I dig my fingertips into her hips, snapping them into mine faster and harder. Losing what shitty little control I've strung together for her.

She doesn't mind, though. Her sweet, perfect perfume—the real shit that makes my entire body come to life—spikes just as hard as my thrusts. When it blends with the smokey cloud of my pheromones, everything in me *sings*.

Higher and higher, the notes rising until my *soul* is screaming. *Bite her. Knot her. Claim her.*

Fuck. I don't know if I can knot her without sinking my teeth into her neck. Does it even matter anymore?

I start to do it. My jaw drops, and I lurch at her, going for the blank side of her throat—

But those goddamn green eyes.

They snag mine mid-lunge. Swirling with lust and need and something I want to say might be love.

None of that is the reason I stop.

It's the *trust*.

From the moment she met me, this omega's trusted me. Turned to me, leaned into me.

Most people see me and go running in the other direction. I've had omegas actually cry just from crossing my path—feeling how unhinged my Alpha is, the tattoos, the way I can't seem to stop glaring.

Not Serena.

The more she's looked at me, the more she's trusted me. And I have to deserve that.

I'll fight myself to the death to deserve that.

No, I decide. *Not here*. She deserves the whole fucking thing. In the nest, with our pack.

Besides, we don't need to be knotted to be connected. Our souls snap together while we stare at one another. Bodies grinding, climaxes building, orgasms burning us both up.

It's all incredible, but I know that isn't what I'll remember later.

It's this moment.

The certainty of it, sinking deep.

The second Serena wants a place in my fucked-up heart, *it's hers*.

IT SEEMED like a good idea at the time.

After two days of listening to the memory of Serena's gratitude swirling through my brain, all I wanted was to give her *more*. When I saw Jonah's game coming up on the calendar and remembered Avery's comment about taking Serena shopping somewhere nice, I figured this might be an opportunity.

Across the back seat of our limo, Serena fidgets with her dress, pulling at the hem discreetly. She's graceful, even when she's clearly agitated.

Keeping our bond closed is becoming more painful by the day. Especially as she's gotten quieter.

She no longer seems terrified when I walk into the room. Just...*frosty*.

Going to the gym with Avery seems to have unlocked something in her. She's suppressing it, but I still catch glimpses of its sharp edges. The heat and bitterness burning through her middle.

I watch the way she avoids my gaze, a realization sinking in. "You're *angry* with me."

The words are a revelation. And a *relief*.

God, I've wanted her to be angry this whole time. What I did to her was *unconscionable*. I deserve for her to hate me.

Her pretty features pucker. "I'm not angry."

But she *is*. I can feel it, seething in her stomach. Layered with uneasiness and maybe even guilt?

I want to grit my teeth and snarl. What the hell could she possibly have to feel guilty about?

When she brushes her hands over the front of her dress, I realize—she doesn't think she *deserves* to be angry.

A sick twist impales my stomach.

"Serena." I wait for her to look over at me. Falling into those luminous green eyes, I urge her, "You *should* be angry."

Which is when it occurs to me—she never has been.

Not when my teeth sank into her perfect throat. Not when she woke up on that cold metal table. Not that first night when I had to tend my mark or I'd go insane.

She's never even raised her voice to me.

Because she doesn't think enough of herself to believe she has the right to.

I don't know what's changed in the last week, but it's clear she's struggling with it. Perhaps Avery taking her to the gym has helped her move past her initial block, and now she doesn't know how to seal the fury back up.

Good.

She shouldn't.

"Tell me," I order, low and soft. "Tell me how much you hate me."

I must be some kind of fucked-up masochist because I really *want* her to.

If she punishes me, maybe I won't have to keep punishing myself. But she doesn't make it easy.

"No," she huffs. "I don't hate you. You brought me here and gave me everything you possibly could. You and your pack are my—

Mates.

It's true.

But it doesn't excuse what happened that night. "I should have courted you," I growl. "Properly, the way you deserve. I had no right to even *touch* you, let alone bond you."

She's so stiff, it looks like she'll crumble. And inside she's... hollow.

"It wasn't your fault," she repeats. "It was only a matter of time. With my perfume being so messed up... and I could never control it. If I hadn't perfumed you wouldn't have snapped like that."

The words coming out of her mouth aren't hers. It's clearly a bunch of shit she was force-fed for years. Removing any and all culpability from the alphas who wanted to prey on her. Because she was "too" sweet-smelling and "too" sexy.

When, really, *they* were *too weak*.

I'll always hate myself for being one of them. She deserves so much more than carrying shame for things that were never her fault.

Things that, really, shouldn't be shameful at all.

"It *is* our fault," I argue. "Alphas... *we're* the shameful ones, gaslighting omegas out of the workforce and their educations. Telling you it's your fault we can't be trusted around you. It's fucked up and inexcusable and exactly what I've spent my entire career combatting."

Serena goes entirely still, staring at me across the backseat of our hired car. When she finally moves, her eyes drop to her lap.

"I didn't ask to be this way," she murmurs. "I never would have *chosen* this."

Fuck. My chest cramps as I reach for her hand, scooping her fingers into mine. "I know that," I tell her. "But even if you *had*—that still doesn't make what happened your fault. I should have had better control of myself before I walked in there."

Every time I think back to that moment, I can't fathom what came over me. I only remember looking into her eyes. And not being able to waste one more goddamn second not being *with* her.

She glances down at our hands, her expression pensive. "Maybe I am angry," she finally whispers. "A little bit." She flicks a timid expression at me—the same one she wore when I first saw her through the interrogation room door. "Does that make you mad?"

My heart heaves and twists, but I force my gaze to stay steady. Needing her to hear me. And *believe*.

"No," I reply. "It makes me proud."

BEING on Tristan Thorne's arm is… *an experience.*

This shopping trip is our first outing one-on-one. Only, not really, because a small troupe of security guards moves in front of us before we even get out of his limo-like Bentley. Tristan doesn't seem annoyed, though. He simply slips out of the car and helps me out, then steps a respectable distance away.

I'm not sure how to feel about that. Ever since biting me, he's always maintained some distance between us. Before, I thought he did it because of his own regret.

But after what just happened in the car—is it possible he really has just been giving me space?

And do I actually find that devastatingly romantic, or is this just my crazy hormones talking?

Because *damn*. They are insane.

I'm insane.

Tristan's brow lowers as he watches me fuss with the skirt of my dress. I wanted to look nice going out with him, since there's always a chance he'll be photographed—but the slinky, asymmetrical black dress feels wrong now.

I'm worried it's cut too high. And maybe my hair is too big, and I probably look stupid in these designer sunglasses—

"Serena."

I stop fidgeting, doing my best to settle into a blank mask. "Mm?"

Tristan's frown deepens. "Are you all right?"

I keep my features smooth for any hidden cameras. "It's nothing. Just my Omega being a bitch."

Well, shit. So much for acting sophisticated for the senator.

Surprise quirks his features for a second before he flashes an unexpected smile. "Tell me if she gets out of hand. My Alpha might know a few tricks to get her under control."

Double shit.

Now I'm perfuming. Out here, in public, with people around who will know I'm his omega, and I can't control myself, and—

Silly little slut.

I tilt my face down and open my mouth to apologize, but Tristan steps smoothly in front of me. With his back to the world.

He reaches for my cheek, cupping it gently. "Dr. Monroe told you this is all perfectly normal. It's healthy for an omega your age who has never been on suppressants. And your heat is coming up. There's nothing for you to be ashamed of."

I've given up trying to figure out how he always knows what I'm feeling when I can never quite read him. At the moment, I'm just grateful he understands.

I slip my sunglasses over my eyes and nod, hating that the motion trembles.

His handsome features always look so much hotter, somehow, when he's broody. We haven't spent any time alone together, but I've started to see that, of all the alphas in the Thorne Pack, their leader is actually the quietest. He only speaks when he really has something to say; and he *listens*.

The scowl on his chiseled lips quirks tighter as he reads my expression, ocean eyes slowly moving over every part of me. "I could scent-mark you," he offers, dropping his voice low. "Would that help?"

Shivers of arousal quiver in my core as slick soaks into the special extra-absorbent panties I'm wearing. Spence got them for me to wear; surprisingly, he's been the most obsessively possessive about making sure others only smell me *on him*.

Or on his desk. Or his chair. Or his bed—

"Serena?"

I blink out of my horny haze, thankful for the cover of my dark lenses. "Sorry. Um. Sure? If you think that would help."

His smile is warm and masculine. Knowing but kind. It reminds me of the way he was when he tended his claiming mark —so proficient and confident yet utterly gentle with me, even when he was on the edge.

"I think it might."

I hold my breath as he leans over me, bending to graze his mouth across his bond mark before rubbing his cheek against it. My pussy gives a warm, wet squeeze, clamping on nothing.

When more perfume pours off me, Tristan...

Purrs.

His silken, rolling rumble sinks through his suit and my dress, past the lacy black bra cupping my tits. Everything inside of me gels, melting and smoothing and *aching*.

A large hand cups the back of my head, stroking tenderly when I sway into the hard muscles of his pecs. "Shhh," he murmurs, "You're okay, sweet baby. I'm here."

His fingers sift through my hair, finding his claim to stroke it softly. "Would I ever let you hurt?" he asks, flexing a wave of calm dominance.

He never has. Even on that first horrible night, when it seemed like he wanted to get as far away from me as possible... he didn't. He stayed in the room the whole time Dr. Monroe examined me. He loomed in the hallway while I met the guys. And he tended his bite with perfect thoroughness.

Shh, sweet baby.

He said it then, too.

I like it even more now.

♥

MY OMEGA TURNS OUT TO be even more unhinged than I previously thought.

The articles Spencer provided to help prep me for my pre-heat symptoms as a semi-bonded omega mentioned a lot of what I'm experiencing. Shakiness, the constant urge to whine.

It did not, however, warn me about the whole wanting-to-claw-other-women's-eyes-out thing.

Maybe that's just a "me" problem?

Either way, it's a definite issue. Especially since this fancy store has only female employees—and they're *all over* Tristan.

While they simper and giggle, he keeps a handsome smile on his face. Ordinarily, the fact that I now know him well enough to know it isn't his true grin—but some vacant, polished politician version—would help.

Not today, apparently.

The silent sense inside of me whines and nudges. Desperate for me to claim him. Yank him away. Rip his pants off and climb him.

An-y-thing.

But I just keep sifting through the racks, looking for something sexy to wear to Jonah's pre-season game... and maybe Avery's first big fight in a couple of weeks. Most of the ones I like are in my pack's signature black—short and close cut, with metallic accents or glittering beadwork.

Jonah will love being able to see so much of my legs, I think, distracting myself as the shop girls giggle some more.

I almost smile at the thought of my big man. Having finally mastered basic cooking, gardening, and swimming, he's now firmly determined to teach me to drive. So far, I've backed his Bronco in and out of the garage about eighty times, but still. He's so sweet to me.

Not for the first time, I wish I could reach out to him internally. He's become my safe place inside the pack house and—usually—out in the world. I wonder what he would say if he knew I'd thought about giving him a place inside of me, too.

Probably something dirty.

Followed by something devastatingly beautiful.

I find three dresses that seem like good options and glance at Tristan to tell him. When I find him making small talk with a gorgeous blonde pixie of a saleswoman, my stomach sinks.

His Serena Radar must ping because he instantly snaps his gaze across the room. "Ready, sweet one?"

Ooh. Why do I like that he called me that? In front of *her*. *Them*.

Either way, a bit of the tension crowding my lungs evaporates. "I think so. Can I try these on?"

By the time I'm ensconced in one of the plush, cream-colored fitting rooms, my mood has edged past insecure and into a more Avery-like headspace. Every time one of the girls hanging around Tris laughs, I want to scream.

My shoulders hike higher and higher each time I flinch. Until Tristan's deep voice cuts in.

"Excuse me, ladies. My *mate* needs me."

Did I imagine the subtle emphasis on that one word?

Maybe that's just how he says it. I don't think I've ever heard him call me that before.

Before I can process the soup of feelings swirling in my stomach, a quiet knock hits my door. I don't answer, but it cracks open anyway.

Gusting out a weary sigh, Tristan steps into the plush changing room and shoots a glare at the door. "Endlessly irritating," he mutters, more to himself than me.

Another word starts to form on his lips, but he turns to face me. And freezes.

A growl whips out of him, so deep and quick, I know it was beyond his control. I clutch at my boobs, holding up the open bodice of the shiny onyx minidress draped around me. Not that hoisting it into place does much—the cups at the front have a sweetheart neckline with a deep slit between them.

"*Serena*," he snarls, ocean eyes flashing urgently. "Dear *God*."

I'm not melting at the moment—in fact, I'm cold and a little worried about the manic look on his face. Not to mention the way his summery scent has already filled this entire room.

"*Turn around.*"

Tristan never—*never*—barks at me. Not since the night we met. Part of me gets even more worried when I hear it. I know he wouldn't have done that if he had the ability to stop himself. And the other part of me...

Or, really, my Omega...

Well.

I instantly turn around, but it's too late. Piña colada perfume swells into his, drowning the room in our pheromones. A quiet whine vibrates in my throat when I inhale the mixture.

"Shh," he hushes, stepping up against my back and peering over my shoulder at the mirror we're both facing. "*Look.*"

The couple standing across from us is beautiful. A tailored, statuesque alpha in silver-gray. And... *me*.

Could that really be me? My hair isn't limp and over-styled anymore. I don't look weak or frail. My skin glows golden brown, complementing the lustrous tresses draped over my shoulder and the even shinier dress.

The only thing wrong with our reflection is Tristan's face. It's wild. Almost... pained?

He steps back slightly and drops his focus to my naked back. I think he's about to zip the dress up, but instead, he reaches inside it and skims two warm palms over my bare waist. I watch his eyes squeeze shut in the mirror.

"I—" he stammers, hoarse. "I need a moment to touch you. Please. Can I—"

There's no use even trying to pretend I don't like that idea. My scent brightens, and he groans quietly, dropping his forehead to my shoulder while his touch glides further down my body.

Instead of giving him a verbal reply, I tilt my neck to the side, exposing his bite. He moans again, diving for it. Latching on like it's the only way for him to survive his next breath.

His thick, hot tongue swirls over the silvery scars. Another grumbling groan skitters across my sensitized skin. My nipples pebble against the fabric grazing them, and I stab another whine before it escapes.

Tristan must feel it, though, because while one of his hands skates lower, the other slips up to graze the underside of my breast. He pauses there, blue eyes snapping back to mine in the mirror.

Asking permission.

Later, I can blame my hormones. My Omega. My upcoming heat.

Because it can't be me wanting this. Craving the touch of this alpha who has *never* wanted me.

Never *liked* me. Never thought I was good enough but *bit me anyway.*

Bonded me anyway, and now—now—

I nod.

Heat strikes his gaze. Lightning on a storm-tossed sea. He palms my right breast but doesn't touch the hardened point. The hand hovering on the lower curve of my belly stretches just a bit—until his middle fingertip brushes the very top of my slit.

I'm appallingly wet. So soaked that one slight flick of his wrist, rubbing one of my pussy lips into the other, makes an obscene sound. He covers it by sucking on my neck.

I start to moan, but his fingertips clamp around my nipple at the same second his teeth scrape my skin. "Hush, baby," he whispers. "They're not allowed to hear you come. Only me."

I choke on a squeal, and he rumbles his approval, a growly purr roaring to life against my bare spine. "The others might like flaunting you. Showing that you're theirs with your screams and your marks. But not me, omega."

Before his words can sink in enough to hurt, he groans again, slipping his soaked finger between my folds. "*You're* going to possess *me*. Everywhere I go, I'll smell like your sweet slick. And everyone will know that *I* belong to *you*."

Pain and pleasure squeeze my lungs, vaporizing my voice. "*Tristan...*"

His eyes fall shut while he strokes up to my clit, rolling his fingertip around it in a firm circle. When I buck and fight another cry, he exhales shakily. "God, there you are. So fucking perfect, aren't you, sweet baby girl?"

I whimper, instinctually nuzzling my face against the side of his. He catches the motion and releases his bond mark, turning to put his lips in my reach.

"*Kiss me.*"

It only just manages not to register as a bark. The command is there, but so is pure, raw pleading.

My eyes fly to our reflection, seeing the way his have closed. The way his chest heaves. And I realize—I have power over him now.

"No," I breathe. "You can't kiss me."

Yet.

Those fierce eyes snap open, pinning me. "Then I'll just make you come all over my fingers."

Tristan Thorne keeps his word. By the time I'm done gushing all over his hand, I'm sure the fact that he bit me every time I even squeaked is meaningless.

I have no doubt all those smug bitches heard us.

Good.

Without an ounce of shame, Tristan takes his slick fingers and dabs them at the base of his throat like he's applying cologne. When he sees my gape, he flashes a cocky smile.

"I warned you."

He did, but it doesn't make me any less dazed. What is *happening*? Does he just want me because he's tired of resisting my scent and my body? Or is there something else, blooming between us?

Do I care?

Yeah, unfortunately, I think I do. Maybe I wouldn't have a month ago. I would have taken any scrap of respect or affection and been damn grateful for it.

But these alphas have told me, again and again, how precious I am. How good and sweet and smart and worthy.

A queen.

Their queen.

And I want more than scraps.

"I think we should buy this dress," I mumble, unsettled, "since it's basically soaked in perfume."

He nods, every inch the commanding senator once again. No trace of the desperate man who needed me in order to breathe.

"We will," he says. "We'll buy all of them."

He pulls out his wallet and extracts a credit card, flashing me a look that could almost be described as teasing. "I'll let you deal with the *ladies* out there while I get the car."

I'm suddenly so pissed. How dare he just... seduce me like that? With his *need* instead of his charm. And so *easily*!

No fair.

My eyes narrow at him, spoiling for a fight. "I don't need three dresses, *Senator*."

"I don't care," he shrugs. "You're getting them."

I snort, tossing my hair back and cocking my hip. "You gonna make me?"

Tristan strikes like a cobra. Sweeping me into the wall and stretching his arm over my head, boxing me in with his perfect scent and the hard body under his suit.

His face drops, looming inches above mine. A dark brow lifts.

"I bit you," he roughs out, the low words sinking straight between my hips, sparks shivering over the embers of the blaze he just extinguished. "Sunk my teeth into your perfect little throat without even *asking*."

Slick slips into my panties the same second I catch myself nearly panting. Clearly, something is deeply wrong with me. Because, for one insane moment, all I can think is...

Yes. Again. More.

A small smile quirks the side of his sculpted mouth. He holds up the black AmEx again. "Take the damn card and buy the damn dresses."

I ALREADY FEEL every second of my thirty-five years.

And there are still three hours before I even have to be at the stadium.

Damn, I think, ignoring the twinge in my knee and an answering throb in my shoulder.

I'm agitated and exhausted, but I have to get it together. It may only be a pre-season game, but it's the first time my omega will see me on the field, and I don't want to look as ancient as I feel.

Honestly, now that Archer's gotten me off the rut-blockers, I expected to feel better. Instead, I'm foggy and more anxious than usual.

I've been doing this NFL shit for fifteen years. You'd think I'd be used to it by now.

Spencer seems to think we'll all be more on edge because of Serena's impending heat. But I don't know if we should listen to him, given that he might actually be an impostor impersonating our packmate.

This morning at breakfast, he *stopped reading his research* just to kiss Serena's forehead. And then *he let her touch his arm.*

Tristan almost choked on his coffee.

That was new, too—Tristan and Serena eating breakfast at the counter like there was only a barstool between them and not a whole damn ocean.

Who knows if that has anything to do with what I find when I come downstairs.

Maybe it's just her hormones or her instincts Her scent has been lighter day-by-day—sweeter with a high sort of sharpness instead of that deep, dark sting she arrived with.

Maybe she's just... happy. Comfortable.

The thought puts a smile on my face as I turn down her hallway.

And see the impossible.

Our gorgeous omega. Building our nest.

She looks so cute, wearing one of Avery's black hoodies, shuffling on her knees from one section of the circular floor mattress to the other.

Long legs bare, face makeup-free. I think this is my favorite look for her. Natural and somehow still so glamorous—she just has that way about her, even on the days I find her elbow-deep in our flower beds.

She likes to look polished—blowing out her hair, waxing her body, wearing little skirts and platform heels.

But I don't think she has to even try. She's glorious just like this.

Especially in her nest.

I hope her scent is sinking into every fucking fiber.

It's been years since I saw the inside of the small, rounded room. I know it has a side door that connects to her bathroom and the suite on the other side, but that's all I really remember.

I guess that wouldn't matter anyway. She's changed everything.

And I love it.

From my vantage point in the hall, I can just barely see the curling tendrils of hanging plants, gently swinging over the nest. She's strung up several, tangled with soft strings of twinkling lights.

It's beautiful. Because it's *her*. The dark, sensual fabrics. The moody lighting. The greenery she loves so much.

When I get close enough to see the whole room, the plants make more sense. She's hung them to absorb the sunlight streaming in through the dome of windows overhead.

I don't remember it being so bright. Will that upset her during her heat? Hanging more plants might help. Knowing Tris, there's probably some remote that tints the glass or releases a shade.

If Serena is bothered by it, I can't tell. In fact, I know from her creamy, golden scent that she's content. Tucking rich purple cushions into plush piles, fluffing out matching blankets, and arranging them into specific swirls.

I watch closely, memorizing the movements in case she needs me to help her rebuild anything later. My scent swells without me noticing—but the second she senses it, she pauses, turning to raise a brow at me.

"Ready for your game, big man?"

God, I am so in love with this woman.

It fills my throat, turning my voice into a rasp. "As I'll ever be." I gesture around the beautiful nest. "Looks like you've been hard at work, little hummingbird."

Her expression turns shy as she shrugs. "I woke up this

morning and just felt like I needed to start." A tiny quiver moves through her. "Shit, should I have asked you guys first?"

I smile wider. She has a filthy mouth, just like me and Ave. I love it.

"You never have to ask us, *manamea*. This is your home. You do whatever you want."

That slight grin grows, cracking my heart in half. *Goddamn.* She's so *pretty*. Sweet and smart and almost mysterious, with so many depths hidden behind those glittering green eyes.

An omega who can charm Spencer out of his shell.

Calm Avery's cyclones of cynical rage.

And connect with this level of me I didn't even know existed.

She does it effortlessly, waving a casual hand and gracing me with that grin. "Come in."

I'm in my pre-game suit, but fuck it. My jacket and shoes end up in a pile next to the door, and I lumber to my knees, carefully finding her in the middle of the rounded mattress.

She gives a nod of approval when I manage not to knock anything down. Then, a wince. "Sorry," she peeps, looking around. "I guess I need to make our free space bigger, huh?"

I'd never criticize her nest-building. Sure, there are three more big guys who will need to fit in here with us, but if my hairy ass has to sit naked on Avery's lap so she can have her pillows the way she wants them, so be it.

"Your Omega will know what to do," I assure her, running my hands over the fuzzy blanket under us. "She's done a great job so far."

Serena sits up, preening a bit. Which pretty much makes my game later a waste of time—I've already won today.

I lean back carefully on my palms, looking up at all the lights and leaves over us. It's perfect. I couldn't imagine anything better.

A deep sigh rolls out of me when I realize I really don't *want* to leave.

Serena's instincts are closer to the surface than usual—because the next thing I know, she's climbed into my lap. Her bare legs stretch to straddle my thick thighs, and she sinks down, melding her scorching heat with the hardness already pressing into my pants.

When she wraps her arms around my torso, a gentle vibration sinks into my chest. I hold my breath, listening...

...to her purr.

It rattles softly but hits me like a ton of bricks. My stomach flattens. My heart pounds. The lump in my throat expands along with my knot.

My omega built me a nest. And now she's purring.

For me.

Which makes me wonder why I ever thought anything else would make me happy.

forty-four

LISTEN, *bitch*, I tell my Omega. *We don't have time for this shit.*

As per usual, I don't get any words back. Just the general sense that someone is narrowing their eyes at me in exasperation.

Which is rich, coming from the one who can't pick a damn shirt.

Half of my new wardrobe isn't here yet, but each of the guys went through what I have and took it upon themselves to provide an option for our first public appearance.

Jonah left me one of his jerseys, which I figure I could tie into a knotted crop top and throw on with some shorts. That seems too casual; the same way the collared black dress and headband Spencer laid out seems way too formal.

Avery just left out underwear.

They're blood-red lace and made to cover scent/absorb slick, but still.

That menace.

Biting back a smile I'd never admit to, I wiggle into the panties and a black denim mini-skirt before throwing on Jonah's enormous jersey. Once I tie it at my waist, it actually looks sort of cute.

The neckline is wide enough to slip off one of my shoulders, leaving the bare skin on display. I work my hair into a messy fishtail braid to sweep over that same shoulder and carefully situate the black bow headband from Spencer on my head.

My selection of shoes is now endless, but I somehow end up in a pair similar to the ones I arrived at the Thorne house in. Platforms with a thin ankle strap—only black velvet instead of worn pleather.

When I come out of my room, Tristan, Spencer, and Avery are waiting in the kitchen. All three of them drop their conversation and snap their focus to me.

Flashing me his quick, feral grin, Avery is the first one to approach. He claps his big, beat-up hand around the back of my thigh and slides it straight up to cup a handful of my ass, squeezing much more tenderly than he'd ever let the others see.

When he feels the panties he picked, victorious adoration glows in his ghostly blue eyes. "Bad little kitten."

To my surprise, Spencer actually comes over next. He stands behind Avery for a long moment, looking me over before offering a nod.

"Jonah will like this," he tells me, matter-of-fact.

The sudden, needy whine in my throat startles me. Spencer's eyes soften, though, the dark pools warming.

He slips around my back and finds my wrists, holding them at my sides as he skims his lips up my exposed shoulder, stopping to properly kiss the fading bruise he left on my neck.

"You look very good, Miss Swanson," he adds, a wave of approval washing over me. Soothing me. "I'm pleased."

Lord, I should not *crave* his praise like I do, but I can't help myself. Feeling dazed—and a little bit betrayed by own brain—I find Avery staring at me, his beautiful face smirking while he nods at the professor.

"Can you believe this fucking guy?"

Laughter breaks the tension crowding my chest. Avery's smile splits into something more genuine, just as he dips forward to steal a kiss from my lips.

I'm covered in de-scenter, but they can still sense the small burst of perfume spinning off me. Spencer's fingers stroke reassuring circles along the insides of my wrists while Avery nips my lower lip lightly.

"Mm," he rumbles. "There she is. Perfect."

But I'm *not*. So I bite him back. His jasmine and amber darken, weaving with the humid freshness rising behind me. The two alphas are arguably the most difficult to get along with—but, somehow, their scents merge into the most peaceful, all-consuming *rightness*.

I feel my body relax, falling back against Spencer's, welcoming the press of Avery's lean hips and warm abdomen. Tristan catches my gaze, smiling softly across the island while he watches his pack-mates embrace me.

It's the first time, in a room full of alphas, that my perfume hasn't caused a frenzy or some sort of faux pas. Instead, as both of the guys lean in closer and slowly breathe deeper, we're just...

At home.

Ourselves.

———————❤———————

I **EXPECTED** Avery to be the most overprotective alpha in such a huge, crowded place. Or, maybe even Tristan, if the half-bond did weird things to him.

But, no.

Spencer is the one who snarls at practically every person we pass.

Halfway along the long, curved hallway outside the stadium's private boxes, I slip my hand into his and squeeze, shooting him a look. Most of the hostility drains from his face, his dark eyes going soft when they land on mine, but his lip stays curled in irritation.

It's cute. I grin at his sour expression and his white-blond brows lift, that stern mouth twitching into a smirk.

"Do I amuse you, Miss Swanson?"

I give a breezy shrug. "Immensely."

He drops my hand, only to reach back and swat my ass hard enough to send me forward a step. "You know what I do to brats, Miss Swanson."

Yeah, that's sort of the point. Flashing a grin, I keep my voice as sweet as can be. "Yes, Professor."

His scent spikes while his nostrils flare. Avery chortles, slipping his arm around my waist. "Getting the professor all hot and bothered?"

Tristan gives me another of those slight, approving smiles, then tosses his brother a smirk. "I think the student is quickly becoming the master."

I'm still giggling when a hand closes around my arm. "Hey—"

A hard spike of fear stabs my gut, forcing a whine up my throat. Spencer unleashes a roaring growl while Avery immediately snaps into action, ripping me off my feet and holding me against his chest, baring his teeth.

A small blonde blinks at me from my former place on the ground, the older, black-suited alpha behind her gnashing his teeth at mine. "Oh," she says. "Sorry."

I hate the shiver that racks my body, but there's no help for it.

Ave tenderly tucks my head under his chin, glaring at the beautiful omega with a frown on her face.

Tristan steps in front of his packmates, extending his hand—to the *omega*.

A lot of alphas would ignore her and reach over to shake the tattooed hand of the man at her back. But Tristan offers her his handshake instead. "I'm Tristan Thorne. You're the Ash Pack's omega, yes? The one who does media for the team? Jonah has mentioned you."

When the woman doesn't move, her alpha shakes Tristan's hand. "Senator Thorne," he says. "I'm Ronan Ash. I believe we met at a mixer last summer."

Tristan nods, his expression losing some of its tension. "Serena," he says, looping me in. "This is the owner of the Ospreys and his omega…"

At my alpha's lifted brows, the blonde snaps out, "Meg." Her pretty blue eyes narrow as she runs them over my face. "Sorry to come stomping over here. I didn't mean to freak you out."

I cringe. "It's a little too easy to do lately. Not your fault."

"Serena's about to go into heat," Spencer informs the pair, still every bit as forbidding as he was a moment ago. "Archer is treating her."

Tristan's earlier introduction finally sinks in. I gasp. "Wait, you're *Dr. Monroe*'s omega?"

Meg pauses but smiles slightly. "Um, yeah. I take it you've met him?"

I nod quickly. "He helped me when—" I only barely catch myself. "He was there when I really needed some help. He's an amazing doctor."

Pride beams all over her face. "He really is."

The air around us suddenly feels awkward. I try to squirm out of Avery's arms, but he just hugs me closer. "Well… sorry for freaking out."

Meg grins. "Happens to the best of us," she says, tossing her alpha a secret smile. "Trust me. I'll tell Archer you said hi!"

They wander off, leaving me wondering if I might have just met a potential... friend?

But then, of course, Avery drops his pout into the crook of my neck, nuzzling. "That was fucking weird."

I smack his side, which only makes him hold me tighter. "Mmm, baby. You want me to fuck you in the skybox?"

Spencer starts to glare, and Tristan's expression darkens, but the faint burst of perfume that makes it past all of my de-scenter pauses both of them.

Avery flashes a feral grin. "See? I know what my girl likes."

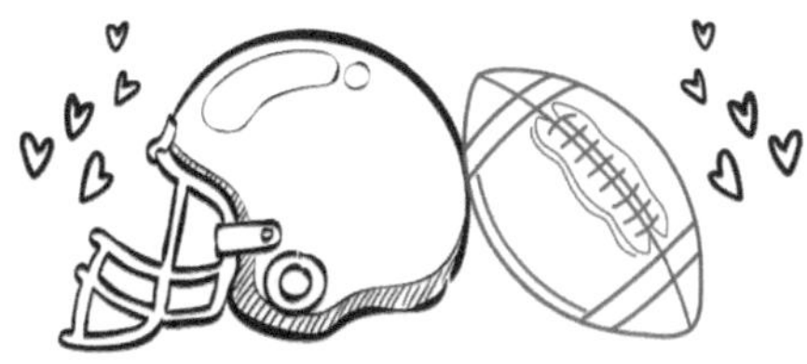

LISTENING IS NOT my strong suit.

If I weren't so shit at it, I might have snapped this whole thing together a lot sooner.

Jonah bitched all day about how bad he felt. I thought he was just *old*—and too stubborn to admit it. But Serena... she suddenly woke up today and *needed* to start on her nest.

Why today? When her heat isn't for another week or two, and she isn't really a big "planner"?

It was also weird that she wanted to leave the game and come straight home. We were supposed to go to dinner, and Jonah was supposed to come home, change, and meet us.

Yeah.

I suck at this.

All the signs were there, but as soon as we walk into the kitchen, my hackles fly up.

Jonah is here, which means he beat us home. There's no other way to explain the thick haze of s'mores globbing up the air.

Which pins my kitten in place the second she steps inside.

Oh fuck.

Her green eyes fly wide, a little shriek catching her throat before she stops it, reaching up and fisting her necklace while her gaze darts around.

"What?" Spencer asks.

"*Jonah,*" she whispers. "He's—"

A low growl from the living room cuts her off. Spencer snaps out a vicious curse. "In a *rut.*"

He and Serena look at each other, then both of them turn to—

Tris.

Oh FUCK.

He's standing in front of the closed elevator, gripping the black metal trim like he's about to rip it off the goddamn wall. His chest heaves under his navy shirt, panting so hard I think he's about to pop some buttons.

Serena freezes even more, locking herself into the perfect stillness of a hunted animal.

I know all about that shit now; all her nature documentaries have taught me what prey looks like before it's about to be eaten.

Pretty much this.

The scent of her fear fills the kitchen in seconds. A deep snarl answers from the other room.

Fuuuuuuck.

As soon as his Alpha senses her freaking out, he'll be clawing through all of us to get to her. I know the motherfucking feeling —since I'm actively muscling it back *right now.*

Usually, I have an understanding with the rabid beast inside me. We like each other. And, yeah, I don't exactly keep him on the shortest of leashes.

But right now?

Fuck that guy.

I didn't even know two alphas in the same pack could go into rut at the same time—we're not adding a third fucker to this situation.

Spence seems to agree. He whips his focus from his brother to his best friend, then down to our trembling omega.

Shit.

"Is it me?" she quivers. "D-did I do something to—"

He shakes his head, eyes blazing. "No, darling. You didn't do anything wrong. Jonah has been on edge since he came off his rut-blockers. I know the two of you were taking things slowly, but waiting so long might have been too much for him."

Serena doesn't move a muscle, but her eyes slide to our pack leader. "B-but—"

"The half-bond would make it virtually impossible for an alpha to know his omega was about to be rutted by someone else without forcing a rut of its own." Spencer shakes his head, getting more intense. "This is *not your fault*, Miss Swanson. Do you understand?"

"Yes, Professor," she answers.

Which—

I'm going to have to unpack later.

Because the second one drop of her sweet arousal touches her scent, Tristan gives a serrated growl, and Jonah fucking *roars*. He suddenly tears into the kitchen, sightless black eyes snapping right to her.

My body moves on instinct, stepping up to block his path, jostling him back. On her other side, Spencer does the same to Tristan, holding him off to give Serena room to make a decision.

A full-body shiver shimmies down her spine, a fresh burst of perfume winding off her. When our eyes meet, I see the scared baby kitten and my fierce little fighter, all swirled together. Layered with some hesitation that doesn't make any sense until it hits me—

"You want them."

Her teeth sink into her lower lip. Spencer frowns in disbelief, nodding at Tris. "*Both* of them, omega?"

"I-is that even possible?" she whispers. "Won't they both want to knot me at the same time? I-I've never—I don't think I could take *two* the first time."

Spencer reaches over and skims his thumb across her mouth, freeing that bitten-up lip. His hand slides down, fingers flexing over her throat. "You trust me?" he asks, then flicks a look at me. "*Us?*"

Serena nods right away, transfixed on his swirling brown eyes. He nods, pure alpha approval rolling off him. "Very well, Miss Swanson. Let Jonah take off your clothes. I have a plan."

IF IT WERE JUST the pain or the desire, I could manage them.

If it were just the daze or the fear, I'd find a way to fight through both.

But all four at once prove the exact recipe for my undoing.

Maybe I should have known this was inevitable.

The face of some other alpha—one with glasses and concerned expression—flashes to mind. Did he warn me about this? Why didn't I listen?

Now, I'm barreling toward the omega who has my entire

world on a string. Or maybe she *is* my entire world, the one thing tying me to existence.

It feels that way, right now, when every thought and instinct and need begins and ends with *her*.

I stagger forward, fighting myself on every step. I'm in a rut, but I'm more aware than I ever have been while in this haze before. Probably from those shots I take.

What do those do, again? Weren't they supposed to help this somehow?

I suppose the fact that I can think at all *is* a help.

At this point, I'd take anything—*anything*—to stop myself from rutting this omega. With one last desperate attempt to gain control, I fling my gaze over to her face. Looking for shock or horror. Fear. Pain. Disgust.

God, please, anything *to make me* stop—

But she's already looking at me.

In another alpha's arms, letting him tear clothes off her and pull her into his waiting lap.

But *looking at me.*

When the alpha under her nuzzles his face between her bare tits, a feral sound rips out of my lungs. The omega shakes, turning her green gaze to one of the others. I can't remember anyone's name, but I recognize him as my brother.

"He can't help himself," he mutters to the omega. "His Alpha must be going crazy. Letting another alpha rut you while your bond is incomplete would probably cause him extreme pain and—"

Her dark brows crease. "P-pain?"

My brother's face softens. "Yes, omega. The half-bond can be very painful for the one who's been rejected. Especially when there's no physical or emotional intimacy and the bond sits empty."

There's a reason I don't want her to know all of that. Something important that I can't see the edges of, like this. But it's too late, anyhow.

The way she's looking at me is full of confusion and sadness and maybe even betrayal. She blinks, and I see that her lashes look wet. "Is that true, Alpha?" she asks, turning to me. "Do you—does it *hurt*?"

Her hand smooths over the burly alpha's long hair, gentling him while he kisses her skin. Tasting her. Tasting *my* omega, and *goddamn it, I'll kill him*.

Another growl rends the air, and he pauses, but only until the omega starts to pet his head again. The look she slants at me goes from wary to angry.

"None of that," she orders, the words echoing through the fog filling my head. "If you need me, you'll have to work with us, not against us."

If I—

Before I can wrap my mind around her words, my brother steps behind the couch, coming to stand next to the inked one. "Are you sure, darling? You don't have to let Tristan touch you. Avery and I will make him leave if you want us to."

Fuck. No. Please.

But it's too late. The familiar pain hits, goring into the place just above my stomach, below my diaphragm.

I usually know her rejection is coming. I can normally brace for it. But this time all I can do is clutch my clawed hands over my abdomen, doing my best not to roar again, holding onto the beast lunging inside of me by my aching fucking fingernails—

Until, suddenly, I'm not.

And the pain is *gone*?

I open my eyes and find the omega's hand stretched over my stomach, lightly tracing the muscles bulging there. When her perfume gets even sweeter, I swear I might die.

Instead, she traces lower, skimming whatever scratchy fabric covers my lower half, while her free hand continues lavishing the other alpha with similar affection.

Fuck. I hold back the urge to fight, ignoring my Alpha's hisses.

It would be so easy. He hasn't even noticed we're here yet.

The fingertips lingering between my hips still. "Alpha," the omega whispers, her eyes big and nervous. "Can you share or not?"

For her? I can do *anything*. As long as she lets me touch her. Lets me have her.

"Yes, omega," I answer, not recognizing my own voice. It's gravel and smoke, but she seems to like it. Her spine arches on a shiver as more perfume spins into the air.

The alpha at her breast groans as I rip my pants off, growling. The sound finally brings me to his attention, his black eyes snapping up, brows crouching low.

But the omega murmurs to him sweetly, guiding his gaze back to hers. "Shh, it's okay. I want him, too. Is that okay, Alpha? Can I have you both? I promise not to let him knot me."

My instincts rage against that, but the small, sane part of me is relieved to have some boundaries. And even more relieved that these rut-blockers are working well enough for me to understand them.

The tattooed alpha, who already has his dick out, gathers the omega's chin in his long fingers, turning her head to him. "Why don't you kiss Jonah and work your clit against his big cock, kitten? Tristan can take you from behind. Get you ready to take both of these cocks at the same time."

Oh *fuck*.

But the omega listens, sinking her mouth against the alpha under her while repositioning herself. Her arms stretch up around his neck while she pushes her bare, rounded hips back.

I don't even think before my hands land there, feeling the plush curves.

The room is holding its breath. And a sense of awe swoops through me.

Is this the first time I've ever done this?

Dear God—*why?*

There was a reason. I can't remember it right now, though, so

I let myself feel her body, molding my palms along the outsides of her thighs, skimming them inward.

Paradise perfume expands between us, the scent making my mouth water and my cock jerk. But then I feel it, under my hands.

She's *shaking*.

And somewhere under all the fog floating through me, there's sadness.

Have I made her *sad*?

I start to back away, bracing myself for the pain that will hit me the second I remove my hands from her perfect body. But the omega looks at me over her shoulder, her eyes pleading.

"Please," she says. "I know you don't want to, but I don't want you to hurt, Alpha."

I do, though. *I do.* Because the way she's looking at me is enough to stop whatever's left of my heart.

She wiggles her hips a little, pressing back far enough for my weeping cock to brush between her legs. My vision blurs, air heaving out of me on a pained grunt.

And then I'm in her.

There isn't a moment where I can stop myself. Or pause to remember why I *need* to stop myself. There's just—

Her.

forty-seven

PART of me wants to hate it.

The thick shove into my slippery, clenching core. The deep, throaty growl that raises goosebumps on my skin. The swelling scent of summer and the way it perfectly meshes with the sweet, toasty alpha under me.

I want to hate it.

But that would be like hating oxygen. Or sunshine. Or the traitorous, aching heart that's somehow keeping me alive as it slowly, painfully kills me.

Because, beat by beat, I want this alpha *more*.

The one who bit me and bonded with me. The one who left me to feel like he wanted nothing to do with me for *weeks* and may only be coming around now because his body is forcing him too.

He might not even like me. Hell, he doesn't really *know* me.

But he's also the man who was willing to sacrifice his career and his pack's reputation to make me happy and keep me safe. He's apologized and admitted he deserves my scorn.

No matter how much I wish I hated him, I don't think I do.

He can't remember all the minefields between us now. Is that the only reason why his hands are stroking me so tenderly? Why he's huffing audible breaths as if he can't inhale enough of me?

His knot is already so full, there isn't even a chance he'd be able to work it into me.

That's just as well. Spencer said he had a plan.

Although, how I'm expected to do *anything* with these *two monster dicks* is beyond me.

I didn't get a chance to really look at it, but Tristan's cock feels big. Not as huge as Jonah's, maybe—but it's as wide as it is long, making it large enough to rip the air out of my lungs every time he pulls out and slams back in.

I was already embarrassingly wet, primed by the scents of my mates. But the second his girth starts to pound against the place inside of me that begs for a knot, my clit echoes the pulse, beating desperately.

All four alphas stare at me while I whine, lowering myself to work it along Jonah's leaking length. He snarls, his teeth scraping the fingers I've placed over his lips.

Avery looms behind my big man, every inch the beautiful demon. Swirling ink on pale skin, muscles cinching and flexing as he grinds his silver-studded cock into his fist again and again.

A special display just for me.

Love swells in the pit of my stomach, and I catch his eye, trying to show him how I'm feeling without words. When I find my favorite fire snapping in the ghostly blue, another whine squeaks out of me.

Jonah licks the cords of my throat, the motion soothing and sweet in an animalistic way. That's how he's been this whole time. Nosing at me. Licking my skin and scoring me with his teeth. It all makes me even more desperate.

He may be out of it, but it's still *him*, my kind-hearted, gentle giant.

Slick squelches out of my pussy, dousing Tristan's thick knot with slippery warmth. When he growls, I press down harder, grinding my clit into Jonah, chasing the pound there.

Jonah groans, his huge hand gripping the back of my neck. He tries to yank me away from Tristan, and a twinge of panic stabs my gullet.

How do I stop him? *Should* I stop him? I want him so badly I can barely breathe, but I can't let Tris *hurt*.

Avery's brows fold, his fist slowing. He opens his mouth, but before anyone can speak, Spencer's hand covers my throat.

For a second, everyone freezes. Spencer is putting himself in the middle of *this*? With his wrist crossed over Jonah's?

My handsome professor doesn't seem bothered at the moment. When I whip my head in his direction, his dark gaze lands on mine, intent. Demanding, even. He flexes his fingers gently.

"You're going to take both of these cocks at once. There won't be room for either of them to knot you."

I whine, equal parts relieved and distressed. His gaze softens.

"I know, omega," he murmurs. "If you want more when you're done, I promise you'll get it. Right, Ave?"

Avery's tattooed fingers find my hair, sifting a few stray pieces behind my ear. "Of course," he rasps. "You know this knot is all yours, kitten. Whenever you're ready for it to stretch that little pussy."

Shit.

My breathing stutters as I choke on a whimper. My inner

walls squeeze Tristan's thickness until the hands slowly rubbing my hips and thighs begin to curl into claws. He snaps me back, hammering into my body and setting a punishing pace.

The aching nub grinding against Jonah's slicked-up length starts to throb urgently. I whine, keening around the palm pressed into my neck while all the tension inside of me seizes and bursts.

Tristan curses and snarls, plunging into my pussy while it tries to clamp around him. Spencer raises his voice, barking, "*Take her ass, Tris.*"

My thoughts swirl and blur as the alpha behind me snarls his displeasure. Which just makes Jonah more agitated.

Damn these alphas and their enormous cocks and all their *growling*.

I really wish it didn't turn me into a human Slip N Slide.

Cutting Tris a look, I prepare myself to give him a piece of my mind. But then our eyes meet. And all I see is *desolation*.

With our gazes locked, the dam holding his emotions back collapses. This time, part of me is ready for it. And when everything sweeps into my center and expands, I finally understand.

His Alpha is desperate. Not for my body—but for the *connection*.

He doesn't want to pull out because he doesn't want to *leave me*.

Not just my smell or my body. *Me*.

I slow to a stop, ignoring the way my body sobs in protest. Spencer loosens his grip on my neck, letting me reach back and touch Tristan's abs again, hoping the motion is as soothing as the emotions I try to push at the frayed tether between us.

I blink, looking right into his dazed navy eyes. The shifting seas of longing and pain and *fury*.

"No one's ever taken me there before," I whisper to him. "Avery's been prepping me, but... you'd be the only one. To claim me there."

The pack leader groans deeply—and he's not the only one. All four of them grunt, my words affecting them all. Avery will be especially pissed, I think. He's been doing all the work to get me ready…

But when I chance a glance over Jonah's head at my tattooed alpha, his ghostly gaze glows with pride and lust while his wrist snaps, jacking his studded cock faster.

I don't have a chance to say anything else, because Tristan rears back. I brace for pain and the jolt of his thickness, *there*…

Instead, his thumb grazes me. *Gently.*

Rubbing slick and the pearly essence dripping from his cock into my puckered hole.

Ah!

Suddenly, my big alpha has had enough of this whole sharing plan. The second he scents Tristan's release on my skin, he yanks me upright and impales me on his cock.

Oh holy—ahhhhhhhhh!

He's so *huge*. Now I see what he's been fussing about—always telling me we needed to wait, work me up, get me ready.

I thought he was maybe exaggerating, but, *um*.

The width and depth of him instantly steal my breath, forcing another pitiful whimper out of me. Avery's beautiful features lift into a smirk while Tristan replaces his thumb with the broad head of his dick, slipping the first inch in. Spencer goes back to collaring my throat.

"That's a good girl," he praises, nodding at Jonah. "Ride your big man for us. We want to see you take his cock, too."

I look down at the enormous erection buried between my thighs. Bigger than my forearm. And that *knot*.

Avery truly could not be any more gorgeous than he is when he actually *smiles*. Genuine joy is so rare for him. It hits my heart like an arrow as he cups his fingers around my jaw, tilting my face up.

"It'll fit, baby," he promises, just as Jonah bottoms out and Tristan forces the next couple of girthy inches into my ass. "You can take it."

The words remind me of that sunny day Jonah and I spent in

the pool. The tender heat in his topaz eyes when he told me, *"You're my mate, manamea. We will fit together."*

He'll be devastated about missing this moment after waiting so long, but he *needs* me.

With a trembling sigh, I set my cheek against his, scent-marking his thick beard and absorbing the purr that rattles under his growls. "I'm here," I soothe, "I know you're in there, too, Jo."

His answering snarl is ragged and desperate. Both of his hands flex at my hips, dragging me down until his entire cock almost splits me in two.

He groans, head falling back. Spencer's hand flexes at my throat, thumb brushing reverently along the pack alpha's bite.

My core clenches, drawing in another bit of Tristan's wide hardness. I squirm, whining while I work to take him deeper without shoving Jonah out. Slick pours down my thighs as perfume rushes off my skin, filling the whole room. Somewhere behind us, a deep moan sends a shiver through me.

Tris.

He's getting close, rutting my ass almost as hard as he did my pussy. My body clamps tighter and tighter on every plunge, getting ready to strangle both of the alphas inside of me.

I hear Spencer's belt tinkle as he opens it one-handed. The rain-drenched scent of his arousal winds into Jonah's toasted sweetness and Avery's incense, melding with Tristan's soothing freshness so perfectly that I could cry. The combination glazes my eyes as they roll back, sobbing and taking Jonah all the way down to the root again. And again.

Ho-ly. Fuuuuu—

I've never been so full. Stretched and slick and pulsing around these big, solid cocks while they rub at every sizzling nerve inside of me.

A scream tears from my lips as my core convulses, sucking them both until stars burst across my vision. The tension inside me releases in a gushing torrent, soaking Jonah and Tris while the grind of both their knots against my entrance tugs at the base of my clit, and I come *again*.

"Shit." Avery's curse is rough, his next command nearly a bark. "*Open up*, kitten."

Head spinning, I only barely manage to glance over at Spencer, worried about letting Avery into my mouth while my professor's already holding my neck.

But I find him barring his teeth in a snarl, tugging at his own dick with impressive fluidity. He nods, and I instantly turn back to Ave, opening my lips for him.

His patterned skin is swollen and hot, highlighting just how cool those metal balls at the bottom of his head are. I roll the tip of my tongue between them before lapping the smokey taste of his pre-cum off each of the bars studding his shaft.

Avery hisses, shoving deeper. When I reach up and cup my hand around his knot, pressing some of my weight into it for balance, he gasps. "Fuck, Serena. *Yes*."

Jonah's hazy brown eyes watch me work. His brawny fingers dig into my hips, circling me around his monster cock harder and faster.

The rolls of his hips force me to suck Avery deeper than I ever have before. He puts a hand on my head, helping hold me steady while he takes full advantage.

Spencer spits out a curse. "Fuck her throat, Avery," he grinds. When he tightens his hold on me, I feel his fingertips press into the glide of Avery's piercings. "Harder."

Avery obeys, snapping his hips, panting as I whine. Spencer's dark eyes drip approval and burning, prideful *lust*. He grips me tighter, letting me focus on the friction for myself.

"Feel that?" he breathes, jacking himself furiously. "I'm going to come feeling him in your tight little throat. Imagining it was *me*, choking you with my cock instead of my hand."

I've been so preoccupied with Avery in my mouth, I didn't realize a new climax was sneaking up on me. Now, as Tristan roars and ruts even *faster*, I veer into another orgasm.

This one blinds me, whiting out the entire room. A keen catches around Avery's dick, which immediately spurts hot and hard down my throat. Behind me, Spencer shouts and paints my bare back in cum, glazing me the way he likes.

Tristan erupts. Scorching lashes of cum fill my backside until I'm dripping down my thighs and onto Jonah's lap.

The big man rolls into my pussy's desperate squeezes one last time before jerking and growling. Quick as a flash, he lunges for the blank side of my neck, but Spencer catches him, taking his hand off my throat...

And putting it onto Jonah's.

I gasp, watching him squeeze the burly alpha's neck, holding him down while my pussy flutters all around him.

Jonah careens over the edge. His balls draw up so hard, I feel them through his throbbing knot. Scorching jets of cum paint my pussy as he moans.

"I'm here," I whisper, panting and laying my forehead against his. "I'm right here, Jo."

Spencer lets him go the second he starts to shake. But they all keep their hands on me as the room slips away.

forty-eight

"SERENA."

Nope. I'm way too warm and comfortable to wake up.

Snuggling into the solid, naked alpha in front of me, I shake my head and turn my face, hiding against a muscled wall of chest hair.

Jonah.

His name brings a flood of memories.

The fierce lines of his face when he lost control. How scary it was to be swept up by an alpha as big as him. The way I had to make a snap decision about how much to give him. How I passed out almost the second he finished.

Shit.

I never got to talk to him about what happened. If it was okay for me to do that with him when he'd been so careful about waiting.

I gasp, scrambling to open my eyes and find his, pushing on his chest for purchase. To my shock, he instantly slides away from me.

Shit, shit, shit.

My frantic eyes scan his face in the pre-dawn gray, finding his golden eyes doing the same to me.

Oh. Is he worried *he's* upset *me*?

"Serena," he starts again, rough with emotion. "I am so sorry. I—I can't even tell you how fucking *sorry* I am."

I open my mouth and try to reassure him, but he's more frantic by the second, running his shaking hands over my arms, my sides, my hips.

"Did I hurt you?" he mumbles, squinting to see my skin... and the bruises splotched on my thighs. "Jesus. Of course I hurt you. I'm almost three hundred fucking pounds, and you—you're—"

Horror flashes through his gaze. "Oh fuck. I didn't knot you, did I? Serena, I swear to God, I will go and drown myself in the fucking pool if I knotted you or tried to bite or—"

"*Hey,*" I snap, then soften. "Whoa. Slow down, big man. I'm okay. See? I'm fine."

There's a moment of tense stillness. Then he snatches me into his arms, snuggling me tightly and dropping his face to mine.

"God," he breathes, kissing my cheeks, my eyelids, my nose. "I'm so fucking sorry, hummingbird. So sorry. I love you so much, I never would have—"

I go rigid in his arms, suddenly fighting to breathe. "Y-you —*what?*"

He rolls onto his back, bringing my body with his. Cuddling me sweetly. "I love you," he murmurs, certain and steady. "You're *everything* to me. Maybe I should have told you before. I just wanted you to feel ready."

Ready for him. Ready to accept all of the things he's been trying to give me since the first night he attempted to wrestle Avery out of my room. And every day after—with each plate of food and every patient life lesson. All of his cuddles and his jokes and the reverent way he touches me all the time.

He loves me.

My heart swells and soars as tears well in my eyes.

Because, well.

No one has ever said that to me before.

I know Avery has, in his way. Without words. But this feels different.

Splatters spill over my lashes and Jonah softens even more, cradling me against him so tenderly.

"*Manamea,*" he sighs. "I love you so much. I'm so sorry. I'll do anything to make this up to you. I'll talk to Doc about taking rut-blockers. They can bench me if they have to, I don't fucking care—"

I press my fingertips into his lips, feeling his facial hair against the pads. My nipples prick, but I ignore them, mumbling my plea.

"Say it again."

His sweet scent deepens as he rolls us back, putting me underneath him and stretching his arm over my head to pet my hair. His warm gaze sinks into mine, all sincerity and devotion. "I love you."

When more tears stream from my eyes, he says it again. And again. He whispers it into my skin as he kisses me, then settles between my legs.

Again as I nip at his neck, and again when he gently presses into my pussy.

My core trembles, welcoming him back without any complaint. We move together while he leaves love all across my skin. Until I swear I can *feel* it sinking into my soul.

This time, he works himself into me much slower. The ledge of his brow folds over his amber eyes, betraying hesitation.

"I'm too fucking big," he mutters, worry singeing the edges of his toasty scent.

I smooth my fingers over the creases in his forehead. "No, you were right. I'm your mate—and we fit *perfectly*."

I swear I catch a bit of mist in his eyes before he bears down, finally giving me what I want. And—*God*—it really is perfect.

Once I'm gasping and moaning around the earth-shattering thickness of his cock, he goes rigid, holding himself still.

Holding himself *back*.

"I want it," I beg, breathing hard. "I want you to knot me."

But he shakes his head. "It's too much," he mumbles. "I don't want to knot you alone. I want one of the guys here in case something happens, and I—"

I can't exactly argue with him. He is huge. Twice as wide as me, over a foot taller. Solid muscle and plenty of padding, to boot.

Still, I press my pussy up into the mass expanding at the base of his length. "I want you, though," I practically cry. "Please."

His eyes flare with panic, even as his face crumbles, the longing plain in every feature. "*Manamea*, I—"

"Knot her, Jonah."

We both still at the low, even voice that speaks from the threshold of the room.

Tristan stands there in nothing more than a pair of gray sweatpants. Arms crossed, leaning into the doorjamb, he looks rumpled and gorgeous in the half-light.

Did he... stay up all night? Sitting in the hallway? To make sure we were okay in here?

One glance into his deep blue eyes tells me *yes*. He did.

He approaches the bed slowly, each step measured and smooth. "I'm right here, Jonah," he says, calm. "I'll make sure you don't accidentally hurt her."

Part of me wants to tell him there have been dozens of times when *he's* hurt me and he couldn't even tell. So why he thinks he's qualified to act as my emotional barometer is beyond me.

Then again, if it will make Jonah more comfortable, how can I say no?

Especially right now. When his huge, thick cock is *splitting me in half* for the *second time tonight,* and all I can think is *more, deeper, now.*

Until that horrible voice hisses, *Just a silly little—*

But no.

I tell it no.

Because Jonah *loves me.* He *said* so. And even if I hadn't believed him, I would now, when he examines every curve of my features for any trace of hesitation.

I love him, too. And I know how much it will mean to him to have this memory with me.

"The Senator can watch," I whisper, trying for a teasing smile that must look a little crazy, considering how desperate I feel with his thickness lodged wide and hard and way too still inside me.

Tris drifts closer, and Jonah exhales against my neck. His rough palm practically covers my entire thigh while he rubs sweetly at the trembling muscles.

"You sure, hummingbird? You want my knot?"

I twine my arms around his neck. "Yes. *Please,* Alpha."

With a quiet groan, Jonah shifts his hips, reminding me just how deep and thick he really is. *Fuck.* I really hope I'm not being too cavalier about—

Oh.

OH!

A shrill whine splits the air when Jonah tilts his hips and shoves the top half of his knot past the tight ring quivering at my entrance. An odd mix of pain and pleasure buzzes through my body—my internal muscles singing with joy while the ones stretched around his girth scream in protest.

When Jonah turns to stone again, the pain wins out, and I whimper. He tenses, bracing to rip himself out.

But Tristan's hand lands on his packmate's shoulder at the same second his other palm finds the crown of my head. "Shhh, sweet one," he soothes, gazing down at me. "Jonah's not going to stop."

Then, to his packmate. "If you pull back now, you'll only hurt her more. Press all the way in and she'll be much better."

I whine again, nodding frantically and biting my lip to keep from crying. Tristan's long fingers pet my head in slow caresses. "I know," he murmurs, "I know, baby. Your alpha is going to make you feel better, okay?"

He infuses a bark into his voice. "Jonah, *now*."

With a sloughed growl, Jonah's pained eyes fly to mine, and his body bears down against me. Finally, the lower half of his knot pops into place.

And I *explode*.

Into a million shimmery pieces. Into stardust and shining euphoria.

The feeling is so incredible, it doesn't even make *sense*. It's impossible. Too perfect. Too glorious and complete and full.

Jonah roars, the deep sound vibrating against my breasts while he buries his face against my shoulder. "Fuck, Serena," he roughs out, the words nearly a sob. "You're so fucking *good*."

I can't understand what he's talking about when, clearly, he's the one who's hit the reboot button on my very *existence*. And now I'll just be glitter, floating around in space for eternity.

Or so I think.

Until he *moves*.

Holy. Fuck.

His knot tugs on every nerve inside of me, grinding into the sizzling pleasure points with every nudge of his hips. I moan, my pussy gushing slick and perfume until I swear I feel a puddle underneath me.

"There's a good girl," Tristan murmurs, softer. "Squirting all over your big alpha. You're so beautiful, stretched like this."

Thinking about his obscene view only makes me tremble

harder, my body wound to the breaking point. Jonah noses at my pulse, sucking at my neck while he works me in circles. His groin hits my clit every time he finishes a rotation, bringing me to the edge of a cliff I'm afraid to jump from.

But Tristan is there, solid and steady, pumping reassurance into the air with that unflappable calm of his. "You're going to come all over that huge knot," he tells me, blue eyes flashing. "And he'll be locked inside you for the rest of the night."

After spending years dreaming of this—*needing this*—the thought alone is enough to push me over. My core cinches, squeezing everything Jonah has with enough force to rip a scream from my lips.

"Fuck," he gasps, snarling my name. "Fuck, Serena."

With a final growl, the solid weight inside of me doubles—pressing out, rubbing around. Filling every nook until throbbing heat strokes the pulse echoing from my clit to my inner walls.

One climax rolls right into another, both of us coming twice before we manage to find one another again. His lips brush mine, reverent and panting.

"*Manamea.* You're really mine now, yeah? My omega?"

Fresh tears rise in my eyes while I squeeze him with my arms and legs, nodding into his broad shoulder.

"Yes," I cry quietly. "Yes, your omega."

He nestles into the crook of my neck, breathing shakily and squeezing his eyes shut while I nuzzle his bearded cheek.

He stays locked deep while we settle into one another, my hands roaming his back as he calms. Tristan is gone—and I don't know when he disappeared from the bedside to let us have our moment, but I find it touching how much he respects his packmates.

Jonah sinks against me, settling. But in my middle, there's a quick flicker of light. Just enough to make me turn my head and look toward the doorway, where our pack leader has paused to watch me comfort our big man.

The flare inside sparks into a full-blown feeling. The first one he's ever *voluntarily* shared.

And it's...

Gratitude.

For me.

He doesn't say the words, but I see them on his face and feel them inside, as clear as any said out loud. *Thank you, omega.*

forty-nine

THE DUMBEST ASSHOLES ALIVE

JONAH

everyone better be extra fucking sweet to my omega today

SPENCER

Why? Is she sick? Did you hurt her?

I told Tristan it was too much for you to spend the night with her.

She was probably sore, and I doubt you held back.

JONAH

Fuck off, she's PERFECT.

I cleaned her up and fed her another dinner before we went back to sleep.

But I had to leave her in bed to go to practice.

So you all better step up your cuddle game QUICK

AVERY

say less

didn't get to kiss her all night

some other motherfuckers have been hogging her.

SPENCER

I can see to her, Avery. I don't have class today.

JONAH

Ave, it's *morning* what the fuck are you doing up?

And, Spence, did you SKIP A CLASS?

AVERY

I don't know what you're talking about.

I love mornings.

SPENCER

I canceled a class.

I did not skip it.

There's a difference.

JONAH

Are we all just pretending we're not complete and total simps now?

AVERY

yep.

SPENCER

Yes.

TRISTAN

The motion carries.

"GOOD MORNING."

Spencer sits in the sunken living room of the townhouse with his ankle casually crossed over his knee. He turns the page of his newspaper and glances at me over the top of his reading glasses.

As if this is *completely normal*.

Like I didn't get railed while they all watched last night. And he isn't missing work.

"You aren't in class," I say, feeling dumb.

His mouth pinches. I can't tell if he's holding back a scowl or a smile. "No, I'm not."

On the couch perpendicular to Spencer's, a black blob suddenly moves. I bite back a scream when I see that it's just Avery, fighting his way out of a blanket. Naked, aside from his boxer briefs. And, apparently, awake?

Well, sort of. He's downstairs, anyway.

Avery is *definitely* scowling. But he opens his arms and makes a grabbing motion with his hands. "Get your ass over here, kitten. Before I strangle someone for fun."

Spencer turns another page. Lord, he's a fast reader. "Avery."

My inked alpha rolls his gorgeous eyes. "Sorry, sorry," he mutters. "But it's *eight a.m.* This is disgusting."

Chuckling, I shuffle over to him and try to sit beside his hip.

He isn't having it, though. Two seconds later, I'm lying on top of him.

"Mm," he mumbles, sleepy. "That's better."

I shake my head, smiling. When I glance over at Spencer, I find him staring back, his eyes as intense as ever. "You're feeling well?" he asks, brow folding.

He's worried they permanently broke my brain.

I nod, feeling shy. "I'm okay."

His mouth almost ghosts up. "Good. I hope Jonah let you get some sleep. Because we have to be at the dean's office in an hour and a half."

I try to jerk upright, but Avery snarls softly and pets my head while pushing it back down to his chest.

"Dean?" I croak. "Of... your college? For what?"

He snaps his paper. "It's a university, not a college. And we're meeting with the dean so I can call in some favors and get you enrolled."

I'm stunned speechless, my mouth hanging open. Avery sees it through the one eyelid he has cracked and smirks, reaching up to close my jaw.

"You said that was the worst part," Spencer explains, his dark eyes roiling when they land back on mine. "Not being able to go to school. Now, you can take any classes you'd like. Although, I do have some suggestions, of course."

My mind reels, but Avery snickers. "Whatever he says, don't take any of his classes. He's a dick."

I'm still not sure I believe what's happening, but I mumble back, "It's probably not a good idea, anyway. I wouldn't be able to concentrate."

A flare lights Spencer's dark eyes. He arches a brow. "I can't imagine why not, Miss Swanson."

———— ♥ ————

I WEAR the little black dress Spencer set out for the game yesterday. It's posh and pretty, with a rounded white collar and the matching bow headband.

The Professor might prefer this preppy look, but I've decided I like to mix things up when it comes to my clothes. For better or worse, sexy stuff is what I'm comfortable in, and I walk better in heels than I do wedges or sandals.

I worry Spencer may not approve of the short, pleated skirt for school, but his gaze radiates approval when I rush out of my room—until he sees the platform-heeled Mary Janes strapped to my feet. Then I get a flash of white-hot electricity.

His scent swells as his eyes trace my legs, but he simply offers me a gentlemanly elbow. "Shall we?"

Even with a noticeable bulge in his tweed trousers, his proper courtesies never waver. He opens my car door for me in our garage, and again after we glide into a special reserved parking spot that literally has his name on it. The second the Volvo door locks, he has my arm wound through his again.

He gives a steady lecture on the university's history and its reputation as we turn for a winding brick walkway. Without missing a beat, he ushers me between two ivy-covered buildings and nods at various places as he gives brief run-downs of each.

My heart flutters while I gaze up at his sharp profile, only absorbing his words half as much as I soak in the feeling his tour gives me. On his arm, for all to see, his approval and respect feel like a cloak around my shoulders.

And, for once, I'm not just a slut. Or a hot piece of ass. Or even a precious omega in need of protection.

Right now? With Spencer? I feel like a *lady*.

His lady.

The most particular alpha in the universe picked *me*. And he's squiring me around his workplace like I'm a duchess.

When I cuddle closer into his side, he reaches over to grasp the hand wound around his forearm. The soft curve of his mouth is the only hint I get that he's pleased, aside from a fierce flex of alpha approval.

I love that it's just for me.

No one else would ever know.

Is this how he feels when I tell him I like him?

We finally reach a big building with stone pillars and carved archways. He stops in front of it, turning me to face him.

"Now, then." I expect him to inspect me for lint or maybe fuss over my hair, but instead, he cups my face between his long-fingered hands. Stepping up against my body, he only pauses for one small second when he feels my hands slide under his blazer. I carefully smooth my touch down his sides, moving slow enough for him to stop me at any moment.

A silent breath quivers out of him, ruffling my bangs. "We have an appointment," he husks, but it isn't one of his usual chastisements. More a lament.

I lean my head back to tease him with a smirk. "Oh, you didn't want to make out in front of the dean's office?"

Another wave of pride washes over me, along with an undeniable flare of affection. To my delight, he plays along, raising both silver-blond brows. "No, actually. I wanted to do this."

My pulse skips as he bends over and nuzzles his cheek against mine. The motion is deliberate and careful, his eyes guarded as he switches to rub the other cheek.

Butterflies swarm my stomach.

He's scent-marking me.

Here. On campus. Right before we meet with his boss.

My eyes feel wet as he pulls back and studies me. Softer electricity snaps through his dark gaze. Seeing me, understanding me.

And still wanting *me*.

In spite of my scent and my past and all the alpha-omega dynamics he dislikes, Spencer wants me.

One of his thumbs catches a teardrop just before it smears my makeup. His lips curve fondly as he re-tucks my hand into the crook of his elbow. "Come along, darling."

PRIDE ISN'T NECESSARILY a foreign emotion for me.

I felt proud when Jonah's team won the Super Bowl last year. When Tristan won his election. Even when Avery got called up to the UFC.

But nothing compares to watching Serena shake hands with the dean of my university. Watching him smile and nod while she shyly tells him she's always wanted to study psychology. And my delighted surprise when she shares the idea of becoming a mental health counselor one day.

She'd be fantastic at that. Her special blend of kindness and sharp humor would probably help people feel comfortable. She's also been through a hell of a lot more than the average person—which would make her uniquely qualified.

It only takes a couple of hours to get her squared away. Since the semester is just beginning, she's able to choose two beginner psych classes to start with. They're simple courses, taught by some of my kinder colleagues. A perfect place for her to start.

And, I note with an unfamiliar burst of wicked satisfaction, if she stays on this track, she'll have to take one of *my* courses next spring.

Her class has its second lecture of the semester today, so I walk her over and drop a kiss to her cheek before stepping away. Shock blinks across her features, as if she's surprised that I'm leaving her alone, giving her the freedom to go into her class and find me afterward.

When I think about what she's told me, I guess that makes sense. She's probably never been allowed to walk around a public place to her heart's content.

Which is why I want to give her this.

It's also why I wait outside the building for ten minutes before secretly peering into the lecture hall to make sure she's safely inside. When I find her sitting beside another omega, chatting with a timid smile, my chest gives a hard twinge.

Is this what a heart attack feels like?

No, I think. I'm fairly certain a clogged artery wouldn't make me grin like an idiot.

WHATEVER SATISFACTION I felt at seeing her happily ensconced in class is long gone two hours later.

The *longest* two hours of my entire career.

Haven't I spent countless days sitting in my office, at this very desk, without so much as glancing up? Now, I can't seem to last longer than ten minutes.

My focus constantly shifts to the arched window behind me and the clouds rolling overhead.

Damn it. I should have left her an umbrella. But surely, she'll call me if she needs me to come collect her? Maybe I should just wait for her, either way. Or would that be overbearing?

The tracking app I snarled at Tristan about is shamefully handy. I keep it open while I attempt to work, glancing at it and the gathering storm until finally—*blessedly*—her glowing blue dot starts to move toward the building that houses my office.

A light sprinkle has just begun when I hear a quiet knock on my door. "Come in, Miss Swanson."

Our omega slips into the dim room a moment later. I see she did get a little wet, but not much. Her hair is slightly damp, and a few beads of water cling to her perfect skin as she shuts the door behind her.

"Lock it."

The command snaps out before I can stop myself. I don't know why I said it, but she casts me one of her surprised little smiles and obeys anyway, turning the deadbolt.

While I drink her in, reassuring the beast inside me that his mate is here and whole and safe, she turns to the bookshelves built into the nearest wall, running her eyes over them.

"A lot of your textbooks are part of my library already," I realize. "We can use the copies I keep at home."

She bites the corner of her lip and nods. Those big green eyes sweep over to the worktable stationed opposite the books. They land on the chessboard laid out there—and the abandoned match set on top of it.

A charge snaps between us, her curiosity lighting my blood. "Who are you playing?" she asks, eyes dancing.

I narrow my gaze slightly. "Myself."

No doubt she'll wrinkle her nose at me. Or just nod and pretend I'm not odd.

But her pretty lips spread into an even lovelier grin. "Who's winning?"

For the first time in as long as I can remember, I *laugh*. The startled sound scrapes out of me before I can help it, and Serena's gaze twinkles in reply.

"If you ever want a real match, I used to play against myself all the time, too," she adds, stroking over one of the ivory pieces. "I bet I'd win."

With anyone else, I might scoff. But that sharp, curious glint in her gaze reminds me how intelligent she is. And gives me the distinct notion that she may be correct.

Even more unthinkable—I *hope* she's correct.

That strange, prideful feeling swells inside of me again. Only, this time, it's layered with fondness. Appreciation, really, and—

Hell. I'm pretty sure it's just love.

I... *love* her.

Even without her scent permeating the air, like it does at home. Even after losing a full day of work to show her around and get her settled and worry about her for no good reason...

I love her.

As if to protest the very first romantic notion of my life, her scent begins winding through the small office. With rain soaked into the creamy coconut, she smells like a perfect summer storm. Fresh and bright, but lush and sweet.

It's *mythical*.

Ambrosia and sunlight and some piece of me that got lost, somehow, somewhere—but it's back now. Returned to make me whole.

Instead of overriding my feelings, it adds a sensual bent to the emotions swirling through me. My cock hardens before I even swivel my desk chair, leaning back and opening my arms.

"Come."

Serena obeys, sauntering over on her sexy heels and gracefully settling sideways across my lap. Like a tease, she angles a taunting smirk at me. But she's still a good girl, keeping her hands in her lap, waiting for my subtle nod before she smooths them down my dress shirt.

It's getting easier for me to let her do as she likes. Maybe because I trust her now.

Instead of fear or aggression, all I feel as her fingertips trace my buttons are the tingles they leave in her wake. On the other side of my sternum, a purr rumbles to life, layering my words with rough reverberations.

"How was your first class, Miss Swanson?"

She flashes a sweeter smile, her eyes dropping to her bare legs. "It was good, I think. I met another omega, and she invited me to a study group. I—If that's okay?"

My chest burns for her, the purr deepening while I tuck her closer. "Of course it's okay, darling. I'll bring you to your study group any time."

When our eyes meet again, all traces of humor flee her face, leaving it stark with emotion. Her hand trembles as she reaches up and strokes over my cheekbone. "Thank you, Spencer."

My darling girl.

I cup her hand in mine, turning it to press a kiss to her knuckles. "It was my pleasure."

Gradually, her expression turns from sincerity back to teasing. "Your pleasure, huh?" She flicks her gaze pointedly to the erection trapped under her thighs.

I see the exact moment an evil idea hits her. "Professor," she starts, running her hot little hands down my chest again. "Didn't you say you wanted me to come to your office after class for *a special lesson*?"

The way I scowl isn't put on—at first. I'm embarrassed that it takes me a moment to realize she's playing a part, acting for the ongoing game between us.

But once I catch up, I keep the disapproving expression in place. "You kept me waiting."

The reprimand isn't entirely false. I truly got no work done while I waited for her.

She must see the honest frustration in my face because hers is instantly contrite. "I'm sorry, Professor," she replies, sweeping her gaze to the side in supplication. "I didn't mean to keep you waiting."

"Hmm," I hum, unimpressed. My hungry gaze roves over her body. "I was going to ease you into today's lesson, but now we have no time for that. I suppose we'll just have to get right to it."

Her pupils expand, edging out her gorgeous green-gold irises. "Yes, Professor."

Fuck, but that makes my knot *throb*.

I've tried to make sense of this too many times to count. Hundreds of students have called me Professor and I've never so much as blinked.

But Serena is special. Something about the honest trepidation and carnal interest filling her face—the way she knows *exactly* when to look me in the eye and when to demur.

She's just... perfect.

Perfect for me.

My mate.

Ignoring the fresh ache tugging at my chest, I lift my chin. "Go stand at the side of my desk, Miss Swanson. And remove your panties."

A shiver moves through her as a burst of sweet perfume wafts into the air. She moves off my lap, leaving my dick aching in protest, and gingerly makes her way to the side of the large mahogany desk.

With her usual sleek grace, she glides her hands under her skirt and shimmies her underwear down, stepping out of the ivory lace before turning to me for further instruction.

I slide a stack of books to the other side of my desk and point to the wood.

"Today's lesson: Presenting."

Her quiet gasp makes my shaft jerk. As I push to my feet, she does her best to follow my unspoken command, hinging at the hips to present as best she can while standing. Her breasts flatten into the unforgiving wood, along with her stomach. Her dress rides up, barely keeping her bare ass covered while she turns her head to wait.

She's so pretty like this.

But not quite perfect.

I *tsk*, circling her with my hands behind my back. To her, it probably looks as if I'm inspecting a troublesome sight, but really, I have to lace my fingers together to keep from running them up the backs of her trembling thighs.

I finally allow myself one caress, smoothing my palm from her ass cheek to the back of her knee as I hum, "Hmm. No. This won't do."

The way her scent shifts—edging into something darker— only adds to our game. As does the way she looks to the floor. "Teach me, Professor. Please?"

A current snaps up my spine, drawing a growl from my chest. "Very well."

"To present properly," I begin, dropping into my typical lecture voice. "An omega must be on his or her knees. Chest flat, arms stretched out overhead."

I hear her breath catch, but a moment later, she moves. Carefully folding her knees up onto the desk, tucking them close to her abdomen while she follows my instructions.

When she settles, her dress is halfway up her naked ass. And, from behind, I can see every inch of her wet, wanting pussy.

While I stare at the dark, glistening lips, her tight little entrance quivers. I want to see her asshole do the same. And technically, proper omega presentation would give me the perfect view of *everything*.

"Lift your rear," I murmur, too husky to snap. "Push your hips back."

She obeys beautifully. A textbook presentation that puts her glorious cunt and rounded ass just over the edge of the desk, hovering above the cock-teasing heels she has crossed under her.

Fucking hell.

Serena whines, but there's no distress in it. Only soft pleading. I smooth my hand over her warm, perfect skin again, sliding her dress to the small of her back.

"How does it feel, omega?"

"Good," she swallows. "Professor."

"Mm. Tell me: Do you like presenting for your professor, Miss Swanson? Showing him this pretty, slick cunt?"

"Y-yes."

I can't decide if I should spank her for that or reward her. What starts as a firm slap to her ass ends with me trailing my fingers through her heat, sucking in a gasp of my own when I feel how wet and *soft* she is.

Goddamn it.

Well, I did tell her this would be quick.

Stroking my thumb against her clit, I drop my voice lower. "This cunt pleases me, Miss Swanson. That means you get to come on my fingers before I fuck you."

She whimpers, rearing up slightly. "*Please, Professor.*"

I unhook my belt with one hand, pulling it through the loops. "Give me your wrists. Place them against your back."

She shifts, balancing carefully while she moves into position. I secure the leather around her wrists in a loose loop, stroking her pulse as I go and pausing to check in with her. "Good, darling?"

Her nod is fervent. "Yes, Professor."

My voice stays quiet. "I want to knot you," I say, admitting it to myself as much as her.

She moans softly. "Please, Spencer. *Please.*"

I can see how much she wants it—how her body literally flutters at the thought. My thumb slides up from her clit to tease the clutching muscles. "Okay, darling girl. You can have my knot, hmm? Take it in this beautiful cunt until you scream for me."

Her sloping spine rises on an inhale. "W-won't everyone hear us, Professor? All your colleagues... and my—"

"Yes," I grit, shoving at my pants until they bunch around my quads. "You'll scream while I knot this pussy, Miss Swanson.

You'll scream loud enough for every one of your other professors to hear you and know you're *mine*."

Possession roars through my blood. I'll be damned if any of the assholes I work with think they can take what's *mine*. And she needs to know, too.

I'll show her.

Teach her that this game is only for me.

Starting with my hand around her throat.

The second I close my fingers around the claim mark branded into her neck, her perfume explodes. A dense fog of arousal, so sweet I swear I can taste it in the air.

My pulse throbs in my dick and my knot, twitching in the open air behind her exposed pussy. I slip my touch back over her clit, licking my lower lip and pulling it between my teeth while I watch her clench and writhe into the pressure.

When she comes, a gush of slick slips out of her sex. And I can't restrain myself one second longer.

"Very good, Miss Swanson," I growl, lining myself up at her pulsing core. "Now, can you pull my knot into your pussy?"

She pants, nodding. The hand at her throat tenses as I press forward, sinking the first few inches into her glorious warmth. She starts to whine but muffles the noise against the desk.

I strangle a groan, speaking over it while I land a slap to her ass. "What did I say about hiding your moans?"

"Sorry, Professor," she demurs, shifting to take more of me. But I hold still, making her beg. "I'll be good," she breathes. "I promise."

I smile, knowing she can't see me. "Hmm. All right then."

Plush heat slides around my cock as I push deeper. Another snarl sloughs out, met by a gorgeous keen from Serena.

I ordinarily hate noise—but *this*? The fact that every cry from her lips means she's mine, screaming and gushing on my dick for every last person in this building to hear?

My Alpha roars with approval and desperation. She feels the twin sensations beating in the air and perfumes again, a fresh burst of slick swirling around the head of my cock like a silken whirlpool.

Fuck. FUCK.

When she squeals, I realize I've clamped my fingers around her throat again. I let up, dizzy as I smooth a soothing touch over her hammering heartbeat.

She whimpers, trembling with want but doing her absolute best to stay still. To be good for me.

"I know, darling girl," I husk, pride and tenderness bleeding into my chest. "I know."

She pants as I slip my free hand underneath her, pressing two fingertips flat against her clit. The swollen bud throbs against my touch while I snap my hips, bottoming out.

Goddamn it. How does she feel so *good*? It's beyond perfection. Mythic, just like her scent.

The smooth, slick glide. Heat and snugness that slips over every inch of my hardness, right down to the knot twitching fuller by the second.

I grind it against her pussy lips, groaning when their warm wetness kisses my stretched skin.

Her next moan breaks off in a high-pitched cry. "Please, Professor. *Alpha! Please.*"

Knotting isn't foreign to me, but this is the first time I've done it without a single thought in mind. It was an experiment before. Data, not desire.

But this? Now?

My instincts lunge, sinking my knot past the tight ring of muscle at her entrance.

Good. Holy. God.

All the pressure and heat bathing my cock absolutely *strangles* my knot.

It's *incredible*. Almost *too* incredible. Every thought I've ever had evaporates. And—for one long moment—I'm lost. My spine locks straight as my lungs heave, fighting to breathe. Waiting for my mind to blink back online.

The brush of fingertips against my dress shirt brings me back into my body. I glance down, finding Serena's hand twisted in its belt cuff. Gently touching my forearm. Grounding me.

When I look into her eyes, though, I don't just find Serena. Her pupils are completely blown, her expression caught between dazed pleasure and something much deeper.

It's her... *and* her Omega. Comforting me. Knowing that I need it.

That bursting, bleeding sensation floods my abdomen again.

Love.

It has to be. Nothing else could feel like this.

It's the only emotion I've ever had that I don't feel the need to question or understand. The single strand of chaos that I *want* to allow in my existence.

I feel it pouring out of her, too. Serena—and her Omega. They love me.

And my Alpha.

The beast I've kept chained for decades.

But, for her...

I let him snap forward for the first time in as long as I can remember. Ready to rip the reins right back. Ready for him to rut or ruin this, somehow, because that's what beasts *do*—

But he doesn't.

He just... looks. Our eyes connect—her soul to mine. And the hand around her throat moves without my permission—

Soothing her. *Loving* her. Caressing down the beautiful line of her spine. Over to the side of her hip, the small of her back.

"Mine," I say.

We say.

Her dark eyes glitter with approval and tenderness. "Yours, Alpha," she breathes, pressing back slightly, her body begging along with her mouth. "*Please.*"

Yes.

The thought belongs to both parts of me—enemies who finally agree on something.

One thing. *This.*

I knot her deeper, shoving the last bit of myself into her glorious heat, groaning when her inner muscles tug at the thick swell expanding inside of her.

I pump my hips harder, and Serena shrieks again. The sound echoes through my office, blending with the patter of rain. Fitting, since my scent has swelled to fill the room like a thundercloud all its own.

Knowing we don't have much time before we're sealed together, I rut her faster and reach back down to stroke her clit. It beats between my fingertips as I rub her in firm circles, snarling when her pussy clamps around everything I have.

"Spen-cer!" she cries, kneading my knot and drawing my cock as deep it will go. "Alpha! I—I—"

"*Come,*" I command. "Come on my knot."

Her body obeys, slick heat caving around my cock in fierce spasms. I loose a shout of my own, bending over and sinking my teeth into the blank stretch of her shoulder, jaw shaking while I barely manage not to break her skin.

Fuck, fuck, fuck.

I've never come so hard or so long. My release *blasts* her cunt, filling her depths until she's squelching. Squirming. Whimpering my name. Flooded with my scent.

Mine.

MINE.

The thought lights up every receptor in my brain as I snuggle into Serena's back. She's standing at the kitchen counter beside our sink, humming while she moves a succulent into a new container.

I squeeze my arms around her, wincing when I recall the way I snatched her up during my rut. My lips skim her shoulder in silent apology.

We're starting to have moments when it feels like we're

already bonded. As I nuzzle her skin, she fits herself more firmly against me, turning to catch my lips with a reassuring sound.

Mm. Practice was endless today and having her in my arms feels like heaven.

I don't even have to worry about sharing her with Avery and his grabby paws—he's entered the really intense part of his training for the fight next week. It will be hours before he comes crawling in here, but I'll leave dinner in the fridge for him and a place in our omega's bed, too.

Can't guarantee either of us will have our clothes on, but...

Behind us, I hear the Thorne brothers coming, each from their own sides of the house. This time, though, Spencer sounds focused, and Tris is dragging.

As Spence walks into the room, his dark eyes are focused and intent. And he's—

Smiling.

"Ah," he says, ignoring me as he comes straight to Serena.

The fact that he doesn't bitch about the newspapers spread over the counter or the small black pots full of soil is a miracle. Let alone the fact that he glances over at Serena's dirty, working hands with *pride*. He presses right past me, brushing my arm like it's not even there.

"There you are, darling," he murmurs, bending to kiss her head. His gaze finds hers, warmer and softer than I've ever seen it. "I have that textbook you need. I'll go leave it on your dresser, and we'll review this week's lessons later, hmm?"

"Yes, Professor." Serena beams at him but keeps her hands off, even when she tilts her face up.

And my best friend doesn't skip a beat, dropping a soft kiss on her parted lips.

Damn. I guess he was serious last week when he came home after Serena's first day at school and told the rest of us that he was going to start reviewing bonding techniques for her heat.

Which is so soon that I swear I can feel it beating in the air sometimes.

Like now, as Spence whispers too low for me to overhear, leaving Serena with an even brighter grin. He strides off toward her bedroom, and we both turn to watch him.

Putting us face-to-face with Tristan.

Things have been less stilted between them ever since the rut. He still holds himself back, and she still feels hurt by it, but at least they can share space easier.

And when her heat comes...

Well. I hope she'll choose to bond with him first. That way, we'll be able to form a pack bond, too. But that's entirely my hummingbird's decision. And Tristan has forbidden any of us to ask her for anything.

I see why as I watch the way his eyes sweep over her face.

He *loves* her.

Maybe from seeing the way she's melted his iceberg of a brother. Or the way she took on all of us last week and somehow left every member of our pack feeling cared for.

Maybe he always has—and this is just the first time I can *see* the longing pulling at his features.

The poor bastard.

When he catches me watching, his mouth curves into a grim smile. He's the only one she hasn't kissed. He never complains, but it must be rough.

Especially since their bodies are outright begging each other to get closer. The entire room is suddenly drenched in summertime sweetness—Tristan's grassy orange blossoms and Serena's piña colada perfection.

As her scent winds into the open air, I hear him wheeze. And I start to wonder—what if this isn't just *hard* on him?

What if it's *harming* him?

Our pack alpha seems determined not to let his pain show. He clears his throat and drops his gaze away from our omega's.

"I called Dr. Monroe," he says. "I've asked him to come do a pre-heat check-up for you this weekend, Serena. Is that all right?"

She sighs quietly and nods, clearly less than thrilled. I've noticed she gets that way about her heat. Avery and I have both tried to bring it up—mostly because I think neither of us can wait —but she usually changes the subject. Or her glorious perfume burns up instantly.

Sort of like now.

A stranger wouldn't notice the way Tristan's shoulders fall, but I do. He thinks it's his fault and starts to turn away. Backing off. Giving her space. *Again*. Like he can't see that this shit *isn't working* and—

"Senator."

He pauses mid-pivot, turning back to the beautiful girl between us. She picks up the pot she's been fiddling with, which now holds a perfectly packed assortment of succulent plants. After a beat, she thrusts it out to Tristan.

"For your office."

He blinks at the pot, then at Serena. "You got me a plant?"

She shakes her head. "I *grew* you a plant. Well, there are a bunch of them in there actually. But, um..." She shrugs, adorably awkward. "Yeah."

The corner of Tris's mouth ghosts up. "You grew this?"

She nods, and he gives her a self-deprecating smirk. "Then I would hate to kill it, sweet one. You keep it and let it live."

I expect Serena to accept the pot back. Another tiny rejection to add to her pile.

I really need to talk to Tris about this. It must hurt her feelings so—

But she gets the fiery look in her eye that she usually reserves for Avery. The one I see when I peek into our home gym and catch her beating the shit out of his punching bag.

"*You* keep it," she insists. "And figure out how to take care of it."

With a final kiss to my cheek, she turns and flounces right out of the room. My pack alpha and I look at each other, then down at the plant.

"Well, damn," I chuckle. "I don't think she could have been much clearer."

SPLIT LIPS ARE ONE THING, but have you ever had a split eyelid?

Shit hurts like a bitch.

By the time I park the Mustang in our garage, I've taken off my tank top and have it balled at the bleeding corner of my left eye. I sit there for a second, wondering how I'm going to hide my face from our omega if I sleep in her bed.

Our bed.

I'm pissed it's so late. I wanted to get home in time to have her ride my fucked-up face. I can't think of anything better for the bruises that will be all over it tomorrow.

Now it's midnight, and when I wake up tomorrow, I have to get serious about saving up my Alpha's energy for the fight this weekend.

Serena's being a cute little tease about my self-imposed celibacy, promising she'll make it as hard as possible for me to stick to my guns.

When I strung together a lame-ass apology for needing us to take a break so close to her heat, she just shrugged and slanted me one of those gorgeous, cock-teasing smirks. *"I have three other cocks to play with, Menace. Not even sure I'll miss yours. It's not like it's* special *or anything..."*

Considering just the memory of that taunt makes me hard enough to drive nails, I'm pretty sure I'm going to be a rabid beast by Friday night.

Ha.

It's funny because I already am one.

Stepping off the elevator, I walk into a wall of my kitten's lush brightness and Jonah's toasted smell. Their scents are tangled up and all over the counter, which means I missed a helluva time at dinner.

Growling under my breath, I start to trudge to the stairs, but the light in Spencer's study stops me.

I've never asked him to stitch me up before, but fixing my own eye is going to be a clusterfuck. And now I have someone who has to look at me for the rest of eternity, so.

"Hey, teach."

I push the door open and find Spencer lying on his lounge chair, holding a sheaf of papers over his face while our omega snuggles into his chest.

She's fast asleep, but I clock the way his shirt hangs open and her hands rest against his sternum.

When he follows my eyes. I expect him to snarl at me or pull his usual icicle act, but instead he sighs. "It's easier when I'm awake and she's asleep. Less chance I'll be surprised."

That makes sense. He's got to get used to her touching him before her heat.

"I know she's worried about it," I admit, scratching the back of my head with the hand not holding my bloody shirt to my eye.

Spencer looks down at her face, watching the way her eyelashes twitch. The quiet purr rattling under her cheek ramps up.

"It's not her fault," he murmurs, snapping his intense eyes up to mine. "Tris and Jonah are always giving me space, so I can't ask them this—but if I start to have an issue during her heat and I need my ass kicked..."

A smile cracks the half-healed cut in my lower lip. "I'll trade you. You fix my eye, and I'll kick your ass."

Spencer actually smirks. "Deal. Here, hold her while I fetch the first aid kit."

We get Serena settled into my lap and he strides off. Watching her curl up against my bare, inked-up chest brings my own purr out. The rusty roar isn't nearly as smooth as Spence's, though, and our girl stirs, nuzzling into the white claw marks branded over my heart.

Bleary green eyes blink up at me, big and beautiful and *mine.* Especially when they flare with that sharp, teasing warmth. "Mm. Should have known. You steal me from my professor, Menace?"

I smile, bending to kiss her forehead. "Little bit."

She gives another sleepy hum, hunkering down against my pecs. "Did your training run late?"

The truth is, it started late. "I had to fill out all sorts of bull-shit paperwork. They wanted my title and my entrance song and all that stupid shit."

"Hmm." She scent-marks my skin. "If you had a trainer, I bet they'd do all that for you."

She's not wrong. I grumble quietly, remembering what I marked on my papers. "The Ghost works alone."

Her pout is especially adorable, with her nose wrinkled and her eyes shut. "I don't want you to be a ghost," she complains, half out of it. Talking nonsense.

Only.

Maybe not.

I look down at her soft features, the long sweep of her gorgeous hair. All snuggled in Jonah's T-shirt, soaked in Spencer's scent. Cuddled up with me like I'm not the monster *I know* I am.

Fuck.

Maybe I don't want me to be a ghost, either.

Is that name even true anymore? I hear those two pussies from the gym, whispering behind my back. "*They call him the Ghost.*"

Because I fought like I didn't have anything to lose—like I was already dead.

I look down at Serena's face and know, down to the bottom of my shitty, ripped-up soul. "I'm not, kitten. Not anymore."

Mollified, she makes a content sound and huddles even closer. By the time Spence walks in, she's back to sleep.

He opens the first aid kit and examines my eye, wincing at the cut. "Was this strictly necessary? You could have lost your eye."

I snort. "Then you'd have one less thing to worry about."

He glares. "I'm serious, Avery. This is the reason I've never been able to stomach coming to your matches. What if you're seriously injured one day and—"

He keeps talking, but I can't focus. My brain skips over what he's said, replaying it.

"Wait, wait," I huff, scowling as he presses an alcohol swab to my split skin. "That's why you've never come to a fight? You're, like..."

Worried about me?

Spencer pauses long enough to parse out the words I don't say. His answering nod is brusque. "Of course. You think I want to watch my packmate get hurt? My Alpha practically climbs the walls every time I even consider it."

Fuck. And here I thought he'd been avoiding the matches

because he couldn't stand being linked to something so crude and repulsive.

Who knew the guy actually cared about keeping me in one piece?

Using a butterfly bandage and some sterile skin glue, he meticulously seals the cut while I stare at the side of his face, my jaw ticking.

Ah, hell.

"It would be cool," I finally force out. "If you'd come watch sometime."

Spencer sways back, blinking at me as he wipes his hands on a fresh sanitizing wipe. "It didn't occur to me that you ever noticed either way. But if you'd like me to come, of course I'll be there."

I bob my head, swallowing. "Okay."

He clears his throat and looks away. "That's settled, then."

"Cool."

Serena nestles closer to me, her lips twitching ever-so-slightly.

Just enough for me to know my brilliant little omega had this in mind all along.

chapter
fifty-three

"I'M COMING, I'M COMING," I mutter, tripping into my left heel and scurrying out of my room.

Geez. Jonah usually isn't so intense. I didn't even know he was home, and now he's down in the garage, laying on his horn like it's a hammock.

Avery took me to get my driver's license today, and my big man told me we were going to grab dinner to celebrate my newfound freedom after he finished practice.

Come to think of it, taking me anywhere super fancy really

isn't like Jonah. The fact that he texted to tell me to wear my best de-scenter and a fancy dress were both out of character too.

Now I'm wondering why I didn't ask more questions. Probably because I was so excited by the concept of an actual real-life date, I didn't want to discourage him.

I feel a little giddy about finally being able to drive us there, too. The form-fitting dress I dug out of the middle of my new wardrobe is short and tight enough not to distract me like a flowy skirt around my knees would.

Jade isn't a color I would normally pick, but Jonah loves my eyes so I figured I'd try to make them pop tonight. With all the craziness, this is the first time I've been out with my big man one-on-one, so I also took extra time with my hair and makeup.

But when I finally rush out of the elevator and into the garage, Jo isn't waiting next to his shiny white Bronco.

He isn't here at all.

Instead, Tristan Thorne stands there with his expression unruffled and his hands in the pockets of his gray suit.

Next to... the Batmobile?

It sure looks like the car from the movie Avery made the whole pack watch last Sunday. All sleek and matte black, slung low to the ground with the sorts of sexy angles that give the sense it's already in motion.

I stop up short, my platforms scraping against the concrete floor. "Um... hi?"

The corner of Tristan's mouth pulls up. "Hello."

I chance a few steps forward, eyeing the beautiful beast idling beside him. "What, um—what is *this*?"

Tristan's smile takes on a wry quality as he surveys the vehicle and turns back to me with a shrug. "Your car."

A startled guffaw jumps out of me. "My—*what*? This isn't a car; this is a missile. I barely have a license, and I'm pretty sure that's only because Avery threatened the guy at the DMV today."

No sex for my fighter has definitely turned him into a bit of a lunatic. But my heat hormones are almost as bad, so, you know—gotta find the ones who can match your freak.

Tristan's shoulders lift in another blasé roll. "I did make some calls. But you would have passed your test, anyway. You got a perfect score on the written exam and the practical. So I thought you deserved a gift."

He waves an arm at the car again. And gradually, it sinks in.

He isn't kidding.

This car is here *for me*.

I float closer, mouth hanging open. "Tristan—how did you —*why did you*—"

"I noticed you eying one at the valet stand when we went shopping. This model is top of the line, though. And it's a convertible."

I just gape. At the car. At him.

Why on earth would he do this? Is it his way of trying to get closer to me? Or yet another in an endless string of apologies?

Because—*I get it*. He's *sorry*. He's sorry he bit me and bonded me and brought me home. And it doesn't seem to matter that *I'm not* sorry anymore. Because he's remorseful enough for the both of us.

My head shakes. "I—I don't need this, Tristan. If it's some apology or a way to make yourself feel better I just—"

But he strides right to me. Closer than the polite distance he used to maintain so carefully. Fervor lights his features as he sinks those ocean irises into mine.

"It's not an apology or a bribe. I won't lie and say you don't deserve both, but that's not why I wanted to do this. It's a *gift*," he husks out. "Because you deserve beautiful things. And I want to be the man who gets them for you."

Oh. My. God.

Can I ask—how, exactly, does one argue with that?

No? Stop? Please?

I blink down at the sleek, outrageously beautiful convertible, trying to come up with any way I can possibly object.

And I only come up with one.

"You guys won't fit."

Tristan's dark brow creases. "You mean..."

"All of you," I murmur, brushing my fingers over the flawless matte-black hood. "I love this car, Tristan. It *is* beautiful, and it means a lot that you noticed how much I liked it, but... I won't be able to drive with everyone in the car. Like for..."

Family time.

The words sound so stupid in my head that I can't get them out.

I don't even know what I'm saying. I've never had a real family—and if we really wanted to be one, that would mean completing the bond with Tris before the others claim me.

Sometimes, I swear he can read my mind. It would bother me more if he weren't so damn kind about it.

As it is, Tristan just smiles—and God, it *isn't fair* how gorgeous he is when he does that. "Then I suppose I'll have to buy you another," he says. "For our family."

— ♥ —

WHEN TRISTAN ADMITS that Jonah's texts were a ruse and, really, the senator is the one taking me to dinner, I'm not even surprised. Of all my guys, Jo is definitely the softy. Of course he wanted to help Tris with...

Whatever this is.

I try to figure it out as he steers my car through the posh, brick streets surrounding the townhouse. He tried to convince me to drive, but I was too chicken. Besides, there are a lot worse things than this view...

The houses here are beautiful we pass French-country mansions, stately colonials, and a huge modern-Gothic estate that turns my head.

Good Lord—do those people have their own *greenhouse*?

Where *are* we?

Tris drives the Lamborghini like he was born to—which, I guess, he sort of was. Still, though, his casual handling and inherent sex appeal would be enough to have the interior soaked in my perfume if I hadn't bathed in de-scenter.

As much as it bothers me that he clearly had Jonah ask me to neutralize before we went out together, this time, I get it. What happened in that fancy store last week was beyond embarrassing.

When I mention it, though, he nearly jerks the car off the road before casting me a scowl.

After a long, furious beat, he curves two fingers at me. "Serena. Come here."

Brow creasing, I lean across the center console, wondering if he's about to try to kiss me or...

Instead, he tilts his head. Letting me get a good read of his scent, which—

Isn't there?

When I blink at him, he explains, "I thought it would be nice for us to spend some time together without that element in play. You know—not as mates or alpha and omega. Just... Tristan and Serena."

I'm... speechless. Not because my Omega is freaking out, but because I am touched beyond words.

We roll up to a stop light, giving him ample time to see the tears gathering in my eyes. Thinking he's upset me, he starts rambling, "Not that I don't love your scent, omega. You know I do. I only—"

He can't finish the sentence.

Because my lips are suddenly covering his.

I HAVEN'T STOPPED STARING at this woman's face since she kissed me.

And she knows it.

I'm so distracted, I can't even take in our surroundings. The upscale Japanese eatery is renowned for its high-class aesthetic and fantastic food—but my eyes can't see beyond Serena's face as we walk through the artful Zen garden space at the center of the restaurant.

As the hostess seats us, I catch Serena smirking. When our

eyes meet, she arches one thin black brow. "Something distracting you, Senator?"

God, she's such a sharp little brat.

Spencer might like bringing her to heel, but I think I love her just like this. Quick-minded and in control, teasing me with her goddess-green eyes and those smartass smiles.

It's been a long time since I've *wanted* to laugh. And even longer since I felt this bubbling swirl in my center.

Joy.

I don't know if it's hers or mine.

At this point, I'd argue they're one and the same.

She slinks into her chair and picks up her menu. When a sudden lurch of panic grips her gut, I find myself flinching toward my phone.

But there's no one else to call now.

I'm the alpha who's with her.

"Everything all right?" I ask, eyeing her over the long list of options. "The chef here offers omakase if you'd like to be surprised."

The dread deadening her insides only gets stronger. When her eyes start to leap around the menu, I realize—she doesn't know what anything is. She's never been out for sushi before.

Finally, a problem I can actually *solve.*

I relax, a fond smile curving my mouth as I reach over and splay my palm across her menu. When she frowns over at me, I just grin wider.

A flirtatious remark pops into my head, but it's too much. Too close to home.

I don't deserve to flirt with this beautiful woman—don't deserve to make her smile.

But then I remember what Jonah said when he pulled me aside the other night. How every time I push her away to punish myself, I'm still *pushing her away.* Rejecting her.

So I say it anyway.

"Think you can trust me?"

The words don't come nearly as casually as I wanted them to. Serena's gaze sharpens as it lands on mine, taking my measure.

"I think I can," she finally whispers. "But if you order anything that still has eyes, I'll definitely send it back."

Abiding by her rule, I order us a sampling of everything I can think of. By the time I finish, she's turned her attention to the large cherry blossom mural painted on the wall. Awe fills her features as she slides shy eyes to mine.

"Are there really that many flowers there? When they bloom?"

Sweet one. She's really never been allowed to go anywhere or see anything. No wonder she loves those nature documentaries so much—she probably had no idea a lot of the things she's learned about even existed.

My mind races, easily coming up with ten places I could take her that would blow her mind. The gardens at Versailles. South American rainforests. Hawaii's world-famous waterfalls.

A whole lot of locales I've promised myself I'd see for years.

Now, I'm glad I didn't have time before. Because maybe she'll let me take her. And maybe she'll like that we're both experiencing everything together.

I slip my hand over hers and give it a tender squeeze. "Yes," I reply. "We can go see them, if you'd like. Or you can come with me to Washington in the spring. There are cherry blossoms up there, too."

She snorts a quiet laugh. "Let me guess—on your private jet?"

I've actually never seen the need for one. But if Serena is interested in traveling... "Do you want a private jet?"

She freezes, blinking. Another guffaw tumbles out of her. "Um... no?"

That isn't true, though. Because I can feel the curiosity and amazement she's working to conceal.

Instead of ruling it out, I shrug. "We can go look at them after your heat. My omega gets whatever she wants."

Throwing up her hands, she sputters, "You can't just—why

would you—if you keep buying me every single thing I want, I'm going to be a spoiled brat!"

I grin. "Mm. Tragic. Terrible plan."

My sarcasm earns me a true, beautiful laugh. The sound is melodic and every bit as stirring as her strongest perfume. I'd happily trade the scent of paradise forever if I got to listen to her laugh every day.

When she finishes, she crosses her arms under her breasts and pouts at me over the table. "But I said I *didn't* want a plane, Senator."

"And I know better," I tell her.

Something about the way I roll my shoulders must not be as casual as I think it is, because her eyes fly wide. A swoop of horror free-falls through her abdomen, sending me scrambling for my phone again.

Fuck. I really need to stop doing that.

It's too late—*goddamn it*—because she's every bit as brilliant as I thought. Her big green eyes clock the twitch of my hand and grow even bigger.

"Tristan. Oh my God. Have you been able to hear me this *whole time?*"

TO HIS CREDIT, Tristan doesn't try to make excuses. Instead, he sighs, "Well, I can't *hear* you, but I can feel whatever you're feeling, yes."

"And you didn't tell me?" I shriek, drawing some concerned scowls from fellow patrons. I drop my voice into a hiss, "Real respectful, *Senator*!"

He cringes. "I did try to tell you, that first night, when I said you shouldn't lie to me about how you feel. But you were so upset, I didn't want you to feel worse. And then, sometimes, it almost felt like you *knew* I could feel whatever you were feeling.

Like you maybe *liked it*, even."

Is that true?

Oh God.

What does it say about me if that's true?!

I never get a chance to decide. Because he isn't done.

With complete, honest humility, Tris looks into my eyes and admits, "*I* liked it. And I hate myself for that. Because I was so *wrong*, biting you, and I haven't done one single goddamn thing to deserve you. But having you *with me* like this—even though it hurts—it's been the first time in as long as I can remember that I haven't felt alone."

I've been keeping a catalog of Tristan Thorne's secret traits. How he's much quieter than I ever expected a public figure to be. So smart and deep. Calm. Kind. Unyielding in his dominance— without ever needing to show his teeth.

Now, a new word joins my list. One that fits him better than I want it to.

Lonely.

He spends his life working for everyone else. Fighting for the rights he thought his brother might not have; making sure all of his packmates had their dreams come true.

Who does the same for him?

No one.

He watches me realize the truth. Unflinchingly honest and humble, even in this.

Better than me. Because I spent years surrounded by people, knowing I was completely alone—but I don't know if I would have had the courage to tell anyone that.

Especially him.

I don't understand one thing, though. "M-me? I don't—I've basically been a hot mess this whole time. Scared and confused and"—*falling in love and fucking nonstop*— "everything else. How could that possibly be a good thing?"

He lifts his shoulder, smiling softly. "It hasn't always been easy," he concedes. "But it's always been *good*. It also made it a lot easier to make sure you always had what you needed."

He taps his phone, sending a cold wash of realization through me. My mind skips back to that day at the nest store—the way the guys' phones went off every time I started to freak out.

He's been texting them. Checking on me.

Our eyes lock again as he adds, "I didn't want you to feel alone, the way I used to."

It doesn't matter that I have no words to reply to that. He feels the bittersweet amazement swelling in my center and reaches over to clasp my hand again.

When I sniff back a rush of emotion and squeeze him back, he flashes the soft smile again. "Mind if I try something?"

I manage a shaky nod, losing the battle with one of the droplets clinging to my lashes. He watches it roll halfway down my cheek before reaching his free hand over, moving his chair close enough to swipe it away.

Something shifts in that indistinct place that somehow feels like the very center of my being, even if I can't pinpoint where exactly it is. The feeling slowly fills me. Bright and gentle, with shaky edges.

It feels... a lot like hope.

His hope, I realize.

He's showing it to me; so carefully, I know it must be something he practiced after the night he accidentally knocked me out.

I suspected as much after his rut, when he somehow sent me that one little beat of gratitude. This time, it's more than one feeling, though. It's a swirl of typical Tristan and the completely unexpected.

His guilt and regret feel so familiar, it would almost be wrong *not* to sense them. But everything else?

That whisper of hope. Then, gratitude—the same soul-deep kind he showed me in the shadows after I told his packmate I would be their omega.

Uncertainty—he doesn't know if he's doing the right thing, being here with me, but he wants to try.

Because, above and below everything else, there's *longing*.

So much—so deep, so *raw*—it instantly pricks my eyes all over again.

He wants me; more than he wants to *breathe*. His body *aches* with it. His heart *hurts*. His lungs can barely expand enough to keep him going.

The night he bit me, he left a piece of his soul embedded in mine. And now there's a throbbing hole where I should be.

Only I'm not there. Because he refused to ever press any advantage. Refused to take one more speck of freedom from me.

And there's the guilt again. The shame of not deserving me, or this. The deep, unshakable sense that he never can because he ruined us right from the start and—

I shove to my feet. Take three steps.

And settle into his lap.

He blinks his surprise, his sculpted lips falling open slightly when I cup my hands around his face and stare into him as fiercely as I can.

"Enough."

In all my years at Wally's, I could never summon an omega bark. No matter how scared or desperate I got. But it comes naturally now. *"Enough, Tristan."*

And my alpha shudders, absorbing my words. The chagrin in his gut starts to wither as I hold his square jaw between my palms and stare into him. Showing him how strong his pack has made me.

"Do I look broken to you?" I whisper.

A devastating pang of *want* zings through him, turning his voice into a rasp. *"No."*

"That's because I'm not. You *didn't break me*, Tristan Thorne. Nothing has."

The truth of that soaks into my bones as it slowly sinks into his. Soothing him. And giving me a feeling I've never felt before.

I'm... proud. *Of myself.*

Instead of stuffing it down or picking it apart, I let the sensation swell through me. Wanting him to feel it. Wanting him to see.

"I'm proud of you, too," he murmurs, leaning his forehead into mine. "You have no idea how much."

I do a moment later, when joyful, awed feeling sparkles into me, bubbling through my veins like champagne. His hands chase the feeling, trailing down my arms and back up again, sliding into my hair.

His eyes bounce between mine, giving me time to pull away. I start to roll my eyes at him, but he strikes, sealing his mouth over mine.

Unlike our brief kiss in the car, this time, he's in complete control. Tilting my head just so, smoothing his tongue over mine in a toe-curling glide that leaves my lips tingling.

Dizzy shivers rush down my spine, dampening my panties as his suit jacket teases the hardened points of my nipples through the thin fabric of my dress. He can't scent me, but he feels my arousal spike through our bond and hums, settling me closer.

Right where I want to stay.

THERE'S some funky energy in the locker room tonight.

Our real season starts next month. Usually, that wouldn't ramp tensions up for another couple of weeks. I can't speak for the others, but my mood has less than nothing to do with football.

I check my phone for the hundredth time, hoping there won't be any messages. Tristan told me he would let me know if our surprise switch really upset Serena. We had a plan where I would come take over the date, if she wanted me to.

As it stands, no news is good news, but I'm fucking anxious about it.

I hated misleading her. Even for a surprise. Makes me wonder whether all alphas feel like this or if I'm just a complete simp.

I take comfort in the fact that I am not alone.

Meg Ash stands at the exit of the lockers, hand on her hip, giving Declan Howard a piece of her mind. She waves her other hand and scowls while she snaps at him. And—unlike the attitude he always gives Coach—Dec nods, hanging his head.

Theo stands between them, wincing, but nodding, too. I do my best not to listen to their business as I approach, bag slung over my shoulder.

"Jonah!" Meg stops me, leaning around her two big alphas to catch my eye.

"Hey, little lady," I smile. "What's up?"

Theo shifts on his feet while Declan does everything he can not to look at me. *Pussies*—their omega has no issue meeting my gaze with her blue eyes, giving me a shrewd look. "Your pack found an omega, huh?"

My hackles rise, but I do everything I can to stop my scent from burning to hell. I don't like anyone talking about Serena when she isn't around, but I also don't want to ruin her chances of making friends with Meg one day, if she wants to.

Usually, the Ash Pack's little blonde is sweet and bubbly. Right now, though, she's looking at me like she's a detective and I'm a witness.

"What was her name again? Sabrina?"

"Serena," I say. "Why?"

Meg narrows her eyes. "I looked for her on socials, to add her to our team pages and stuff. But I couldn't find her anywhere."

Shit. My hummingbird has been nervous about making any accounts. She's still afraid someone from Wally's might recognize her and out her past before Tristan can get his law passed. It never occurred to me that not having anything up at all might look suspicious, too.

"Weird," I hedge, forcing a shrug. "I can ask her about it if you want."

Meg nods. "We do brunch every month for the omegas of the bonded alphas on the team. My friend Remi comes, too. It's fun —she'll like it."

I'm not sure how true that is, considering how shy and wary our girl can be. But Spencer did mention that she'd joined a study group at school... so maybe this is another step forward for her.

I want her life to be like that—*rich*. Full of friends and fun things she enjoys.

Thinking this, I agree and give Meg Serena's phone number. Once she has it saved, the blonde omega beams. "Perfect! By the way, do you have a picture? Maybe I did see her profile and just didn't recognize her."

My stomach sinks, knowing that wouldn't be possible, but wanting to save face for my girl. I swipe my phone open, flipping to the one selfie Serena's allowed me to take with her. In it, I'm grinning like an idiot, and she's looking at my face with that sweet little smirk on her pretty lips.

When I show it to Meg, she blinks twice and nods. "Got it. Mental image saved."

Behind her, Theo is even whiter than usual. Declan knocks his shoulder pointedly, until they both nod their goodbyes.

I walk away shaking my head.

That was fucking weird.

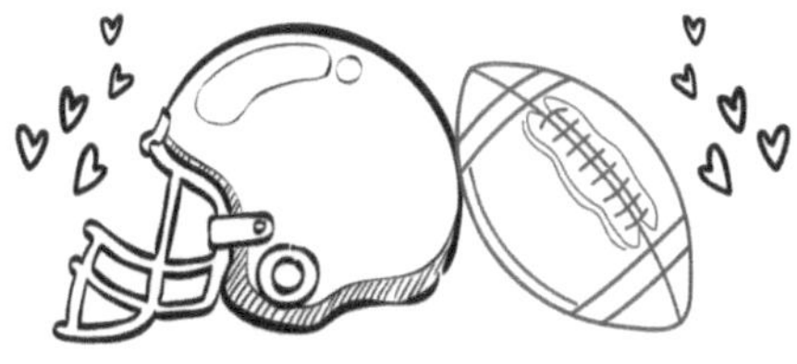

AT THIS POINT, it honestly doesn't matter if Serena never completes our bond. If she chooses to claim all of my packmates and doesn't claim me. If she punishes me for all eternity.

That's okay.

Because I'll always have *this*.

Tonight has been the best night I've had... ever. When I think about the evenings I spent at presidential galas, state dinners, exotic, exorbitant restaurants—I'm *angry*. Furious at all that wasted time. When I could have just been here, with her.

Right in my own goddamn backyard.

That's where we end up, after dinner and an impromptu driving lesson where I teach my beautiful baby how to drive her new toy. She truly does love it, despite feeling distinctly guilty about loving it.

Which only tells me I need to find more gifts to lavish on her. Until the last of that shame falls away—and she knows she's worth it.

Once we got home, she asked if the plants she gave me were still alive. When I told her, miraculously, yes, she shyly led me out to her garden to see the rest.

After pulling me through rows of garden beds and pointing out all her favorites, she just keeps holding my hand. I watch the way she bites her lip, luminous green eyes gazing up at the moon.

"Tell me something," she starts, speaking quietly. "You helped Avery get into the UFC. Got Jonah his shot in the NFL all those years ago. Made sure Spencer had his dream job..."

She trails off, turning to me with an arched brow. "What about you? What do *you* want?"

My answer is automatic. The one I've been giving reporters, my colleagues, and my pack for as long as I can remember. "I want to pass my Omega Workplace Protection Act."

Serena's face doesn't move, but I feel a distinct thud of doubt in her middle. "Hmm... anything else?"

For a second, my mind reels. Aside from my work, and making sure everyone in the pack had what they needed, I'm not sure I've ever thought very much about what *I* want.

The first image that comes to mind is too much. I shake my head, immediately chucking the notion aside; unwilling to even *mention* it to the omega who's already given up her whole life because of me.

For me.

Whatever she feels through the half bond makes her eyes soften as her brows lower. "Do you ever wonder what would have happened if we'd met... some other way?"

God. I've thought about that a thousand times. Agonized over it.

But at least I have an answer prepared, this time.

"I would have walked out of whatever room we were in," I start. "To call the guys. I would have told them that I'd found our mate and asked them what they thought we should do."

A smile tips my lips. "My money would have been on Jonah for a good date idea. Once we'd made a plan, I'd have asked you for your number and begged you to come out with us. Then I would have sent you flowers every morning and a gift every night until you agreed."

Serena smirks. "And you think that would have worked on me?"

I flash a grin. "I buy very nice gifts."

Her gaze warms as she reaches up to cup my jaw in her dainty hand. "Do you want to know a secret?"

I step closer, nodding. "Yes."

Pure sincerity fills her features while trepidation beats through our bond. "You wouldn't have needed any presents to win me over, Tristan."

My heart cramps. Air quivers out of my lungs as I drop my forehead to hers and scent-mark her. A languid roll of need swoops between us—

And I grab her.

She gasps as I sling her up into my arms, snapping her gaze to mine. I let my purr loose and bend to kiss her crown, murmuring, "I told you. Whatever you want, I'm going to give it to you. Even when you don't know how to ask."

Right now, she wants a knot. It's taken me weeks, but I can finally differentiate between all her various strains of arousal. This kind—where there's a skittish, desperate undercurrent—usually means her heat symptoms are melding with her general desire, but she's too nervous to ask one of us for help.

Now that she knows we have this connection, I'll make sure she never has to ask again.

The patio door falls shut behind us and we step into the still, silent living room. I don't know where my pack is. I suspect they're trying to give us privacy. I appreciate it, but my sweet baby needs to be knotted.

"Who should I get for you?" I rough out over my purr. "Anyone sound particularly good?"

Avery is out of commission, but I'm sure he could be tempted if she felt like a challenge. Or Jonah if she wants someone comforting and nurturing. My brother is arguably the most thorough and efficient, though, so if we're going purely on her *need*, then—

Her little hand lands on my cheek as her lips slant up in the sweetest half-smile. "Tristan."

"Yes?"

This woman has my whole fucking heart. I could look at her forever and never get over the gold woven into her irises, the way her smirk teases while still feeling so soft and kind. And those silver half moons branded into her flawless golden skin. Calling to me like a beacon.

As our gazes connect, she runs her thumb along my cheekbone. "No, I mean *you*. Tristan. That's who I want right now. The *only* alpha I want tonight."

When she feels the way shock bottoms out in my stomach, she laughs quietly. When I just stare at her, not daring to believe she could possibly be serious, her expression softens again, though she raises one arched brow.

"Whatever I want, right?"

Suddenly, it feels like I won't live if I don't find out what that is.

I start striding toward her bedroom, but her hand drops to my collar. She tugs at it, shaking her head. A balloon of nervousness expands under her diaphragm as she hesitates.

She's changed her mind, I think. Which is completely understand—

"No," she whispers, interrupting my thoughts. "I want you in the nest."

———————— ♥ ————————

I **STILL CAN'T BELIEVE** how fortunate I am, even after Serena finishes removing all of my clothes and pulls her dress over her head. In a pair of ivory lace panties and a matching strapless bra, she looks like an angel. Especially when she smiles gently and tugs me into her nest.

Her *perfect* nest.

It's every bit as gorgeous and mysterious as her. Smooth purple velvet on the walls, matching silk cushions in every shade of violet, lavender, and the deepest plum. All laid out beneath a beautiful canopy of greenery.

The soft lights woven through the leaves glow off her skin as she sinks to her knees and crawls to the middle of the round mattress built into the floor. When she hugs her knees and looks up at me, tenderness pierces my heart.

I drop down to her level, immediately going to her, cupping my hands around her uncertain face. "This is the most beautiful nest I've ever seen, sweet one," I tell her, letting our bond echo my complete sincerity. "I'm honored that my pack will be in here with you for your heat."

She blinks up at me, her eyes impossibly big and full of the fear I feel creeping up her throat. "A-and you? Will you be here, too?"

Fuck, the *relief*. I've never felt any so strong. I pick her up and hold her in my lap. She closes her eyes while I rub her back, hiding her face against my purr.

"Yes," I reply, hoarse and hard and so goddamn *hopeful*. "My sweet baby, of course I'll be here. I'd never let you hurt. And I couldn't stand to be away from you when you need me."

Serena whimpers, squirming in my lap. "I—I think I need you now."

I know she does. She's still covered in de-scenter, but now that she's down to her panties, I'm starting to pick up the edges of her luscious perfume.

It isn't enough, though. I want to taste her, right from the source.

"Let me make you come," I rumble, suppressing a growl. "Then you can have my knot if you want it."

She rolls her lips together but nods. "How do you—"

I raise a brow at her, and she freezes, then flashes a smile. "Oh. Right. Whatever *I* want, right?"

So smart, our omega. I pet her satin-soft hair back, watching the way light glimmers off it while she thinks. She's so goddamn gorgeous, and the cute pensive scowl on her face only makes me happier. And harder.

Finally, she lightly pushes at my shoulders until I'm lying on the padded floor of her nest, gazing up at her. She clearly isn't confident, but determination steals across her face as she reaches behind her and unclasps her bra.

Fucking hell. Her tits are glorious. Round and tight, tipped with dark nipples that match her pussy lips. My mouth waters as she hooks her thumbs into her underwear and nods down at mine.

By the time we're both bare, her perfume is permeating the air, thickening it with that lush scent of paradise. When she shuffles closer, I see why—her thighs are absolutely coated in slick.

I groan, dropping my hand down to fist my raging cock. It's already purple and roped with throbbing veins. When she sees me strangle it, Serena licks her lips.

"What are you going to do to me, little omega?" I ask, kneading my knot so she can see it swell. "You want to watch?"

She nips her lower lip again, nodding. "But... I think I need a good seat."

Holy God.

I grab her hips and yank her on top of me in one breath. She squeals, but the sound quickly drops into a moan as I settle her glistening lips over my mouth and run my tongue between them.

Fuck. Fuck. *Fuck.*

I didn't realize I'd been walking around—*starving*—for weeks until I have her in my mouth. She tastes better than I ever could have dreamed. Better than anything, surely, that has ever existed.

Ripe sweetness, tangy and bright, bursts over my tongue while I gently kiss each of her lips, sucking and nipping at them. Fresh slick pours out of her, dribbling down my chin, filling my mouth with absolute heaven.

I fist my dick with a white-knuckle grip to keep from spilling, but a jet of pre-cum still shoots out, the hot release splattering over my abs.

Serena goes rigid as she watches before gasping and moaning louder, sinking herself down onto my face with an intensity that makes me want to grin as much as it makes my knot pound.

From her position, she can balance her hands on my chest and reach down to swipe her fingers through my pre-cum. When she brings it to her own mouth and sucks me off her fingers, my balls tingle, begging for relief.

I ignore my body's demands and focus on the gorgeous cunt riding my mouth. Working my tongue into her opening, sucking at her swollen nub, letting her work herself against my face until she's trembling.

My hands roam her body, petting her sides, caressing her thighs and her ass, reaching up to roll her nipples. When I finally skim my touch over the claiming mark I left on her neck, she bucks into my tongue and comes all over my face.

"*Tris-tan!*"

She squirms, begging me for more. "You want my knot, baby?" I grunt, wiping my lips against her thigh and coming up with even more of her sweet slick. "Is that what this pretty pussy needs?"

Serena gives a true omega whine. The sound breaks my brain.

Before I can think, my hands snatch her hips again, turning her to face me and sinking her right on top of my cock.

Which is when I realize I must be dead. Assassinated maybe, or perhaps I simply dropped from the broken heart that's been slowly killing me. I don't know how or when it happened, but there's absolutely no way I'm not in heaven right now.

Serena's pussy is too good to be anything but some sort of eternal reward. Smooth and so slick, but tight and textured enough to tug at my pulsing cock until my knot fills with burning blood.

She screams as she takes me all the way to the top of the thick swell, her head falling back until her long hair brushes my thighs. For a moment, neither of us can move.

Then I feel *her*, inside. A little whisper of self-doubt. Like maybe this isn't the very best moment of my entire life.

I push myself upright and wrap my arms around her, shifting so she can feel how swollen I am for her. "Sweet baby," I whisper, kissing the mark on her throat. "I love you."

She trembles in my arms. "Y-you do?"

I've never felt so certain. Sending that steely assurance through our bond, I nuzzle into her hair. "Yes. And I want you so much I can barely breathe. Will you show me what you want? What you like?"

When another niggle of apprehension worms through her, I know she isn't sure what to say. "Here, sweet one," I murmur, leaning back onto my palms and swallowing a grunt as she shifts on top of me. "You work that pretty cunt all over my cock. Do whatever feels good. And when you're ready to come again, I'll knot you so deep, I'll be in you until morning."

Her eyes light up, and my heart *flips*. Goddamn it. I would do anything to put that look on her face. She's completely correct— I'm going to spoil her beyond all reason.

And I'll *love it*.

Moving carefully, she starts to bounce on my pounding girth, squeezing me in slick clenches that have me panting praises to her.

"That's it. Good girl. So fucking beautiful while you take what you want. Does my knot feel good rubbing against that pretty, throbbing clit?"

Within minutes, she grips my shoulders and grinds up and down my length. Our mouths brush in a filthy, fucking sort of kiss. Licking and nipping at each other.

A burst of want soars through her and I pull back, cupping her chin to force her to look into my eyes. "Anything. Ask me."

She moans, her eyes bouncing between mine. "I—I want you to bite me again. On your mark."

Fuck. My balls draw up as my abdomen clenches, right on the edge just from the *thought* of tending her mark while she comes.

But I nod, gliding my hands down to palm her breasts and letting her stretch to give me access to the side of her throat. The second I latch onto her skin and start to suck, her pussy echoes my pulls, drawing me in *hard*.

"Tristan, yes! Oh God—please!"

With one rock of my hips, my knot is buried in her sweet heat, surrounded by slick, kneading muscles. Pleasure explodes through my base, up my back and down my straining thighs.

Serena comes, her inner walls fluttering and flexing while I spurt into her depths and clamp my teeth around her neck.

Absolute *rightness* flashes through my entire being. As if my entire life, every breath and every step has been for *this*. To get *right here*.

The same sensation reverberates through our bond, so strong the emotion doesn't feel frayed at all.

FOR THE FIRST TIME EVER, I wake up in my nest.

It's a relief, honestly.

The plants overhead absorb most of the sunlight glowing dimly behind the tinted dome above me. Above *us*.

Because Tristan is still here. Spooning me so thoroughly, there isn't a single place we aren't touching. Not *one single place*—because he's also, still, very much inside me.

We fell asleep knotted together, but we aren't anymore. Now, as he sleeps, the thick swell that locked us together has gone down. He's still a semi-hard, weighty stretch in my pussy, though.

Coated in a thin layer of my slick, with his balls nestled firm and heavy between my lower lips.

The second I snuggle back into him, solid arms flex around my body. "Mm," he hums, voice rough with sleep. "Sweetest fucking thing. Good morning, baby."

The way he rasps reminds me how loud we were last night. A flutter of chagrin flits through me while I hide my face against the nearest pillow. "Morning..."

It's hard to stay embarrassed when the gentle glow of adoration rolls through him, funneling into me. He huddles closer, finding his mark and brushing a soft kiss over the fresh bruises layered on top.

An awkward giggle clogs my throat. "I was really into you biting that last night, huh?"

His chest rumbles on a growly purr. "Did you hear me complaining?"

No, I heard him *roaring* every time he went over the edge. And felt, bit by bit, some deep pain inside of him easing.

I couldn't focus on it while we were all wrapped up in each other, but now, with the periwinkle morning light streaming in and a songbird warbling somewhere nearby, I close my eyes and try to stumble my way through the half-bond.

It definitely doesn't feel natural, the way I imagine full bonds do. But I can still get a sense of what's going on. And under all the happiness and relief floating there, I find the point of connection, where we're partially tied together.

And it *hurts*.

I know Spencer told me not having me during his rut would be painful for Tristan, but it never occurred to me...

"Tris," I whisper, clutching his forearm. "You're in *pain*."

For a moment, he seems genuinely confused. He lets me turn as much as I can in his grasp, slipping out of my wetness and frowning down in consternation.

When I brush my fingertips over the place above his stomach, below his lungs, he understands. A crease rumples his brow. "It actually doesn't hurt right now. Not nearly as much as usual, anyway."

He thinks he's comforting me, but I'm horrified. When he feels my blood turn to ice in my veins, he blows out a breath and settles on the mattress beside me.

"I guess I didn't want to think about how bad it had gotten," he admits. "It's been progressively worse, but nothing compared to how it feels when I have to be away from you physically. I've been working from home because the few times I tried to go in..."

He cringes slightly. "Between the pain and the way I can sense your... *urges*—it was very difficult to get anything done."

Tris must feel me preparing to apologize because his scent smolders slightly. "Don't apologize for that, omega," he murmurs. "If I hadn't been fighting myself every step of the way, I would have loved that part."

That part; because the *other* part is some worse version of this pulling, pinching *pain*.

"Tristan," I whisper. "Why didn't you tell me how badly this was harming you? I never would have let you hurt like this."

He gathers me into his side and kisses my forehead. "That's exactly why I didn't want to tell you, sweet one, or let you into my half of the bond. My pain was never your burden. It's the consequence of what I did. I never wanted you to feel pressured to complete the bond because of guilt."

And I *want* to argue with him... but I already see his point. Because I don't feel quite ready to bite him, but the impulse is there, thick enough to block the air from reaching my lungs.

I know I'm going to complete this bond, now, right? So what's the harm in doing it today? Putting him out of this misery?

But Tristan feels everything I do now, and an answering flare of outrage fires in his gut.

"*No*," he barks quietly. "*Absolutely not*. If you want to complete the bond, we'll do it during your heat, when you're ready. Not randomly. And *never* because you're worried about me. I'll be fine."

It isn't a lie because he believes it. But I sense the doubt lurking underneath his optimism. The fear.

He refuses to lose me by keeping me.

But will that mean *I* lose *him*?

THE DUMBEST ASSHOLES ALIVE

TRISTAN

How is our omega today?

She woke me up at dawn and kept me in bed until I had to leave at nine.

Has she needed more?

SPENCER

I took her for two hours after you left.

She's with Jonah now.

AVERY

if I wasn't about to murder you all, I'd be impressed

JONAH

water.

SPENCER

Serena needs water?

JONAH

NO I NEED WATER

our omega fucked me to death

TRISTAN

Then how are you texting?

AVERY

I've decided I *am* going to kill you all

JONAH

jealousy isn't very demure or mindful, ave.

TRISTAN

You already booked your night with her after your fight tonight, Ave

She's very excited about it.

AVERY

that's cute as hell

I might let you live

SPENCER

Everyone please be gentle with her

She's very sensitive today

I made her take a break after three rounds with me in the shower because she felt faint and she got upset.

AVERY

I'm going to kill you.

JONAH

aaaaand we're back.

THIS MUST BE a circle of hell.

The jeers, the lights. The *thousands* of different scents.

And mine, getting worse by the *second*.

My heat should start any day now, and I'm basically a lunatic —climbing the guys like a horny spider monkey, crying over every tiny thing, and losing my ever-loving shit if any other omega even *looks* at one of my alphas.

After class yesterday, I thought Spencer would have to call for an exorcism when a *bonded male omega student* came to his office to drop off papers. I spun out so completely, he only managed to calm me down by knotting me against the office door, then carrying me to his leather sofa and holding me against his chest until I passed out to the sound of his purrs.

When I woke up, I was at home, in my bed, with Tristan rubbing my feet, Avery nuzzling his face into my belly, and Jonah ready to force-feed me chicken noodle soup.

So maybe we're *all* a little nuts?

Especially the usually-composed Tristan Thorne.

He's barely left my side for three days, and he still has a very I'll-rip-off-another-alpha's-head energy. According to Spence, this is normal for pack leaders after knotting their omegas for the first time. He also thinks the half-bond is making Tristan extra posses-sive and protective.

After spending three nights with Tristan's cock and knot buried in me until late morning, the guys finally put their collective foot down.

Avery practically rolled his pack alpha out of my bed, then proceeded to spread my legs and dive in for a morning feast. After which he spent hours lying with his head on my sternum and his chest pressed into my belly, purring to break up my pre-heat cramps and snarling at anyone who dared to wander within a foot of the mattress.

Afterward, Spencer took a bath *with* me. He let me have his knot while he cleaned me, tutting his disapproval for all the bruising bite marks littered across my skin. As if he isn't the worst offender of all—a fact he proved when he sucked his own mark into the opposite side of my throat.

Jonah seems determined to feed me up before my heat starts. Today, after Ave left to go prep for his fight, Jonah made enough comfort food to sustain a family of ten. He put me in his lap and sweetly massaged every bit of my body he could reach while also feeding me mashed potatoes and fried chicken.

By the time we all had to leave to get to the arena, Tristan was practically vibrating. I still feel his impatience and feral protectiveness throbbing through the half-bond as we walk into the arena.

When I glance up at his face—square jaw loose, dark brow smooth—I don't see the cool mask he's giving the world. I only see the mania in his eyes.

They snap to mine immediately. Almost like he was just waiting for me to look at him.

His gaze slides to his healed bite mark, then back to my face. And, I swear, I can *feel* how much he wants to send me a thought right now.

But there are about thirty cameras trained on us at the moment, so he just nods at the Octagon.

I force my head to bob up and down, ignoring the way my skin crawls when my ponytail brushes my bare back. The dress

Tristan defiled at the store is sexy, but the tight fabric mashing my breasts down *hurts*.

Flashes pop around us while people call their names. *Senator Thorne. Tristan. Jonah. Professor.*

Some of them shout questions about the fight: How is Avery? Is he ready? What's his headspace been like lately? Have we seen the odds?

Others have *different* questions.

"Senator Thorne, is this your omega?"

"Where's your bond mark, Senator?"

"Where are *her* bond marks, Senator?"

Tristan only winds his hand around mine and keeps staring straight ahead. Jonah wedges his big body between me and the cameras, blocking me from view as Spencer steers us toward our ring-side seats.

I miss Avery. He'd never let people shout at me. One flick of his murderous glare and they would all leave us alone.

I've never been in a gym like this without him, and I feel stupidly out of place here, in this sexy dress and a face full of makeup. I just want to be back *home*, in our own gym or in our bed...

Jonah feels me tense up and notices the tears gathering in my eyes. Instead of letting me sit between him and Spencer, he pulls me directly into his lap, where all three of them can reach me.

His chin fits against my shoulder, a deep purr vibrating into my back. "Do you want to go?" he murmurs. "We can leave right now, hummingbird."

They've all told me that a hundred times today. Even Avery, who texted me just three minutes ago to tell me I should go home and wait for him in bed. Naked.

Before we walked into the actual arena, I felt confident I could make it. But now...

"This is so important to him," I whimper, turning to hide my wet eyes in Jonah's neck. "Please help me stay."

Spencer hears me, leaning around Jonah's shoulder to take my hand. He cuffs my wrist with his fingers, squeezing rhythmically. I don't know what kind of omega magic he's weaving, but I can suddenly inhale. The scents of all three of them sink into my lungs.

I crack one eye open, finding Spencer's intense stare waiting for me. "I'm going to embarrass him," I whisper. "He'll be distracted by me. What if I perfume while he's up there and—"

I hate that I feel so panicked. Just weeks ago, I couldn't *wait* to see Ave in action. Part of me still can't. But I don't trust my body right now. And once the heat sets in... I know what the pain will do to me.

In the end, it's Tristan who stands up.

"*Enough,*" he barks quietly. "This is inhumane. You two stay and watch. I'm getting Serena out of here."

I protest weakly as he bends and plucks me out of Jonah's lap. My big man rubs his thumb over my cheek, reassuring me Avery won't be upset at all. Spencer nods his agreement and promises they'll stay for the entire fight and keep an eye on my menace.

Instead of wading back through the crowd of cameramen, Tris carries me the wrong way down the tunnel Ave is supposed to emerge from. He doesn't seem to care much that people are star-ing. His eyes flash from the path in front of us to my face, concern shifting behind his flawless poker face and swelling through his stomach.

I close my eyes and turn my cheek into his lapel, not wanting to hear the shouts or see the faces blurring past. I only open them again when I hear Avery growling roughly.

"*What the fuck?*"

For a second, I think he's angry with me for being so weak. Or for being back here, near the locker rooms, at all. Then I feel his taped-up hand land softly on my head, petting my hair gently.

God, he looks so good. The tight black shorts molded to his body display all of his ink and muscles perfectly. They also do nothing to disguise the enormous bulge at his groin.

His fallen-angel face is full of rage as he growls at Tristan. "I told you this would be too much. She needs to be home, in our nest. I'll kick this guy's ass and then I'll come knot her myself."

When I whine, the hand on my head tenderly cups my cheek. His voice loses every last edge as he murmurs to me, "I love you for trying so hard, kitten. But I'm going to be distracted up there, worrying about you, yeah? Go wait for me. I'll come for you the second this fucker hits the floor."

I'm a bad omega. A silly little slut who can't do anything except perfume and ruin everything and make all the alphas hate me and—

"Hey." Avery kisses me so softly, I almost don't believe it's really him until he pulls back and his gorgeous face comes into focus. "I want you home and safe and happy, baby. Fuck everyone else."

That last bit has my lips curling up a little. He flashes his wild, crooked grin. "There she is. You give Tris hell, and I'll take care of this motherfucker in the cage. Meet you back in our bed."

He scent-marks my forehead before backing away. Out in the arena, the lights have dimmed and the music pounds as they announce his opponent. Tristan cups his hand around my head to protect my ears, but I still hear Avery call out one last thing as he backs toward the doors.

"Hey, kitten!"

I lift my heavy head and turn to find him, a dark silhouette outlined by the flashes and spotlights beyond the doors as they swing open.

He shoots me one final, feral smile. "I decided on a new name."

Avery's preferred metal music screams to life over the speakers just as an announcer intones, "And tonight's challenger, weighing in at two-hundred-fifteen pounds of rage and ink, Avery Thorne. *The Menace.*"

MY SWEET BABY is in so much pain, and her heat hasn't even started yet.

I do my utmost to keep everything on my side of the bond calm and smooth, purring as evenly as I can while I rock her in my lap.

"Shh," I murmur. "I know it hurts, baby. I know. The heating pad is almost ready."

Spencer did an incredible job making sure we had everything we could possibly need to keep her as comfortable as possible.

True to form, he left detailed instructions with each item. His tilted script says the heating pad should be 114 degrees and applied directly over her lower abdomen in twenty-minute intervals.

His asterisk almost makes me laugh.

May be combined with easing for maximum effect.

Jonah would have thought that was hilarious.

I'm surprised how bittersweet this all feels. Our omega, going into heat. Knowing she will definitely bond with the others. *Not* knowing what will happen with us.

As much as I want us to have a pack bond, I don't think I can let her do that for me. She needs to be one hundred percent sure. She shouldn't feel any pressure at all—which is just impossible, as it stands.

I'll have to have a talk with the guys once the heat sets in for real. I don't want any of them to pressure her, either. Even inadvertently.

It will be the hardest on Spencer. He and I have been through *everything* together—and he's the one with the best understanding of just how hellacious this half-bond has been for me. After her heat passes, if we aren't completely bonded, he says the pain will increase exponentially.

I can't quite fathom that, so I focus on the other hurt rolling around my middle; the thought of never having a pack bond with the guys.

We didn't plan to have one at all, so it isn't as though I'll be giving up some lifelong dream. But I've realized more and more over the last few weeks, while we've dedicated ourselves to our love for Serena, we're not nearly as strong a pack as we could have been. And I regret that immensely, because each of these alphas has made me so proud to be their leader.

Serena whimpers in my arms just as the heating pad beeps. It's cordless, thanks to Spencer's forethought. I slip it right under her dress, nuzzling the side of her head as I whisper directions.

"Arms up. I'm going to put you in one of Jo's T-shirts, okay? If it isn't warm enough, I also have one of Avery's hoodies here."

She nods, letting me maneuver her arms and torso until she's snuggled into her layers. I tuck her into her bed and pull the sheets up, trapping most of her mind-melting perfume under the duvet so I can keep a clear head.

I've already alerted Myles to the situation. Aside from making any necessary food deliveries, he'll be steering clear of the house altogether. In the meantime, he'll inform my aides, Jonah's coach, and Spencer's TA's not to expect any of us until next week.

Serena is my sole focus. I take her temperature and brush out her hair, quietly telling her any funny pack stories I can think of. Like the time we tried to take a road trip and Spencer developed a tick in his eye after three hours of listening to Ave and Jonah bicker. And the one wedding we all attended as a pack, where a much younger, much scarier Avery accidentally panicked the bride and she fell into her own cake.

Serena's little giggles fill me with satisfaction so much sweeter than her scent. For a long moment, while her chuckles die down, we just stare at each other. Our eyes lock in the low light of her celestial bedroom.

"Tris," she whispers, gazing up at me. "Come here for a second?"

She frowns and points at her nape, like maybe some of her hair is tangled in her hummingbird necklace. I lean around her to investigate, my focus trained on the thin gold chain.

It looks fine to—

Every single thought I've ever had evaporates.

Because her teeth have found my neck. And they sink right into it, breaking the skin once and for all.

JONAH GIVES AN EVIL CHUCKLE, counting the stack of cash he just won.

Or, rather, *Avery* just won.

"Every damn time," Serena's big man mutters, shaking his head with a grin. "The kid never lets me down."

He's full of shit. We all know he gives the money he bets right back to Ave. He's done it that way for years. Though, maybe, this time, they'll use it to take Serena out instead.

We should celebrate, after her heat. Avery's debut was a resounding success. Even without a trainer or a coach, he took his opponent down in two rounds, thrashing him so completely that he couldn't even stand for the third.

TKO—a technical knockout. I researched all the proper terminology before coming along tonight.

Jonah's been snorting ever since the other fighter went down. I admit, it *was* a bit humorous to watch the announcer try to bestow victory on our packmate while he glared daggers at him.

Avery clearly just wants to get home to our omega. The notion is a relief. I've never been so worried about anything or anyone before, and my anxiety is becoming intolerable. My Alpha looms nearer to the surface with every breath and only settles when Serena is in my arms.

I have two baskets of our sheets. Worn clothes from all four of us. All the cleaning products are hidden in her bathroom. Watering cans for the plants—

My mind restlessly repeats the same to-do list I've reviewed a thousand times while we wait outside the locker room. Inside, a medic is stitching a deep gash under Avery's left eye. He grumbles and growls the whole time but allows it, knowing having an open wound would upset our sensitive darling more than usual.

The doors at the end of the tunnel-like hall swing open, revealing a blond alpha who's altogether too well-dressed for a place like this.

His eyes scan over us, clearly absorbing every small detail. My tapping foot, Jonah's fist full of cash. The fading love bites we both have on prominent display.

I don't see any bites on him, but he has a gold wedding band and the distinctly settled air of a bonded alpha. When he clips closer, my instincts recoil from the scent tucked into the front of his suit jacket. It looks like a powder-blue pocket square to match his suit, but the scrap absolutely reeks of another omega.

I'd forgotten how indifferent I used to feel about their scents, generally. Now, though, everything in me balks. It isn't Serena, so it's *wrong.*

My Alpha and I have been agreeing more and more lately. At

first it was disconcerting, but as time has gone on, I've started to take comfort in it.

The certainty feels good.

Neither of us wants anything to do with any omega but ours.

We never will again.

Jonah finally realizes we're being approached and folds his cash into the back pocket of his jeans. His broad shoulders expand as he squares up to the stranger, sliding his eyes over his outfit and clocking that strange pocket square the same way I did. He's more subtle than I was, but I notice a slight wince under his dark facial hair.

The alpha comes to a stop right in front of Jonah and me. I sense shuffling behind us in the locker room, but I can't focus on it with a more direct threat staring me down.

The man's shrewd, dark eyes jump from my face to Jonah's. He frowns mildly. "Are you the Thorne Pack?"

All the commotion at our backs suddenly makes sense when a sweaty, shirtless Avery steps between us. His wild, pale eyes flash. "Who's asking?"

If this alpha is off-put by my packmate's obvious bloodlust, he doesn't let on. His head tilts slightly, assessing all of us carefully before he says, "My name is Smith Pierson. This is my omega."

He extracts a cell phone from his inner jacket pocket, swiping at the screen to reveal a photo.

Of Serena.

All three of us immediately snarl. *Is this one of the despicable alphas from that godforsaken club? Has he been following her or watching us—*

But, no.

I raise my hands to my enraged packmates, leaning closer to the image glowing up at us.

Because it *isn't* Serena.

This woman has the same face, the same coloring, and a similarly breathtaking smile—but her eyes are blue. Her hair is curly. And she's surrounded by other alphas, happily snuggled between them in a way our omega would never allow with anyone but us.

Smith Pierson watches me realize what I'm looking at: *his* omega. Who is identical to mine.

His mouth pulls into a scowl as he sighs, "I think we need to talk."

sixty-two

I DON'T KNOW why I'm here.

Naked. Running.

Scrambling is maybe a better word.

I remember being in my bed with one of my alphas. The tall one who never lets me do anything for him. Except this time, he had to. Because this time, I didn't give him a choice.

Is that why I feel so panicked? Was he mad? Did I stay there long enough to find out?

Nothing makes any sense at all, which is the very worst sign. That means everything—including the burning, terrifying *pain*—

is about to start. I have to get somewhere dark and safe. Maybe find a pillow and a blanket if Wally's left one anywhere...

My mind doesn't know what I'm doing, but my feet carry me to a room that's *perfect*. Sumptuous dark fabrics, satin cushions, low light. Maybe, if we stay hidden here until our heat starts, Wally won't come get us and make us go in the basement closet.

I huddle under the first blanket I find and say a little prayer, begging whoever is listening not to make me leave this room. It smells *miraculous* in here. Like summertime and thunderstorms and torched sugar and night jasmine. All of my favorite things.

"Omega?"

Oh God, is he coming? Did he find me already?!

It doesn't *sound* like him. This voice is too quiet and echoey. When I hear it again, I jump, realizing it isn't coming from outside my cocoon... but *inside* my body.

Serena? Can you hear me, sweet one?

I whine, so confused and hot and *OH MY GOD, WHAT IS RUBBING AGAINST MY SKIN*?!

Is it a straitjacket made of nails that someone set on *fire*???

"That's Jonah's shirt, baby," the warm voice says out loud. "I can take it off for you. Would you like that?"

Another shrill noise blares up my throat, piercing my ears. I cover them with my palms, shrinking into my knees, trying to burrow away from the sound.

There are so many *feelings* in me. Fear and pain and desperate need—but there's also euphoria and gratitude and...

Love?

What the hell is that doing in there?

I hear a soft chuckle. "That's me, baby," its owner says. Something inside me shifts, and then I hear the voice there, at my center. *You completed our bond, Serena. I think it triggered your heat.*

Oh *no*. That means it's too late. There isn't any way to escape. *I have to brace for all the pain and—*

"Fuck," he growls. "No, Serena. I won't let you hurt, sweet baby. Just come out and let me help you."

But he sounds angry. Angry alphas aren't safe. Especially not now, when I'm like this.

A soft nudge inside of me accompanies a slow tide of adoration. *I'm not angry, baby. Just worried about you.*

There's a beat of tight silence, then a thump of dark, heated excitement. When he speaks again, he sounds gravelly. "Do you want to come tend your bite?"

A bolt of white-hot want strikes my core like lightning, leaving frantic tingles in its wake. Slick and perfume gush out of me as everything below my navel pulses—empty squeezes that have me clawing my way out of whatever is covering me and launching myself at the swelling scent of orange blossoms.

I crash into a beautifully bare alpha chest, strong arms snapping me up immediately. I start to panic, a whine building in my chest, until my head falls back and I see—

It's *him.*

The one who saved me by accident and couldn't forgive himself for not doing a better job.

My alpha.

He hears me think the words and his square, gorgeous face softens. "That's right, my sweet little mate," he rasps. "You need this knot. Let me give it to you, hmm? Take this shirt off. Have you tend this mark you made."

He does all of it within seconds, stripping me bare and situating me over his big alpha cock. The second my gaze snags on the half-moons bitten into his neck, I moan and fall against his body.

"Good girl," he murmurs, tilting his head to let me latch onto the mark. "God—*good girl*, Serena."

Pleasure pours through him while I lick his skin, inhaling the fresh, rich smell of summer as it floods the nest along with my perfume. Strong hands grip my hips and pull me right down, sinking his cock and knot all the way inside me in one go.

And it—it doesn't hurt.

It doesn't hurt anymore.

Instead of the horrible emptiness, there's his solid girth, rubbing at every sparkling nerve with heat and hardness.

"Beautiful baby, taking your alpha's knot. So perfect."

I love you, I love you, I love you.

Praises pant out of him and swirl inside our bond while our hips grind, bringing us both to the brink within seconds. His head falls back as my teeth scrape my claim. A screech echoes off the walls and he circles me on his knot even faster.

He growls as he comes, the heavy swell buried in my pussy expanding to fill every aching inch of me. My muscles clench and flutter, the ball of tension coiled in my middle popping as the warm lash of his release cools the flames climbing my insides.

"There," he whispers. "Right there. I've got you, sweet one. You can let go now."

The haze smothering the edges of my mind sweeps in. Only, for the first time, it doesn't feel like I'll drown in it. Because my lifeline is under me, holding me close, filling me in every way there is.

And I can finally drift instead of sinking.

I CUT my Mustang's engine and fall back against my seat. Tomorrow, I'm going to be as sore as my backed-up balls have been all week.

I'm tired, and I'm pissed. Tonight was supposed to be very simple—win my match and come home to fuck my girl until one of us passed out.

Now there's all this shit...

Spencer sighs, frowning out the windshield the same way he has been the whole way home. "We need to—"

But Jonah snaps forward, filling the space between our seats and *snarling*.

Which is usually *my* thing, but okay.

I toss him a glare, but then Spencer stiffens, too. He curses viciously and *moves*, throwing his door open. Jonah's right behind him.

Why the fuck are they—

Oh.

Oh *fuck me.*

That's why.

———————— ♥ ————————

LATER, I'll have to replay this mental image for our girl. Three grown men, tripping out of their clothes and over each other's bare asses to get into her nest.

There's no help for us, though. Not with the tangy succulence of her scent filling the whole fucking house.

We reach the door and find it cracked open. The pitiful whimpers inside have me gnashing my teeth, ready to say 'fuck nest etiquette' and burst in there. Spencer is too quick, though. He shoots me a severe look and slowly opens the door so we can look in.

Goddamn, it's pretty. There are cute-ass fairy lights in there. Our baby's beloved plants and her favorite plush purple.

Jesus. I care about *decor* now?

Guess so. Because when I see what a perfect job my kitten did building us a nest, my hard cock *throbs*. My knot echoes the pulses as I finally catch sight of Serena and Tristan.

They're in the center of the mattress built into the floor, clutching one another like they're keeping each other afloat. Tris lifts his head from her shoulder, where he's been tending his mark. Serena huddles closer to his throat, though, her own lips rubbing at—

Holy shit.

She bit him.

I haven't seen Tristan smile like this in—well, *ever*. He grins at us and nods, confirming what we're all trying to wrap our minds around.

They're bonded.

Which means we all will be if she accepts us.

Or should I say, if her Omega accepts us.

That's who's here now. The wordless Omega skirting wide, fearful eyes over to us is every inch the girl we met in that interrogation room.

I still see my fighter in there, though. I just have to coax her out like I did that night.

Tristan whispers to Serena, petting her hair. She tucks herself closer to his chest, shaking. Beside me, Spencer's scent takes on a crackling, electric edge.

"Her Omega has been traumatized," he intones, watching her with heavy sadness in every line of his face. "She was locked up before, all alone. No toys or aftercare. I'm not surprised her Omega doesn't want to speak, especially right now. She's been taught to associate heats with extreme distress."

Jonah's purr kicks up, triggering mine. "She—" He swallows, the sound thick, "She told me how scared she was. I didn't think that her Omega could be worse."

Tristan isn't deterred, though. "Can they come in, baby?" he asks, nuzzling her bare, shimmering shoulder. "I promise they're going to help you, too. They all love you, omega. Just like I do. They can make you feel just as good with their knots."

He drops his voice into a whisper. "I bet they'd even let you bite them if you want to."

She clearly does. Her heavenly perfume pours into the nest, a visible gush of slick slipping down Tristan's balls to pool under them. He groans, leaning his forehead into hers.

"Good girl," he praises. "Feels so good every time you do that, omega."

Jealousy and need and just... *heartache* rage through me. And for a second, I'm untethered.

Then I remember.

You bow to her.

I let my knees go out, falling to the floor. Bending my head in supplication.

Jonah and Spencer follow suit, each lowering themselves behind me. When I chance a glance across the room, she's staring right at me. The recognition lighting her eyes might be the sweetest sight I've ever seen.

"Alpha," she breathes. She looks at Tris and starts to squirm, those green eyes flashing back to me. "*Mine.*"

They're *words*. Her Omega, finally speaking to us. To *me*.

Tris nods, carefully sliding her off his deflating knot. "Yes, sweet baby. He's yours. We're *all yours.*"

I'm about to fucking crawl to this woman—and I don't even care. All that matters is that light glowing in the thin band of her irises.

Seeing me, knowing me, wanting me.

Needing me, I think—because, fuck, her perfume has never been this incredible before. Just *breathing* is enough to start a frenzy, my blood thrumming faster the closer I get.

When I jump into the nest and pick her up, her scent *slices.* Carving down my throat, giving me the exact kind of pain I like most. "That's it, kitten," I moan, gathering her into my body. "Fuck, you hurt so good, baby."

She whines, looking lost as she skims her dazed eyes over my throat. Tristan comes up behind her, his hands cupping her shoulders while he levels his gaze on mine. "She wants to bond with you now. Are you ready?"

Um.

Fuck, *yes.*

Spencer scowls, muttering the way he does when there's a

shitty equation he can't solve. "There are health benefits if we all wait until the end of her heat. Though, with her perfume this strong…"

Serena whimpers, and Tristan nuzzles her hair, murmuring, "Shh, it's okay. None of them are saying no, baby. We just need to decide what's best to keep you taken care of."

To the rest of us, he sighs, sadness clear in his eyes. "She's terrified we'll all leave her."

Jonah muscles his way around our pack leader, cupping his enormous hand at the back of Serena's head. "*Manamea*, I will *never* leave you," he whispers.

When he looks at each of us, his decision is all over his face. "She needs to feel all of us with her. Once we've bonded, we'll be able to *show* her how we feel and help her feel secure. I don't want to make her wait."

Thank *God*.

"I *can't* wait," I bite out, bending to lick a path up the unmarked side of her neck. "I need my claim on this omega. *Now*."

She bucks and whines, nodding hard. Spencer's face softens. He reaches between all of us to hook his fingers under her chin, looking into her eyes.

"All right," he agrees, hushed. "We're all going to bond with you, darling girl. Are you ready for us?"

Her head bobs again, but we all glance at Tristan for confirmation. He smiles, clearly beyond ec-fucking-static that he can hear her thoughts. "She *really* is."

I've never seen Jonah so happy. His broad grin takes up half of his face as he tells Tris, "Ask who she wants first."

The way she shimmies over me and flashes those blown-out green beacons my way, I have a feeling it's me. Even before Tris tilts his chin in my direction, smiling wider. "She says, '*the menace*.'"

Shit.

Say less, baby girl.

With a low snarl, I snap her away from the others, rolling to press her under me, into all the silkiness of her purple cushions. When our eyes meet, I can't help but smirk. "Me first, huh? You sure?"

I should have known she would shock me. She always has, right? From that very first moment. And she's still doing it.

Because just when I think—I *know*—I can't love her any more... She does something that blows my fucking mind.

With eyes so cloudy, I'm not even sure she can really see, she glances down at my chest—and lifts both of her hands. Fitting her fingers into her claw marks, the ones I branded onto my skin.

Fuck.

My *heart*.

I don't know if it stops, or shatters, or burns to the ground. Maybe all three. But for the first time in my entire life, my eyes are... wet?

I feel them shining as I gaze down at her, absorbing the feel of her fingertips curling against my white ink.

"You remember me, kitten?" I rough out, dropping my face to nuzzle hers. "I know my girl is in there. I love you so goddamn much, Serena."

So much that I've almost forgotten about the delicious, perfect perfume that's practically *gutting* me. When a fresh burst erupts from her body, I remember.

Oh *fuck*.

She's never had my knot before, but she's about to. She needs it—and I won't last one more motherfucking second without claiming her in every possible way.

This is still my kitten, though. So while I'm plunging my aching cock into her slick cunt, I reach down to rub at the bud pulsing at the top of her slit.

The wet squeeze of her pussy knocks the air out of my lungs. Her inner muscles have never clamped this hard, this fast. Almost like they're sucking me in deeper. *Begging* for the swell of my knot.

Before she can pull me in on her own, I tilt my hips and pop into place.

Holy.

Fucking.

Shit.

An inhuman sound rips out of me as Serena *strangles* my cock and my knot, slick gushing around *everything*.

Fuck meeeeeee.

I can't move or I'll come. She's too good. *Everything* good.

Paradise.

While my knot pumps fuller, curbing her cramps, my forehead grazes her cheeks, her chin, her shoulder. Covering her in my scent while I lick her skin, deciding where I'm going to leave my mark.

In the end, her throat is too tempting. The idea of all of us marking her there, giving her a collar of bites, makes my balls tingle.

She must like the idea, too because when I start to nose at the spot across from Tris's, she squeals, perfuming so hard the others all groan.

I can't fucking take it. I have to have her. So I start pumping my hips, popping my knot in and out of the tight ring of muscle that desperately tries to keep me inside her.

Serena screams, dragging her nails down my back. "Fucking perfect, kitten," I snarl. "*Yes.* Squeeze me just like that. You like this big, pierced alpha cock? Does it feel good so deep in your pussy? You gonna take this knot too?"

"*Alpha,*" she cries, "Yes!"

And she does. On my next thrust, her body locks around mine, milking my cock so hard my vision blurs and my knot *explodes*. While spurt after spurt fills her pulsing pussy, I find the perfect place to claim her, and I strike.

Sweetness rolls over my tongue, snaking down my throat and punching into the very middle of my soul. Gouging deep, burying itself into the dark, desolate place I abandoned a long time ago.

But now—*now*—

"*Ungh,*" I grunt and groan as Serena's teeth dig into the side of my neck. Placing her mark in the exact spot on me that I took on her.

The tether burrowed in my center pulls taut as it comes to life. Light and color and sound, all in a chaotic swirl every bit as beautiful as the omega working her body against mine.

And then... she's there.

In me. With me.

And she's just... all the good I've ever lacked. All the softness and sweetness and understanding. Everything I wanted to be but couldn't find.

It's her.

My gorgeous fighter. My goddamn glorious mate.

And I can only send one thought through to her. The only one that matters. The best one I've ever had.

There she is.

WE ALL WATCH as Avery collapses, rolling himself and our omega onto their sides, tucking her in close. He's knotted deeply, giving them limited mobility while she tends her mark, and he returns in kind.

Beside me, my brother's voice is hushed. "I can feel them both," he says, amazement and tenderness in his gaze while he stares. "They're—the way they *fit* is just—"

He shakes his head in awe. I wish I could feel the same, but there's a hard lump of fear lodged in my gullet and a sick squirm in my stomach.

Secretly, I've been dreading Serena's heat every bit as much as she has. For one thing, I abhor the idea of not being able to give her what she needs—and I know my usual boundaries won't be enough when she's so dazed and needy.

And, secondly, I've been scared of losing *her*.

Her scent, her body. They're lovely. Perfection, even.

But I fell in love with *her*.

The girl who rolls her eyes when confronted with an unhinged cage fighter, but pales at the thought of hurting someone's feelings. The brilliant mind that beats me at chess and quips out sharp little jokes while she does it. The omega with a heart full of compassion and eyes that sparkle with intelligence.

I was afraid we'd get in her nest and she wouldn't be there anymore.

I was afraid of how I would react if that happened.

When she and Avery finally disengage, though, the green eyes that flash over to me aren't strange or unfamiliar. They're just a little different.

Tristan whispers, telling me what I already know. "It's you next, Spence."

My Alpha is rabid, lunging against his binds. Begging me to let him loose.

I might not have a choice. Because when her creamy, tropical essence winds its way into my lungs, I can barely keep breathing, let alone hold on to the leash being ripped from my grasp.

Avery rolls up onto his elbow as our omega crawls across the nest. His black brow raises, reminding me of our deal, but his voice stays calm. "She wants you to let your Alpha out."

Right. He can hear her, too.

It's a relief more than anything. I like knowing someone will stop me if I upset her.

Tristan nods, agreeing with Ave, but it's Jonah who somehow knows I'm reeling. He moves a little closer, hesitating for a long moment before curling his hand around my shoulder.

We both go still for a long beat before he finally says, "I can help you, Spence. What if I take her from the back and you take her from the front? That way, if you have to tap out, she won't feel abandoned."

It's a kind offer—because he's a kind person. He always has been, from the day we met, when he didn't laugh in my face while I spiraled over my sock drawer.

I still don't like having his hand on my shoulder, but, for once, it isn't making me feel violent or violated. Possibly because my Alpha has muscled his way to the surface, needing to be as close as possible to the little omega approaching us.

"Okay," I rasp out. "Thank you."

Jonah simply nods, dropping his palm from my arm and turning to catch Serena's hips. He grins at her, all joy and encouragement. "Hi, beautiful. How do you feel about taking two alpha cocks at once? You up for that?"

She whines desperately, nodding so hard her hair falls into her face. My lips tip up fondly as I brush it back, cupping her cheeks. Then, I slide one of my hands lower, flexing my fingers around her throat, touching both of her bond marks.

Tris and Avery both hiss as she moans, more slick pouring down her shiny thighs. I reach down to collect it, stroking my fingers back to her tight ass.

She feels *hot* there and much softer than I ever expected. When I imagine the snug heat stretched around Jonah's enormous cock, my mouth waters.

It will make her pussy so goddamn *tight*. My dick will barely fit. And when we work my knot in...

The leash holding my Alpha snaps. And I expect him to lurch at her or fight Jonah off. But just like that day in the office, he only wants to stare at his omega.

Rightness expands in my middle, quelling all of the apprehension crouched there. My rainy scent swells, and her eyes blink, dilating even more.

Coconut sugar and golden cream drift into the air. Jonah

groans, adding his own toasty pheromones to the mix as his forehead falls to her shoulder from behind.

"Fuck, hummingbird. I love you so much. Can't wait to work my cock into this pretty little ass. Think you can take me? I promise I'll go slow."

Her bare, beautiful breasts bounce while she nods, rearing up. My Alpha reacts before I can, closing my fingers around her throat and growling low, "*Behave.*"

Serena whimpers, her perfume darkening into the delectable scent that makes my teeth throb.

"You want me to bite you, omega?" I snarl, letting Jonah arrange her body between ours. She lets out a squeak as he lines himself up against her back entrance.

My thumb presses above Tris's mark. "Right here? Where you'll feel me every time I hold this gorgeous throat?"

Her keen echoes off the round walls. My heart stutters and cramps, pounding fiery tingles through my veins. The heat pools in my groin, filling my knot and lengthening the erection that already grazes my navel.

Serena eyes it with a whine, licking her lips.

Which feels like a compliment, especially with Jonah's monstrous dick making its way into her ass.

A smile I can't quite hide curves my lips. As soon as her bleary gaze roams over it, her small hands float up to touch my cheeks.

The motion is sweet—and the way her thumb automatically traces my cheekbone reminds me of all the other times she's done this. My Alpha practically sighs in relief, loving the feel of her touch so much that I can't feel anything but pleasure.

It's incredible, being able to enjoy her without any of my demons clawing holes in the moment. I think, for the first time ever, I might be *grateful* for the instincts I've always loathed. The piece of myself I tried to break and bury and beat into submission.

I'm so glad I didn't succeed.

Because now I can do this—*be this*—for the woman I love.

Emotion swells in my stomach, nerves simmering in the

bottom of my lungs while I press closer, whispering, "I'm here. I'll give you what you need, darling."

"Do it now," Jonah grits out, fingers denting her hips as he gnashes his teeth at me. "Trust me. There won't be room in a second."

Using all his brawn, he spreads his knees to balance on his shins and holds her steady, half-skewered on his obscene length. As he leans them both back, I can see her entire slit—the way he splits her open, her wet pussy clenching on nothing, the swollen bud of her clit begging to be touched.

Fucking hell. She's absolutely *gorgeous.*

Inhaling her golden scent sets my canines to aching. I shuffle up against her, kissing her forehead as I slide the first inch of my cock into her slick core.

My brain blinks off, but this time, there's no panic. My Alpha has the reins, guiding my hands to her thighs and tugging her down.

All three of us shout as the motion lodges Jonah even deeper than before. I feel him—a thick ridge pressing through the thin wall of her pussy. The extra friction has me panting while I shove myself upward, bottoming out in her cunt.

She trembles around me, her inner muscles twitching and spasming. Her clit is so needy, pressing into my knot, pounding dully. When I wreath my hand around her throat, she sucks at both of us.

Jonah grinds out a curse, snagging my wild eyes with his own. When I nod, he pulls out, letting me push up.

Fucking—

The friction of him against the underside of my shaft makes my balls tighten. Serena feels it, too, perfuming in a dizzy rush that sends slick streaming down all of our thighs.

And all I can think is that I want *more.*

Need her scent all over me.

Need her soul inside mine.

My knot grinds the underside of her clit harder when Jonah's presses into it. Serena bucks and gasps. My fingers press into both of her bites and she comes, cinching in tight, rhythmic squeezes. My head falls back on a snarl as Jonah pulls out, gliding against me through the fluttering wall of her cunt.

The world dips and disappears as my knot pops into place. I can't see or hear or sense anything that isn't her, holding me in the most intimate way possible, her body begging for everything I have.

Limbs clasp around me. My back hits a soft surface. My cock erupts, dousing her depths with thick streams of cum as my hand slides to her nape and holds fast, exposing the exact spot I've dreamed of biting dozens of times.

My teeth break her skin, filling my mouth with tangy sweetness. I feel my *self* reach into hers. Gentle and slow, unfurling from a tight coil to a loose tether. When her cold little nose grazes the same, precise spot on my neck, I smile into her hair, pressing her closer.

"My darling girl. Right there is perfect."

She finds her mark, the motion painless and perfect. The cord I've offered her connects, pulling into an unbreakable bridge. But instead of linking two distant points, the bond blends them into one—until pieces of each of us are embedded in one another.

It's... seamless.

Beautiful in the simplest, truest way.

And as all of her feelings flow into me, they whisper like peace.

I HAVE a feeling we all need to get used to Spencer smiling.

The expression of pure, pride-filled happiness hasn't left his face since Serena burrowed into his neck. He lies on his back, petting her hair while he murmurs to her.

Like this, she's fully spread on top of him, with his knot lodged inside, and her legs spread wide around his thighs so we can all see.

Tristan feels whatever is going on between them and grins. Avery tries to hide it, but fails, smiling to himself as he reaches over and lazily tosses a rag to me.

I'm covered in our omega's slick and my own cum, having spilled twice already—once from watching her bond with Avery, and again right after I pulled out of her plush, tight ass.

Now, I feel my knot and balls fill again, just from admiring this insane view.

Most alphas would probably be feral at this point. Or at least jealous as fuck.

But my *manamea* must know me better than I know myself, because I'm not. In fact, I suspect her Omega picked me last on purpose, knowing I'd want to be the one to do her aftercare.

And I'm... *honored*.

To be chosen by her at all, but also, to be trusted to catch her at the end of all this.

I always want to catch her. Be her safe space, her soft place to land. The arms that hold her when she's sad or scared. The reassuring voice in her head when she doubts herself. The one who teaches her heart what unconditional love feels like.

God, she's so tired.

I can feel it in the lines of her body as Spencer's knot releases and slips free. They deflate more quickly during omegas' heats to allow us to fill them as many times as they need.

I'm grateful for that now.

Our omega needs to rest.

I mutter my assessment to Tristan and Avery, but Ave snorts. "Uh, yeah, try telling her that."

Tris chuckles, looking me in the eye. "Serena very specifically saved you for last."

"Like dessert," Avery chips.

Spencer's voice is more languid than I've ever heard it. "No," he puts in. "Everything she's done makes perfect sense. She bit Tristan without warning or permission so they would be even and he wouldn't feel guilty anymore. She took Avery first because she knew he wouldn't be able to wait."

He pauses, scent-marking her forehead and grazing it with his lips. "She put me in the middle in case I needed help. And she wanted Jonah last because she knew holding her after would mean the most to him."

Spence gives a hearty nod, as if he's confirmed something he always suspected. "She's a genius."

Avery reaches over to flick her foot. "An *evil* genius, maybe."

"Beautiful, evil genius," Tristan agrees.

My heart cracks when I see the small smile curving her lips. Even in the thick of her haze, she can understand them because of their bonds.

The air in the nest suddenly shifts as all three of them stiffen. Purrs break out. Serena whines, the sound small and pitifully exhausted.

Tristan's voice drops. "She's having more cramps."

Avery's eyes glow with restless worry. "Needs another knot. You ready, big man?"

I surge up to my knees, holding my arms open.

"Shh, darling," Spencer whispers into her hair, sitting them both up. "I know it hurts. But your big alpha is waiting for you. Remember how huge his knot gets? That will feel so good inside you, hmm?"

My best friend hands me our omega, laying her in my outstretched arms bridal-style. Her head lolls back as her eyes search sightlessly for mine. I balance her in the crook of one arm so I can touch her cheek with my free hand.

"I'm right here, *manamea*," I murmur, bending to brush my lips over hers. "How's my girl?"

The vulnerability and pain in her eyes tear me in two. She tries to speak, but only manages a little moan.

"Okay, sweetheart," I hush. "Let's fix that for you. I'm going to fill this sweet pussy with my knot. You just relax and let me make you feel good."

She stares into my eyes with her blown-out pupils, the look in them unfathomable. When Tristan explains, he sounds hoarse.

"She's... *grateful*, Jonah. That's what she feels when she looks at you. *Gratitude*."

My throat tightens while I absorb that, running my eyes over her face. Needing to remember every second of this.

"I'm grateful, too," I tell her, nuzzling my temple into hers. "You're my dream, omega. I love you so goddamn much."

She whimpers, fighting her exhaustion to try to stretch up and kiss me. I help her straddle my lap, holding most of her weight with my hands balanced under her perfect ass.

There's so much slick pouring out of her, there's no need to work my cock into her slowly. She takes the whole thing in a single glide, leaving me panting as I hit the end of her snug heat and feel her pussy lips suck at my knot.

It's tempting to work her up and down my length, taking time to feel the way she grips me. But she needs me right now. And that will always be the most important thing.

Circling my hips, I press my knot past the entrance of her pussy. Her slick heat tugs at the swell, instantly doubling my girth until she mewls.

A growly purr revs in my chest, and she throws her limp body into it, clasping her arms around my torso with what little strength she has left. I stroke my fingers into her hair with one hand and use the other to work her around my knot, letting her feel the way it fills her.

We don't last long before we're both gasping and grasping at each other. She comes with a soft cry that pierces my heart. I hold myself stiff inside of her, letting her body use mine to soothe her pain.

There's one spot left on her throat, right above Avery's bite, opposite Spencer's. I take it between my teeth while she's still coming, knowing the bite will help extend her pleasure.

The second I break her skin, I feel myself lose control. Some distant part of my mind registers that she's biting me, too. Simultaneously taking my bond and giving me hers. So that one moment, one blink later—

She's there.

She's *here*.

A glowing tether stretches between our centers. Filling me with contentment. Giving my life a whole new purpose.

Her. This. *Us*.

And I know I'll never need anything else.

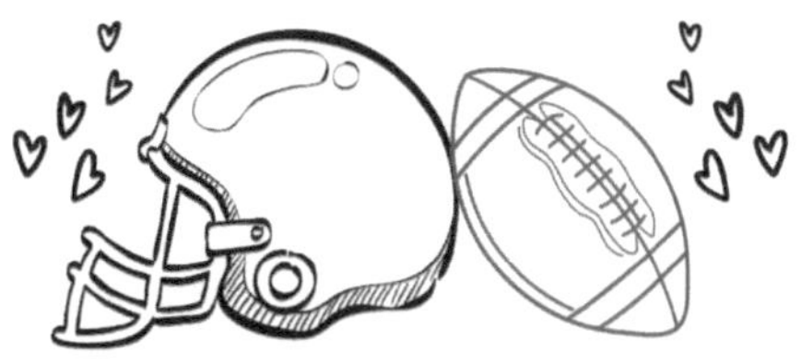

I CAN'T BELIEVE *I almost gave this up.*

It's a thought I've had every day since Serena bit me. The utter disbelief that I nearly forfeited a pack bond as some sort of penance.

She's been in heat for nearly five days, and every hour only makes me more thankful that our omega knew better. She knew that *we* needed this, somehow, and made sure to give it to us.

It's taken this long, but I'm almost used to being able to tune into the guys' thoughts. We all occasionally shut each other out, but for the most part, we've needed our lines open to keep Serena well cared for.

Right now, she's dreaming about her garden. We can only see flickers—lights, colors, sometimes scents. But I can tell Spencer is listening as hard as I am because his lips keep twitching up. He doesn't even seem upset about being distracted from the equations on his mind.

Avery is half-listening. That's the way his mind works, I've noticed. He can only give complete focus to a handful of things—going over every step of his latest match, looking for errors; and pack stuff—like how secretly grateful he is that Spencer sat through his fight and how excited he is for Serena to see the next one.

Right now, he's mentally blocking out all the workouts he'll have to do to make up for his time in here—though, he notes, he won't need to catch up on cardio. If anything, he might need to reduce that a bit...

Jonah would usually be thinking along similar lines, working overtime to catch up on practices he's missed, but he's pretending to sleep. We let him get away with it, even though it's obvious he's busy behind his curtain. He has his eyes shut, but a heavily pensive frown pulls under his beard.

The fact that we've all gotten more than six hours of rest makes his ruse less convincing. For the first few days, Serena needed one of us every hour—sometimes more than one of us. Yesterday, she started to go for longer stretches, just needing to be held or purred for.

Today, she finally started sleeping more, which Spencer says is a good sign. Her Omega must finally feel satisfied; we should see our sweet baby again soon.

Which means it's time to discuss what happened outside the locker room after the fight.

According to the alpha who approached my pack, his omega, Remi, is best friends with Meg Ash... who met Serena in the stadium at the pre-season game and instantly knew something was amiss. A fact she confirmed with her alphas by asking Jonah to show them all a picture last week.

Apparently, Remi and Serena are identical. And both of them were placed for adoption at birth.

We should talk.

Beside me, Spencer sighs, leaning his head back on the edge of the nest and shutting his eyes. Jonah's eyes snap open right away, proving he really wasn't asleep.

And Avery is the first one to complain, burying his head between two of Serena's nest cushions with a grumble. "Do we *have to?*"

I'm about to say, "yes"; because we have to figure out what we're going to tell Serena when she wakes up. Which will be soon, apparently.

I've spent a long time trying to shoulder everything for all of us, but we clearly work better as a unit. They deserve a say in how we move forward here. And I'm grateful as hell not to be in this alone.

I open my mouth, but urgency suddenly flares through the bond. We all sit up, looking at each other for an explanation.

Was that—

Are you—

No, it wasn't—

Serena.

We think it at the same time, all four of us turning to the little omega bundled up between Jonah and Ave. A moment ago, her beautiful features were smooth. Now, they're pinched, reflecting the pain that rips at her lower abdomen as a sharp burst of perfume fills the air.

Our pack moves as one, closing in on her. Jonah starts up his deep purr, pushing against her back as Ave cups her face, slowly kissing her awake.

"Time for another knot, gorgeous," he whispers. Serena whimpers, pressing closer to him.

"She's exhausted. The pain *should* be subsiding by now."

Spencer frowns as he checks her temperature, tutting at the thermometer. "She's cooler but not enough to break the heat."

I'd normally feel a jag of alarm, but the bent of his thoughts stays calm, so I do, too. "Does that happen?"

He nods, quirking his lips to the side. "She might need us to try something new. Sometimes, toward the end of a heat, especially if it's the first one an omega's had with mates, their instincts are reluctant to let go. A big shock to their systems can be effective in breaking that grasp."

There's no time for me to wonder what he's talking about, because he instantly shoots all of us a mental image of the exact configuration that immediately came to his mind.

Jonah looses a low growl of approval, but Ave *groans*. "Oh *God*."

And Spencer actually *laughs*. "I'll direct, of course." He shoots me a customary nod of deference. "If you're good with that, Tris."

Jonah snorts a smirk over Serena's dark head. "You'll be a bit busy, alpha."

Yeah, no shit.

Serena starts to whine, the sound much softer than it was at the beginning of her heat. It has something to do with how tired she is, but more to do with how safe she feels. She knows she barely has to make a sound, and we'll all trip over ourselves to get to her.

My spoiled baby girl.

She's perfect.

Which only makes what I'm about to do all the better. I raise a brow at Avery as his inked-up body slinks over. "Front or back?"

He cocks a glower. "You have to ask?"

He has a point. I don't think there's been a single time he's missed the opportunity to take our omega while she presented or hold her from behind while the rest of us worked.

I move to lie on my back as Jonah bundles Serena into his chest, purring louder and kissing her forehead before he carries her over. "Who's going to knot her?" he asks, being a shit-stirrer.

Avery smiles menacingly. "Whoever lasts the longest."

Jonah gently places Serena on top of me, her breasts rubbing against my chest hair as she moans and rocks against me. "Hi, baby," I whisper. "We have a treat for you."

Brilliant green eyes blink at me, trying to understand through her brain fog. When I send her the mental image Spencer came up with, though, she instantly perks up.

Ave chuckles fondly, straddling my thighs and smoothing his hands down her back. "Yeah, kitten? Look good?"

She nods emphatically, putting grins on each of our faces. Jonah looms at one of her sides while Spencer closes in at the other.

He spreads his palm flat over her heart and kisses her softly, nosing her cheek. "Hello, darling. You've done so well. I'm very pleased."

She lives for his praise, the same way she loves Jonah's reverence, Avery's wild obsession, and my protectiveness. When a flutter of joy and a burst of confidence soar through her, we all smile wider.

I love the way she preens as she kneels, tossing her thick, lustrous hair back. Avery promptly grabs a fistful and tugs her into his inked muscles, leaning over her shoulder to whisper in her ear.

Whatever he says has slick pouring down her thighs, dribbling onto my throbbing erection. I ignore my curiosity, knowing it's better for us all to keep our interior curtains drawn while we tend to our omega.

We learned pretty quickly that leaving them open and sharing all of our arousal in the bond was a recipe for things ending quickly.

And the mess wasn't ideal, either.

There will be no help for that, with what Spence has in mind.

He holds her steady as Avery works on getting everyone ready

—fingering her slick pussy until his hands are covered in shiny wetness. He gives no warning before clamping one of them around each of our dicks and *tugging*.

Fuck. I snarl quietly, loving the feel of her need coating my skin and the fact that Avery isn't gentle in the slightest.

He pulls at my aching cock until all the veins along the sides rub against his callouses. Buzzing tingles race to my balls, tightening my abdominal muscles as pre-cum pools at the bulging head of my dick.

Serena moans, watching his tattooed hand move over me. Finally, he reaches all the way down to knead my knot. It's already pounding, but she watches it grow and keens, tweaking everything below my navel even tighter.

Jonah smooths soothing hands down her back and belly, rubbing a slow circle where she aches to be filled. "Doesn't your alpha look good with Ave's hands on him?"

She whimpers, eyes flashing down to mine. This isn't the first time during her heat that one of us has lent the other a helping hand, but it's the first time she seems to *get* it.

And she loves it.

Biting her lip, she starts to buck against the open air. Spencer hushes her, sliding his hand up to her throat.

"I know, darling girl. Let Avery get them both as hard as possible. Then you can take two alpha cocks at once, hmm? Show us what a good omega you are for us?"

Serena sways closer, whining for a kiss he immediately gives her, murmuring more praises against her lips while Jonah strokes down to thumb at her clit.

In her haze, Serena can't put up her curtain, so we all feel the jolt of pleasure that bolts through her core. Jonah licks his lips as she moans, dropping his other hand to fist his cock. She'll need that later, too.

Avery's fingers slides down my girth faster, pressing into my knot until I finally growl at him. He releases me with another evil smirk and starts positioning us.

My chest is already heaving, but I feel fairly confident I can last.

Until he bends her forward and uses his shaft to shove mine into her clenching heat.

And I remember—the *piercings*.

Holy fucking—

Serena and I both shout, my head falling back to the mattress and hers dropping forward. Jonah holds her around the waist, allowing her to hover half-folded over my body while Avery tunnels deep from behind, pushing me in as far as we can both reach.

Her pussy shudders, gushing slick down to my knot and the full balls dangling under it. It creates a whirlpool effect—wet heat swirling, pressing us together until I feel the metal balls pierced through his head stimulating mine. When she cinches tighter, the bars studding his length roll against me, too.

Which explains why he was so cocky about outlasting me.

He may have overestimated his control, though. After half a minute, he's gnashing his teeth every bit as hard as I am, roughing out growls to match mine on every plunge.

Serena begs for more, whining and moaning, squirming in the thick circle of Jonah's arm.

"She needs more," Spencer decides, kneeling upright. His cock bobs in front of her face as he flexes his fingers into all four of her claiming marks.

She screams, her core spasming around both of us until my knot ticks wider. It bumps Avery's and he groans, gasping, "Fuck me. Fucking *fuck me*."

I can't tell if he's talking to me or our omega, but all three of us move faster and harder, grinding together as our knots press and glide, so perfectly slicked up by Serena's sweet, creamy cunt.

Spencer guides himself into her mouth, petting her hair back as he pumps against her tongue. When he moves the hand around her throat down to support her weight, Jonah drops his arm and fists himself harder, watching our omega swallow her alpha down with desperate moans. His free hand falls to the place between Serena's body and mine, finding her clit and rolling it between his fingers.

Shit.

"She's gonna come," Avery bites out. "Fuck, kitten, you feel so goddamn good when that little pussy squeezes us. Just. Like. *That.*"

He gives a vicious thrust with every word, the friction between us building until I know I'm about to lose my battle for control.

But just as I'm gritting my molars, ready to admit defeat and pull out to come all over both of them, Avery spits out one final curse and explodes.

The thick spurt starts inside of her, lubing her up for my knot as he drags those piercings and his pounding shaft out of her body. He comes across her ass while I shove all the way in, my knot popping into place as Serena's inner walls massage it.

She drains Spencer with her mouth while her pussy empties my cock. Jonah bellows, adding to the mess of scents decorating her skin with his own load.

Our omega comes longer than she has yet, her orgasm rolling through her body long after all of them have gently pulled out or way from her. Spencer catches her limp body as she falls into another daze, already reaching for the nearest clean blanket to wipe her up.

Jonah staggers back while I stare up, my blurry brain rebooting.

Holy fuck.

Avery looks just as fucked up, chortling as he sinks backward like a stone. "Weren't we," he pants, "supposed to talk?"

THE FIRST THING I see is Jonah's monster cock.

It's been tamed, apparently, because it's resting against his thigh innocently enough. Though I notice it twitch the same second his fingers pause in my hair.

He sets something aside—a hairbrush—and fits his other palm around my cheek, turning my head so it's cushioned on his upper thigh like a pillow. He bends forward, grinning widely behind his burly beard. "*Manamea*, is that you?"

My smile feels shy as I nod, stretching lightly. A warm, hard body bumps my backside while I reposition, and I find Spencer there. He's fast asleep, with his face inches from where my spine was and his hips tucked in a spooning position.

Right, I think, feeling slow. *He had me present last time. To get me to calm down long enough for Jonah to brush my hair.*

A pang of chagrin hits my stomach as I try to recall exactly how many times they'd needed to do things like that. My Omega didn't like to speak—and taming her had been an ordeal until Spencer thought up his big idea and had Avery and Tris both take me at the same time. That seemed to settle her down.

I woke two or three more times after that, but each time, my need was more emotional than physical. It was a lot harder than I expected, going from so much intimacy to a normal level.

Jonah reads my bittersweet wistfulness and picks me up, meeting my eye for permission before slowly sliding me down his length. He isn't hard as stone, but he's halfway there, and his cock is thick and warm inside of me. More a comfort than a temptation.

We both sigh and he gathers me into his chest, purring effortlessly.

Fresh memories flow through my mind, and I cringe, thinking he can't see me. But then I hear him inside. *Can't hide that easily, little hummingbird.*

With a surge of dizzying joy, I remember—*we're bonded.* They'll *all* be able to hear me. And each other.

"It's wonderful," Jonah rasps into my silky hair. "You did an amazing job, *manamea*. I don't think any of us even realized how much we needed this until you gave it to us."

I know exactly what he means. Now that they've all claimed their places inside me, I truly cannot imagine ever being alone again. Just thinking about it makes me whimper.

"Never again, baby," Jonah murmurs, holding me closer, his heft growing more rigid inside me, letting me feel him. "*Never.*"

I burrow into his neck, kissing my claiming mark. I don't need to see his face to know he's smiling—I can *feel* the joy swoop through his chest. It echoes in my own, bringing my tiny purr out for him.

He *loves* that. His cock hardens as he moans into my hair, nuzzling his cheek against my forehead to leave his scent-mark behind.

Instead of speaking, he gives me a moment to adjust, working through my hazy memories and the twirl of giddy happiness braided into them. I feel him listening, caring about every little thought as if it's vital. When he sees flickers from my dreams, he grins again.

"You dreamed about our garden a lot, hummingbird. We'll take you out there as soon as you have your strength back. Maybe a picnic?"

I rub my own scent between his pecs, smiling as I admit, "I wasn't dreaming about the garden, I think. It was... you guys."

For a long beat, confusion clangs in his head. With a sigh and a pinch of embarrassment, I do my best to show him what I mean instead of telling him. Taking his hand and leading him, metaphorically, down into my bond.

Our bond.

To me, it *is* a garden. I've heard central bonds described as a room with doors to each alpha, but mine feels more like a little patch of peaceful grass. An oasis, with gates for each of them to come to when they need me or want to cross through to one another.

It's more than that, though. The way they each make me feel —they've *grown* me. From a tiny, broken seed into something too fierce to be a flower and too soft to form thorns. I'm somewhere in the middle—maybe even something I don't quite know yet.

But I know that Spencer is my rain. Steady and cool, nourishing me with every drop of praise and every bit of knowledge. He can be stormy—or gentle. And I love him either way.

Avery is the wind, whipping around me in a whirl of chaos and color. And then, sometimes, whispering to me in the sweetest ways. Bringing me things I never thought I'd want or need.

Carrying pieces of me off to plant them far away, in the unknown. Always keeping me guessing which direction we're going in.

There's joy in that mystery and beauty in the trust it takes to enjoy it. He and I both have that.

Jonah and I have a similar sort of happiness; only the type we share is brighter. Warmer. He's my sunshine—so constant and *vital*. The steady, vibrant heat that encourages growth. There every day, no matter what.

Tristan is just as consistent in his own way. Like roots and soil. Anchoring all of us, protecting the parts of me I don't want anyone else to see. Letting me slice through him if it means I can flourish. Giving and giving—because that's who he *is*.

Jonah listens while I try to explain without words, his head finally turning to look at our pack leader. He's stretched out, asleep, with his arm thrown over his face.

My big man's chest rumbles deeper. "I wanted to talk to you. About that."

But he's... embarrassed? It's such an odd feeling, coming from my most easy-going alpha. I let it flow through our bond, anyway, wanting to listen to him as attentively as he does for me.

I feel Avery and Spencer starting to stir, but that doesn't seem to bother Jo. He wants them to hear, too, I think. It's just easier to pretend I'm the only one paying attention.

He shows me what it's been like this season, preparing to play for the fifteenth year in a row. How he didn't ever want to stop because it felt like football was all he had—all he was.

Until me.

"Over the last few days, I've realized how much purpose you've brought to our pack. To me. And I think I want to retire. To be home. With you."

It would help Tris, too. That's why he's bringing it up now. He felt me worrying about my senator alpha and all the weight on his shoulders. If Jonah is willing to take on more of our pack business so Tristan doesn't have to carry as much...

"Are you sure?" I ask, peering up at his wide, handsome features, touching his face. "Won't you be bored?"

He grins and shakes his head, showing me memories through the bond—the days he spent building our garden, hours cuddling me on our couch to treat my touch starvation, evenings in the kitchen.

And along with every single image? A burst of true, deep satisfaction. Of *purpose*.

We make him happy.

A hand claps around Jonah's shoulder, squeezing. I'm shocked when I find Spencer at the other end of it, staring at his best friend with solemn appreciation in his gaze. "This is an inspired idea."

Avery shuffles over next, smiling crookedly as he presses a kiss to my bare shoulder. "Yeah, Jonah, you're old as dirt anyway. Time to pack it in."

"Fuck off, kid," Jo chuckles, "I still fucked you under the table at least five times this week."

A throb of heat hits between my hips, and my fingers clutch at Jonah's beard. Which reminds me...

"Oh *God*," I groan. "Did I—push you between my legs again?"

"Only every day," my big man replies with pride, then bounces his bushy eyebrows at me. "Ave was jealous. But I told him that's *our* thing."

My fighter rolls his eyes before smacking another kiss onto my arm, flashing me his bedroom eyes. "In case you were wondering, kitten, *our* thing is doggy style."

I cut him a look. "How *romantic*."

Of course, the barb only makes him smile more. Spencer laughs quietly as he sits at Jonah's side, turning to his brother. As soon as Tristan's eyes blink open and he sees us, a rush of new emotions floods our bond.

There's joy and love and gratitude. Pride for his pack. And then a complicated mix of things that make no sense to me.

Whatever it is, the humor falls off all of their faces. Jonah sighs, lifting me off his lap and turning me to face them as Tristan meets each of their gazes.

"What's wrong?" I ask, turning from face to sober face. "Guys?"

It's amazing how calm I feel.

When I first came to this house, the smallest hint of unhappiness from any of them would have sent me spiraling. Now, I know it isn't anything to do with us.

But it turns out to have everything to do with *me*.

Tristan kisses me slowly and then frames my face in his hands as he stares into my eyes. "Sweet baby," he sighs, "there's something we need to tell you."

DUMBEST ASSHOLES ALIVE

AVERY CHANGED THE GROUP CHAT NAME TO
THE *LUCKIEST* ASSHOLES ALIVE

JONAH

yeah, good call.

THE SUNDAY after my heat is warm and sunny. A perfect day

for a picnic—which is exactly what the guys have planned for all of us.

This park is lovely. A large patch of greenery and ancient oak trees, sprawled between picturesque brick streets, lined with sunny little shops and posh restaurants. Off to the side, I spy a pretty peacock fountain surrounded by a colorful rose garden.

I wish the setting were enough to help me feel better. But my stomach seethes, protesting the panic churning there.

I have my interior curtain up, not wanting to swamp the guys with my anxiety. Besides, if they know how upset I am, they might try to talk me out of this. And it's taken seven days for me to talk myself *into* it, so.

Soft kisses sink through the hair on my crown. "Beautiful baby girl," Tristan hums, tucking me into his suited-up side. "You look so gorgeous today."

It's just a crop top and a black denim skirt. I didn't know what to wear to meet the omega who might potentially be my long-lost sister.

Twin, my mind corrects.

That little piece of info was added after the initial batch. When my heat broke, and my alphas told me about the man who had approached them at Avery's fight, they only knew his omega was friends with Meg Ash, a fellow orphan, and, apparently, identical to me.

It wasn't until a couple of days after my heat, when he started slowly getting back to real life, that Tristan reached back out to the Pierson pack and got a copy of their omega's birth certificate.

Not only do we have the same woman—Alana Skyes—listed as our birth mother. We also have the same birthday.

Jonah is, of course, the first to see past the mask I'm wearing. He sighs, bending forward to balance his forearms on his knees. His warm eyes trace my face from his place across the limo while his features crease, wincing.

"Come here, *manamea*."

The apprehension climbing my insides gets harder to hide by

the second. By the time Jonah settles me into his big body, it's a relief to feel his thick arms close around me.

"You're only sisters if you *want* to be," he murmurs.

It's the one sentence that's brought me any measure of peace over the last few days.

Beside us, Avery nods. His fiery blue eyes meet mine, and the rage burning there somehow soothes me. "You know as well as I do that names on papers don't mean jackshit, kitten. If you don't like this chick or this pack, we never have to see them again. Ever."

Spencer nods, his cool control flexing to fill the backseat along with his brother's reassuring dominance.

"We can turn around and go home," Tris offers. "Or we can meet them another time. It's all up to you, baby. We'll do anything you want."

I know I have to do this. Because I have to *know*—all that time, was Wally doing more than keeping me in cruel isolation? Was he keeping me from my sister? The only real family I ever had a prayer of having?

Well, until my pack, anyway.

I blow out a deep breath, trying to fight off old fears. And failing. "Her alphas... did they seem nice when you talked to them?"

My senator's eyes soften while he reads whatever's pulsing through our bond. "Yeah, baby," he says quietly. "They did."

Jonah hugs me tighter, nuzzling my temple with his forehead. "We'll be with you the whole time," he says into my hair. "And you know Avery will gut anyone who looks at you wrong."

"There will be no *gutting* in a public park," Spencer snaps, slanting Avery a warning look before flickering back to me. His shy half-smile appears—just for me. "Besides, I think Miss Thorne can throw her own punches now."

Miss Thorne.

It's the first time he's ever said that. I've been waiting, hoping he would soon. And, maybe, one day, it will be *Mrs.* Thorne...

Maybe? Jonah bellows in my head, affronted.

Avery guffaws. *The fuck you think you're getting out of marrying us, too, kitten.*

Yes, Spencer chimes dryly, *I'm afraid that's a foregone conclusion, darling.*

Tristan pumps out a bit more of that big-knot dominance. *Of course it is. I already ordered rings for her to choose from.*

I feel myself smile despite the tangled mess in my middle. *Rings.* Of course he wouldn't just pick one. He's going to get me whatever I want. Even if I want a different one for each of them.

Thinking this, my fingers find the one piece of jewelry I arrived with, the hummingbird charm resting against my sternum. I fist it, remembering where it came from. Wondering if Remi has one, too.

"Okay. I'm ready."

⸻ ♥ ⸻

IT'S easy to spot the Pierson pack.

Or, I should say—it's impossible to miss them.

Their pack leader is every bit as put-together as mine—wearing a navy suit with a frilly pocket square that does *not* match his scowl. For a second, I'm *almost* intimidated... until I clock the huge alpha behind him.

Now *that's* a frown.

Wow.

Not quite up to Avery's standards, but he's pretty close.

The only one smiling is the most handsome—a dark-haired, blue-eyed alpha who looks coiffed despite being in gray joggers and a white T-shirt. His expression glows as he talks to the small woman at his side, smoothing his thumb over her lower lip to release it from her teeth. She just pulls it right back in, though.

I know the feeling, sis.

The blond one—Smith—spies us first. He speaks to the others and then strides over, stretching out his hand.

To me.

I blink, taking it and shaking as he says, "I'm Smith Pierson. You must be Serena."

I manage a shaky nod as Tristan steps into my back, hugging me around my middle as he extends his right hand. "Tristan Thorne. I apologize for taking so long to get back to you. It was our first heat as a bonded pack."

Smith almost smiles. "I understand. We just bonded four months ago."

That makes sense. They all look young—and they have the same harmonious energy the guys behind me share now.

Her alphas wander over, keeping her safely behind them while they all introduce themselves and shake my hand. I swallow the lump in my throat, hoping my voice doesn't abandon me.

It almost happens when the big one and the pretty one step aside, revealing—

Well.

My twin.

There's just no other way to say it. She literally *has my face*.

Wide blue eyes blink at me, cut with the same gold patterns carved through my green irises. Her scent—some cake-like honey aroma—singes a bit, but she doesn't look away.

Her mouth opens, but nothing comes out. Which is way too fucking relatable, honestly.

I think about how it felt to choke on my words that first night. How it hasn't happened in so long, I barely remember the last time.

I think about how many people tried to break me.

And how I'm not.

I'm not broken.

I'm *Serena Thorne*.

So, I do my best to smile and hold my hand out to her. "Hi. It's nice to meet you."

♥

"IS THIS NORMAL?"

Remi squints across the lawn, watching while Avery and Jonah somehow maneuver a soccer ball around Damon and kick it toward the trash cans they're using as a makeshift goal. When Cassian blocks it, Avery roars in frustration while Damon laughs.

"Yes," she confirms, snorting quietly. "Just thank God there isn't a pool nearby. They'd be trying to drown each other."

I believe it. Her alphas seem every bit as extra as mine. Right now, we're laid out on a picnic blanket fit for a pair of queens—there's even a duvet under it for "padding."

The spread her pack assembled is incredible. Mostly baked goods—courtesy, shockingly, of the pretty alpha with the scoundrel's grin.

I heard Remi call him Trouble, and that totally tracks. I bet if we left him alone with my Menace, property damage would be involved.

Our pack alphas are off to the side with Spencer. The three of them murmur to each other with serious expressions that I'm trying not to think about too hard. Their shades are up, anyway, trying to give me privacy. The anxious look on Remi's face makes me think she's in the same boat.

For a moment, awkward silence threatens to descend. Then her gaze catches on my necklace. Before she can ask, I reach up to touch it.

"It was... from her," I whisper, holding it out to show her the charm. "Our mother. I was wondering... did she leave you anything?"

For a second, Remi looks stricken. But she reaches into her thick, curly hair and pulls out a sparkly pink butterfly clip.

"This," she says softly.

It's the strangest, longest, hardest moment of my life. Seconds stretch on as we stare at each other. And I have the sense she's thinking the exact same things I am.

Why did it have to be like this?

What if we had been allowed to know each other?

What will happen now?

Tears well in her eyes, but she sniffs them back, raising her chin primly. "She liked things that could fly," Remi points out. "I wonder why."

I think I know. Because I *get* it—being rooted to a life that's all wrong, wishing you had wings to spread and soar away. "Maybe she felt trapped."

Remi sniffles again, wiping at her nose with her wrist this time. "By us?"

"No."

I'm surprised how easily my answer comes. Ordinarily, I don't think of myself as someone who struggled or went through something traumatic. *But I did.* And if I'd found out I was pregnant while living under Wally's roof? Well, I would have felt trapped, too.

But not because of the life inside me.

Because of the life around me.

"I think she loved us," I murmur, looking up into the leafy canopy swaying overhead, tapping into the little oasis inside me for strength. "Whatever was going wrong in her life that made her an unfit mother, she still carried us. And kept us safe while she could."

Remi fingers her clip, considering. "I suppose you're right. She probably wouldn't have left us pieces of herself if she didn't care."

A necklace and a clip.

I remember the night I wandered into the police station, off the street, with only that red rubber bodysuit and the thin gold charm strung around my neck.

Was it the same way for our mom at the hospital? Did she

come with just the clothes on her back? Were these trinkets the only ones she had to give?

"Do you think—" Remi starts and then has to pause to swallow. A tear tracks down her cheek, but she just lets it fall.

And I decide I like her.

Even before she finishes.

"—do you think she did it? Do you think she flew away? To freedom?"

And I decide I *really* like her.

My sister, I think.

It suddenly occurs to me—maybe our mother never meant for us to be alone. Maybe we were always supposed to do this together. Have one another. Maybe that's why she felt like we would be okay without her.

Maybe, now that I know that, I can finally forgive her.

"I hope so," I say, smiling up at the sky, letting my own tears fall. Feeling happy and sad, but mostly just *hopeful*. "I really do."

two years later

WHAT THE FUCK am I doing here?

I know I said I was past all that shit, but seriously.

How did I end up with this tight end's hairy ass *in my face*?

From her place across my old bedroom, Serena smirks at me like the naughty little kitten she is.

You think this is sooooo funny, huh? I gripe internally. *Maybe I should tie you to my chair again.*

She knows I'm not bluffing. Her sweet, creamy scent is still soaked into the black leather recliner that currently has the Ospreys' star player draped over it.

Since we all started sleeping in the Omega Suite together every night, this place has basically become our own personal tattoo parlor.

It sat empty for a couple of months before our girl came to me one day and shyly asked if I'd meant what I said the day I told her I would ink her. Now, a couple of years and half a dozen designs later, she knows I don't make idle threats.

They're called "promises," Ave, Tristan chimes.

He's downstairs, being a stick in the mud with the other pack alpha, the doctor, and the professor—while the cool kids get tattoos.

For good measure, I send both Thornes a nice, long mental image of Theo Matthew's bare ass and get an internal wince back.

Jesus Christ, Avery, Spencer snaps. *I am _eating_*.

I start to pan my gaze over to a particularly bloody line I just inked, but a soft, tinkling laugh fills our bond.

Menace... Green eyes glance up from where she and Meg are sitting crossed-legged on my former bed.

The makeshift curtain I have up to keep my girl from having to witness this atrocity makes it hard for me to see her whole face, but I catch the teasing light in our omega's gaze as she asks, *Why are we torturing Spencer?*

Anytime she interrupts one of my mean streaks, she always says "we." Because, in her mind, I'm her permanent accomplice. And she's mine.

Which is how I got roped into this clusterfuck.

It was supposed to be one piece. Her sister's goalie alpha, Cassian, wanted a blue butterfly like the monarch I have in the center of my chest.

I like the guy, since he tends to keep his yap shut, unlike their other packmate Damon. Plus, it was some romantic shit for my sister-in-law. So I said *fine*.

Little did I know.

"Peeeeeachessss," the burly blond football player whines. "It buuuuurns."

The Ash Pack omega snickers. "I told you, big guy: This is *allll* you."

From their spot on the floor, Declan and Jonah both snort. "It can't be that bad," Declan grumbles. "Unlike what this animal did to my spine."

An *animal*? As I stand here tattooing his packmate for nothing but a good time?

I press harder on the needle and Theo actually *whimpers*.

"Menace," Serena calls out loud, her soft voice full of mischief. "Behave."

Jonah scratches his beard and laughs. "Fat fucking chance."

I flash her half a smile. "What do I *get* if I behave?"

Gold sparkles in her green gaze. "I'll let you finish my thigh piece tonight."

Oh fuck. I've been steadily working on it for *months*. A detailed, shaded vision of the garden she envisions as the center of our bond. I drew it for her as part of her birthday gift, and she's been sitting for sessions ever since.

It's been slow work... probably because I stop to lick her cunt every few minutes.

My pheromones flex, filling the room as Declan rolls his eyes, Jonah chuffs, and Meg chortles. Theo shoots me a dirty look. "Are you and your omega *flirting* while my *ass* is out?"

"Yep," Serena and I answer together, then grin at one another.

Fuck me, she's so beautiful. Even in a ripped-up Ospreys T-shirt and those little exercise shorts she likes to wear when she's kicking ass at our gym.

There's no time for that today. As soon as I finish this piece, we'll be on the go.

And I have to wear a fucking suit. Although this might be the *one time* I won't mind.

Or won't *complain*, at least.

Much.

I can tell my girl is listening to my thoughts when a soft tendril of love creeps through our tether. I grin to myself, showing her an image of me kissing the hell out of her as soon as I'm done.

Which will be right... about... now.

I click my machine off, setting the needle aside. "Alright, you big blond pussy. You're done."

And I'm officially responsible for the fact that there's a fat, fuzzy peach tattooed on a grown man's ass.

The things I do for love.

I barely have a second to stretch and try to dial down my glare before my omega senses my mood. Casting Meg a knowing look, Serena flounces right over and jumps into my arms.

"Thank you, Menace," she says, wrapping her lithe legs around my hips. "Now I owe you."

I glower at her gorgeous face. "Everyone in this damn room owes me, kitten."

Meg scrambles up from her spot and runs over, ducking around the partition to see the finished product before I slap a bandage over it. She squeals, bouncing in place while Serena hides a smile against my neck.

Theo's face has lost all traces of pain. He grins back at his omega and then bounces his eyebrows. "Sexy, right?"

"Soooo sexy," Meg gushes, bending to kiss his furry face. "The hottest tattoo in the pack *for sure*."

Declan rises to the bait, coming over to sweep her into an openly suggestive kiss. Meg giggles against his lips before breaking away, winding one arm around her quarterback and dropping her free hand to pet Theo's long hair.

She looks over at us, suddenly remembering something. "Oh! Serena! I have something for you."

She moves to the purse she left beside the bedroom door and drops to rummage through it. "Really, it's a gift from me and Remi. I know you're going to see her later, but I wanted to be the one to give it to you before you leave on your trip!"

Meg fishes out a rectangular box and hands it to Serena, paying no mind to the way I'm snuggling my omega into my chest.

"They're sort of a tradition," Meg chirps, returning to Declan. "It took us a while to find the right ones for you, though."

My girl flips the lid open and reveals a pair of gold, heart-shaped sunglasses. They're shiny, with exaggerated angles and the words "bad bitch" engraved along the side.

Serena laughs. "Oh my God, thank you! I *love* them. They're just like yours and Remi's!"

Meg shrugs. "We've wanted to get you some forever, but you only wear bougie accessories—Remi finally custom-ordered those because we couldn't find any other gold ones! Now you'll have them when you're lying on the beach next week."

Jonah, Serena, and I all share a beat of excitement at the mention of our vacation. For good reason.

It legit took us two years to agree on a place. Spencer wanted something historic. Jonah wanted to surf and lie on a beach. I wanted to do some adventure traveling. And Tristan was aiming for a romantic angle.

In the end, Serena picked the locale—two weeks traveling from Japan down to Thailand. Plenty of culture, designated beach time, *and* we get to ride elephants.

Not to mention the moony way she and Tris look at each other every time someone mentions the cherry blossoms in bloom this time of year.

We've been on lots of little trips since we bonded, but this one is supposed to be a "honeymoon."

Two years late. Though, lately, I got the feeling our girl knew exactly where we were going all along—she just liked listening to us bicker and the way we all spent an hour after every pack meeting huddled around Tris's laptop, researching together.

Sparks fly through her gaze while she settles her new glasses on top of her hair and leans back to look into my eyes. *Only took you a year-and-a-half to figure it out,* she thinks. *This is why you're my partner-in-crime.*

She's mine, too.

Usually. But today we have a major surprise for her, too.

When she feels my inner curtain drop suddenly, her brows fold in suspicion. *What are you up to, Menace?*

I grin. *You'll see. We have plans for you.*

Glowing green orbs narrow at me. *Does this have anything to do with how secretive Tris has been recently?*

I pout, knowing she'll sense my lie even before I think, *What?! No!*

Instead of getting annoyed, she shakes her head, fondness filling her eyes. "And here I thought you worked alone."

"Not anymore, baby," I admit, unable to help the way genuine happiness touches the words when they echo in our bond.

Not anymore.

"JUST HOLD STILL," I grunt, shooting Ave a glare. "Goddamn, kid. It's a suit, not a straitjacket."

He fidgets with his solid black sleeves, flashing his signature murderous look. "I take it back. I'm officially complaining about these dumbass clothes."

Yeah, no shit, I chuckle internally. *This is important to our girl. Just a couple more hours...*

I hope.

Truth be told, I have no idea how long this ceremony is going to last, and I'm not exactly a huge fan of wearing a suit in the Florida heat, either.

It's warm, for an April day. Serena and Spencer get to wait inside, along with all the other graduates. The rest of us are fine baking in the sun, but I hope this weather won't be too much for Remi...

As I have the thought, Tristan steps up beside me, hiding a smirk as he nods at the solid figure cutting through the university quad. Cassian stands as tall as I do, easily noticeable over the heads of all the other attendees.

He's frowning, but what else is new? I've started to suspect he's grumpy on purpose, sometimes, to earn himself extra time with our sweet sister-in-law.

That would never work on Serena, Tristan thinks with pride. *She'd figure us out in two seconds.*

He has a point. It's a miracle she hasn't unriddled her surprise yet. Tris has been killing himself to keep it completely secret, but our omega is brilliant.

Case in point—we're at her graduation, and she's only been in school for two years.

It helps to have your professor inside your head, Serena quips. *Makes it sooooo much easier to cheat.*

All three of us snort at Spencer's internal scoff of outrage. *As if I would ever allow that, Mrs. Thorne.*

Serena's musical laugh fills our bond, lighting everything up. Oblivious to the way we all grin at each other like idiots, she asks, *Is Remi here yet?*

Tristan sends a mental image of Smith Pierson melting the flesh off of someone's face as they accidentally step in her sister's unsteady path.

Oh, yes...

Damon brings up the rear, turning and offering charming smiles to everyone Cassian and Smith have just growled at.

Relatable, I think, casting Avery and Tris a glower.

Avery pulls at his collar again and Tristan rolls his eyes. "I'm not that bad," he mutters, watching while Smith runs his anxious eyes over Remi's profile.

All four of us blare back at him in the bond.

Um, yes you are, I laugh.

HA! Avery exclaims. *You're hilarious.*

No, Spencer puts in drily. *You're worse.*

Serena's tether glows with happiness. *Don't listen to them, Senator. I happen to like it.*

Tris still hasn't wiped the shit-eating grin off his face when the Piersons finally make it over. He shakes hands with Smith and gives Remi a careful once-over.

Avery slaps Damon's shoulder and exchanges grunts with Cassian while I hug Remi from the side, careful not to get my scent on her or squeeze her enormous middle.

"How are you feeling, little sis?" I ask, grinning down at her huge baby bump.

Well, *babies* bump, I guess.

When everyone found out Remi was having twins, Serena was overjoyed. I think, in a way, the two sisters getting to go through this together has been healing for them.

Tris and Smith haven't had any luck finding out what happened to their mother. But my hummingbird once told me, while we were lying in our garden, that not knowing didn't bother her as much as she thought it would. She likes to imagine Alana flying free, wherever she may be.

In the meantime, knowing that she'll get to watch her sister's twins grow up has really helped Serena make peace with all the time they lost. I wonder—if our girl is ever ready for babies—whether having some of our own will be another big step in coming to terms with her past. The same may be true for Spencer and Avery, too.

Seeing Remi carry her babies has definitely gotten all of us thinking about the future. We're in no rush, though. The most important thing is that Serena gets where she wants to go and has everything she needs.

That's clearly the Pierson's only goal for their omega, too. If having two humans inside of her distresses Remi at all, I can't tell. So far, she's been one of the happiest pregnant ladies I've ever met.

A wide smile graces her slightly drawn features. "I'm good! A little tired. They were playing tetherball with my bladder most of the night."

Avery can take all the gore and violence in the world, but he looks a little squeamish as he cringes at Remi's big belly and the purple pleated sundress draped over it. "You guys are done after these two, right?"

Damon snorts, wrapping his arms around his omega. "Hell no! We all have to have a turn!"

Serena told me they don't know which alpha fathered these particular babies, but I guess we'll find out fairly soon. Still, three alphas and two babies a piece…?

Remi rolls her eyes. "If you each get your own set of twins, that's *six* babies, Trouble."

He grins at her. "Exactly! We'd have our own hockey team!"

The wash of horror that floods Avery is enough to have Tristan and I hiding snickers. And then, a moment later, we're all swallowing a bit of longing, too.

Spencer's voice interrupts my musings, announcing that it's time for us to find our seats. Thankfully, they're reserved and we don't have far to walk.

Cassian winds up between Remi and me while we shuffle into the second row of folding chairs. "So, how are you doing?" he grunts in his grumbly way. "Missing the field yet?"

Last fall marked my first season as a retired NFL player. And, really, I was surprised how much I *didn't* miss playing. The game will always mean a lot to me, and I definitely miss seeing my teammates every day—but we're around the Ash Pack so often, these days, it honestly doesn't seem like I've given very much up.

Especially when our house and our pack run so much better with me available to help Tristan and care for Serena every day.

"You know," I tell him, sitting down. "It's actually been really good."

It helps that our omega is so appreciative of every small thing I do for her. There's never been a single day where she's let me doubt my value—to her or the others.

Once everyone is settled, "Pomp & Circumstance" begins to play. That shuts everyone up—even Avery, who finally stops fussing with his damn shirt.

The graduates file in. And for once I'm grateful I'm the biggest guy in the whole damn crowd because I get a perfect view of our omega, draped in her white graduation robe.

She's nervous. I can feel her heart fluttering through our bond. The moment our eyes meet over the rows of people between us, though, a burst of confidence and joy fills her.

This is it, she whispers, just to me.

I swear, I must look like the world's biggest sap, getting misty-eyed just from *looking* at her and hearing her voice. *This is what?* I reply.

She shows me an image from a long time ago—the day I showed her the garden I made for us and told her I didn't care where she'd been.

This is where I wanted to go, she tells me. *And you got me here.*

TWO YEARS AGO, shaking hands with three-hundred graduates would have been my own personal version of hell.

This year, I volunteered.

I had to, for one very important reason: I truly couldn't picture anyone else handing Serena her diploma.

She looks lovely in her cap and gown, the white fabric setting off her luminous eyes and the golden shimmer of her skin. I watch her out of the corner of my eye for the entire ceremony, my instincts pacing inside of me.

Making peace with them has been a process. Still, it's no longer a shock when my Alpha's voice rises from the place where we're connected.

Mine.

Ours, I correct. *You possessive bastard.*

He almost seems to shrug, conceding. His pride blends into mine as I look around, noting how many more omegas Serena's class has than previous grades.

I know that's partially due to my brother. His law protecting omegas' rights in the workplace passed nearly eighteen months ago and, ever since, we've had a huge influx of omega students, staff, and applicants.

Sending this thought to him through the bond, I add, *Good work, Tris.*

He nods at Serena, whose row stands to file up to the stage. *Back at you.*

I wish I could take even a crumb of credit for our omega's brilliance, but it's truly all her. She's blown me away, taking on enormous course-loads and leaping through her school work with flying colors. Next fall, she'll start her doctorate, which will make us colleagues, of sorts.

I catch the flash of her grin as she lines up along the side of the platform, thinking, *You'll always be my Professor, Mr. Thorne.*

Those words still have me grinning after twenty-six more handshakes. Until finally—*finally*—our omega sweeps across the stage.

The dean announces her name, and I hear our family cheer, inside our bond and out loud for the whole assembly to hear. Serena's bright sweetness swells between us as she steps in front of me, her smile beaming from her beautiful face.

The black diamond on her ring finger sparkles as she reaches for the diploma I hand her, curling my other hand around her free fingers. "Congratulations, Mrs. Thorne," I say out loud.

And, inside, where no one else can hear, the words I've been thinking all day. *My best student. My wife. My mate. I didn't know I could love anything as much as I adore you, darling.*

Serena squeezes my palm and leans up to kiss my cheek, not caring who sees. "I love you, too," she whispers, her eyes warm, even as her lips quirk into my favorite, smart smirk. "*Professor.*"

TRISTAN

AFTER SIX MONTHS OF RENOVATIONS, the hinges on the back door still creak.

I frown at them as I push out of the house, stepping down into the grand backyard. I have no idea how she managed to spot the house with the biggest lawn in the whole damn city, but I'm beginning to think my omega can do just about anything.

Here's hoping I'm still alive to enjoy that fact once she figures out what I've been up to.

Keeping secrets from her is next-to impossible. For one, our whole pack likes to keep our bond as open as possible. But, moreover, Serena is exceptionally perceptive.

She'll make the most amazing counselor, just as she's made an incredible student.

Pride lingers in my chest despite the fact that her graduation ceremony ended hours ago. In accordance with the plan the guys and I came up with, they all went with Serena and the Pierson Pack to a celebratory dinner while I pretended to get an urgent call.

Really, I've been here.

At our new house.

It's the one I saw her staring at the night I took her out on our first date—a sprawling, modern-Gothic estate with an old-fashioned greenhouse tucked behind the imposing black home.

The truth is, I tried to procure it for her right after the end of her first heat with our pack, but it took nearly eighteen months and a hell of a lot of negotiating to get the previous owners to give it up.

After a series of minor updates, it's finally ready. We figured it would make the perfect graduation gift for our perfect girl.

Standing in the backyard, I survey the acres of polished lawn spread in every direction. Instead of a pool, the property backs into a quiet pond, layered with lily pads. They're blooming, covering the peaceful water with white blossoms.

I hear a car door and feel a shove at my closed internal curtain. Serena, trying to nudge me for an explanation. Even though I can feel that she already knows what's going on, deep down.

I turn in time to catch her rounding the side of the house, running in her heels like she was born with them strapped to her ankles. When she spots me, her eyes go wide.

Tristan Thorne, she thinks, _what_ have you done?

I stride forward, smiling as I sweep her up into my arms and carry her toward our new home.

"I've told you; my wife gets whatever she wants."

I TOTALLY KNEW what was happening the whole time.

But they're so damn proud of themselves, I just let them believe I'm as blown away as they think I am.

I guess on some level, I *am* sort of stunned.

I had a notion that whatever Tris had up his sleeve was something grand like this—and a new home makes sense, since we've been outgrowing the townhome ever since Jonah retired and each of the guys started spending more time at home with me.

But the fact that Tristan got us the *exact* house he saw me swoon over before we were even really *together*…

That's my alpha. Providing for all of us, making sure we all have exactly what we want.

Which is why I've made it my mission to make sure he has everything *he* wants, too.

Mission accomplished, I hear him whisper, just to me.

Our gazes meet across the picnic blanket laid out in the middle of the new house's empty living room. Candlelight illuminates the huge, dark space, sending flickering shadows across all the black walls. I smile as I look around, imagining how cool this place will look once we add our pack's signature blend of class and badassery.

My Omega is already humming in contentment, plotting our new nest and basking in the scents of our mates, swelling to fill this new place for the first time.

Spencer pops a bottle of champagne, passing glasses to each of us while Jonah lifts me into his lap and Avery lies with his head on my thigh. Tristan squeezes my hand, grinning down at me.

"So, tell me, did we really surprise you?"

I bite down on my amusement and nod, wide-eyed. "Oh yeah. You totally got me."

I feel all four of them pause, realizing I have my curtain drawn and assuming it's because I'm fibbing. Shocked indignance sparks in each of them. Jonah's jaw drops to my shoulder while Spencer sighs and Tristan narrows his eyes.

Avery groans into my thigh, "*Seriously*? All of that for *nothing*? You weren't even *really* surprised?!"

"It's not that." I shrug. "It's just that... you guys aren't the only ones with a surprise."

Another roaring silence fills the bond. Loud enough that I nearly laugh.

Instead, I pull up the mental image I've been dying to show them all week. The reason I haven't taken a sip of my champagne yet.

Awe and joy light up the oasis inside of me as they all focus on the collection of positive pregnancy tests looming in my mind's eye.

I toss them all a smirk and lean back into Jonah, as smug and happy as I could ever possibly be.

Which is when they all tackle me.

"*Manamea*," Jonah breathes, his voice full of reverent amazement. "This is *incredible*."

"Are you *kidding me*, kitten?!" Avery shouts, rolling me out of Jonah's arms and kissing me all over my face. "You are *such* a bad girl."

Spencer bends over to scent-mark my face, grinning. "I thought I was proud before," he whispers. "But you always find new ways to amaze me, darling."

Tristan is last, still sitting frozen in place when Spencer pulls me back up. Our eyes meet and I crawl to him, settling in his lap while he blinks at me.

I can feel everything he does—the longing, the love, the all-consuming gratitude.

Because this?

This was *his* dream.

After the night he refused to tell me, I took my time coaxing the truth out of him. When he finally confessed that he'd always wanted to have children, it was almost as if he'd plucked the secret desire straight from my own heart.

And now, I get to give him his dream. The same way he's given all each of us everything he could.

"Serena..." he whispers, nestling our foreheads together, "I—"

His words choke off, but he says them through our bond. *I'll never be able to thank you, sweet one. But I'll never stop trying.*

I close my eyes, showing him how happy he's made me—today, and every other day since we bonded. "Thank *you*, Alpha."

I love that he lets me say that to him, now. Once he felt how sincere my appreciation was, he slowly stopped feeling guilty about accepting it.

It helps that the others all started making a bigger effort to tell him, too. It's important for him to know how much we all love him.

It's important for all of us.

Our bond is awash in it, at the moment. All of them dazed and punch-drunk on this newfound joy. I soak it in, feeling like a flower in full bloom. Bursting with color and life and possibilities, all because of them.

My alphas huddle closer, purring and reaching out to touch me. I smile, shooting each of them a look.

"For the record," I preen, "*that's* how you plan a surprise."

a note from ari

Hi!!

Thank you so much for reading Knot Her Fight!

As with all my books, this one was inspired by our main character, Serena.

Her specific story might not be something many women face, but I truly believe she shame she was made to feel regarding her body and her sex appeal is all-too familiar for so many of us. I really wanted to write a story about overcoming that narrative, and highlight how difficult it can be when one's mind has been conditioned for blame and shame.

Serena's strength and undefeatable sense of humor definitely make her one of my favorite MFC's to date!

And I'll definitely never be able to eat pizza rolls again.

Until next time—sending you love and gratitude!

xx,

Ari Wright

acknowledgments

Writing these books has been the most incredible experience for so many reasons, but the first and foremost are the people who read them and love them. I want to thank my readers for being here with me on book three of this wild ride! I'm loving every minute of it and I hope the next installment brings you all the joy it gives me to create for you.

To Kelly, who is absolutely a fighter. I know this year has tried to kick your ass in every possible way—I'm always in awe of how you get back up and keep going. Thank you for being by my side for everything, especially when it's hard 🩶

All the gratitude and credit goes to Katie, my editor and friend (and so much more!). I love you so much and I genuinely could not have written this story without you! Thank you for taking my crazy calls and even crazier ideas and helping me turn them into something great. Watching you grow in your career while I grow in mine has been one of my favorite parts of this journey!

To Kendra, who worked so hard (and quickly) to get this book ready for me. Your voice notes gave me life... and the confidence to hit submit on this manuscript. I love working with you and can't wait for the next round!

There is a small group of really special people in my DMs— they know who they are—who are always there for encouragement. I cannot tell you all how much it means to me!

Last, but never least, is always my husband. He does so much for me and our family, which allows me to live this dream. Thank you for hanging in here with me, babe! I love you!

about the author

Ari Wright was once entirely sane, but then she realized sanity is overrated and decided to write sporty Omegaverse smut.

Because life is short, you know?

When she isn't writing unhinged romances, she enjoys drinking coffee to the point of excess, kitchen experiments, raising her littles, and trying to keep her plants alive (just kidding, her husband does that).

She loves really embarrassing music, moody weather, and any story where the bad guy gets the girl.

Because what's Happily Ever After without a little (or a lot of) spice?

You can follow her works in progress, favorite reads, and very pink aesthetic on Instagram—or check out her exclusive reader Facebook group!